PETALS OF BLOOD

Ngugi wa Thiong'o—who originally came to international
fame as James Ngugi and is still known simply as Ngugi—
was born in Kenya in 1938. He studied at Leeds (England),
taught at Makerere (Uganda) and Northwestern University,
Evanston, Illinois, and has been chairman of the literature
department at the University of Nairobi. Ngugi is married
and has six children.

Petals of Blood

By the same author

NOVELS

Weep Not, Child
The River Between
A Grain of Wheat

PLAYS

The Black Hermit
The Trial of Dedan Kimathi
(with Micere Mugo)

ESSAYS

Homecoming

SHORT STORIES

Secret Lives

Petals of Blood

Ngugi wa Thiong'o

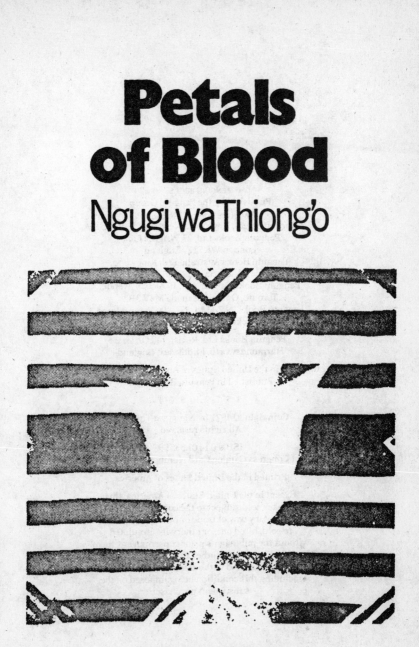

PENGUIN BOOKS

PENGUIN BOOKS
Published by the Penguin Group
Penguin Books USA Inc.,
375 Hudson Street, New York, New York 10014, U.S.A.
Penguin Books Ltd, 27 Wrights Lane,
London W8 5TZ, England
Penguin Books Australia Ltd, Ringwood,
Victoria, Australia
Penguin Books Canada Ltd, 10 Alcorn Avenue,
Toronto, Ontario, Canada M4V 3B2
Penguin Books (N.Z.) Ltd, 182–190 Wairau Road,
Auckland 10, New Zealand

Penguin Books Ltd, Registered Offices:
Harmondsworth, Middlesex, England

First published in the United States of America by E. P. Dutton 1978
Published in Penguin Books 1991

3 5 7 9 10 8 6 4

ISBN 0 14 01.5351 9
Library of Congress Catalog Card Number: 78–60717 (Dutton)

Printed in the United States of America

For my mother and Nyambura
In memory of Njinju wa Thiong'o who died on 6.4.74

Acknowledgments

Thanks to:
    Nyambura for the songs on pages 264 and 265.
    Elijah Mbŭrŭ for *Hŭni Cia Gita* on page 287.
    PCEA Gathaithi choir for the hymn on page 135.
    DK for his song quoted on page 102.
    Josh White for his song quoted on page 165.
    Mrs Lee and Mrs Keval for typing the MS.

And also to:
    The Soviet Writers Union for giving me the use of their house in Yalta in order to finish the writing of this novel.
    Dr Samuel Kibicho – for introducing me to the joys of literature, the novel in particular.
    Mr Stephen Thiro – for efforts in the past without which I might never have written.

And to:
    Many others
    One in the struggle
    With our people
    For total liberation
    Knowing that
    However long and arduous the struggle
    Victory is certain.

Fearful, original sinuosities! Each mangrove sapling
Serpentlike, its roots obscene
As a six-fingered hand,

Conceals within its clutch the mossbacked toad,
Toadstools, the potent ginger-lily,
Petals of blood,

The speckled vulva of the tiger-orchid;
Outlandish phalloi
Haunting the travellers of its one road.
Derek Walcott, from *The Swamp*

Part One: Walking...

And I saw, and behold, a white horse, and he that
sat thereon had a bow: and there was given unto him a crown:
and he came forth conquering, and to conquer ...
And another horse came forth, a red horse: and to him that
sat thereon it was given to take peace from the earth, that they should
slay one another: and was there given unto him a great sword ...
And I saw, and behold, a black horse; and he that sat thereon
had a balance in his hand ...
And I saw, and behold, a pale horse: and he that sat
upon him, his name was Death ...
And there was given unto them authority over the fourth part of
earth, to kill with sword and with famine, and with death.

Revelation, Chapter 6

The people scorn'd the ferocity of kings ...
But the sweetness of mercy brew'd destruction,
    and the frighten'd monarchs come back;
Each comes in state, with his train – hangman,
    priest, tax-gatherer,
Soldier, lawyer, lord, jailer, and sycophant.

Walt Whitman

Chapter One

1 🍀 They came for him that Sunday. He had just returned from a night's vigil on the mountain. He was resting on his bed, Bible open at the Book of Revelation, when two police constables, one tall, the other short, knocked at the door.

'Are you Mr Munira?' the short one asked. He had a star-shaped scar above the left brow.

'Yes.'

'You teach at the New Ilmorog Primary School?'

'And where do you think you are now standing?'

'Ah, yes. We try to be very sure. Murder, after all, is not irio or ugali.'*

'What are you talking about?'

'You are wanted at the New Ilmorog Police Station.'

'About?'

'Murder, of course – murder in Ilmorog.'

The tall one who so far had not spoken hastened to add: 'It is nothing much, Mr Munira. Just routine questioning.'

'Don't explain. You are only doing your duty in this world. But let me put on my coat.'

They looked at one another, surprised at his cool reception of the news. He came back carrying the Holy Book in one hand.

'You never leave the Book behind, Mr Munira,' said the short one, impressed, and a little fearful of the Book's power.

'We must always be ready to plant the seed in these last days before His second coming. All the signs – strife, killing, wars, blood – are prophesied here.'

'How long have you been in Ilmorog?' asked the tall one, to change the subject from this talk of the end of the world and Christ's second coming. He was a regular churchgoer and did not want to be caught on the wrong side.

'You have already started your routine questions, eh?'

'No, no, this is off the record, Mr Munira. It is just conversation. We have nothing against you.'

'Twelve years!' he told them.

'Twelve years!' both echoed.

'Yes, twelve years in this wasteland.'

*Irio and ugali are the most common Kenyan foods.

2

'Well, that was – you must have been here before New Ilmorog was built...'

2 🌸 Abdulla sat on a chair outside his hovel in the section of Ilmorog called the New Jerusalem. He looked at his bandaged left hand. He had not been kept long at the hospital. He felt strangely calm after the night's ordeal. But he still could not understand what had really happened. Maybe in time, he thought – but would he ever be able to explain this fulfilment of what had only been a wish, an intention? How far had he willed it? He raised his head and saw a police constable looking at him.

'Abdulla?'

'Yes.'

'I am a policeman on duty. You are wanted at the station.'

'Now?'

'Yes.'

'Will it take long?'

'I don't know. They want you to record a statement and to answer a few questions.'

'That's all right. Let me put this chair back inside the house.'

But at the station they locked him up in a cell. Abdulla protested against the deception. A policeman slapped him on the face. One day, one day, he tried to say in sudden resurgence of old anger and new bitterness at the latest provocation.

3 🌸 A police officer went to the hospital where Wanja had been admitted.

'I am afraid you cannot see her,' said the doctor. 'She is not in a position to answer questions. She is still in a delirium and keeps on shouting: "Fire ... Fire ... My mother's sister ... my dear aunt ... put out the fire, put out the fire!" and such things.'

'Record her words. It might give us a clue in case—'

'No, she is not in a critical condition ... just shock and hallucinations. In ten days' time ...'

4 🌸 Karega was fast asleep. He had come late from an all-night executive meeting of Ilmorog Theng'eta Breweries Union. He heard a knock at the door. He leapt out of bed in his pyjamas. He found a heavily armed police contingent at the door. An officer in khaki clothes stepped forward.

'What is the matter?'

'You are wanted at the police station.'

'What for?'

3

'Routine questioning.'

'Can't it wait until tomorrow?'

'I am afraid not.'

'Let me change into something . . .'

He went back and changed. He wondered how he would contact the others. He had listened to the six o'clock news and so he knew that the strike had been banned. But he hoped that even if he was arrested, the strike would go on.

He was hurled into a waiting Landrover, and driven off.

Akinyi, preparing to go to Ilmorog Church for the morning service, happened to look in the direction of his house. She always did this, automatically, and she had promised herself to cut out the habit. She saw the Landrover drive away. She rushed to his place – she had never been there – and found the door padlocked.

Within a few hours word had spread. The workers, in a hostile mood, marched toward the police station demanding his release. A police officer came out and spoke to them in a surprisingly conciliatory manner.

'Please disband peacefully. Karega is here for routine questioning. And it is not about your last night's decision to take a strike action. It's about murder – murder in Ilmorog.'

'Murder of the workers!' somebody retorted.

'Murder of the workers' movement!'

'Long live the workers' struggle!'

'Please disband—' appealed the officer, desperately.

'Disband yourself . . . disband the tyranny of foreign companies and their local messengers!'

'Out with foreign rule policed by colonised blackskins! Out with exploitation of our sweat!'

The crowd was getting into an angry, threatening mood. He signalled his lieutenants. They called out others who came with guns and chased the protesting workers right to the centre of Ilmorog. One or two workers sustained serious injuries and were taken to hospital.

Workers were waking to their own strength. Such a defiant confrontation with authority had never before happened in Ilmorog.

5 ❀ One newspaper, the *Daily Mouthpiece*, brought out a special issue with a banner headline: MZIGO, CHUI, KIMERIA MURDERED.

A man, believed to be a trade-union agitator, has been held after a leading industrialist and two educationists, well known as the African directors of the internationally famous Theng'eta Breweries and

4

Enterprises Ltd, were last night burnt to death in Ilmorog, only hours after taking a no-nonsense-no-pay-rise decision.

It is believed that they were lured into a house where they were set on by hired thugs.

The three will be an irreplaceable loss to Ilmorog. They built Ilmorog from a tiny nineteenth-century village reminiscent of the days of Krapf and Rebman into a modern industrial town that even generations born after Gagarin and Armstrong will be proud to visit ... etc ... etc ... Kīmeria and Chui were prominent and founding fathers of KCO ... etc ... etc ...

Chapter Two

1 ❁ But all that was twelve years after Godfrey Munira, a thin dustcloud trailing behind him, first rode a metal horse through Ilmorog to the door of a moss-grown two-roomed house in what was once a schoolyard. He got off and stood still, his right hand akimbo, his left holding the horse, his reddish lined eyes surveying the grey, dry lichen on a once white-ochred wall. Then, unhurriedly, he leaned the metal horse against the wall and, bending down, unclipped loose the trouser bottoms, beat them a little with his hands – a symbolic gesture, since the dust stubbornly clung to them and to his shoes – before moving back a few steps to re-survey the door, the falling-apart walls and the sun-rotted tin roof. Suddenly, determinedly, he strode to the door and tried the handle while pushing the door with his right shoulder. He crashed through into a room full of dead spiders and the wings of flies on cobwebs on all the walls, up to the eaves.

Another one has come into the village, went the news in Ilmorog. Children spied on him, on his frantic efforts to trim up and weed the place, and they reported everything to the old men and women. He would go away with the wind, said the elderly folk: had there not been others before him? Who would want to settle in this wasteland except those without limbs – may the devil swallow Abdulla – and those with aged loins – may the Lord bless Nyakinyua, the old woman.

The school itself was a four-roomed barrack with broken mud walls, a tin roof with gaping holes and more spiders' webs and the wings and heads of dead flies. Was it any wonder that teachers ran away at the first glance? The pupils were mostly shepherd boys, who often did not finish a term but followed their fathers in search of new pastures and water for their cattle.

But Munira stayed on, and after a month we were all whispering – was he a little crazed – and he not so old? Was he a carrier of evil? – especially when he started holding classes under the acacia bush near the place rumoured to be the grave of the legendary Ndemi, whose spirit once kept watch over Ilmorog Country before imperialism came and changed the scheme of things. He is mocking Ndemi, said Mwathi wa Mugo, who divined for both the ridge and the plains and prescribed a deterrent. At night, under the cover of darkness, the old woman shat a mountain between the school building and the acacia bush. In the morning the children found a not-so-dry mound of shit. They ran back to their parents and told a funny story about the new teacher. For a week or so Munira galloped his horse the length of the hills and plains in pursuit of the disappearing pupils. He caught up with one. He got off his horse, letting it fall to the ground, and ran after the pupil.

'What is your name?' he asked, holding him by the shoulder.

'Muriuki.'

'Son of?'

'Wambui.'

'That's your mother?'

'Yes.'

'What about your father?'

'He works far away.'

'Tell me: why don't you like school?'

The boy was drawing marks on the ground with his right toe, head bent to one side, holding back laughter with difficulty.

'I don't know, I don't know,' he said, making as if to cry. Munira let him go after getting a promise that Muriuki would return and even bring the others. So they came back cautiously: they still thought him a bit odd and this time would not venture out of the closed walls.

She waited for Munira outside the school kei-apple hedge. He got off the metal horse. He stood aside, thinking she only wanted to pass. But she stood in the middle of the narrow track supporting herself against a twigged stick.

'Where you come from: are there tarmac roads?'

'Yes.'

'And light that comes from wires on dry trees to make day out of night?'

'Yes.'

'Women in high heels?'

'Yes.'

'Oiled hair, singed goatskin smell?'

'Yes.'

He looked at her furrowed face, at the light in her eyes. His own wandered past her, over the empty school, for it was after four o'clock, and he thought: what did she want?

'They are beautiful and wise in the ways of the white man: is this not so?'

'That they are: too wise, sometimes.'

'Our young men and women have left us. The glittering metal has called them. They go, and the young women only return now and then to deposit the newborn with their grandmothers already aged with scratching this earth for a morsel of life. They say: there in the city there is room for only one ... our employers, they don't want babies about the tiny rooms in tiny yards. Have you ever heard of that? Unwanted children? The young men also. Some go and never return. Others sometimes come to see the wives they left behind, make them round-bellied, and quickly go away as if driven from Ilmorog by Uhere or Mutung'u.* What should we call them? The new Uhere and Mutung'u generation: for was it not the same skin diseases and plagues that once in earlier times weakened our people in face of the Mzungu invasion? Tell me: what then brings you to a deserted homestead? Look at Abdulla. He came from over there and what did he bring us? A donkey. Now imagine, a donkey! What have you really come to fetch from our village? Is it the remaining children?'

He pondered this a few seconds. He plucked a ripened yellow kei-apple and crushed it between his fingers: *isn't there a safe corner in which to hide and do some work, plant a seed whose fruits one could see?* The smell from the rotting fermenting kei-apple hit into his nostrils. He felt a sudden nausea, *Lord deliver us from our past,* and frantically fumbled in his pockets for a handkerchief to cover the sneeze. It was too late. A bit of mucus flew onto the woman's furrowed face. She shrieked out, *auuu-u, Nduri ici mutiuke muone,†* and fled in fright. He turned his face aside to hold back another sneeze. When a second later he looked to the path, he could not find a trace of her behind the kei-apple bush or anywhere. She had vanished.

Strange, mysterious, he muttered to himself. He got on his metal horse and slowly rode toward Abdulla's shop.

Abdulla was also a newcomer to Ilmorog. He and little skinny Joseph had come into our midst in a donkey-cart full of an assortment of sufurias and plates and cheap blankets tightly packed

---

*Uhere is measles; Mutung'u is smallpox.
†A curse expressing shock.

into torn sisal sacks and dirty sheets knotted into temporary bags. This was going to be an eventful year, Njogu had exclaimed sarcastically on seeing the odd trio, and listening to their even more odd request: how in this desert place could anyone even think of rescuing the broken mud-walled shop that had once belonged to Dharamshah of Ilmorog legends? You can take the ghost ... memories, curses and all ... old Njogu had said, pointing to the building, whose roof and walls leaned to one side and looked indistinguishable from the dry weed and the red earth. We used to crowd his little shop and look curiously at his stumped leg and his miserable face and listen to his stream of curses at Joseph. Soon we were glad that at long last we had a place from which we could get salt and pepper. But we were rather alarmed at his donkey because it ate too much grass and drank too much water. Within a month Abdulla had added bar services to his supply of Jogoo Unga and pepper and salt. On a Friday or a Saturday the herdsmen from Ilmorog plains would descend on the store and drink and talk and sing about their cows and goats. They had a lot of money from the occasional sale of goats at Ruwa-ini Market, and they had no other use for it, carrying it hidden inside their red cloths in small tins hanging on strings from their necks. Afterward they would disappear for days or weeks before once again descending on Abdulla.

Munira entered the place through the back door and sat on the edge of a creaking bench. It's strange, he muttered to himself again, recalling the encounter with the old woman as he waited for Joseph to bring him a Tusker beer. No sooner had he started drinking than three strongly built but elderly folk joined him at the table. Muturi, Njuguna and Ruoro were prosperous peasants, and as such they were the wise men, the athamaki, of the farming community. They settled disputes not only between the various families but also between this community and that of the herdsmen of the plains. For more serious disputes and problems they went to the diviner, Mwathi wa Mugo. They greeted Munira and started talking about the weather.

'Where you come from: is it as dry as this place?'

'It is ... well ... it is always hot in January.'

'It's the same season of course – githemithu season.'

'Is that the name of it?'

'These children ... You have too much of the Foreigner's maneno maneno* in your heads. Did you have a good gathano harvest in your place? Here it was poor and we don't know if the grains of maize and beans can last us to the end of the njahi rains. That is, if the rains come ...'

*talk

'I am not really a farmer,' Munira hastened to explain, all this talk of njahi, themithu, gathano and mwere, confusing him.

'We know, we know ... the hands of a Msomi are themselves a book. Don't I see those town-people when they come to visit us? Hands untouched by soil, it's as if they wear ngome.'*

Njuguna's ambition had always been one day to wear ngome on his fingers' knuckles as a sign that he had said kwaheri† to soiling his hands. He would then be like some of the mbari‡lords of his youth. Some of the famous houses had had so much wealth in cows and goats they would get ahois and hangers-on to work for them. The ahois§ and the ndungatas** ofcourse hoped to get a goat in payment and strike out on their own in the virgin common lands or unclaimed grassfields. Other heads of big houses and clans and mbari had had enough wives and sons to do the work or enough daughters to bring in more wealth. But such prosperity had always escaped Njuguna. The land seemed not to yield much and there was now no virgin soil to escape to as in those days before colonialism. His sons had gone away to European farms or to the big towns. Daughters he had none: and what use were they nowadays? Old Njogu, after all, had several and they had only brought him sorrow instead of goats. So, Njuguna, like the other peasants in all the huts scattered about Ilmorog Country, had to be contented with small acreage, poor implements and with his own small family labour. But he kept on hoping.

'We did not get enough rains last mwere season,' Muturi was explaining. 'Now we look at the sun and the wind and the thungururi birds in the sky and we fear that it may not rain. Of course njahi rains are still two moons away ... but these birds, we fear.'

Munira was not interested in farming. And this talk of possible droughts and rain he had heard since his childhood. Farmers always talked of being threatened by droughts, as if giving voice to their fears would keep out such calamities.

'I am sure it will rain,' he said, just to assure them that he was interested. He tried to steer the conversation along different lines, and it was Abdulla who came to his rescue.

'Do you think you can manage the school alone?' Abdulla asked.

'I hope that once Standard I and II classes start going I can get more teachers.'

'Standard I and II, how?'

'Well, Standard II in the mornings only. Standard I in the afternoons,' he said.

'You must be very dedicated,' Abdulla said, and Munira did not know if it was said in sarcasm or in compliment. But he tried to answer it sincerely.

*rings
†good-bye
‡family
§beggars
**servants

'Some of us who had a schooling . . . we tended to leave the struggle for Uhuru to the ordinary people. We stood outside . . . the song I should say. But now, with independence, we have a chance to pay back . . . to show that we d . . . did not always choose to stand aside . . . That's why . . . well . . . I chose transfer to this . . . to Il-morog.'

'I am not sure that some have not already started looking after their stomachs only,' Abdulla said, and once again the tone made Munira slightly uncomfortable. It was as if Abdulla was already suspicious of, or else antagonistic to his . . . well . . . his rather missionary posture and fervour.

'I can't speak for everybody – but it seems that there is still enthusiasm and a belief that we can all do something to make our independence real . . .' he said.

'That's the way to talk,' said Muturi in compliment. 'Those are good words.'

Munira now seized this chance to elaborate on the future prospects of the school and begged their co-operation. Kamuingi koyaga ndiri,* he said, not believing it, but noting that the words impressed them. Later, after dusk, the three peasant farmers staggered back to their homes, but not before reporting their findings to Nyakinyua. They leaned a bit too heavily on their walking-sticks, eyes a little red, voices a little blurry: he is all right, they told the others who had gathered in Nyakinyua's hut: he's all right, they said, and looked at one another with knowing eyes.

He became one of us. The children sang *a e i o u ĩ ũ* in loud voices. They also sang: *Kamau wa Njoroge ena ndutu kuguru*: and thought of their own jiggers eating their toes and scratched them against the floor in earnest. Some ran away from the school to whistle the true herdsman's tune to their cattle or simply to climb up and down the miariki trees in the open fields. Others blubbered on for a week or so and they too rejoined the cattle trail. But this is the 1960s, not the 1860s, Munira reflected, a little disappointed.

Once more he ran about the ridge, caught up with a few and asked them to tell the others that he had called a School Assembly. Only five pupils turned up. He addressed them from the raised mud rostrum: 'Listen, you have shown more than average diligence and even intelligence by attending this meeting. You are therefore promoted to the English beginners' class. But you will need to get a teacher who can and will endure all this hostility and indifference of a people opposed to light and progress.' He closed his first School Assembly by silently swearing never to come back to this God-for-

*Unity is strength.

10

saken place. His first conscious attempt to keep in step with the song seemed to have ended in yet another failure and defeat.

Spurs, stirrups, metal horseback, rider in a cloud of dust. Munira was aware of the many eyes that laughed at his failure behind the hedges. Nyakinyua, the old woman, stepped into the dusty track and shouted at him, at his retreating back. Further in the fields women mockingly sang to a gitiro tune of another horseman long ago, when Ilmorog was truly Ilmorog, and they chorused: Sons of Munoru we see; where now the stock of Ndemi?

He did not care. For a month they had made a fool of him. And even Abdulla, whose store and bar had become a daily refuge, would not help. 'They are a bit suspicious of strangers and strange things. At first they did not like my donkey. They still don't like it. And why? Because of the grass. Imagine that.' He would turn to pour curses at Joseph before continuing, leaning toward Munira and assuming a conspiratorial voice: 'Mwalimu, is it true that the old woman shat a mountain in your compound? A deed without a name. Ha! ha! Joseph, Gatutu Gaka, bring another beer for Mwalimu. But is it really true?' And the crippled fellow would laugh at Munira's discomfort.

The laughter, other memories, and now the road to Ruwa-ini, capital of Chiri District, did not improve Munira's humour. The road was as treacherous as those hags and brats and cripples, he thought, riding through ruts and bumps and ditches.

The road had once been a railway line joining Ilmorog to Ruwa-ini. The line had carried wood and charcoal and wattle barks from Ilmorog forests to feed machines and men at Ruwa-ini. It had eaten the forests, and after accomplishing their task, the two rails were removed, and the ground became a road – a kind of a road – that now gave no evidence of its former exploiting glory.

He smiled once when he came to the tarmac-ed last stretch which zigzagged through coffee farms previously owned by whites. Even here there was no respite. He kept on diving into the bush to avoid the oncoming lorries whose drivers only laughed and made obscene gestures: let the cycle suckle the udder of the lorry.

The buildings of Ruwa-ini came to view and it suddenly occurred to him that he had not yet thought of an alternative. He remembered why he had earlier so readily chosen Ilmorog and all sounds of fury inside were replaced by the fear of going to work in Limuru against the shadow of his father's success compared to his own failure, and so admitting to failure.

The thought suddenly made him stop. He got off the bicycle. He leaned on it and watched the scene over the hedge. Stretching for a mile or so outside Ruwa-ini was a golf course of neatly trimmed green lawn. Three Africans were laughing at a big bellied fourth who kept on swinging the stick without hitting the ball. Caddy boys, in torn clothes, stood at a respectful distance weighed down by bags of golfsticks and white balls. Aah, this world, Munira roused himself and quickly rode his bicycle into Ruwa-ini.

Mzigo's office was a specklessly clean affair with a tray for incoming mail, a tray for outgoing mail and one for miscellaneous mail plus numerous pens and pencils beside each of the three enormous inkwells. On the wall hung a map of Chiri District with the location of the various schools marked in with drawing-pins.

'How goes your school?' Mzigo asked and, swaying ever so slightly on the swivel chair, he glanced at the pin-dotted map.

'You sent me to an empty school. No teachers.'

'I thought you wanted a place of peace? A challenging place?'

'No pupils even.'

'I honestly don't know what's wrong with that school. No teacher wants to stay there. One year, two years, and they leave. If you should find a teacher, even UTs, we shall certainly employ them.'

'But ...'

'I'll shortly be coming there, I'll shortly be coming round. Do you have good roads? You know these damned cars – a real nuisance, the true black man's burden – believe me, Mr eeh, eeh – Munira – a bicycle is so much less trouble.'

He now glanced at Munira, his lips split into an ironic smile as if to say: You should have known – trying to escape ... but then, thought Munira, how could Mzigo have known? And suddenly, remembering the lorries and the matatu drivers who had forced him into the bush on his way here, he saw great wit in Mzigo's condescending compliment on bicycles. His inward rage gave way to laughter. He laughed until his ribs pained and he felt better, lighter inside. 'You don't believe me, eh?' Mzigo was asking. Munira was now thinking of Abdulla, the cripple; Nyakinyua, the old woman; the children who preferred herding cattle and climbing up miariki trees to going to school. He contrasted their direct approach with this pomposity; their atmosphere of curiosity with the fear behind the faces that sat in the back corners of sleek Mercedes Benzes, behind the walls of the once for-Europeans-only mansions and private clubs; their sincerity with the bellies pregnant with malice and cunning that walked the length of a golf course negotiating business deals, and recalling Abdulla's words he felt kindly toward Ilmorog.

Maybe he had not understood Nyakinyua, Abdulla, Njogu, Njuguna, Ruoro and all the others, he now reflected. He did not say a word about resigning or asking for a transfer. He collected chalk, exercise books and some writing paper.

'Mr Mzigo, are you serious ... do you mean what you said just now? That I could recruit UT help?'

'Yes, Mr Munira, provided you bring them to me for formal appointment. I want to see that school grow. I would like to see all the classes going.'

❀

He stayed the night at Furaha house in Ruwa-ini. The following day he crossed over into Kiambu District. He wanted to spend a day or two at his home in Limuru before pedalling back to Ilmorog.

He had until now practically lived all his life at Limuru. After leaving Siriana in 1946, he had taught in many schools around Limuru: Rironi, Kamandura, Tiekunu, Gatharaini and for the last six years or so at Manguo. Hence he felt his heart quicken at his return to a seat of his past. But it pained him that he still depended on his father for a place in which to set a home. He had always thought of striking out on his own but he had remained circling around his father's property without at the same time being fully part of it. This was unlike his more successful brothers. The one following him had even gone to England and returned to a successful career with the banks. The other had just finished Makerere and was PRO with an oil company. Yet another was in Makerere doing medicine. The first two sisters had successfully completed their high schools: one was in England training as a nurse: the other was at Goddard College, Vermont, U.S.A., taking a B.A. in Business Administration. One, Mukami, had recently died and he still felt deeply saddened at the memory because, although she was much younger than himself, yet he felt that she somehow sided with him, and did not look upon him as a failure. She was of a lively, rebellious spirit: Mukami had once or twice been beaten for joining the children of the squatters in stealing plums and pears from her father's fruit farm. Often, even after she had been admitted to Kenya High School, she would, while on leave, join the gang of workers and she would help in picking pyrethrum flowers. Her mother would remonstrate her with: 'They are paid to work!' Her committing suicide – she had jumped off a quarry cliff overlooking Manguo Marshes – must have been her act of saying a final 'No' to a trying world.

His father Ezekieli, tall, severe in his austere aloofness, was a wealthy landowner and a respected elder in the hierarchy of the Presbyterian Church. He was tall and mean in his austere holiness.

He believed that children should be brought up on boiled maize grains sprinkled with a few beans and on tea with only tiny drops of milk and no sugar, but all crowned with words of God and prayers. He was, despite his rations, especially successful in attracting faithful labour on his farm. Two of the labourers had remained in his father's employment ever since Munira could remember – still wearing the same type of patched up trousers and nginyira* for shoes. Off and on, over the years, he had engaged many hands – some from as far as Gaki, Metumi, Gussiland – to help him in cultivating his fields, picking his pyrethrum flowers all the year round and drying them, and picking red ripe plums in December, putting them in boxes, and taking them to the Indian shops to sell. They nearly all had one thing in common: submission to the Lord. They called him Brother Ezekieli, our brother in Christ, and they would gather in the yard of the house after work for prayers and thanksgiving. There were of course some who had devilish spirits which drove them to demand higher wages and create trouble on the farm and they would be dismissed. One of them attempted to organize the workers into a branch of the Plantation Workers' Union that operated on European farms. He argued that there was no difference between African and European employers of labour. He too was instantly dismissed. He was even denounced in a church sermon. He was given as an example of 'the recent trials and temptations of Brother Ezekiel'. But Munira even as a boy was quick to notice that away from his father's house, in their quarters down the farm, the workers, even as they praised the Lord, were less stilted, were more free and seemed to praise and sing to the Lord with greater conviction and more holiness. He felt a little awed by their total conviction and by their belief in a literal heaven to come. It was at one of their meetings that Munira once during his holidays from Siriana had felt a slight trembling of the heart and a consciousness of the enormity of the sin he had earlier committed, his very first, with Amina, a bad woman, at Kamiritho. He had felt the need to confess, to be cleansed by the Lord, but somehow, on the verge of saying it, he felt as if they would not believe his confession – and how anyway would he have found the words? Instead, he had gone home, convinced that inwardly he had given himself up to the Lord, and decided to do something about his sins. He stole a matchbox, collected a bit of grass and dry cowdung and built an imitation of Amina's house at Kamiritho where he had sinned against the Lord, and burnt it. He watched the flames and he felt truly purified by fire. He went to bed at ease with himself and peaceful in his knowledge of being accepted by the Lord. Shalom. But the cowdung had retained the fire

*sandals

14

and at night the wind fanned it into flames which would have licked up the whole barn had it not been discovered in time. In the morning he heard them talking about it – saying that maybe some jealous neighbours had done it – and he decided to keep quiet. But he felt as if his father knew and this had added to his consciousness of guilt.

One woman Munira always remembered: although she never went to church she stood out as holier than all the others and more sincere in her splendid withdrawal and isolation in her hut surrounded by five cypress trees. Her hut was exactly halfway between their big house and the other workers' quarters. Old Mariamu had a son who used to be Munira's playmate before he went to Siriana. And even after Munira had come back from Siriana they kept some kind of company – not much – but enough to have made Munira really shocked when in 1953 or so he heard that Mariamu's son had been caught carrying weapons for Mau Mau and was subsequently hanged. But the main reason he remembered her was because she would protest against low pay or failure to be paid on time where others trusted his father's word and his goodwill. She was respectful to Ezekieli but never afraid of him. Yet he never rebuked her or dismissed her. He had once heard her name mentioned in connection with his father's missing right ear – it had been cut off by Mau Mau guerrillas – and more recently in connection with Mukami's suicide. But he himself never forgot his childhood escapades to tea and to charcoal-roasted potatoes in Mariamu's hut.

Now Munira stood for a while by the cypress trees where her hut used to stand before she along with the others were moved to the new Concentration village of Kamiritho. What had happened to her? It surprised him how, in his self-isolation, nursing his failure at Siriana, he had lost touch with and interest in active life at Limuru ... he was of it ... and yet not of it ... everything about his past since Siriana was so vague, unreal, a mist ... It was as if there was a big break in the continuity of his life and of his memories. So that taking a definite decision to go to Ilmorog was like his first conscious act of breaking with this sense of non-being.

He played with his two children, wondering for a time what image he presented to their young minds. Did he have the same austerity and holy aloofness as his own father? He told them about Ilmorog. He dwelt on the flies that massed around the eyes and noses of the shepherd boys until his wife exclaimed: 'How can you—?' He told them how Ilmorog was once haunted by one-eyed Marimu; funny old women shitting mountains; morose cripples with streams of curses from their foul mouths, until once again his wife exclaimed: 'How can you—?' without finishing the sentence. He was not being very amusing and he felt ridiculous in their unlaughing eyes. O.K., I will read you something from the Bible, he told them, and his wife's face beamed with pleasure. And Jesus told them: Go ye unto the villages and dark places of the earth and light my lamp paraffined with the holy spirit. So be it. Aamen.

When the children had gone to bed she immediately turned to him with half-severe, half-reproachful eyes. She could have been beautiful but too much righteous living and Bible-reading and daily prayers had drained her of all sensuality and what remained now was the cold incandescence of the spirit.

'You should be ashamed, blaspheming to the children. You should know that this world is not our home and we should be preparing them and ourselves for the next one.'

'Don't worry, I myself have never belonged to this world ... even to Limuru ... Maybe Ilmorog ... for a change.'

❦

So Godfrey Munira once again galloped his metal horse into Il-morog, and this time people actually came out to greet him. The old woman went to the school compound and said: You have indeed come back, God bless you: and she showered a bit of saliva into her hands in blessing. He shrank a little but he was glad that Nyakinyua was now not hostile.

He resumed his teaching, now warming to their apparent accept-ance of him. The listening silence of the children – those who turned up for classes – thrilled him. All Ilmorog seemed suddenly attentive to his voice.

He became a daily feature in Ilmorog, a guardian knight of knowl-edge for part-time pupils. Standard II or what he called the English beginners' class met in the morning: Standard I in the afternoon. The pupils came in and out as they liked and he took this lack of expected order, this erratic behaviour, even the talk of drought with an aloof understanding and benign indifference. It was enough for him that to the old men and women and others in Ilmorog he was the teacher of their children, the one who carried the wisdom of the new age in his head. They appreciated it that he from the other world had agreed to stay among them. They could see his readiness to stay in his eyes, which did not carry restlessness: the others had always carried wanting-to-run-away eyes and once they had the slightest complaint they always went away in a hurry and never returned. Munira stayed on. They anxiously watched him, at the end of every month, prepare to go to Ruwa-ini to fetch his salary, but they saw that he always came back, and they said amongst themselves: 'This one will stay.' Now they brought him eggs, occasionally a chicken, and he accepted this homage with gratitude. He strolled across the ridge following the paths scattered all over. The people would stand aside, in reverence, to let him pass and he would accept this with a slight nod or a smile. He was amused by their ndunyu*which was more of a social gathering of friends than a place for exchanging commodities and haggling over prices. They met on the ridge whenever the need arose on an evening before sunset. Those from the plains would bring milk and beadwork, occasionally skins, and they would buy or exchange them for snuff, beans, and maize. One could more or less do without hard cash except when one went to Abdulla's shop or to Ruwa-ini. Money or food or an item of clothing: any of these would do as a basis of exchange. Money anyway was saved only to buy other articles for use. Once he saw one or two spears and knives being sold and he was surprised to learn that it was the work of Muturi. 'But he can only make them at Mwathi's place,' Nyakinyua confided in him, 'for in beating and bending iron with bellows and hammer, he must be protected from the power of evil and envious eyes.' And he came to know that Mwathi wa Mugo was the spiritual power over both Ilmorog ridge and Ilmorog plains, somehow, invisibly, regulating their lives. He it was who advised on the best day for planting seeds or the appropriate day for the herdsmen to move. Munira had never seen him: nobody below a certain age could see him: but he was shown his homestead hedged round with thabai, and he was grateful to know this, for in future he would avoid passing anywhere near the place. Otherwise he felt secure: to be so liked, honoured, venerated, without the mess which comes from hasty involvement in other people's lives: this struck him as a late gift of God. He tried to forget his fears, his guilt, his frozen years: he stifled any unpleasant memories of his father or his wife or of his childhood and youth with a drink or so. He liked it especially when the herdsmen from the plains came to Abdulla's store. They would plant their spears outside and drink and talk about cows and make jokes about those who lived like moles, digging the soil. The peasant farmers of Ilmorog, though they were worried and anxious about the lateness of the rains, would hold themselves ready to defend themselves and their calling. Then a heated debate would follow between the tillers and the herdsmen as to which was more important: animals or crops. Cattle were wealth – the only wealth. Was it not the ambition of every real man, especially before the white man came, to possess cows and goats? A man without a goat would often plant fields and fields of sweet potatoes, vines, millet or yams, sugarcane or bananas. In the end, he would try to sell these for a goat – one kid,

*marketplace

even. And had it not been known for people to hire themselves as ndungata in the hope of one day getting a goat? People sold their daughters for goats, not for crops: smiths, workers in pottery and basketry or in beautiful trinkets would more often than not only exchange their wares for things of blood. And why did nations go to war, if not to secure these things of blood? But the others argued that goats were not wealth. Since wealth was expressed in goats and cows, the same could not be the wealth. Wealth was in the soil and the crops worked by a man's hands. Didn't they know the saying that wealth was sweat on one's hands? Look at white people: they first took our land; then our youth; only later, cows and sheep. Oh no, the other side would argue: the white man first took the land, then the goats and cows, saying these were hut taxes or fines after every armed clash, and only later did he capture the youth to work on the land. The line of division was not always clear since some owned crop fields and cattle as well. These said that both were important: a person paid goats for a girl, true: but he looked for the one who was not afraid of work. And why did wealthy people keep ndungata and ahoi? Not only to look after cows and goats but also after the crops. And why did the colonial settler and his policeman capture the youth? To cultivate his fields and also to look after the cows. The foreigner from Europe was cunning: he took their land, their sweat and their wealth and told them that the coins he had brought, which could not be eaten, were the true wealth! And so the debate would go on. Munira did not take part in such talk: he felt an outsider to their involvement with both the land and what they called 'things of blood'. Any talk about colonialism made him uneasy. He would suddenly become conscious of never having done or willed anything to happen, that he seemed doomed to roam this world, a stranger. And yet, yet, why this ready acceptance of undeserved homage, why this secret pleasure at the illusion of being of them?

He would try to change the subject. Who was their MP? A heated exchange would follow. Some could not remember his name. They had heard of him during the last elections. He had visited the area to ask to be given votes. He had made several promises. He had even collected two shillings from each household in his constituency for a Harambee water project, and a ranching scheme. But they had hardly seen him since. Nderi wa Riera-aa, that was the name, somebody remembered. What was an MP? A new type of government agent? But why had he needed votes? Even such a talk would make Munira fidgety. He would ask yet other questions hoping for a conversation that would not make demands on him to choose this or that position in politics. Didn't they ever get visitors from the outside? Yes, yes, they used to have teachers. But these ran away (back to the cities) just before independence. The few who later came never stayed. Also at the end of every harvest, some people, traders, would come with lorries. They bought some of the produce. Sometimes too, at the beginning of each year, the Chief, the tax gatherer and a policeman would come and they would terrorize them into paying their dues. Thus the money from the seasonal traders would end up in the hands of the tax gatherer. But this was nothing new. It had always been so, these many many past years, and the only thing that pained them was this youth running away from the land. The movement away had started after the second Big War ... No ... before that ... No, it was worse after Mau Mau War ... No, it was the railway ... all right, all right ... even this had always been so since European colonists came into their midst, these ghosts from another world. But they of Ilmorog ... they now would have to find a way of avoiding those taxes ... *Politics!* Couldn't one escape from these things, Munira thought impatiently?

He developed a working pattern: classes all day; a walk to the ridge; then a stroll to Abdulla's place. In time, even Abdulla came to accept him and he would curse Joseph into bringing a chair for Mwalimu at the sight of Munira in the distance. Only his tone in conversation – between friendly hostility and playful contempt – sat disagreeably in Munira's stomach as he sipped beer in this land of easeful dreams. But occasionally Abdulla would get into one of his vicious moods and would remind him of his first reception in Ilmorog. Abdulla would lean towards him and assume an intimate tone of false conspiracy:

'These people – you know – too suspicious. Have you seen their anxious faces raised to the sky? I bet that if it refused to rain they would blame it on my donkey. They would even go to Mwathi's place to ask him about the donkey. Have you ever seen this priest of theirs? Actually he has a reputation. A good reputation. But I have never seen him. A mystery, eh? Look at Muturi, Njuguna, Ruoro and even old man Njogu: they don't like my donkey. Do you know why? They say it eats grass enough for several cows. It cannot be slaughtered. But I know they are really envious of the appetite of my donkey. It can even eat roots, you see: it can find water where no cow or goat will find any. That's why there is that look in the eyes of these people. Have you seen the old woman's eyes? The glint ... evil, don't you think? You should know. But tell me, Mwalimu: is it true that she once shat a mountain in your compound? And the children thought it was you? Ha! ha! ha! Brought all that shit from out there? Ha! ha! ha! Joseph – you lazybones – have you ever met a little nigger that was so lazy? Another beer for Mwalimu – but tell me, was it really true?'

'Listen, Abdulla,' Munira would say, trying to steer the conversation away from this delicate area, 'now that you have brought up the question of education, why don't you let Joseph enrol in the school?'

'And bring my donkey to run errands in this shop as it does outside?'

Excepting for such small irritations Munira had come to like Ilmorog, and now he even tended to view the other world of his wife and Mzigo and his father with suspicion and hostility. At home he hardly every stayed more than a night, suddenly feeling his new sense of 'being without involvement' threatened by their inquiries. Mzigo's routine questions came to acquire menacing edges in Munira's own mind: might he not actually carry out his own promises and visit Ilmorog? Munira had worked out a routine answer: 'That place ... hell ...' and he hoped this would deter Mzigo from a visit. He did not want anyone to interfere with his teaching rhythm, and with his world. Sometimes he made them sing nonsense songs like: *Mburi ni indo; ngombe ni indo, mbeca ni indo; ngai muheani.* Sometimes he would give the children addition or subtraction sums and go out into the sun.

He would watch the peasants in the fields going through motions of working but really waiting for the rains, and he would vaguely feel with them in their anxieties over the weather. But the sun was nice and warm on his skin and he would suddenly be filled with a largeness of heart that embraced all Ilmorog, men, women, children, the land, everything. His home and its problems were far, far away!

At the beginning of April it started raining. The eyes of the elders beamed with expectation of new life over Ilmorog: their wrinkled faces seemed to stretch and tighten with sinews of energy. Everybody was busy about the fields. Muturi, Njuguna, Ruoro, Njogu: even these, for a time, would not come by Abdulla's shop for they were tired out after the day's involvement with planting or walking their cows and goats in muddy fields. Time was when men did no planting except for things like yams, sugarcane and bananas, but times were changing, and the elders had been unable to prevent the youth from going away. So during the period of planting, Munira drank alone or with only Abdulla and Joseph for company. He now missed their idle gossip, their anecdotes, and even their comments and debates on unsettling issues.

He walked or cycled to his house, an outsider to their activities on the land, and he felt sad and a little abandoned.

The women only threw him hurried greetings as they rushed to the fields between bouts of heavy downpour.

But he tried to understand and he even made a lesson out of it all: 'There is dignity in labour,' he told the children. He made them sing even more fervently:

> Cows are wealth
> Work is health
> Goats are wealth
> Work is health
> Crops are wealth
> Work is health
> Money is wealth
> Work is health
> God the Almighty Giver
> God Bringer of rains!

❊

So within six months he came to feel as if Ilmorog was his personal possession: he was a feudal head of a big house or a big mbari lord surveying his estate, but without the lord's pain of working out losses and gains, the goats lost and the young goats born. When the rains had come and seeds sprouted and then, in June, flowers came he felt as if the whole of Ilmorog had put on a vast floral-patterned cloth to greet its lord and master.

He took the children out into the field to study nature, as he put it. He picked flowers and taught them the names of the various parts: the stigma, the pistil, pollen, the petals. He told them a little about fertilization. One child cried out:

'Look. A flower with petals of blood.'

It was a solitary red beanflower in a field dominated by white, blue and violet flowers. No matter how you looked at it, it gave you the impression of a flow of blood. Munira bent over it and with a trembling hand plucked it. It had probably been the light playing upon it, for now it was just a red flower.

'There is no colour called blood. What you mean is that it is red. You see? You must learn the names of the seven colours of the rainbow. Flowers are of different kinds, different colours. Now I want each one of you to pick a flower ... Count the number of petals and pistils and show me its pollen ...'

He stood looking at the flower he had plucked and then threw the lifeless petals away. Yet another boy cried:

'I have found another. Petals of blood – I mean red ... It has no stigma or pistils ... nothing inside.'

He went to him and the others surrounded him:

'No, you are wrong,' he said, taking the flower. 'This colour is not even red ... it does not have the fullness of colour of the other one. This one is yellowish red. Now you say it has nothing inside. Look at the stem from which you got it. You see anything?'

'Yes,' cried the boys. 'There is a worm – a green worm with several hands or legs.'

'Right. This is a worm-eaten flower ... It cannot bear fruit. That's why we must always kill worms ... A flower can also become this colour if it's prevented from reaching the light.'

He was pleased with himself. But then the children started asking him awkward questions. Why did things eat each other? Why can't the eaten eat back? Why did God allow this and that to happen? He had never bothered with those kind of questions and to silence them he told them that it was simply a law of nature. What was a law? What was nature? Was he a man? Was he God? A law was simply a law and nature was nature. What about men and God? Children, he told them, it's time for a break.

Man ... law ... God ... nature: he had never thought deeply about these things, and he swore that he would never again take the children to the fields. Enclosed in the four walls he was the master, aloof, dispensing knowledge to a concentration of faces looking up to him. There he could avoid being drawn in ... But out in the fields, outside the walls, he felt insecure. He strolled to the acacia bush and started breaking its thorn-tips. He remembered that his first troubles in the place had started because of taking the children into the open. How Nyakinyua had frightened him! and at the thought, he instinctively looked to the spot where she had once stood and questioned him about the city and ladies in high heels.

For a few seconds Munira's heart stood still: he could hardly believe his eyes. She left the village path and walked toward him. A bright coloured kitenge cloth, tied loose on the head, fell wide on her shoulders so that her face was half veiled from the sun.

'Are you well, Mwalimu?' she called out boldly. Her voice had a studied vibrant purity: the tone was rich and pleasant to his ears. There was a calculated submissive deference in her bearing as she stretched out a small hand and looked at him full in the eyes, suddenly lowering them in childlike shyness. He swallowed something before answering.

'I am well. It is a bit hot, though.'

'That is why I came here.'

'Ilmorog?'

'No. Here in your place. Have you any water to spare? I know that water is like thahabu in these parts.'

'It has rained recently. Ilmorog river is full.'

'I stopped at the right place then,' she said cooingly. Her words and voice lingered in the air, caressing the heat-filled silence between them.

'Come into the house,' he said.

The water was in a clay pot in a corner of the sitting-room under a bookshelf. She drank from a cup and he watched the slight motion of her Adam's apple along the bow-tightness thrust toward him. Her neck was long and graceful: she-gazelle of the Ilmorog plains.

'Some more, if there is,' she said, panting a little.

'Perhaps you would like some tea,' he said. 'They say tea heats the blood in cold weather and cools it in hot weather.'

'Tea and water go down different gullets. I would like another cup of water. As for tea, don't trouble yourself. I will make it.'

He gave her another cup of water. He showed her where the different things were. He felt a little generous within, even a bit warm. But he was suddenly shaken out of this mood by her vigorous laughter. He instinctively looked at the zip of his trousers and he found it in place.

'Men, men,' she was saying. 'So it is true, what they say of you in the village. You are indeed a bachelor boy. One saucepan, one plate, one knife, two spoons, two cups: don't you ever get visitors? Don't you have a teacher's darling girl?' she asked, a wicked glint in her eyes.

'Why! How long have you been here?'

'I came yesterday evening.'

Yesterday! and she already knew about him! He was tense ... he felt his six months' security threatened: what did they really say about him in the village? Was there nothing that could cleanse him from doubts, this unknowing? He excused himself and walked toward the classroom. Let her spy on him, on his doings, the defiant thought gave him momentary relief: what did it matter? He was only an outsider, fated to watch, adrift, but never one to make things happen.

He heard feet bustling and books rustling. The brats had been watching the whole scene through windows and cracks in the wall. Their exaggerated concentration on their books confirmed his suspicion. He now put the question to himself: what did the children really think of him? Then he dismissed it with another: what did it matter one way or the other? He had taught for so many years now – teaching ready-made stuff must be in his blood – and one did all right as long as one was careful not to be dragged into ... into ... an area of darkness ... Yes ... darkness unknown, unknowable ... like the flowers with petals of blood and questions about God, law ... things like that. He could not teach now: he dismissed the class a few minutes before time and went back to the house. He wanted to ask the stranger girl more questions: what was her name? Where did she come from? And so on, carefully, gingerly toward the inevitable: had she been sent by Mzigo to spy on him? But why was he scared of being seen?

He found the floor swept: the dishes were washed and placed on two sticks as a rack on the floor to dry. But she herself was not there.

2 ❀ Munira's life in Ilmorog had up to now been one unbroken twilight. It was not only the high esteem in which the village held him: he cherished and was often thrilled by the sight of women scratching the earth because they seemed at one with the green land. He would always remember that period when the rains came and everybody was in the muddy fields, sacks on their heads – not to protect them really from rain but to cushion its fall on the body – and they were all busy putting seeds in the soil, and he had watched them from the safety of his classroom or of Abdulla's shop! There was a cruel side: this he had to admit. A few roads and a reliable water system would have improved their lives. A dispensary might have been a useful addition.

The children especially were often a nauseating sight: flies swarming around the sore eyes and mucus-blocked noses. Most had only tattered calicoes for clothing.

But transcending this absurdity was the care they had for one another. He would often meet them, a handsome trio: one rocked a crying baby strapped on the back; the third would pat-pat the crying baby to the rhythm with a rocking lullaby:

Do not cry, our little one.
Whoever dares beat our little one,
May he be cursed with thorns in his flesh.
If you stop crying, child of our mother,
She will soon come home from the fields
And bring you gitete-calabash of milk.

Their voices – two, three or more – raised in unison emphasized the solitude he associated with his rural cloister. It reminded him of similar scenes of rocking, lullaby-singing children on his father's pyrethrum fields before the Mau Mau violence.

24

Otherwise the village never intruded into his life: why should he – stranger-watchman at the gate – interfere in theirs?

Today as he walked to Abdulla's place he felt slightly uncomfortable at the elusive shadow that had earlier crossed his path. Yet Ilmorog ridge was quiet, serene: let it be, let it be, world without end, he murmured.

As he was about to knock at the back door to Abdulla's shop, he felt blood rush to his head: for a second he felt as if his brain was drugged ... perhaps ... not too old ... oh hell ... yes ... hell is woman ... heaven is woman. He steeled himself and entered:

'This is your other hiding-place, Mwalimu,' she said. 'You see, I am finding out all about your secrets.'

'This ... no secret ...' he said as he sat. 'I only come to wet my throat.'

'Your tea chased away my thirst. It was really good—'

'But beer is better than tea. Ask Abdulla. He tells me: *Baada ya kazi, jiburudishe na Tusker.* Won't you have another?'

'That I'll not refuse,' she said, laughing, throwing back her head, breasts thrust out in a fatal challenge. She turned to Abdulla. 'They say that if you don't drink your share on earth, in heaven you will have too much in stock.'

Abdulla shouted at Joseph to bring in more beer. He himself hobbled about and brought a paraffin lamp, cleaned the glass and lit the lamp, and sat down to drink.

'What is your name?' Munira was asking the woman.

'Wanja.'

'Wanja Kahii?' Abdulla joined in.

'How did you know that? It is what they used to call me at school. I often wrestled with the boys. I also did some drills only done by boys. Freewheeling. Walking on my hands. Wheelbarrow. I would tuck in my skirt and hold it tight between my legs. I also climbed up trees.'

'Wanja ... Wanja ...' repeated Munira. 'And you don't have another?'

'I have never asked: maybe I should. Why not? My grandmother here would know.'

'Who is your grandmother?' Abdulla asked.

'Nyakinyua ... don't you know her? She it is who told me about you two: that you are strangers to Ilmorog.'

'She is well known,' Munira said uncertainly.

'We know her,' Abdulla responded.

'I suppose you have come to visit her?' added Munira.

'Yes,' she said quietly, almost inaudibly. There followed a silence.

Abdulla coughed, cleared his throat and turned to Munira ... beginning to lean toward him, putting on that intimate air of conspiracy. Munira's stomach tightened as he saw the malicious glint in Abdulla's eyes. Does he need to tell the story? Does he? He suddenly felt a murderous hatred well up in him: at the same time, he desperately searched for fitting words with which to ward off the blow.

'Do you, Mwalimu, think I am too old to join your school?' Abdulla unexpectedly asked, almost as an afterthought. And Munira was grateful, so relieved that he could not help a loud sigh. 'Then I can persuade Wanja also to join the school. I would not mind wrestling her to the ground, or playing wheelbarrows together.'

Wanja laughed and turned a grave face to Munira.

'This one – with a crippled leg ... he is wicked. But I would floor him a thousand times.'

Joseph brought them more drinks.

What fascinated Munira was the subtle, quick changes on her face: from a suggestion of open laughter to an unconscious gravity and back again, yet the face somehow remaining basically unruffled.

'What can I teach a big man and a big woman?'

'Read ... write ... speak English through the nose,' Abdulla retorted.

'And geography and the history of lands far away from here,' chimed in Wanja.

'What good would you do the school? You would turn the children into rebels. One of my teachers used to say: Discipline maketh a school.'

'Make us prefects,' said Abdulla.

'Class monitors. Write down the names of those that make noise.'

'Or those that backbite their teachers.'

'Or those that smoke.'

'Or those that write letters to girls ... but I know why Mwalimu is scared of enrolling us. We might lead a strike. We might tear books and beat up the teachers. Down with our teachers ... There will be a riot, the school will close and ...'

Abdulla became absorbed in his mythical school strike. He unrolled idea after idea: image after image.

'Why,' he went on, 'I know of a school where the children went on strike because a teacher had confiscated a love-letter.'

And suddenly he was seized with an irresistible urge to tell that story of a school which almost closed because the headmaster had been suspected of erecting a mountain of shit. He was about to start when he remembered that Nyakinyua was Wanja's grandmother.

He also noticed that Wanja and Munira were quiet, very quiet. They seemed to have inexplicably withdrawn from the drunken irrelevance of a few minutes before. He looked from one face to the other: what had gone wrong? The lamplight flickered. Shadows passed over the walls: shadows passed over the faces. Maybe also over their lives, Abdulla thought: the two after all were strangers to him, and only Ilmorog had brought them together. Munira's voice when later he broke through the shadow of silence was reflective, sober, but underneath it, bitter.

3 🌑 To be made a prefect, Munira started slowly, looking to the ground, absorbed in thoughts he did not know he had, speaking from a past he should have forgotten, crossing valleys and hills and ridges and plains of time to the beginning of his death, you must be able to lick the boots of those above you, you must be able to scrub a dish to a shine brighter than the original, or as we would say in Siriana, outpray Jesus in prayers of devotion. Siriana: you should have been there in our time, before and during the period of the big, costly European dance of death and even after: you might say that our petty lives and their fears and crises took place against a background of tremendous changes and troubles, as can be seen by the names given to the age-sets between Nyabani and Hitira: Mwomboko ... Karanji, Boti, Ngunga, Muthuu, Ng'aragu Ya Mianga, Bamiti, Gicina Bangi, Cugini-Mburaki. But you understand we were protected from all that at Siriana, then both a primary and secondary boarding school. But I am straying. I could never quite lick anybody's boots. I could never shine dishes to brightness brighter than bright, or out-Jesus ... eeh ... Mr Christ. To be sure I was never prominent in anything. In class I was average. In sports I had not the limbs – I had not the will. My ambition and vision, unlike that of Chui, never would carry me beyond what the Lord had vouchsafed to me. Ambition, the same Chui used to say, quoting from an English writer called William Shakespeare, ambition should be made of sterner stuff. He himself was made of a different stuff from most of us. He was a tall youth with prominent cheekbones, a slightly hardened face, and black hair matted but always carefully parted in the middle. He was neat with a style all his own in doing things: from quoting bits from Shakespeare to wearing clothes. Even the drab school uniform of grey trousers, a white starched shirt, a blue jacket and a tie carrying the school motto, For God and Empire, looked as if it was specially tailored to fit him.

It was Chui who first introduced the tie-pin to school: it became the fashion.

He was the first to wear sports-shorts with the bottoms turned up: it became the fashion.

He was the star in sports, in everything: Chui this, Chui that, Chui, Chui, Chui everywhere. The breezy mountain air in which English settlers had found a home-climate had formed his sinewy muscles: to watch him play football, to watch that athletic swing of his body as he dribbled the ball with sudden swerves to the left or to the right to deceive an opponent, that was a pleasure indeed. Shake, shake, shake the ball, the looking-on crowd would shout themselves hoarse. He was a performer, playing to a delirious gallery. Shake, Shaake, Shaaake ... spear the ball somebody added. And Shakespeare he remained until, again through him, we heard of Joe Louis and his feats in the ring. He then became Joe, especially when our school was playing against some European teams. Joe, Joe, shake them, shake them: if you miss the ball, don't miss the leg. That was his best moment. His footwork would then be perfect. I believe that in such moments he was us, playing there against the white colonists.

Now when I come to think of it, it was strange that with all the hate we had for white people, we hardly ever thought of the Rev. Hallowes Ironmonger as a white man. Or maybe we thought of him as a different sort of white man. He was, despite his name, a gentle old man who looked more a farmer than a missionary headmaster. He was rather absent-minded and he would often forget his gold-laced black gown in the classroom or in the chapel. Walking across the grass lawns hand in hand with his bow-legged wife – we used to say that if she were to be made a goalkeeper, all the balls would go through her legs – they looked as if they were pilgrims resting on earth for a time, before resuming their journey to heaven, where they would eternally plough cotton-white fields, drink milky tea and eat vanilla cream chocolates. Rev. Ironmonger liked Chui and used to call him Shakespeare (but never Joe Louis) affectionately to the amusement of us all. They used to take him for long rides in the country in their choking Bedford. They also took him to musical concerts and puppet shows in the city. He was probably the son they had never had. We were not surprised when Chui, in his third year, was made the school captain, previously a prerogative of those in the fourth forms.

That was just before the Ironmongers retired to their home somewhere in England to wait for death, as some students rather ungraciously remarked, and a Cambridge Fraudsham came to the scene. Before we had any time to know him, he changed our lives. Fresh from the war, he already had firm notions how an African school had to be. Now, my boys, trousers are quite out of the question in the tropics. He sketched a profile of an imaginary thick-lipped African in a grey woollen suit, a sun-helmet, a white starched stiff collar and tie, and laughed contemptuously: Don't emulate this man. There was to be no rice in our meals: the school did not want to turn out men who would want to live beyond their means. And no shoes, my boys, except on the day of worship: the school did not want to turn out black Europeans but true Africans who would not look down upon the innocence and simple ways of their ancestors. At the same time, we had to grow up strong in God and the Empire. It was the two that had rid the world of the menace of Hitler.

The strength to serve: sports, cross-country races, cold showers at five in the morning became compulsory. We saluted the British flag every morning and every evening to the martial sound from the bugles and drums of our school band. Then we would all march in orderly military lines to the chapel to raise choral voices to the Maker: Wash me, Redeemer, and I shall be whiter than snow. We would then pray for the continuation of an Empire that had defeated the satanic evil which had erupted in Europe to try the children of God.

Chui – who else? – led us in a strike. We wanted all our former rights restored: we would have nothing to do with khaki shorts and certainly not with mbuca and other wadudu-eaten beans,* no matter the amount of proteins in the insects. And why should teams from European schools get glucose and orange squash after a game while our own teams only got plain water? Bring back Rev. Ironmonger, we shouted.

Today, now, I wonder what came over me. It was probably the emotion of the hour. But for those three days of defiant refusal to salute the British flag, I felt more than my usual average and I must have unnecessarily brought myself to the fore. Chui and I plus five others were expelled from Siriana. The rest returned to classes, after fierce-looking riot police with batons and tear gas and turai-shields came marching to the school. Fraudsham had played it tough and won ...

Munira paused. His voice had become more and more faint with the progress of the narrative. But it retained the weight and power of a bitter inward gaze. He had not quite realised that a school incident in the early forties could be so alive, could still carry the pain of a fresh wound. Maybe the drink and Wanja's presence had mellowed him. Maybe that or something else. He raised his face from the past of his days at school and looked at the grotesque shadow images on the wall. Wanja cleared her throat as if to say something, but she

*Mbuca and wadudu are East African insects.

didn't speak. Abdulla called out to Joseph to shut the counter. Munira continued.

'Chui was later heard of in South Africa and then America. For me the whole episode was a lesson. Ambition should be made of sterner stuff. Mine was of soft material. Withdrawal into self ... depersoning myself before a crowd demanding passionate commitment to a cause became, thenceforth, my way of life. Let me remain burrowed into the earth. Why should I dare? I say: Give me a classroom; give me a few attentive pupils and leave me alone!'

Abdulla started cursing Joseph and asking him why he had not yet brought more beer. Joseph quickly brought the beer. Abdulla shouted at him to clean and clear the table.

Joseph was about seven years old with bright eyes but a hardened, expressionless face. His presence was a kind of distraction and they all looked at him. Wanja noticed his untucked shirt; she was quick to see that as he cleaned and cleared the table he was avoiding turning his back to her. The table was big with a huge crack in the middle. He tried to lean across but he could not reach her side.

'Bring the cloth,' she said. 'I'll help you.'

'Let him do it. He is a lazy mass of fat and idle bones.'

She took the cloth all the same and cleared the whole table. As he left the room she saw that his shorts were torn at the seat and she understood.

'Is he at your school?' she asked, turning to Munira.

'No, no,' Munira said quickly, as if he would absolve himself of the responsibility.

'Why not?'

'Ask Abdulla,' he said, gulping down his drink.

'Look at this leg: I can't run round the shop on one leg. I'm not a magician.'

Unpleasant memories seemed to be interfering with an evening which had started so well.

'Listen, Abdulla,' Wanja said after minutes of silence. 'I'll be here for sometime. Let him go to school. I will help in the shop. I've done this kind of work before. Now I must go. Mr Munira, I am scared that I might meet a hyena in the dark. Walk me to my grandmother's place.'

Abdulla remained at the table and didn't look up as the two said kwaheri and left. He called out to Joseph.

'Go and shut the door. Bring me another beer and retire,' he said in a softened voice and this time he did not curse him.

4 ❀ Within a week she too had become of us, the new object of our gossip. She was Nyakinyua's granddaughter, this we knew – she often helped the old woman in the daily chores about the house and in the fields – but she remained a mystery: how could a city woman so dirty her hands? How could she strap a tin of water to a head beautifully crowned with a mass of shiny black hair? And what had really brought her to the gates of Ilmorog village when the trend was for the youth to run away? We watched her comings and goings with mounting curiosity: for there was little else to do in the fields beyond breaking a few clods of the earth as we waited for the beans and maize to ripen so that we could start harvesting. She would go away, we all said.

One day she disappeared. We were sure that she would not come back, despite the enigmatic smile on the old woman's face whenever she was asked about it. It's strange because we all talked as if we wanted her to stay away: but really we were all anxious that she should come back. This was clear on the people's faces when after a week she returned in a white matatu Peugeot car loaded with her things. We surrounded the vehicle. It was the first time we had seen a real car stand by the door of any Ilmorog homestead and we felt that something was stirring on our ridge. We helped her unload. The driver was all the time cursing the road and saying that had he known, he would not have agreed to the deal. At least not for that kind of money. Why couldn't they build even a track fit for a cattle wagon? We stood aside to let the car pass. We waved and waved until dust buried it in the distance. Then our interest was taken up by Wanja's things, each item in turn becoming the centre of gossip and speculation: the Vono spring bed, the foam mattress, the utensils, especially the pressure stove which could heat water without the aid of charcoal or firewood. But it was the pressure lamp that later in the evening really captured our hearts and imaginations. Ilmorog star, we called it, and those who had travelled to beyond the boundary said it was very much like the town stars in Ruwaini or the city stars that hang from dry trees. She moved to a hut not far from Nyakinyua's, and even a week later people still hung about the courtyard just to see her light the lamp. Still the question remained: why Ilmorog? Maybe now all our children will come back to us, for what's a village without young blood? But for that night of her return we stayed wakeful outside her hut. Nyakinyua broke into Gitiro, for which she had once been famous in Ilmorog and beyond: she sang in a low voice in praise of Ndemi and his wives, long long ago. The other women chimed in at intervals with ululations. Soon we were all singing and dancing, children chasing one another in the shadows, the old men and women occasionally miming scenes from Ilmorog's great past. It was really a festival before harvest-time a few months away, and the old only regretted that they had not prepared a little honey beer blessed by the saliva of Mwathi wa Mugo to welcome these promises of new beginnings.

The other women nodded their heads in appreciative understanding.

'Nyakinyua has found a helper in earthing up crops and later in harvesting,' they said.

'We even would follow her into the fields to see if she could really cultivate.'

The floral cloth over Ilmorog countryside was later replaced by green pods and maize cobs. The peasant farmers of Ilmorog now went into the fields to idly earth up crops that no longer needed the extra earth, or to merely pull out the odd weed. Thistles, marigolds and forget-me-nots would stick to their clothes, and they would now laugh and tell jokes and stories as they waited for the crops to ripen.

But their laughter concealed their new anxieties about a possible failure of the crops and the harvest. When a good crop was expected it was known through a rhythmic balanced alternation of rain and sunshine. A bad crop was preceded by sporadic rains or by a continuous heavy downpour which suddenly gave way to sunshine for the rest of the season. The latter was what had happened this year.

Indeed they could now see that the pods of beans and peas were short: the maize plants were thin and the cobs looked a little stunted.

Still they all waited for their ripeness and harvest believing that God was the Giver and also the one who took away.

❀

Between Wanja and Munira there gradually grew an understanding without demands: nothing deep, nothing to wreck the heart. It was only, so he at first told himself, that her company gave him pleasure. For a time he felt reassured, protected even. She seemed to accept his constant attention with a playful gratitude. It was as if she would have been surprised if he had done otherwise. She often mentioned the coast, the white kanzus worn by men, the milky mnazi beer, the hairy coconut shells strewn along the Sunday beaches, the low cliffs at the water-edges of Kilindini harbour, and the wide blue waters with steamers from lands far away. She talked about the narrow Arab streets in old Mombasa town above which stood Fort Jesus – 'It's funny, imagine them calling it by the name of Jesus' – and when Abdulla asked her if it was true that some Arabs could change themselves into women or cats she only laughed and asked him: but what kind of Mswahili*are you to believe such things? Mswahili Mwislamu wa Bara,† eh? She talked feelingly about all these things as if in every place she had been she had immersed herself in the life there: otherwise she rarely discussed her personal life, or talked about herself. Which of course Munira did not mind, for he was not one to want to tear the veils round another's past. But he was not immune to her fatal glances and the boldness alternating with studied shyness which she bestowed on him and on Abdulla. He was, though he did not want to admit it, a little troubled by that waitingness on her face, by that pained curiosity and knowledge in her eyes. She was of course not bound to him, this he knew, and it accorded well with his spirit: he was scared of more than a casual link with another.

Still he felt that by telling his story, so frivolous, so childish, he had surrendered a part of himself to others and this he felt gave them power over him. He went to his classes with an eye to the end of the day so he could meet her at Abdulla's place. A beer together ... a laugh together ... and in the course of the evening's chatter he would carefully edge toward the night he told the Siriana story, circling round it without actually mentioning it: but their unresponsive faces did not tell him what they had really thought of his failure. She was always near and yet far, and he found that he was getting more and more pained that she talked to Abdulla with the same intimacy: perhaps, weighing him against Abdulla, she found him wanting? He started thinking about Abdulla: how had he lost his leg? Why had he come to Ilmorog? He was surprised how little he knew about Abdulla, about anybody.

An aeroplane flew low over Ilmorog. Children streamed out of their classrooms and all strained their eyes and raised their voices to the sky, trying hard to follow the movement of the plane and also its shadow that so swiftly crossed over many fields, over Ilmorog ridges and into the plains. Abdulla's donkey hee-hawed, frightened, and its voice jarred against the sound of the small plane. Peasants emerged from the fields of maize and grouped in twos or threes in the open paths to look at the aeroplane and gossip about it: what did it want with Ilmorog that it kept on coming back? Wanja walked across to the school and asked Munira the same question. What did it want? Munira did not know but he felt it good that she had come over to seek his opinion. Maybe sightseeing, he pronounced, as the plane now flew straight across and disappeared into the white-blue cloudy distance. It was the first time that she had called on him at school since their first encounter and as she now walked away, he watched, entranced by her slightly swaying buttocks. He felt irresistibly drawn toward her.

*Swahili-speaker.
†A bogus Swahili-speaker.

And then she started appearing to him in dreams: breasts would beat on breasts, body frames would become taut with unspoken desire, eyes would hold onto eyes as they both stood on Ilmorog hill, hideaway from school, away from Cambridge Fraudsham who had fumed, frowned and ground his teeth with anger because of the perfumed garden that was her body. They would start wrestling, but instead of falling on the ground they would tumble into fleecy clouds, waltzing in slow motion over Ilmorog hills and valleys, thighs to thighs, warm bloodpower surging for release and suddenly he could not hold himself. In the morning he saw dry pools on the bed and he felt immeasurable sadness. He was now in danger. What is happening to me, a spectator? he moaned. For a day or two he would hold himself stiff and aloof in her presence. He walked about Ilmorog hill in the twilight, puzzling out the meaning of this new emotion: where was his man's courage? Was he to go through life trembling on the brink because he was afraid of the chaos in the abyss?

Not so many days after the plane visit, other men in khaki clothes came to Ilmorog in a Land Rover. They walked through the fields, pulling a chain on the ground, and planting red sticks. They were besieged by the whole community who wanted to know who they were and what they were doing trespassing on other people's lands. But they were also fascinated by the men's instruments of chains and theodolite and the telescope hanging from one of the men's neck and through which he constantly peered. People argued that the telescope could see from where they were to the end of the world. Munira stood at a distance from the group. Wanja came over and stood by him but her eyes were on the officer-in-charge of the team. The officer walked to Munira and asked for water. Munira sent one of the children to the school to fetch water and glasses ... Munira asked him: What was that all about?

'I am an engineer,' he said. 'We are making a preliminary survey for a proposed road across Africa.'

'To?'

'Zaire, Nigeria, Ghana, Morocco – all over Africa,' he explained and went back to his workmates.

When Munira turned to Wanja he saw her hurrying away, almost running away as if she had been stung by a bee. Later at Abdulla's place almost the whole countryside came to ask Munira what the man had talked about and whether it was the long promised waterway they had come to measure. But Wanja was not among them. Strange, he thought as he tried to concentrate on the chatter and speculation.

'I hope they will not take our lands away,' Njuguna voiced their fear after Munira had talked about the road.

'They would only take a small piece,' Abdulla suggested, 'and they would pay compensation.'

'A lot of money and other lands,' somebody else added.

'And it is good to have a proper road. It will make our travel easy and we can send our goods to markets far away instead of giving it to these scorpions who visit us from the city,' Njuguna now enthused over the prospect.

But in their hearts they did not believe that such things could be. Nderi wa Riera had after all promised water which never came.

Munira was puzzled about Wanja's absence. Was she avoiding him? He now ached for her and he decided to force the issue.

The following night after the departure of the road team, he went to her place, determined that this time he would take the plunge. Pleading eyes, fingers warm with bold bloodness, aah, that this cup would soon be over. He called Hodi and stood at the door leaning on the frame of the hut, rubbing his stomach a little to clear the bitter pool of frustration and disappointment. The light brilliantly lit Abdulla, seated quite comfortably on a stool, his body against the bed-frame.

'Mwalimu ... come in ... I am so happy,' she called.

His heart sank even further as he sat down: the light seemed to emphasize the happy face of Abdulla beaming at him a smile welcoming him to his carefully hidden lair.

'You should have brought us beer to celebrate this day,' she continued, sitting next to Abdulla facing him.

'How are you, Mwalimu?' Abdulla asked. 'I wish I had known you were coming over here. I would have waited for you. As it is, I had to beat all the evening dew by myself and I have only just arrived ...'

'I am fine ...' Munira said, suddenly feeling better at the news. 'What are we celebrating?'

'Guess.'

'I can't.'

'Today Abdulla offered me a job. Do you think I should take it?'

'What job?'

'A barmaid. Imagine that. A barmaid in Ilmorog. Do you think I should take it?'

'It depends on the work. But there are very few customers in Ilmorog.'

'Aah, but that is the job of a barmaid. Really, Mwalimu! A barmaid is employed to get more customers. Or to make the few regulars drink more.'

'Well, if you like it ... have you worked as a barmaid before?'

'But how do you think I came to know all the places that I have been talking about?' and she suddenly jumped up from her seat. 'Oh, I should make tea: let's celebrate with tea without milk ...'

She was very light on her feet. She started washing a sufuria and Munira's eyes moved in rhythm with the motion of her full body and of her breasts. He was still puzzled: why was she so happy about such a job in Ilmorog when she could easily work in any of the cities she talked about? Even Ruwa-ini was much bigger and better for that kind of work. And why had she acted so oddly yesterday? But he could not help but be affected by the light, gay mood she generated. As they drank tea she once again changed from the childlike happiness to a sombre, quieter, composed self.

'I feel I want to cry. I really feel so happy because Abdulla has bought Joseph clothes and a slate and books and now he can start school.'

'That is good, Abdulla. At long last. Joseph looks a bright boy and I am sure he will do well.'

'He should thank Wanja. It was her who made it possible.'

'It was Munira's story. It was so moving ... really so moving,' she said.

The Siriana incident had touched a chord in her past.

Munira was suddenly happy with himself. He turned to her:

'You yourself ... when you laugh ... you look so young, you should be in school instead of working for Abdulla as a barmaid.' She thought a little. She sipped some tea. She fingered her cup.

'It is strange how one thing can lead to another. You yourself: maybe you are here because of that strike in your school. As for Abdulla — anyway I don't know why you are here in Ilmorog. Maybe it is an accident that we are all here. Or an act of God. I don't know ... I don't know ... Do you remember the men who came to survey the road?' she asked. 'Do you remember the Engineer?'

She had started haltingly, but now she suddenly felt the need to tell of this one knot in her life. And they waited also, sensing this in the air. She stood up, pumped more pressure into the lamp to add to the light.

'Do ... you ... know ... him?' Munira faltered.

'No,' she said and then added slowly, 'but he reminded me of my past ...' She paused again and sat down hitting the empty cup with her foot. She picked it up and put it aside. 'Yes, take me, for instance,' she started again in an introspective tone, which was very captivating. 'I sometimes ask myself: why should a silly happening ... a boy's visit ... a girl's and boy's school affair ... why should such a thing affect one's life? You know such affairs – Abdulla talked about it the other night – a gift of a pencil, a stolen sweet, love-letters copied from books ... all ending in the same way ... *maingi ni Thumu: manyinyi ni cukari* ... tear drops on paper circled with x x – kisses.' She raised her head and laughed. 'Maybe they are right: a lot of words is poison: a few words are sugar. Later I was to see cases of sugar words turning out to be poison. Now this boy. His name was Ritho. He and I were in the same class at Kinoo Primary School. Girls can be cruel. I used to read his letters to the other girls. We would giggle and laugh at him, all the way from Kinoo to Rungiri. But his gifts of pencils and sweets – these I did not tell to anybody. It was all childish and a game that amused us. And then we were late in school one Friday. We were watching a football match between our school and Rungiri. We called them KADU and we called ourselves KANU, which they resented. KANU lost to KADU. Ritho walked me home and we talked about the game. Then he talked about Uhuru. He said there would be increased chances, especially for poor people. Therefore he was going to work very hard: go to a secondary school ... university ... engineering. Yes, he was going to be an engineer ... his ambition was to design and build a bridge over a road or over a river. Can you imagine this ... at that age, then? It felt good. But boys were always more confident about the future than us girls. They seemed to know what they wanted to become later in life: whereas with us girls the future seemed vague ... It was as if we knew that no matter what efforts we put into our studies, our road led to the kitchen and to the bedroom. That evening it felt so good to be with one who was so confident in his heart's desires that I seemed to share in his ambitions. I thought I also could see a light and I swore to work harder. He did not appear so funny and clumsy and ridiculous any more and we held hands in the dark. A man coughed as he passed by: I thought he was shaped like my father – but I did not care. I ran home and hung my deerskin bag in itʳ place on the wall and sat down: my mother asked me: why have you not changed into ordinary clothes? I said it was Friday and I would anyway be washing the school uniform the following day. And is that why you have come home late? I kept quiet. I recalled Ritho's letters ... my love is as uncountable as the sands of the sea, the trees in the forest, or the stars in the sky or the cells of my body ... and his ambitions and now I wanted to laugh and tell my mother about Ritho and his dreams of becoming an engineer. I said: I was late watching a football match at school. We were supposed to stay and cheer our side – And with whom were you just now? My boy friend, I said just like that and now I laughed. Mother, he – I started.

But the look in her eyes killed the words. My father said: She is now a woman, she even talks to her mother as equals. They locked me in my room and they both beat me, my father with his belt and my mother with a cowhide strap we used for tying and carrying things. This will teach you to come home holding hands with boys! This will teach you to be talking like equals to your mother. It was so unfair and I was determined not to cry. This seemed to add to their anger. They were now beating to make me cry. At last I screamed for help. I cried: you are people of God: have you no mercy? They now stopped. I continued crying bitterly. I silently cursed at this world. I could not see that I had done anything wrong. I did not feel guilty. When they warned me never to be seen with pagan boys – I don't know – I felt then that they were beating me not just because I was with a boy but because he came from a family even poorer than ours. I also felt that the way they beat me – it was as if they were working out something between them. I had known that my father and mother were drifting apart because of something else that had happened almost at the beginning of the Emergency. I also knew that my father was facing hard times. But I resented that they should use me as a path for their coming together. That time, they whispered long into the night.

'For days and weeks I planned vengeance. My parents had often beaten me, but it was the first time I was so rebellious in my thoughts. How could I get my own back? Was it a sin to be poor? We ourselves were not rich: were we sinners? Was it a sin even not to be a Christian? At the same time I hated the young man who had been the cause of my suffering. I nursed the pain in my soul. I am a hard woman and I know I can carry things inside my heart for a long time. I wanted to find something that would really hurt them and humiliate them as they had done to me. But I was young, the pain faded and thoughts of vengeance were buried by the call of daily living. But I also knew that since that night I, my home, school, the world, nothing was any longer the same. I was aware of a growing impatience with the school and learning: it was as if these were keeping me from a world, a more interesting world beyond the school and the village. Out there, there was life. This was also the years preceding independence when there was a lot of talk of how different life would be ... Aah, you see how I talk as if all this was ages ago. Yet only a few years ... Yes, a few years.

'At about this time a certain man came and bought a plot very near our home, and he put up a stone building with a huge iron tank for catching rainwater. He was married, with two girls. His example was soon followed by others, but his remained the best known for setting the trend. It was also seen as a sign of things to come. Maybe, soon, after independence, everyone would have at least a corrugated-iron roofed house and a tank in which they would catch rainwater. He was also the proud owner of a small lorry and a bus. We did not know where he had come from, but he was probably the first such big man in our village in the last years of the emergency, you know, when Africans started acquiring businesses. He was so different from my father: he was tall and strong and wealthy and envied and respected by every one. I was drawn to him from the very first time I saw him in his bus acting as a conductor. He did not charge me any fare the second time, saying you are the daughter of so and so, and of course I felt good that he knew me. He came home once or twice and my father, whose fortune had declined over the years, was so proud I felt ashamed. He became friends with my father and he soon became a frequent visitor at home. During Christmas he brought us all gifts. He gave me a floral dress and called me his daughter and I looked, or thought I looked, like a cousin of mine who had gone to the city a long time back. Later he gave me a lift in his lorry and took me to an afternoon film show at the Royal Cinema in the city. School could never thereafter be the same. Whenever he came to visit us, I would deliberately go to bed early as if I was shy of company. But his visit was always a sign between us that he wanted to see me the following afternoon. I would put the floral dress into my bag with books on top. In the city I would go to a latrine and change into the floral dress and hide my school uniform in the bag. At four or five I would go back home, of course in my school uniform.

'It was the maths teacher who found me out. I used to be his best student and he had set his eyes on me. My breasts were a little bit more developed than those of the other girls and I had a full body. He used all sorts of excuses to detain me a little longer in school: Go and light a fire in my house: take these exercise books to my house: why didn't you clean your nails, see me after four ... and all sorts of things. Once, I had reported him to my mother and my mother was cross and had threatened to take up the matter with a higher authority. Now he noticed my frequent absences: he spied on me, and he found out. He called me into his house and talked love and said he wanted me and would I? I refused and he confronted me with his knowledge. Either I let him, or I would face my angry parents. I refused. He told my parents. My mother who all along had shown a marked dislike for the man was so shocked she could not even beat me. At first I felt – it has hurt them. But she cried and held me to herself as if she would protect me from a hostile world, and I felt guilty and I wept. This brought their final rupture. She told my father with a tone that cut deep: he was your wealthy friend, after all: and my father was so humiliated and looked so small I felt sorry for him too. My mother threatened that should that man ever set his dirty feet and hypocritical face in the house, she would pour hot water on him. Otherwise they did not say a word to me and for that reason I swore not to see the man again. I became a little more studious and even endured the leering triumphant laughter and snide comments of the maths teacher. I was surprised, and the teacher was probably surprised, when in the mock-CPE results I was number two in the whole area with the best maths results. My awkward boy friend was fifth. Everybody now thought that the actual exams would be a 'walkover' for me, and the teachers started talking of the high schools they would like me to try . . . But the results of my vengeance also followed me. I started vomiting and feeling a little tired. So I was pregnant? I ran back to my lover. I will marry you all right, he assured me, if you don't mind being a second wife, and my first is so harsh she will make you her slave. I thought him a little light-hearted on a matter that was life and death to me. And I knew that my mother would soon find out. No, I could not bear it. I would not be there when she found out. My mind was set. I would force the issue.

'I will always remember that day with shame and guilt. My mother lay in bed, and I was going to school she told me . . . you see, we had two goats in a pen . . . she told me – go and throw the dry dung in the shamba. Here was my chance. I put all my nice clothes under a basket and covered the top with dry dung manure. And I ran away from home . . . to him. He looked at me once and suddenly he started laughing. He told me not to be funny, he was old enough to be my father, and anyway he was a Christian. Something blocked my throat: I could not cry. I just whimpered once and I went to my cousin in Eastleigh.'

She had lowered her voice a little as she said the last words and Munira could somehow imagine a tortured soul's journey through valleys of guilt and humiliation and the long sleepless nights of looking back to the origins of the whole journey. She broke into his thoughts with a cynical little laughter.

'Yes. Many were the times I used to think that I could hear a Lamb's voice calling me across a deep deep valley: come unto me, all ye that are lonely, and I'll give you the final rest. It was really tempting and my cousin could see through me as she tried to make me face the reality I had chosen. And yet had I chosen it? I fought hard against both the Lamb's voice and my cousin's suggestion. I would live to have my vengeance. I was young: I would not go her way. I have tried my hands at various jobs, but work in bars seems to be the one readily available to us girls – dropouts from school and CAPE failures and even some drop-outs from high schools.'

The sad, bitter note dominated the silence for a few seconds. It was clear that no matter what a fight she had put up she had not forgotten the original wound. She had somehow drawn Abdulla and Munira into her world and they seemed also to experience this wound, or maybe it reminded them of their own wounds. Now she suddenly bounced back to life:

'That is why it always pains me to see children unable to go to school ... and that is why tomorrow at the shop we must celebrate Joseph's return to school. Abdulla, I am so happy. Munira, you'll come tomorrow please, you must. It will be my first night as a barmaid in Ilmorog.'

She again carried them along with her boundless energy and enthusiasm. She had a way of making a man's heart palpitate with different emotions and expectations at the same time.

'I am going to see Mzigo at Ruwa-ini tomorrow ...'

'No, you must come,' she interrupted him imperiously. 'And bring me a pound of the long-grained rice. Abdulla saw me home tonight. Tomorrow it is your turn. Or are you afraid of the dark? Look. The moon will be out. It will announce the first day of harvest. Tomorrow ... so many hopes to celebrate!'

Afraid? No, not tomorrow night nor any other night with you, his heart sang joyfully.

'Thank you, Abdulla ... thank you, Munira ...' she cooed as they stood up to go and each felt as if it was said with a special meaning, to him, alone.

Munira said 'Keep well' to Abdulla and continued in the dark. But he would be there tomorrow, he said to himself, he would surely see her home tomorrow, and he was now smiling to himself. Beautiful petals: beautiful flowers: tomorrow would indeed be the beginning of a harvest.

Chapter Three

1 ✿ Twelve years later, on a Sunday, Godfrey Munira tried to reconstruct that scene in a statement to the police, a statement in which he was meant to tell the truth, the whole truth and nothing else but the truth. But he found that although it was still alive in the

memory, the night of Wanja's first narrative, with all its suggestion of inexplicable doom and violence, eluded exact formulation in words. He sat on a hard bench, his elbows planted on the table, his eyes occasionally darting to the Aspro-calendar, the only decoration on otherwise bare walls. But mostly he rested his eyes on the face of the officer: he must be new in the Force, Munira thought. Ilmorog was probably his first big station and he was probably nervous or impatient or both. He tapped the floor with his right foot and drummed the table a little with his fingers. He was losing patience and Munira tried to understand: who could not feel the subterranean currents of unrest in the country? Schoolboys and girls on strike and locking up their recalcitrant, authoritarian headmasters and head-mistresses in office cupboards: workers downing their tools and refusing the temporary consolation of tripartite agreements; housewives holding processions and shouting obscene slogans in protest against the high food prices; armed robbers holding up banks in daylight with crowds cheering; women refusing to be relegated to the kitchen and the bedroom, demanding equal places in men's former citadel of power and privilege – all these could try the nerves of those entrusted by the ruling classes of this world with maintaining man's ordained order and law. They trusted too much in the wisdom of this world: they would not open the book of God to see that these things had been prophesied a long time ago. Karega and his following of Theng'eta factory workers were not any different: they had rejected it is true mere brotherhood of the skin, region and community of origins and said no to both black and white and Indian employers of labour. But they too would fail: because they had also rejected the most important brotherhood – the only brotherhood – of religion, of being born anew in the Lord of the universe and of the eternal kingdom. What other truth did the officer want? Munira wanted to show him that Wanja was the 'She' mentioned by the Prophets, extracting obedience from men, making them deviate from the path, and all the time with a voice that had the suggestive qualities of suffering and protest, hope and terror and above all of promises of escape through the power of the flesh. But the officer – the wise man of this world – he only stood and walked about the room, turning cold eyes on Munira. What had a silly barmaid's cry eleven years back – before a single stone building, let alone an international highway, had been built in Ilmorog – to do with the present? He might as well open that book and start with Adam and Eve. But would it not be better – it would surely save time and energy – if he skipped the years and did not indulge a rather – well – a rather vivid memory? That was exactly the point, Munira thought, slightly amused by the officer's outburst. It – the cry – the scene had everything to do with it: for if Munira had not been blinded by that voice he could have seen the signs, the evil web being spun around him, around Abdulla, around Ilmorog. He tried another approach: he begged for pen and paper and appealed for time: he would write a statement in his own hand and in his own way and later the policeman could ask questions – and with the help of the Lord . . . The officer suddenly banged the table, all patience gone: he wanted facts, not history; facts, not sermons or poetry. Murder was not irio or njohi,* he said and called out to the warders: Lock him in.

He was put in a cell: he heard the chain lock click and he felt a kind of spiritual satisfaction – he remembered Peter and Paul – yes, Paul who used to be Saul – in jail hearing voices from the Lord. Murder is not irio – the same words as were used by the constables who earlier had come for him, Munira thought, yawning. He was tired – suddenly very tired from the night's vigil – and he sank into deep slumber.

They woke him up the following day. He felt fresh in the mind. He was ushered into the same office: but this time the officer was a different man all together: elderly, with a face that was expressionless even when he smiled or laughed or joked, as if the face could never register any emotions.

The officer had come from Nairobi to take charge of the investigation. He had served in various capacities under various heads from the colonial times to the present. Crime for him was a kind of jigsaw puzzle, and he believed that there was a law to it – a law of crime – a law of criminal behaviour – and he believed that if you looked hard enough you could see this law operating in even the smallest gestures. He was interested in people; in their behaviour; in their words, gestures, fantasies, gait: but only as a part of this jigsaw puzzle. He had read a lot and was interested in the various professions – law, politics , medicine, teaching – but only as part of his one consuming interest. He was looking for that one image which contained the clue, the law of a particular crime. From there he could work out the exact circumstances, to the minutest details, and he hardly ever failed.

He had no illusions about his work: he had put this knowledge in the service of whatever power happened to be in the land, and he never took an attitude. Thus he had served the colonial regime with the same relentless unsparing energy that he did an independent African government, and he would serve as faithfully whatever would follow. He was neutral, and his awesome power over politicians, professionals, businessmen, petty criminals, all that, arose

*beer

43

from this neutrality in the service of a law. His secret ambition was one day to set up a private practice in detective work so that, like a lawyer or a priest, his services could be hired by anybody.

This case interested him immediately, especially because of the types of personalities it had brought together. Chui – an educationist and businessman; Hawkins Kimeria – a business tycoon; Abdulla – a petty trader; Karega – a trade unionist; Mzigo – an educationist turned businessman; Munira – a teacher and man of God; Wanja – a prostitute. And all this in what was basically a New Town. He wondered how many other people it would bring together. He would apply himself to a study of the place and the people and he would not start with any prejudices; everything fascinated him, and Munira most of all:

'Mr Munira, please sit down. You slept well?'

'Yes.'

'Like some cigarettes?'

'No, I don't smoke.'

'I should start by introducing myself. My name – you'll be surprised by the coincidence – my name is Inspector Godfrey, and I must apologise about yesterday. You see, he is young – you know youth these days.'

'I understand. He was only doing his work – servicing man's law.'

'That is the spirit, Mr Munira. The law. All of us are governed by the law.'

'Of God.'

'Yes, Mr Munira. But God must also work through man; you, me, somebody else. Listen, Mr Munira, you are a very highly respected man in Ilmorog. You have been here longer than anybody else. Twelve years, they tell me. You know the character of most people in this town. Please believe me, we don't want to deal unfairly with anybody. We only want to serve truth and justice. It may be only man's concept of justice but it is his present concept of justice. Maybe later, when things are fully revealed to us, when we as it were cease to see things through a mirror darkly ... but now, Mr Munira, we must try our best. You see a policeman, just like a teacher, or a priest, is only a public servant; I might have said a public victim. We never get thanks for ensuring the safety of people's lives and property. But that is our lot, our job, and anyway we get paid for it. But we cannot discharge this tremendous responsibility – and it is a fearful trust, Mr Munira – without help from our true master, the public. Now, Mr Munira, we shall provide you with pen and paper and a place to sleep even – for you understand, don't you, that we cannot very well let you leave the precincts of the police station before you have made a complete statement – it is just procedure, Mr Munira, and nothing is implied – and, of course, food. You can handle it any way you like – I myself am very curious about the history of Ilmorog, of your school even, that is, if you have the patience and the writer's energy; but remember that all we are asking you to do is to tell us in a clear simple statement anything you may know about the behaviour, the general mental disposition, and especially the movements of Abdulla, Wanja and Karega on the night of . . . and even during the week or so before this triple murder – of course, it may not be murder – of Kimeria, Chui and Mzigo.'

2   How does one tell of murder in a New Town? Murder of the spirit? Where does one begin? How recreate the past so that one can show the operation of God's law? The working out of God's will, the revelation of His will so that now the blind can see what the wise cannot see?

    Perhaps . . . perhaps this or that . . . what I might have done or might not have done . . . these things we always turn over in our minds at the post mortem of a deed which cannot now be undone. Peace, my soul. But how can I, a mortal, help my heart's fluttering, I who was a privileged witness of the growth of Ilmorog from its beginnings in rain and drought to the present flowering in petals of blood? I who knew Abdulla, Nyakinyua, Wanja, Karega? Have I not leafed through the heart of each? In all our conversations and schemes and remembrance of the past, even on the night that she made me promise that I would surely return the following day, to celebrate, I was always struck by the razor-blade tension at the edges of our words. Violence of thought, violence of sight, violence of memory. I can see that now. In this prison twilight certain things, groves, hills, valleys, are sharper in outline even though set against a sombre sky. Get thee behind me, Satan. Arrogant confidence of hindsight. There was a time I used to think that I was saving him, might have saved her and Abdulla too. Then I suddenly saw Karega about to tumble headlong down the path I myself had gingerly trodden and I was struck by my lack of power to hold him back, though I wanted to. For that one week I would picture Wanja laughing at our frail efforts to extricate ourselves from her vast dreams and visions; for I now knew, God is my witness, that all she wanted was power, power especially over men's souls, young, desperate and lost power, I thought, to avenge herself of the evil done to her in the past.

    And Karega even after his travels was still a child. This is not to denigrate him or to deny the strength of his feelings: the fire, the idealism, the glowing faith in the possibilities of heroism and devotion. He stretched his arms for that elusive beauty, for that yet undiscovered truth of an enduring human relationship. Indeed it was as if in everything, even in his coming to Ilmorog, he was searching for a lost innocence, faith and hope. I remember an entry I once read in one of his exercise books in the days before we fell out:

> You'll laugh and say: oh, these are only the tears of a big baby. You'll laugh and say: he is manchild come to bring ill-omen to the gates of a peaceful homestead. Laugh and sneer. I alone have carried this fear and wrestled with this knowledge in my heart. For how can I say I had not known, even as our hearts beat each to each, that she would later betray me? She was older than I was; She had seen more thabiri birds fly home with the sunset. And really it is not her alone. Alas, the world I hoped for yesterday has fallen from my hands. The people I knew, the people I had seen creating new worlds, are hazy images in my memory: and the seed we planted together with so much faith, hope, blood and tears: where is it now? I ask myself: where is the new force, what's the new force that will make the seed sprout and flower?

I thought then that this was despair and I used to ask myself: could it be this despair, so painful in one so young, which had made him turn to me for – for – what? Or was it the searching hope behind the selfsame words that had made him a wanderer all over Kenya, from Mombasa to Kisumu and back again to Ilmorog, looking for – for – what? Whatever it was it had driven him to Ilmorog, to me, to Abdulla, to Wanja, to this riddle: truth and beauty – what illusions! We are all searchers for a tiny place in God's corner to shelter us for a time from treacherous winds and rains and drought. This was all that I had wanted him to see: that the force he sought could only be found in the blood of the Lamb.

3 ✿ I suppose you can say that Karega had chosen to confide in me on the claims of some shadowy connections in our past. Shadowy, I say, because for a long time after our first meeting in Ilmorog I thought that our paths had only previously crossed once in that impersonal territory of a teacher and pupils. But even that I had forgotten, that day he came to my hideout in Ilmorog only recently discovered by one outsider – Wanja. I asked myself, surprised: who is that stranger standing at the gate?

I was returning from a trip to the HQ in Ruwa-ini. I had not stopped anywhere because I was thinking of Wanja's appeal the night before. I so wanted to take her home – to walk her to her hut –

she and I – alone – in the dark. Inside, I was scared of this possession, of the way she had taken my heart prisoner so that she could say so coolly: *and you'll bring me a pound of the long-grained rice*: and my whole being so ready to obey. I had gone to every shop in Ruwa-ini. I had bought the rice. Everything was so ready for tonight's celebration of a harvest. And now who was this stranger?

'Good afternoon,' I called out in a neutral voice, getting off my creaking bicycle, and leaning it against the white, ochred wall.

'Maybe you don't remember me . . .' he started to say after replying to my greeting.

I waved him to silence with a non-committal smile: we shall talk, we shall talk. Even at that stage in our relationship, there was something about him which irritated me: his apparent self-possession, or was it his ready devotion? He helped me carry two boxes of white chalk and a bundle of exercise-books. I carried a packet of the long-grained rice I had bought for Wanja. The sitting-room, like the rest of the house, was rather empty: one wooden bench, a table with huge cracks along the joints; two folding chairs and a shelf fixed to the wall and graced with old copies of *Flamingo*, *Drum*, *African Film* and torn school editions of *Things Fall Apart* and *Song of Lawino*. I had always thought of improving my library but in this, as in so many other matters, I dwelt in the twilight of doing and non-doing. He sat at one end of the bench, declining my offer of a folding chair. He was small in build, with sad intense eyes: he was a man, but one who had suddenly but painfully grown mature.

'Some tea?' I asked, hoping that he would say no: I stretched my legs and thought of Wanja and her story and her concern over Joseph and the magic she had wrought in Adbulla and myself: I thought of her having to leave and I suddenly found myself asking: but what happened to the child?

'Anything watery and warm will be enough,' he said. I was resigned to the fate of an unwilling host.

'One thing we do not have in this house is milk.'

'Tea without milk is all right. Although we live next to a shopping centre, we cannot always afford milk.'

As I put pressure in the primus stove, I suddenly remembered, somehow or other his words made me remember Old Mariamu, as we used to call her. She was a muhoi*on my father's land and we always thought of her as inseparable from the land. She was very pious in an undemonstrative way: her piety simply lay in how she carried herself; in how she talked; in her trembling, total absorption in her work. She used to make tea without tea-leaves: she would simply put sugar in a spoon and bake it on the fire. When the sugar had turned

*beggar

47

into a sticky mess of syrup, she would dip it into the boiling water. How I loved her tea; I would often hide from my mother's Christian vigilance for a sip of Mariamu's brew. At least it had plenty of sugar and no pretences about milk. I thought of telling this to my visitor but I only said:

'We should be grateful for small mercies: some people take tea without milk and without tea-leaves.'

'Oh, my mother often does that when she cannot afford tea-leaves. She bakes sugar in a spoon: we call it, we always called it, soot. She would say, laughing: Karega, do you want a little sugared soot?'

I looked at him rather sharply and said:

'Where do you come from?'

'Kamiritho. You know, Kwa-mbira. Limuru.'

'You mean: you came all that way, from Limuru?'

'Yes.'

'Not on foot, I hope.'

'Part of the way. I got into a matatu taxi. It was crammed with people. The owner seemed convinced that there was infinite space in the coughing Ford Anglia. He would say: "Mundu wa Uria – Let us love one another and sit up properly, I tell you this car is bigger than even a lorry," and he would pack in yet more passengers. We were more than twenty in that thing, and it so rough a road.'

'All roads to anywhere in this area are rough.'

'Maybe they will one day gravel them with murram or else tar them.'

I remembered the aeroplane, the Landrover and the surveying team that only the day before had planted red pegs in Ilmorog. An International Highway through Ilmorog. I suddenly wanted to laugh at the preposterous idea. Why, I asked myself, had they not built smaller serviceable roads before thinking of international highways? At least my journey to and from Ruwa-ini would have been much quicker and I would have arrived home much less tired and might even have avoided this meeting with a stranger. But as suddenly I became bitter and took the side of the Ilmorog peasant; *they* would never build a road – not unless money was a flowing river. I burst out:

'Yes. Yes ... when hyenas grow horns.'

I was surprised at my words. After all, the peasants and herdsmen in Ilmorog had for years fought the earth and the sun without help from tarred roads and reliable transport. Young men and women had anyway trekked to the cities and left the old to till the land, and the old themselves had not much incentive to farm for the big markets. As for the herdsmen, they usually multiplied their cattle only to see them claimed by the drought or disease. The curse of God, they would probably say as they moved further into the plains. In my mind I now put this wretched corner beside our cities: skyscrapers versus mud walls and grass thatch; tarmac highways, international airports and gambling casinos versus cattle-paths and gossip before sunset. Our erstwhile masters had left us a very unevenly cultivated land: the centre was swollen with fruit and water sucked from the rest, while the outer parts were progressively weaker and scraggier as one moved away from the centre. There is a story of dwarf-like Gumbas who lived long, long before the Manjiri generation, before the iron age in Kenya, and whose heads were over-huge and so sat precariously on the rest of the body. Whenever a Gumba fell, so goes the legend, he could not lift himself without aid from outside.

As suddenly as these thoughts, so alien to my life in Ilmorog, stole into my consciousness, I felt the presence of the young man as a weight on my spirits: what did it matter to me that the peasants here were without decent water? That the herdsmen had swollen eyes and the cattle died of drought? What did it matter to me that the able-bodied had fled Ilmorog in search of the golden fleece in cities of metallic promises and no hope? What had it all to do with me? I was not and I had never wanted to be my brother's keeper.

I was never one for the public limelight or really interested in the affairs of others. My life was a series of unconnected events: I was happy in my escape-hole in Ilmorog, at least before Wanja came. Her face once again rose before me, etched beautiful and sad against the horizon of my being. What was she doing to me? What had happened to her child?

'What work do you do?' I asked the young man rather abruptly, coldly in fact.

'Work? I don't do any ... no job yet ... I've been all over the city ... well, that is why I have come ... you see, until a year or so ago, I used to go to school—'

'Which school?'

'Siriana!'

'Please help yourself to another cup,' I found myself saying, looking at him with renewed interest. He was fingering his empty cup, looking to the ground as if about to continue talking but not knowing how to proceed. I handed him the mbirika*and he poured tea into his cup. The face, his face, now formed a faint silhouette in the memory.

'I am afraid I can't quite – eeh—?'

'It's a long time. My name is Karega. But I don't expect that you
*kettle

would immediately remember me. I think I have grown a bit. I used to pick pyrethrum flowers in your father's shambas.'

He paused but he sensed that I was still unable to place him. He continued:

'My mother was Mariamu and before we moved to the new Emergency village in 1955, we used to live on your father's farm. Ahoi . . .'

'Mariamu,' I said. 'Are you Mariamu's son?'

'Yes.'

'I cannot recall . . . but . . . I knew your brother Nding'uri. He used to be a playmate. We even went hunting antelopes together running through thorny bush in my father's forest. We never caught any . . . But that was long before 1952.'

'I didn't know him . . . I have only a vague, misty impression . . . but I recently heard about him and I built a few more details of him . . . but only in imagination.'

'I am sorry about what happened . . .'

'You mean his being hanged at Githinguri? It was a collective sacrifice. A few had to die for our freedom . . . But it is strange . . . now that you say you knew him . . . I did not even know that I had a brother . . . that he had died – until Mukami told me.'

'Mukami!'

'Yes . . . just before she died.'

'Mukami . . . my sister . . . did you . . . but how could she . . .?'

'Your father I believe had told her.'

I tried to figure out all this: what had this stranger to do with my father and Mukami and Nding'uri's death of years before? I wanted to know more – to know where or how Karega came into all this . . . but how could I ask a stranger and a boy at that, about a mystery involving my own family?

It was he who changed the subject and talked as if the revelations were incidental to his visit.

'But that is not why I came . . .'

'Yes . . .'

'I have come to you because you taught me at Manguo. Don't you remember?'

An urgent insistence had crept into his voice. But how could I remember? So many people had worked on my father's farm and lived there as ahoi. So many pupils had passed through the schools where I had previously taught. A few I could maybe remember. But this young man before me? Ah! who was I to keep a storehouse for all the eyes I had taught? I turned the silhouette in my mind, this way, that way. I looked at Karega. His face was pained, young, eager, and suddenly from the mist his outline, as he was seven or nine years back, rose before me. He was my pupil at Manguo and was one of the first to get a place in Siriana. This was considered a great honour to the school and the region. Although he knew that I was not the headmaster, he had come to me with papers demanding the signature of a responsible elder who could testify to the candidate's character, etc. Who was I to grade people's morality? But for him I suppose it must have been a way of showing comradeship: I who had been there before him had to be a witness of his departure to higher realms. I put my name to the documents and shrugged off the nagging thought that if they ever checked records my name would work against him. And now, many years after, he was back, maybe to tell me of a new departure for even higher realms. Indeed this was the real compensation in teaching: occasionally you found one who later had gone beyond your wildest dreams, beyond your fondest hope, such a one returned to thank you and you were glad. I was suddenly in a light euphoric mood. I forgot my fatigue and Wanja. I put on one side thoughts about Mukami and my father and all tnat. I seemed to like him better, indeed I felt honoured by a visit from a university scholar.

'And you successfully smashed your way through Siriana? Did you go to Makerere or Nairobi? How is life at the university? You don't know how lucky you are: Uhuru has really increased chances for us black people. How many universities now? Three. In our time we only counted that number of high schools. So which university? If I went to university I would like to study law or medicine: nothing else for me – just law and medicine – an advocate or a doctor. You know you can make a lot of money in those professions – but a teacher? We only work for God. I suppose you roamed the Big City looking for vacational employment? Pocket money . . . I know how it is. At Siriana my father used to give me two shillings. What do you study?'

I had so enthused on his success that I interpreted his fidgeting as a sign of modesty. He fingered his cup and then put it on the bench.

'The point is – well, I have not been to anybody's university – well – except maybe the university of the streets. I was expelled from Siriana.'

'Expelled?'

'Yes.'

'From school – Siriana?'

'Yes.'

'But why?'

He was quiet, absorbed in himself, as if seeking some nervous energy for the leap.

'It is a long story. You heard about the strike?'

'Strike? Which one – I mean where?'

'It was last year, toward the end. There were editorials on it in the newspapers – all the dailies.'

I was never really a great one for reading newspapers or for listening to the radio. Whenever I bought a newspaper I just glanced at the headlines: I never read editorial comments or any other features or news stories, especially of a political nature, only advertisements and court stories, especially on murder. Those I would read avidly, sometimes over and over again. Now that he had said it I thought that I had heard something about a strike in Siriana, but in my mind it had got mixed up with the past I would rather forget and I never followed up the matter. I told him:

'I hardly ever read newspapers. I have lived in a world to myself. I did hear something about a strike over food or something.'

'They always attribute every students' grievance to food,' he said rather bitterly. 'And the newspapers never wrote anything about our case: only editorials blaming us – you know, the usual homilies: so much taxpayers' money spent, and all they care about is their stomachs! It comforts them in their blindness. But no doubt you read about Fraudsham?'

'Fraudsham, Cambridge Fraudsham?'

'Yes. You know he went away?'

Gone! Cambridge Fraudsham gone? How? I could hardly believe this: Fraudsham was Siriana and Siriana was Fraudsham. I cursed my lack of interest in newspapers. I suppose if he had been murdered or something – but Fraudsham! My obvious ignorance was to Karega like cold water thrown over a guest on his entering a house. His excited enthusiasm subsided even as my curiosity and excitement rose. Another strike involving Fraudsham, ending in his defeat and final departure!

I have since that night read Karega's own incredulous reaction to the man's departure. His words carried poetry and beauty and sadness and momentary triumph:

> I can't believe it. I can't believe that
> our united strength, untried before,
> could move mountains where the prayers of
> yesterday had failed. Still, he was not there:
> he was not there any more at the blowing
> of the horn and the raising of the flag –

our flag. It is of three colours,
rightly sang the poet: Green is our
land; Black is black people; and
Red is our blood.

But at that moment, sitting in the midst of the neutral gloom of my house, I just felt strange inside: here I was, embers of curiosity stoked to a glowing intensity by his revelations, yet I was unable to ask questions. It was Karega who now unleashed question after question, hardly giving me breathing-time to answer or to react: what years had I been in Siriana? I told him. Did I really know Cambridge Fraudsham? Yes, a little. Well, I must have known Chui — Shakespeare or Joe Louis. I stood up despite myself. What? Chui? I had that eerie feeling of a dead past suddenly being resurrected before me who had been totally unprepared for the second coming. I knew at the same time that I had irretrievably let Karega down, I who must appear an impostor, a cheat, before his interrogating eyes. He too was now on his feet. I tried but could not make him resume his seat. So I stood at the door and watched him go. The sun about to set left shadows of grass and bush long on the ground. What else had he wanted to find out?

I was once again surprised at the depth of my concern. Had I not done away with Fraudshams, Chuis, Sirianas, strikes and politics, the whole lot, years ago? Now and then one occasionally would hear of Siriana's brilliant success at state examinations under its eccentric headmaster, but I could never really become involved in the glory of a school which had rejected me. Why should it follow me to Ilmorog? I felt a sudden nostalgia for that time, not so long ago, when my school and Abdulla's place were my whole life in Ilmorog.

I thought I should make myself another cup of tea before walking over to Abdulla's for the celebration. Tea was a good stimulant, Reverend Hallowes Ironmonger used to say, and he always thought of heaven as a place where there would be an unlimited quantity of tea and sausages. There! I was drifting back to the same past. It had started with Wanja and this last month my life had been lived in broken *cups* of memory between this ghost of a school, the backyard of Abdulla's shop and Wanja's hearth.

No, I must not lose my hold on the present. My earlier trip to Ruwa-ini for instance. Would Mzigo ever make it to Ilmorog? I didn't care now if he came or not, though only recently I had feared he might suddenly turn up and, finding no pupils, or seeing that they were so few or that each class took only half the day, he would transfer me back to places and people I had left behind, denying me the challenge of nation-building in remote Ilmorog, my new-found kingdom.

Try as I might, I could not dismiss from my mind that inconsequential visit by a former pupil. The visit had left too many questions unanswered: what really was the secret purpose of the visit? What could have been behind the strike at Siriana? Behind Fraudsham's departure and Chui's equally sudden return? A cold fear of Karega's visit settled uncomfortably in my belly. But what was it that scared me? That I would have to face something I had forever left behind? Or was I simply afraid of being drawn into somebody else's life and inner struggles, an unwilling witness of another's wrestling with God? ... and Jacob was left alone and a man wrestled with him until the breaking of the day. When the man saw that he did not prevail against Jacob he touched the hollow of his thigh, and Jacob's thigh was put out of joint as he wrestled with him and then he said I will not let you go unless you bless me ... Let me go, let me go, I cried to myself: why awaken voices from the past?

I closed the door and went out. I would now go over to Abdulla's place. As if it read my mind, Abdulla's donkey howled through the air, and it somehow startled me. I stopped. Where would Karega get a matatu at this hour? On the impulse, I went back to the house, took my bicycle from against the wall and raced after him. He might as well shelter here for the night. I would find out more about him: Siriana, Mukami, everything. But I felt what I had felt on my first encounter with Wanja, that this was another threat to my self-imposed peace in this land.

4 ❀ Wanja, too, twelve years later, recovering in the New Ilmorog Hospital, tried to recall this period: the night of her first narrative and her anxious vigil the following day loomed large in her troubled mind.

The idea of celebrating Joseph's return to school; the beginning of the harvest; her own expectation, had all been her own created drama. Now, in hospital, she recollected the details of that day, long ago.

She had woken up early and accompanied her grandmother to the shamba. It was always good to pull out beans in the morning before the sun became too hot. On this occasion they had additional shade from the maize plants which seemed too slow in maturing and ripening. There were not many bean plants to pull out and to thrash and by late the same morning they had finished winnowing. The beans could hardly fill up a sisal sack.

'What a harvest!' Nyakinyua exclaimed. 'Our soil seems tired. It did not receive enough water to quench its thirst. Long ago land the size of this piece could yield eight to ten containers each the size of this sack here.'

'Maybe the maize will yield more,' Wanja ventured to say.

'These strings!' Nyakinyua said depracatingly, and did not add another word.

They took home their harvest. Nyakinyua walked across to other fields to see if her neighbours were faring any better.

Wanja went to Abdulla's shop. It was in the afternoon. She knew that no customers would have arrived yet. But she wanted to start her work as a barmaid in Ilmorog and also to kill time so anxious she was for the celebration before the moonrise at midnight.

Throughout the afternoon Wanja arranged and rearranged things and parcels on the shelves. It was a busy afternoon with the three of them – Abdulla, Joseph and Wanja – somehow finding something to do. Joseph had not started school: it was closed for the day because of Munira's absence in Ruwa-ini. It was a thorough cleaning-up operation. Wanja demanded that Abdulla repair a few of the shelves and also the table in one of the back rooms in the shop that served as the bar. Abdulla said that he himself would do that some day soon. Wanja and Joseph swept the floor of the bar-room and splashed water on the dust. Outside the building she had put up a signboard: SHOP + BAR CLOSED THIS AFTERNOON – STOCKTAKING. But there was very little stock to take and customers, especially in an afternoon, were few and far between. Nevertheless Abdulla was pleased with Wanja's innovations and especially the professional seriousness with which she did her job. She was in command of the situation and she was so involved in dusting up here and there, and writing up things in an exercise book, that she forgot the fatigue of the morning bean harvest. Abdulla could only marvel: so his shop and bar could be something after all.

Toward the end of the afternoon she removed the stocktaking sign and put up another one: SHOP NOW OPEN. They sat behind the counter and waited for customers. But nobody came. She was up again. She put up another sign. PERMANENT CLOSING DOWN SALE and on an impulse drew sketches of a shop and people running toward it in a hurry.

A few children came to buy sweets. They laughed and commented on the little sketches of the men. They tried to spell out the words on the notice-board and recognising the word *close* and *sale* ran to their parents to say that Abdulla's shop was closing and he was giving away things. Within a few hours the place was full of customers who soon found out the mistake of the children. But they liked the new-look shop and a few remained to gossip and sip beer. Wanja took out chairs for them so they could sit outside on the verandah and while away the time drinking and talking about the harvest.

But even these later went away and Wanja sat patiently behind the counter waiting for a new lot. Her mind started wandering. Tonight the BIG moon would come out: tonight was the day for which she had been waiting since she came to Ilmorog and she hoped that nothing would go wrong. Celebration of Joseph's impending return to school was only part of her scheme – a coincidence, although it was one with which she was genuinely pleased. Suppose Munira did not come – but he would, he must. She was somehow sure of her power over men: she knew how they could be very weak before her body. Sometimes she was afraid of this power and she often had wanted to run away from bar kingdoms. But she was not really fit for much else and besides, she thought with a shuddering pain of recognition, she had come to enjoy the elation at seeing a trick – a smile, a certain look, maybe even raising one's brow, or a gesture like carelessly brushing against a customer – turn a man into a captive and a sighing fool. Still in her sober moments of reflection and self-appraisal, she had longed for peace and harmony within: for those titillating minutes of instant victory and glory often left behind an emptiness, a void, that could only be filled by yet more palliatives of instant conquest. Struggling in the depths of such a void and emptiness, she would then suddenly become aware that in the long run it was men who triumphed and walked over her body, buying insurance against deep involvement with money and guilty smiles or in exaggerated fits of jealousy. She would often seek somebody in whom she could be involved, somebody for whom she could care and be proud to carry his child. For that reason she had somehow avoided direct trading, and that was why she had run away from her cousin who had wanted her straight in the market. No, she preferred friendship, however temporary, she liked and enjoyed the illusion of being wooed and fought over, and being bought a dress or something without her demanding it as a bargain. She liked it best at the counter. There, sitting on a high stool away from the hustle and bustle, she could study people so that soon she became a good judge of men's faces. She could tell the sympathetic, the sensitive, the rough, the cruel and the intelligent – those whose conversation and words gave her especial pleasure. But she had come to find out that behind most faces was deep loneliness, uncertainty and anxiety and this would often made her sad or want to cry. Otherwise she did not often brood and she enjoyed involvement in her work so that she was much sought by employers. She liked dancing, playing records, memorising the words of the latest records: on one or two occasions she tried composing but no tune would come. She always wanted to do something, she did not know what it was, but she felt she had the power to do it. When live music was being played – a guitar or a flute – she thought she could feel this power in her, this power to do – what? She did not know. The music would often take the form of colours – bold colours in motion – and she would mix them up into different patterns with eyes and faces of people – but only as long as the music lasted. She wandered from place to place in search of it or for a man who would show her it. And then she thought she knew. A child. Yes. A child. That is what her body really cried for. She had learnt to take precautions because of her first experience. But now she abandoned all preventives and waited. For a year or so she tried. The more she failed to see a sign the more it became a need, until in the end she could not bear the torture and came to seek advice from her grandmother. Nyakinyua had taken her to Mwathi wa Mugo and it was he who – or rather his voice – who had suggested the night, the new moon. But she did not say anything about her first pregnancy.

No other customers came for the evening. She started to fret. Even Munira had refused to come. Despite his promise. It pained her. Something was wrong with today. Something was wrong. Perhaps even the moon wouldn't come. Perhaps – and who was Mwathi after all? A voice! Just a voice from behind a wall. What superstition!

'Abdulla – please – I want to go home,' she suddenly told Abdulla in the middle of a drink.

'I don't know why Munira hasn't come. Perhaps he was delayed at Ruwa-ini. But it is still early and he may yet come . . .'

'All the same, I must go,' she said, and Abdulla was surprised at her many changes of mood. But he was pleased with her work and the look of the shop.

'I will walk with you part of the way.'

'All the way,' she said, suddenly laughing. 'What a celebration! Joseph didn't start school today, the harvest of beans was nothing; Munira didn't come; I haven't sold much beer.' She added pensively: 'Will the moon really show in the sky?'

❁

Karega's father and his two wives had left Limuru and moved into the Rift Valley in the '20s. They had lived as squatters on different European farms providing free labour in return for some grazing and cultivation rights on the settlers' lands. They would be given a piece of land in the bush: they would clear it and after a year they would be driven off and shown other virgin lands to clear for the European landlord. Thus they had moved from one landlord to the next until they ended in Elburgon. By this time their goats were depleted either through death, or fines, through forced sales 'to prevent the passing on of tick and other diseases' and they turned solely to working full-time on settlers' farms for wages.

It was at Elburgon that his father and mother quarrelled. She complained about her triple duties: to her child Ndinguri; to her husband, and to her European landlord. She was expected to work on the European farms; to work on her own piece of land; and to keep the home in unity, health and peace. At the same time she never saw a cent from her produce. Usually her husband would take it and sell it to the same European farmer, their landlord, who fixed his own buying price: and her husband in turn gave her only enough to buy salt. She rebelled: she would not work on the settlers' farm for nothing and she demanded a say in the sale of her produce.

He beat her in frustration. She took Ndinguri and ran back to Limuru where she begged for cultivation rights from Munira's father. At first Brother Ezekiel had refused. But looking at her eyes, he had felt a sudden weakness in the flesh and he had allowed her to build a hut, but he made sure she built where he could visit her without being seen. She had refused him, all the same: and thereafter his weakness and her refusal became a kind of bond between them, a shared secret. He feared that she might expose him to the world.

But she was not interested in exposure. She had her son Ndinguri to look after. He was a tall youth who was splendid in his self-confidence. Nothing could ever perturb him and he, throughout the hardships of the Second World War, and through the famine of cassava, had acted as her main support often laughing away her anxiety and her fears for him. It was he who in fact had suggested a reconciliation with her husband. She had felt ashamed this coming from a son, and she had briefly returned to her husband in Elburgon who had now added a Nandi bride to his others. The reconciliation was good for only one month and the same pattern of quarrels re-emerged. She ran away again but Karega was the product of that brief reunion.

Munira and Karega walked into the shop almost as soon as Wanja and Abdulla had left. They were both rapt in different thoughts about a past they could not understand. Joseph stood ready.

'It is all right, Joseph. Just two bottles of Tusker,' said Munira.

'I don't drink,' Karega said. 'Let me have Fanta, please.'

'Do you know what Fanta means? Foolish Africans Never Take

Alcohol. You see I am an avid reader of advertisements. Occasionally I even try my mind at a few slogans.'

'The trouble with slogans or any saying without a real foundation is that it can be used for anything. Phrases like Democracy, the Free World, for instance, are used to mean their opposite. It depends of course on who is saying it where, when and to whom. Take your slogan. It could also mean that Fit Africans Never Take Alcohol. We are both right. But we are both wrong because Fanta is simply an American soft drink sold in Ilmorog.'

Munira laughed and thought: he is too serious and he is already beginning to lecture me, probably from a book!

So he drank alone and retreated into his own private thoughts. He had caught up with Karega and he had managed to persuade him to stay for the night. But he did not know how to introduce the subject of their earlier conversation. It was obvious that Karega avoided any reference to it. Munira formed mental pictures of Siriana, the Iron-mongers, Fraudsham, Chui, Ndinguri, Mukami: Aah, Mukami – her image was the most alive in his mind: she had been serenely beautiful but with impish eyes, especially when she laughed. She had loved practical jokes. She once placed a drawing-pin on a chair – he had sat on it and jumped up to everybody's laughter, and he had been very angry. Later she told him that it was meant for her father – she had wanted to see how he would react with his holy-looking face. Munira had laughed. How and where did Karega fit into the picture? This was a case of history repeating itself, and indeed for him at that moment the cliché seemed to acquire new significance. Yet did anything ever repeat itself? He opened the next bottle of Tusker and poured beer into the glass. He watched the foam clear into a thin white bubbly ring at the top. He watched the air-bubbles race up to the top. Before 1952 Africans were not allowed this kind of drink and Munira, as a boy, used to think of those bubbles as sugary sweetness. He could not finish the second bottle. There is a depression, an acid drop in the pit of one's stomach that no amount of beer can wash away. His evening with Wanja was ruined. He would not be able to walk her home because she was already there. But he still needed a human voice to remove that feeling inside. He bought six bottles of Tusker.

'Let's go to Wanja's place,' he told Karega.

Again they hardly exchanged more than two words all the way to Wanja's hut. He knocked at the door and he was grateful when he heard the hinges creak because now there would be more company to absorb Karega's resentful silence.

'Karibu, Mwalimu, karibu,' Wanja called. 'Oh, you brought

another guest. You really know how to bring warmth to my hut.'

'His name is Karega: I found him waiting for me at the house and we had a little talk.'

'But don't talk standing. Sit.'

'Karibu, Mwalimu,' said Abdulla. 'You could have brought Karega to the shop to celebrate. It was your turn to walk Wanja home today.'

'Abdulla, you surprise me. You mean you were not glad to walk a girl home?' said Wanja in pretended anger.

'It is only to make sure that my turn tomorrow is still there,' Abdulla said, and he laughed.

The hut was well lit by the pressure-lamp placed on a small table near the head-end of the bed. Abdulla was slightly hidden by a shadow from the folded curtain which Wanja normally used to shield the bed from the sitting place. But his face was aglow, his eyes intensely bright. Munira handed Wanja the six Tuskers he had brought and sat on a cushioned armchair near the small table. Karega sat next to Munira, his shadow falling on Munira's face. Wanja started looking for an opener in a small cupboard by the wall.

'Forget it,' said Abdulla.

'You'll open them with your teeth?' she asked.

'Just bring the beer here.'

He held one bottle firmly on his knee with his left hand: then, holding another in his right hand, he placed the grooves of the tops against one another and opened the first with an explosive plop. He twice repeated the performance with the insouciance of an actor before a captive audience.

'How do you do that?' asked Wanja. 'I have seen it done in bars but I've never found out how.' She filled their glasses while Abdulla tried to demonstrate the act.

'I do not touch drinks.'

'Would you like a glass of milk?'

'It is strange to see a young man who does not drink these days,' commented Abdulla. 'You should keep it up. But I fear that in a few weeks I shall find you completely drowned in wine . . . and women.'

'I hope not to give in.'

'To what? Women or wine?' pursued Abdulla.

'Abdulla, how can you put women and wine together? He'll choose women and leave wine to you two. Milk?'

'No. Let me have some water. A glass of water.'

She fetched him water and sat on the bed between Munira and Abdulla.

'You ought to get a job as a bottle-opener,' she told Abdulla.

'Put an advertisement,' butted in Munira. 'Experienced bottle-opener seeking a highly paid job.'

'Munira, did you tell Karega that we are celebrating an addition to your school?'

'No. But he has just met Joseph. Joseph, who is Abdulla's younger brother, is starting school on Monday.'

Karega looked puzzled.

'There is nothing to celebrate,' Abdulla explained. 'It is true that he is returning to school. But that is as it should be. We are celebrating new life in Ilmorog, and the beginning of the long-awaited harvest.'

'How was the harvest? Did it yield much?' Munira asked.

'Not much,' Wanja said. 'It'll be a lucky farmer who'll fill two gunias of beans.'

'Maybe the maize ...' Munira said.

'That ... it does not look as if it will be much, though my donkey will be grateful for the dry stalks of maize,' Abdulla answered. 'Or what do you think Wanja? You are a barmaid farmer.'

But Wanja did not hear the compliment. She was looking at the still serious face of Karega.

'Karega ...' she said aloud. 'What a funny name!'

'Ritwa ni mbukio,' Karega quoted the proverb. 'Somebody a long time ago asked the question: What's in a name? And he answered that a rose would still be a rose even by another name.'

Talking as if from a book, again thought Munira. Wanja countered:

'Oh, then it would not be a rose. It would be that other name, don't you think? A rose is a rose.'

'Names are actually funny. My real name is not Abdulla. It is Murira. But I baptised myself Abdulla. Now everybody calls me Abdulla.'

'You mean, you thought Abdulla was a Christian name?' Wanja asked.

'Yes. Yes.'

They all laughed. Even Karega. Abdulla took another bottle to open. Munira said: 'Let me try: I too might become an assistant bottle-opener.'

'Oh, Mwalimu,' she cried in ecstasy. She was really in high spirits with not a trace of the troubled voice and face of yesterday or of the earlier part of the evening. 'Abdulla has been telling me such impossible stories. Did you know that he actually fought in the forest? He used to go for days and days without food and water: they had trained their bodies to accept little. I am sure I would have died.

Abdulla, you were going to tell a story about Dedan – Dedan Kimathi.'

Munira's stomach tightened a little at the revelation. He always felt this generalised fear about this period of war: he also felt guilty, as if there was something he should have done but didn't do. It was the guilt of omission: other young men of his time had participated: they had taken sides: this defined them as a people who had gone through the test and either failed or passed. But he had not taken the final test. Just like in Siriana. He looked at Karega who had today brought back that other past. He still held the two bottles. Karega sat up: his body was taut with curiosity. He gazed at Abdulla: he was once again ready to devour the past from one who was then present. Wanja looked at Abdulla: she thought that now he would tell the secret behind his crippled leg. Abdulla cleared his throat. His face changed. He suddenly seemed to have gone to a land hidden from them, a land way back in a past only he could understand. He cleared his throat, a prolonged slow roar. Suddenly a bottle-top flew from Munira's hand. Wanja and Karega threw up their arms to their faces and in the process somebody must have hit the table on which the lamp stood. It fell down with the sound of broken glass. The light went out. They were plunged in darkness. Abdulla was the first to see the other light: a small flame had caught the folded curtain. Wanja in a voice of terror shouted 'Fire!' but by this time Abdulla had sprung up and put out the flames. It all happened so quickly. Munira struck a match. Wanja said: 'Behind you, Karega, there's a Nyitira.'* Karega gave the Nyitira to Munira who lit it: but this was a poor substitute for the pressure-lamp. The light was pale and their faces and their shadows on the wall were large and grotesque. Wanja collected the glass and the pressure-lamp and put it aside and then turned to Munira.

'It is nothing. You will get me another one and also a box of wicks. Abdulla . . . we must do something about the stock in your shop.'

Her voice was shaky and she stopped, cold silence in the hut. The shadows on the wall kept on moving in a grotesque rhythm to the erratic movement of the smoking thin flame from Nyitira. Wanja poured the drinks. Munira wanted to tell of an advertising slogan about beer so that they could resume their drinking and small irrelevancies, but he changed his mind. The drink remained untouched. Karega hopefully waited for Abdulla to tell the story of Dedan Kimathi. But Abdulla suddenly stood up, excused himself and said it was time to go. He might find Joseph's leg pulled by a hyena. Karega was disappointed and stared to the ground as if with Abdulla's departure he had lost interest in the company. Wanja looked at him and something, a small puzzled frown, came to her face and then

*kerosene lamp

passed away. She stood up, looked for her shawl which she now draped round her head, letting it fall onto her shoulders. She once again turned to Karega and for a flickering second her eyes were laughing. Karega felt his blood suddenly rush through his veins. But her voice was serious, and genuinely gentle. 'Please, Mr Karega, keep the house for me for a few minutes.' Then to Munira and a note of slight impatience crept into her voice: 'Come, Mwalimu, take me for a walk, just a little walk. I have a knot only you can untie!'

❁

They walked in silence through the yards of the village, through lanes between the various shambas. They caught one or two voices of mothers shouting to the children to 'hurry up and finish – why did you have to stuff yourself so? – or else you'll be eaten by hyenas'. Otherwise the ridge was generally quiet except for the dogs of the village which kept on barking. In Munira's mind buzzed many thoughts: who was Abdulla? Who was Karega? Who was Wanja? What did she want now? He felt guilty because of his clumsiness which had lowered everybody's spirits. But as they sat down on the grass on Ilmorog hill, his heartbeats drove away unpleasant thoughts, warmth started suffusing his body, as he felt her breathing so powerfully near in the dark. Of all his thoughts the one that came out in words was mundane and sounded odd in the dark.

'I bought you two kilos of the long-grained rice. But I forgot to bring it along.'

'It's all right,' she said in a quiet distant voice. 'You can always bring it along tomorrow. And anyway you had a visitor. Who is he?'

'It was very strange. Some weeks ago I told you about Siriana, and Chui – all that. Today comes this young man whom I once taught in a school in Limuru and he tells me about Siriana and a strike and mentions Chui. Almost a repeat story of my past. But unfortunately he did not finish it.'

And he told her a little about his earlier encounter with Karega. But he omitted all references to Nding'uri and to Mukami. Karega had a knowledge about Munira's past – how could Munira tell Wanja about the fears awakened in him by Karega's visit? 'It was strange his having been to the same school as I had attended and he ending in a similar fate,' Munira concluded and waited for Wanja's response.

But she was only half listening. She sat holding her knees together with both hands so that her chin rested on them as she gazed toward Ilmorog plains below. She was contemplating live mental images of places and scenes to which she had once been. Though she tried to

63

hide this to herself she knew that these scenes were indelibly embedded in her deepest memories of pain and loss, past victories and defeats, momentary conquests and humiliations, resolutions of new beginnings that were only false starts to nowhere. She now spoke quietly, to herself it seemed, holding a dialogue with a self that was only one of a myriad selves.

'You talk of the past coming to visit you ... There is one picture that always comes to mind. Wherever I go, whatever I do ... well ... it follows me. It is a long way back. In 1954 or '55, anyway the year that we were moved into the villages and others into "lines". You know that some people in Kabete side did not go exactly into villages but they built on either side of roads close to one another, but we still called them villages. My cousin – but let me first tell you about her. She had married a man who kept on beating her. There was nothing that she could do right. He would always find an excuse to beat her. He accused her of going about with men. If she had money through working on the land, he would take it away from her and he would drink it all and come home to beat her. So one day she just took her clothes and ran away to the city. Later her husband became a white-man's spear-bearer – you know – Home Guard – and he was notorious for his cruelty and for eating other people's chickens and choice goats or sheep after accusing them of being Mau Mau ... Anyway my cousin would come from the city and she glittered in new clothes and earrings. All the men, the ones who had remained, eyed her with desire. Her husband, it is said, trembled and wept before her as he asked for forgiveness. She had with disdain dismissed his several approaches. We, the children, liked her because she would bring us things ... rice ... sugar ... sweets ... and those were lean years for us all. One Saturday she came home with her usual gifts. Now my aunt – my mother's true sister – traded in the market. That day she must have been delayed in the market. So my cousin came to our house. We all admired her dress, her white high heels – how we would often follow her in the streets – her everything. She looked very much like the pictures of European women we saw in books. Even her gait and the way she held up her chin as she spoke, had "staili". It was now dark. My cousin stood and she said that she was going out to the latrine and also to see if her mother had come back from the market. My mother who was strangely quiet looked at her gait and I could tell disapproval in the eyes. All at once we heard a scream. It was – it was – it chilled words – blood – it's difficult to describe it because it was not like a human cry at all. My father and my mother and us children rushed outside. At the sight a few yards away, my mother screamed, but I couldn't scream or cry, just urine trickled down my legs. "My sister, my only sister," cried my mother as she rushed forward toward the burning figure of my aunt. There she stood, outside her burning hut, and she aflame and not uttering a sound at all ... just ... just animal silence. Now were other screams and hurrying feet and noises ... "put out the light ... put out the light," were her last words.'

Munira looked about him, a little uneasy. It was as if this was happening now in Ilmorog. He felt the terror in Wanja's voice, felt the desperation hidden in the very offhand tone she had adopted in telling it.

'Later it was said she had maybe caught fire while lighting Nyitira which spilt out oil and flames on her clothes. But it was clear that my cousin's husband must have done it. He may have thought that the town wife who had rejected him was inside the hut.'

'But it's a horrible death ... the pain ... the helpless terror.'

'There is no death, unless of old age, without pain. For some reason, I have not wanted to believe that it was my cousin's husband who did it. I have not wanted to believe that any man could be so cruel. I have – it really is so childish of me – but I have liked to believe that she burnt herself like the Buddhists do, which then makes me think of the water and the fire of the beginning and the water and the fire of the second coming to cleanse and bring purity to our earth of human cruelty and loneliness. Mwalimu. I will tell you. There are times – not too many times – but a few times – when I remember a few things – that I have felt as if I could set myself on fire. And I would then run to the mountain top so that everyone can see me cleansed to my bones.'

'Wanja ... stop that ... what are you talking about?'

'My aunt was a clean woman though,' she continued. 'She was very good to us children. Her husband was a hard-core Mau Mau. I was even more proud of her when later I learnt that she used to carry guns and bullets to the forest hidden in baskets full of unga. She was not a Christian and used to laugh at my mother's Jesus ways. But they somehow loved one another. My mother respected her in a certain kind of way – and her death – well – it really affected her. My father once said: "It's probably an act of God ... for helping the terrorists." That was the beginning of their falling apart of which I was later to become a victim.'

She stopped. For a few seconds she dwelt alone within that inward gaze.

'No,' she said as if she was continuing a dialogue with one of her several selves ... 'I don't think I can ever burn myself. Did I frighten you? It was a way of talking. I am terrified of fires. That's why I was upset in the hut when I saw the fire. What I would like is to get a job.'

'Wanja ... tell me: what happened to your child?'

He felt rather than saw her body shudder. He wished he had not asked her the question. He did not know how to cope with her silent sobbing.

'Wanja: what's the matter?' he asked anxiously.

'I don't know. I just feel feverish. I thought the moon would come out tonight. What a fruitless vigil on a mountain! Please take me home.'

They went back as they had come – in silence. They found the light was out. And Karega had gone. He struck a match and lit the Nyitira. Wanja said: 'Please put it out.' They both stood at the door looking out. He knew Karega could not have gone to the house because he did not have the keys. Munira felt cold sweat on his face. The fear he had earlier experienced came back. Karega had gone as mysteriously as he had appeared. He fixed his eyes to the dark out-side hoping to pierce the mystery and so dispel his inner terror.

Twelve years later Munira was to pick on this night as yet another example of Wanja's cunning and devilry.

'Looking back on that night on Ilmorog Hill,' he wrote, 'I can see the devil at work in the magic and wonder and perplexity I felt at that fatal meeting between Karega, Wanja, Abdulla and myself; an encounter dominated by people who were not there with us, who were now only voices in the past. But also for me, then, the night had the changing colours of a rainbow. For even before I could wish her goodbye and go home, I saw emerging from the far horizon a big orange moon half veiled by a mixture of dark and grey clouds. We watched it rise, growing bigger and bigger, dominating the horizon, and my heart was full and I searched for the slogan which would contain the experience – Moon in a Grey Rain Drop, or something like that. Wanja, who only a few minutes back was crying, was now excited like a little child at the first drops of rain and she cried out in ecstasy: The moon ... the orange moon. Please, Mwalimu ... stay here tonight ... Break the moon over me.' Her pleading voice had startled Munira out of his thoughts. He too wanted to stay the night. He would stay the night. A joyous trembling coursed through his body. Aah, my harvest. To hell with Karega and all the un-pleasant memories of yesterday, he thought as he followed Wanja into the hut.

Chapter Four

1 ❀ If Wanja had been patient and had waited for the new moon to appear on Ilmorog ridge – as indeed she had been instructed by Mwathi wa Mugo – she and Munira would have witnessed one of the most glorious and joyous sights in all the land, with the ridges and the plains draped by a level sheet of shimmering moonlit mist into a harmony of peace and silence: a human soul would have to be restless and raging beyond reach of hope and salvation for it not to be momentarily overwhelmed and stilled by the sight and the atmosphere.

Even without the moon Ilmorog ridge, as it drops into the plains along which Ilmorog river flows, must form one of the greatest natural beauties in the world. The river is now only a stream. But there was a time when it was probably much bigger and geological speculation has it that its subterranean streams, buried long ago, feed Ondirri marshes at Kikuyu and Manguo in Limuru. Results of the researches on the recent archaeological finds in Ilmorog may well add to the theories of Ogot, Muriuki, Were and Ochieng about the origins and the movement of Kenyan peoples: they may also tell us whether the river is one of those referred to in ancient Hindu and Egyptian sacred literatures or whether the walls that form the ridges are any part of Ptolemy's Lunae Montes or the Chandravata referred to in the Vedas.

For there are many questions about our history which remain unanswered. Our present day historians, following on similar theories yarned out by defenders of imperialism, insist we only arrived here yesterday. Where went all the Kenyan people who used to trade with China, India, Arabia long long before Vasco da Gama came to the scene and on the strength of gunpowder ushered in an era of blood and terror and instability – an era that climaxed in the reign of imperialism over Kenya? But even then these adventures of Portuguese mercantilism were forced to build Fort Jesus, showing that Kenyan people had always been ready to resist foreign control and exploitation. The story of this heroic resistance: who will sing it? Their struggles to defend their land, their wealth, their lives: who'll tell of it? What of their earlier achievements in production that had annually attracted visitors from ancient China and India?

Just now we can only depend on legends passed from generation to generation by the poets and players of Gichandi, Litungu and

Nyatiti supplemented by the most recent archaeological and linguistic researches and also by what we can glean from between the lines of the records of the colonial adventurers of the last few centuries, especially the nineteenth century.

Ilmorog plains are themselves part of that Great Rift that formed a natural highway joining Kenya to the land of the Sphinx and to the legendary waters of the River Jordan in Palestine. For centuries, and even up to this day, the God of Africa and the Gods of other lands have wrestled for the mastery of man's soul and for the control of the results of man's holy sweat. It is said that the roll of thunder and the flash of lightning are their angry roar and the fire from the fearful clashing of their swords, and the Rift Valley must be one of the footprints of Africa's God.

From Agu and Agu, Tene wa tene, from long long before the Manjiri generation, the highway had seen more than its fair share of adventurers from the north and north-west. Solomon's suitors for myrrh and frankincense; Zeu's children in a royal hunt for the seat of the sun-god of the Nile; scouts and emissaries of Genghis Khan; Arab geographers and also hunters for slaves and ivory; soul and gold merchants from Gaul and from Bismarck's Germany; land pirates and human game-hunters from Victorian and Edwardian England: they had all passed here bound for a kingdom of plenty, driven sometimes by holy zeal, sometimes by a genuine thirst for knowledge and the quest for the spot where the first man's umbilical cord was buried, but more often by mercenary commercial greed and love of the wanton destruction of those with a slightly different complexion from theirs. They each had come wearing different masks and guises and God's children had, through struggle, survived every onslaught, every land- and soul-grabbing empire, and continued their eternal wrestling with nature and with their separate gods and mutual selves.

Memories remained memories of a few individuals who had made some mark on the plains and on Ilmorog before making a dramatic exit to other grounds.

First a white colonist, Lord Freeze-Kilby and his goodly wife, a lady. He was probably one of those footloose aristocrats, but a ruined one, who wanted to make something of his own in what he saw as a New Frontier. To change Ilmorog wilderness into civilised shapes and forms that would yield a million seedlings and a thousand pounds where one had planted only a few and invested only a pound, was a creative act of a god. For this he needed other's sweat and he used the magic of a government, the chit and the power of his rifle, to conscript labour. He experimented with wheat, ignoring the many frowning faces of the herdsmen and survivors of the earlier massacres in the name of Christian pacification by the king's men, and he again trusted to the rifle he always slung on his shoulders. Some of the herdsmen and the peasants were turned into kipande-carrying labourers on lands that used to be their own to master and to rule. They all watched the wheat finger-dancing ballet in the wind, and bade their time. Had they not heard what had happened to the Masai people of the Laikipia plains? At night, on Ilmorog ridge, their leaders met and reached a decision. They set fire to the whole field and themselves ran to the outer edges of the plains, awaiting deadly repercussions. The lord refused to move. But his lady deserted him. The warriors came back and made strange noises around his bungalow late at night. The lone adventurer must have then seen the wailing ghost of the earlier colonist, and a man of God, too, and he quickly retreated to the happier and healthier valleys of Ol Kalou. There he found his goodly wife being comforted in the arms of another lord and shot them both with his rifle. In Ilmorog, the natives burnt down the wooden bungalow and danced and sang around it. Reprisals came. The battle of Ilmorog early this century was one of the fiercest of all the wars of conquest and resistance fought in Kenya.

Then later, in between the two European wars, came a Ramjeeh Ramlagoon Dharamashah, from nowhere it seemed, and sought permission to erect a bungalow that would be a home and a shop. He put up an iron roof and iron walls and settled into business. He sold salt, sugar, curry and cloth and also beans, potatoes and maize he had bought from the same farmers more cheaply during harvest-time. He always sat behind the counter in the same corner chewing some green leaves. Occasionally he would shut the shop to take a trip to the city, trekking along the selfsame plains and bringing back more supplies piled on the backs of the African porters and some on a wagon pulled by bulls. Once he shut the shop and stayed away for a month. When he came back, he had with him a giggling shy girl they took to be his daughter until she started bearing him children. He also got a helper in the shop and around the house, Njogu's daughter from Ilmorog. She was very useful, especially when Dharamashah's wife was away in India or some other place. She too became round-bellied. Dharamashah, it is said, paid her a lot of money and sent her to the city where he would often visit her in secret, half-acknowledging his only son by a black woman. But the son one day after the Second World War came to Ilmorog – a tall coffee-coloured boy – and stayed with his grandparents, only once visiting his father who thereafter quarrelled with his giggling wife about him. In time, the people of Ilmorog came to depend on Dharamashah's shop for everything. Their economy and daily needs became inextricably bound up with the rising fortunes of the shop. They pawned their crops, their milk, their needs to the shop until they started grumbling about the invisible chains that bound them, necks and lives and all, to the shop. In 1953 the black woman, beautifully dressed but emaciated in body, suddenly came to Ilmorog and went to see Dharamashah and soon after went crying to her aged parents. In 1956, Dharamashah received a letter from one Ole Masai with a strange sender's address: *Somewhere in Nyandarura Forest.* He read the letter, hands trembling, mouth frozen in the very act of chewing green leaves, and quickly shut the shop. He and a wife who had borne him more than ten children, all sent to India for their education and marriage, fled Ilmorog and never returned. The villagers broke into the shop and helped themselves to every scrap of food and cloth in the store and on the shelves and blessed those fighting in the Forest.

May the Lord bless Ole Masai and his band of brave warriors.

They suffered. For now they had to trek all the way to Ruwa-ini for their tiniest needs, salt even, until a few took a leaf from Ramjeeh Ramlagoon Dharamashah and started buying more than they needed and selling to others at a profit. But trading remained incidental to their daily struggle with the soil and the weather. None, not even Njuguna, was mad enough to believe that one could really grow to become a man as a mere go-between. It was left to another stranger, Abdulla, soon after independence, to rescue the building from moths, spiders and rats. Abdulla sold more or less the same assortment of things: he sat more or less in the same corner behind the counter, but he used a donkey to pull a cart and cursed Joseph where Dharmashah had used bulls to pull a wagon and chewed leaves and shouted at his wife and children.

And then suddenly they noticed that Abdulla's curses were over: the scowl on his face was gone: instead of terrorising Joseph with curses he had sent him to school; he would even laugh from deep in his stomach. The store had a more cheerful look. The tea packets, bundles of salt and sugar and the curry powder tins were tidily arranged on the shelves. He had repaired the broken table in the bar and added more chairs which could even be taken out into the sun. More and more people now spent a few hours of their evening in Abdulla's shop.

'It is Wanja's doing,' whispered Njuguna to Muturi, Njogu and Ruoro. 'It's that girl's doing. And what is this I hear that she goes to Mwathi's place?'

'It's the way she helps Nyakinyua that moves me, and she a city woman,' said Njogu. Muturi kept quiet, as he nearly always did when Mwathi's place was mentioned.

2 ✿ It was not only under the floodlight of the moon that made Ilmorog a wonder! There was also something soft and subdued and beautiful about Ilmorog ridge between the hour of the sun's death and the hour of darkness. For an inexplicable reason the low, billowy Donyo hills seemed to rise and to touch the sky. Standing anywhere on the ridge one could catch sight of the sun delicately resting on the tip of the distant hills which marked the far end of the grazing plains. Then suddenly the sun would slip behind the hills, blazing out a coppery hue with arrows of fire shot in every direction. Soon after, darkness and mystery would descend on the plains and the hills. The ridge, unless the moon was out, would now suddenly become part of that awesome shadow. Munira relished twilight as a prelude to that awesome shadow. He looked forward to the unwilled immersion into darkness. He would then be part of everything: the plants, animals, people, huts, without consciously choosing the links. To choose involved effort, decision, preference of one possibility, and this could be painful. He had chosen not to choose, a freedom he daily celebrated walking between his house, Abdulla's place and of course Wanja's hut.

Yet he felt guilty about being propelled by a whirlwind he had neither willed nor could now control. This consciousness of guilt, of having done a wrong, had always shadowed him in life.

Munira was a refugee from a home where certain things were never mentioned. His own family life was built and he supposed now broken on the altar of Presbyterian Christian propriety and good manners. He had had his affairs, this he could not deny. Son of man must live. But he always remembered that first time in a house in old Kamiritho, long long before the present Emergency village, with shame. The house was one of several built in what was called Swahili majengo style: a corner house with a huge sprawling roof of rotting tin. The houses were famous, especially because Italian prisoners of war – the Bonos, as they were called – used to fetch murram for the Nakuru road from near there and they would frequent the houses. Amina, her name was: he gave her two shillings, all the money that he had saved. She had really humiliated him. 'He is only a boy,' she said, standing in the doorway, looking him up and down with amused eyes, as if announcing her surprised discovery to another inside the house, and for a second he was full of terror in case she was a married woman and her husband came out with ten sharpened pangas.* 'You know I don't sleep with uncircumcised men. It's a rule of mine. But come here.' She led him into the house and sat on the bed. Munira was trembling with fear and shame and he wanted to cry. His thing had anyway shrivelled. 'Let's see now ... don't be afraid ... you are a man ... I bet you have impregnated one or two.' But she was nice and she had soothed him with the gentleness of a mother and his thing had suddenly saluted, upright and strong, and now he felt he would die if— But she had put him between her fleshy thighs, she spoke in a cooing voice, crossed her legs slightly and, God, it was all over for him and he could not tell if he had been in or not. It was this that he had tried to exorcise by fire in vain. He always recalled that scene with unpleasant feelings, especially when in later years, after expulsion from Siriana, he would pass by the house on his way to Kamandura as a young teacher. Nevertheless he had sworn never to be shocked by anybody's openness to the flesh.

But even with Wanja he found that he was still a prisoner of his own upbringing and Siriana missionary education. It was not that he did not enjoy the experience. On the contrary, despite that upbringing he knew there was nothing so great, nothing so joyous as those few seconds of expectation before entry into a woman's unknown. And Wanja's pained face under the moonlit beams issuing from the window; or her little noises of pain, as if she was really hurt; of pleasure, as if eating honeycombs and sugarcanes; and the waves of her gentle motions made the snake in paradise full with the blood-warmth of expectation before final deliverance from the pain of this knowing, this knowledge. Her scream, calling out to her mother or sisters for help, would give him an even greater sense of power and strength until he sank into a void, darkness, awesome shadow where choosing or not choosing was no longer a question. But he would wake to a terrified consciousness that somehow he had been led on, and he did not feel any victory. He had not reached her and this, ironically, made him hunger the more for her, for a thousand sins with her and more.

He reached out for her. He felt her recoil, recede. He withdrew, baffled. She would come back and she would suddenly carry him, a willing passenger, on a night train to the sindom of pleasure and leave him there panting, thirsting and hungering for more.

Her changing moods were difficult to keep up with and they left him breathless. Sometimes it was her concern for people. She would then be sad, introspective, and would ask him questions that sounded cruel in their innocence. Abdulla especially was nearly always in her mind.

'Mwalimu: do you know why he came to hide in this place?'

*machetes

72

'Who?'

'Abdulla: who else?'

'I don't know. I found him here. He and I never talked much before you came. You release his mouth more times than anybody I know.'

'I look at him sometimes. His face is filled with pain but he tries to hide it. It is as if he is carrying much suffering, not in his crippled leg, but in his heart. I suppose we are all alike.'

'I don't understand.'

'But you do,' she insisted, raising her voice a little. 'What I mean is that perhaps we all carry maimed souls and we are all looking for a cure. Perhaps there is only one!'

Her tone more than the words eerily crept into his flesh.

'I do not – understand,' he said haltingly, afraid.

'You always say you don't understand. But what's there to understand? You too are in flight. What made you run away to an area like this? Tell me truthfully. What were you running away from?'

He winced: he felt prickly sweat in his skin. He panicked but kept his voice controlled.

'Just a simple transfer ... change of climate ... change of places. They say that a too long a stay in one spot attracts lice ... things like that. But after independence ... I felt well. It is time we all did something ... Harambee. ... Self-help. ... Nation-Building ... Return to the land. ... I was obeying the general call in my own way. I have often thought of a good national slogan: Self-help is Help-self!'

'You see!' she said suddenly, triumphantly. 'I did not believe your story when I first came here three months ago ... having no sights ... all that.'

Looking at her involvement in the village life he could not but feel the lie behind his own words or feel guilty at her sudden declaration of faith.

In the two weeks of maize harvest she threw herself into the work, helping Nyakinyua and even some of the other women. It was a poor harvest and the peasant farmers looked at one another and shook their heads.

At the same time she kept on helping at the shop, arranging things: once she even accompanied Joseph in the donkey-cart to Ruwa-ini to buy more stock, instead of Abdulla going. Munira watched her total immersion in work and he felt anxious almost as if the work was a human rival. She would clean up the place in the morning and take stock. In the afternoon she would join a group of women going into the plains to fetch water.

Wanja enjoyed their gossip about everything: from the dirty clothes they had to wash for the men, to the love-making habits of their men. Wambui said: 'Why, mine once came back from Ruwa-ini or wherever he works and found me in the shamba and imagine, he wanted it there in the shamba, on dry maize-stalks under the shade of a mwariki shrub, and he wouldn't hear of waiting for the evening in the hut, and there he was sweating out his power, and I told him that I would cry out "Shame!" and he would not heed my protests and well, can you believe it, that's where that rogue of mine, Muriuki, was conceived ... on a maize stalk under the sun.' 'I bet you did not mind it much, seeing that one is also thirsty under this hot sun,' another retorted, and they all laughed. They would often turn to Wanja: tell us about the men in the city – we hear that they put a rubber trouser on it? And Wanja would only laugh. But they were full of praises for her coming to help her grandmother. Do stay so we can see your man from the city when he comes to visit you.

Later she would return to Abdulla's place to look after the bar, but also to while away the time sipping beer and listening to more gossip and stories, this time from the men. They talked and even sang of the humped longhorns that roamed wild on the wide Ilmorog plains and which once, in a time of drought long before the Ngoci and Mburu and Ngigi generations were even conceived, gave up their horns and humps to God in ritual sacrifice for rain. Wanja was the life and now the major attraction in the place: it was as if they talked in order to catch her ear, to provoke her laughter or to inspire an approving nod from her.

Munira looked at her animated face, at her neck slightly inclined toward a person talking, at her hands that sought for human touch and warmth and he would feel these inward twitches of inexplicable physical pain. She would be so completely absorbed in another person as if he Munira, did not exist.

The poor maize harvest was followed by months of no rain. With little to do in the fields everybody's nerves seemed affected by the dust and the searing sun and people would often quarrel for nothing. They all knew but did not want to accept that there would be only one season that year. As if forewarned of meagre harvest, the traders who usually came and bought the produce to take away to the cities this time did not appear.

Wanja's eyes were more and more turned away from Ilmorog.

Sometimes she would turn her restlessness against the village and flay it and the conditions with merciless fun and mockery.

'Why should anybody end up in this hole of a place? Look at the women scratching the earth. Look at them. What do they get in return? What did we call by the name of harvest? A few grains of maize.'

'It was a bad season. Njuguna, Muturi ... they all say it was a poor harvest because the rains were delayed.'

'It is a bad season. They say that every year. They hope that by saying that the next harvest will be better. But all they'll get is this windfall of dust: and this scraggy earth waiting to be saved from a heartless sun by rain that may never fall.'

During the month of December she became more and more visibly restless: it was as if something were really eating her. Her complaints against Ilmorog became sharper and more bitter. One day, after a stream of invectives and ceaseless complaints, she jumped from the counter, got an exercise book and quickly drew sketches of a group of old women raising dust as they ran from a pursuing lusty young man sun toward thin old man rain with a tiny head and spindly legs.

'They are one with the soil ... peace ... Uhuru na Kazi ... There is dignity in labour, don't you think?' Munira was saying of the peasants.

'One with the dust, you mean?' She said looking at her sketch and then throwing it at Abdulla. 'Haven't you seen the flies on mucus-filled noses? A cowhide or grass for a bed? Huts with falling-in thatches?'

And now she laughed. Not from deep in her stomach but from her throat: a bitter, ironic laugher.

For some reason Munira was angry at this: after all he had accepted the conditions. They were his very protection and now she was laughing at them.

'Why did you leave those places you talk about, the coast, the cities, Nairobi, Nakuru, Eldoret, Kisumu, and come here? Why don't you go back?'

'Why not indeed?' She suddenly said, angry, but somehow Munira felt that she was restless and quarrelling about something else. 'I hate Ilmorog. I hate the countryside – so boring! I could do with clean tap water. Electric light and a bit of money.'

She spoke quickly as if her mind was there and not there: as if she was both there and also in another landscape. She had never spoken harshly to Abdulla but now she turned on him. She took the piece of paper and tore it into small bits.

'What does Abdulla here tell me? I will pay you well. When? Do you know, Abdulla, that all employers are the same? I have worked in many bars. There is only one song sung by all barmaids. Woe. They give you seventy-five shillings a month. They expect you to work for twenty-four hours. In the daytime you give beer and smiles to customers. In the evening you are supposed to give them yourself and sighs in bed. Bar and Lodging. The owner grabs twenty shillings for letting a couple use a Vono bed and torn sheets for ten minutes. Abdulla, do you know you can make a lot of money by simply buying a spring bed, a blanket and two sheets and labelling this place: Ilmorog Bar and Restaurant? Provided of course that you get yet another barmaid to wash the sheets!'

They all watched her expecting her to cry or something. But she had changed. She sipped her beer thoughtfully and then went on dreamily.

'Wait a minute. We should turn this into a church. Those tired of the city can come here. They will wash the pain in their souls with beer and dancing. Or a sanatorium. A big one. They run away from their wives and children for a weekend. Roast goat meat. Drink beer. Dance. Get cured. Go back to the waiting wives. Or, Mwalimu: what should we do to this place? To Ilmorog? Isn't a teacher the true light of the village? Would you light a fire and hide it under a tin? Seriously Abdulla, start brewing Changaa, or Muratina, any of these. Kill me Quick. Truly these drinks kill people but they still go on paying their hard-earned last cent to hasten their death. Buying the right to die sooner. Here in the village people will die under this sun and they'll not pay you for it. So Abdulla, brew Changaa. Get rich on the misery of the poor.'

Her smile as she said this seemed cunning and sinister: it carried mockery and irony at the edges. He felt she was talking about him and his escape from his home to this place. Munira felt her even more remote: as if he had never touched her: her taunt had the same alluring power as the beckoning coquetry of a virgin: he could touch her only by deflowering her by force and so himself flowering in blood. A virgin and a prostitute. Why couldn't she carry an advertising label on her back: Drive a VW: Ride a Virgin Whore. Or VIP: Very Interesting Prostitute. He thought of throwing these insults at her. But the malicious and bitter flow of his thoughts was interrupted by Wanja's next antic. She stood up and went to the door and yawned: why are we all in this hole? Then as suddenly, she wheeled round, jumped over the counter, onto the floor, and faced the men with a hard and set expression. She almost screamed:

'Some music, Bwana Abdulla. Some music: this body is only fit for dancing. Why! this place does not even have a radio! Siiiing! Mwalimu, play the guitar, play a flute, I want to dance.

Without waiting for their responses, she started to dance, gyrating her hips, slow motion at first but in rhythm with some music in her head. The rhythm became faster and faster, her face changing into something between ecstasy and pain. She moved her hips, her breasts, her stomach, so that her whole body was now wave-motions of sensuality and power. Soon the music was over. She sat down exhausted. She spoke quietly now, calmly, as if she had worked out something inside her. She was more relaxed, almost the Wanja they knew.

'Well, that is how we used to lure men. It was our only minute of glory. Two girls could be dancing together on the floor. Men would beg with their eyes and beg with their hands and in the end with their drinks and money. I am really very wicked. I hate a man thinking he can buy me with money. I once made a man spend over two hundred shillings buying me imported cider. Cider can never make you drunk you see. I simply walked out on him. I went with another who had not spent a cent on me. It felt good. The following morning he was waiting for me with a knife. Give me back my money! What money, I asked him? Cider, cider, he shouted. I put on my most innocent face and put sugar and honey in my voice. You mean you wanted me last night? Why didn't you say so? Cider has no mouth to speak. But I must say I am hurt: there I was thinking all the time, at long last I have found a true friend ... so *you* are like all of them! I flashed angry eyes at him. He was so ashamed. He bought me more cider, and he never again molested me. Abdulla ... I am really tired of this wretched hole.'

And now Munira was lost in admiration of her coquetry. She sat there looking so desirable: he wanted to ride a VW to the sindom of pleasure and now, now, he would reach her, he would bind her to himself. But Abdulla looked out past her, past the door to the outer edges of the now dusty land after the cultivation which had followed the harvest. It was as if he was holding communion with memory and distance. What loneliness is here, he muttered to himself. He turned to Wanja: his eyes were kindly and mellow with intense pity.

'Wanja, you also listen to me. I will say this and Mwalimu here can be a witness. I know what it is to carry a live wound. And I am not talking of this leg stump. Stay in Ilmorog. Let us face what you call this hole together. The wages that I would give you will now become shares. You and I will be joint-owners of this business. It is not much to offer, but it is offered sincerely. But don't go away.'

Wanja controlled her tears with difficulty. She understood what he said and even more the sincerity behind the offer. But she could not accept: there was that within her that urged her to go away now that she knew that her visit had come to nought. But even if — how could she stay in Ilmorog?

'Abdulla, you have a big heart. You make me feel I want to cry. I am a wicked woman. Do you know why I came to Ilmorog? Why did you? Why did Munira here? Mine, Abdulla, is a long and a short story. Maybe I'll come back. But I feel as if I've a debt to settle with the world, out there.'

Without another word, she suddenly stood up and walked slowly across the dry fields toward her hut.

Early the following day Nyakinyua went to Abdulla's shop. She refused a seat but she sent Joseph to call Munira. Abdulla's stomach tightened with fear.

'Wanja has gone away,' she now said after Munira had come. 'But she might return since she did not take away all her things,' she added, doubtfully.

Munira and Abdulla did not say anything.

'Aah, this sun,' Nyakinyua said and made as if to move without actually doing so. 'This sun!' she repeated.

And still Munira and Abdulla did not say anything.

Chapter Five

1 ❀ The year that followed Wanja's departure from Ilmorog was momentous for the whole country. It was the year that started with a mysterious political murder in open daylight without the assassins ever being caught. He was a national, of Asian origins it is true, but one famous in the whole country for his earlier involvement in the struggle for independence and after, for his consistent opposition to any form of post-independence alliance with imperialism. He was an implacable foe of wealth gotten from the poor and whether in or outside parliament, he would call for an agrarian revolution. Rumours were rife in the country for the whole of that year: people would meet in groups of three or four to discuss the latest rumour and theory. Was it true that he was in league with this or that politician? Maybe he had been planning something fishy: a coup d'état? But how—? Communism: what was this? Opposition to foreign control of the economy? Call for agrarian revolution? Call for the end to poverty? Asian: maybe that and this. But he had been imprisoned and detained by the British in the years of struggle? So many questions without answers and a current of fear, the first of many others to follow, coursed through the veins of the new nation.

For Ilmorog the year saw yet another rain shortage. For a second year following there was only one harvest more miserable than that of the year before.

So that when the year of assassination ended and still there was no rain people of Ilmorog put on frowning faces and anxiously looked up to the sky. But the sun seemed to mock their inquiring faces.

The sun sent direct waves of heat in exaggerated brightness that almost blinded the eye to look. The wind would suddenly whirl dust and rubbish into the air as if sending an offering to God-sun: but as suddenly the wind dust-storm would subside and the rubbish would fall disconsolately to the ground as if the offering had been found unacceptable. The peasant farmers of Ilmorog felt this headache giving heat-rays on their dry skins, saw the little furious whirling of dust and rubbish and retreated to the verandahs of their huts: in the fields were no more green umbrella leaves of mwariki to give shade and shelter. Still they went to the shambas not because there was any weeding and breaking of the earth to do but simply because they were attracted to their shambas as a moth to light. They could not help it. Now under the eaves of their huts they exchanged gossip and memories and wicked pleasantries but underneath it was a disquietening consciousness that this year might be a season of drought.

Njogu, Muturi, Ruoro, Njuguna were sitting outside Abdulla's shop. Ordinarily they would have taken the cows and goats to the plains. But it was the end of the year and the beginning of a new one and the school was closed for holidays and it was the children's turn. What worried them was that the previous two years had only yielded one harvest in September. Thereafter it had not rained except for a few intermittent falls – the kind of rain that only drove away lazy ones to shelter. So if this New Year's njahi rains were late as had been the case in the last two years the community would almost immediately be faced by famine. But as they sat outside Abdulla's shop they tried many subjects but they always came back to the rains.

'It might still rain ... sometimes it has been known to rain at the beginning of the year or a little bit later,' said Njogu.

'I don't know why, but the weather is becoming less and less predictable. It's as if something has gone into its head,' argued Njuguna. 'Mwathi wa Mugo seems to be losing his power over the rains,' he added with an ironic smile, without looking at Muturi.

'It may be those things that the Americans and Russians are throwing into the sky.'

'It could be. I hear that they might be sending travellers to the moon. Is it possible?'

'There was a time we didn't believe it was possible for a man to walk on a metal horse of two wheels,' Njogu said as he saw Munira riding the metal horse toward them. 'Until Munoru rode on one.'

'You know when the white man first came. He removed his shoes and we thought he had taken off his leg. People ran away saying: what is this new magic?'

They laughed at this and asked for more to drink. Munira leaned his bicycle against the wall, and sat down, asking for beer at the same time.

'Beer will soon be our only water...' he said.

'Mwalimu ... when do you open school?' Njuguna asked him. 'You have now been with us two years. That has been good for our children.'

'I don't know,' he said. 'We are now in the middle of January. Unless I get more teachers, it will not be possible to carry on. The first year I had two classes. The second year, I had three classes. Now it'll be four classes.'

'Where will you get the teachers? Which VIP will want to come and bake in the sun?'

'I will be going to Ruwa-ini. I'll go and tell Mzigo this: unless you give me at least one extra teacher, you better close the school.'

They were silent at his words. For a moment they all withdrew into private thoughts. So Mwalimu was preparing to leave them? Two years had maybe been too long for him

Munira had hoped that with Wanja's going he would recapture his previous rhythm and aloof dominance. But this was an elusive dream, he had soon realised, and for a month after she had gone Munira could be seen galloping all over Ilmorog, a dustcloud following him. 'It is the sun,' some of them said. After four or five months of hoping in vain that she would return, he went to Ruwa-ini on a market day, pretending that he was only looking for something to buy but didn't get anything. He again found a reason to stay the night at Ruwa-ini and drank in almost all the bars. He ended up in Furaha Bar. There he saw a girl at the juke-box. Her back was turned to him. But his heart gave exaggerated wild beats and he could not keep up the pretence: he was looking for Wanja. He sat on a high stool at the counter and waited for her to recognise him. First the guitar: then the choral voices rose and dominated the atmosphere: it was a religious hymn and the girl now turned – oh! it was not Wanja – and started singing with the voices, her eyes slightly shut, as if she was part of the choral voices issuing from the box. When it was over, she came to the counter and asked for a drink. What interested Munira was her knowledge of nearly all the languages of Kenya. When she spoke Gikuyu one thought she really was a Mugikuyu: when she spoke Luo one thought she couldn't be anything else. The same with Swahili, Kamba and Luhya. He soon lost interest in her: but he had liked the hymn and he went over, put a shilling into the slot and pressed it. It was sung by Ofafa Jericho Choir and the hymn was moving. The girl ran back to the box and Munira was so fascinated with her total almost seductive absorption in the hymn that, for a time, he forgot his disappointment at not finding Wanja. He even thought of buying her drinks and asking her to bed for the night. But the religious hymn brought back the memory of his boyhood escapade and later attempt at purification by fire, and he lost all interest in the girl's body.

He had returned to Ilmorog after that fruitless search for a dream and for the rest of that year he threw himself into his teaching and tried to suppress memories of Wanja and their lovemaking in a hut. But things were not quite the same. At least Abdulla's place was different: Abdulla himself hardly ever spoke more than two sentences to him. He was always glad when he found the elders in Abdulla's place.

'Is it true that these people are trying to walk to the moon, Mwalimu?' Muturi asked to move their minds away from thoughts of Mwalimu's possible desertion.

'Yes.'

'These people are strange. They have no fear even of God. They have no respect for holiness. They ruin things on earth. And now they go to disturb God in his realm. It is no wonder He gets angry and withholds rain.'

'Indeed this is true. Look at us. We have always feared God and we have not tried to probe closely into his ways. This is why God was able to spare us from utter ruin. That's why after the Battle of Ilmorog he turned the colonialists' eyes the other way. And you will agree with me that we of Ilmorog did not lose too many sons in war for Uhuru despite Nyakinyua's husband's mad action.'

'Nyakinyua's husband, Njamba Nene. He was a brave man,' Njuguna commented.

'That he was – so old and yet pointing a gun at a white man!'

'He redeemed Ilmorog with his blood,' said Njogu.

'And so did your grandson – don't forget that Ole Masai had Ilmorog blood in him.'

And suddenly they were all startled by Abdulla's stream of curses at Joseph. This was strange because for a whole year after Wanja's visit they had not heard him curse. Again they kept quiet as if they were holding a silence in memory of Nyakinyua's husband and of Ole Masai whom they only knew in name.

'I don't agree with you there,' said Muturi, once again trying to change the subject. 'We have been losing our sons to the cities.'

'Oh yes,' agreed Ruoro and he coughed to clear his throat. 'I don't understand young men these days. In our time we were compelled to work for these oppressing Foreigners. And even then, after earning enough to pay tax or fines, we would run back to our shambas. Now take my sons ... I don't even know where they are. One went to work in Nairobi, another in Kisumu, another in Mombasa, and they hardly ever come back. Only one, who occasionally comes back to see his wife Wambui, and even he hardly stays for a day.'

'Mine too,' observed Njuguna. 'One went to work as a cook in the settled area. He was then detained and even after detention went back to work as a cook for the new African settlers. Imagine that: a big man able to use his hand cooking for others. The other three are in Nairobi.'

'Actually we should not blame them,' rejoined Muturi. 'After that first big war there was no more land in which to move. And also there will always be those who will never resist the call of strange places. My father used to tell me that even before the white Foreigners came, a few people would travel to the waters carrying ivory, and sometimes they would not come back.'

'Like Munoru who sighed after new things,' said Ruoro. They were again silent, for a few seconds, as if all their minds were on this movement of their sons and the calamity which had come over the land. Then Njuguna coughed and looked into space:

'You are right about the shortage of land. I remember the words of my youngest son before he left for the City. It was soon after a harvest like the ones we have had these last two years. He said: "I have worked on this land for a year. My nails are broken. But look at the yield. It mocks the strength in these arms. Tell me father, when the tax gatherer comes round, what shall I give him? When I go to Ruwa-ini and I see nice clothes, where shall I get the coins to give the shopkeeper? I must go to the big city and try my future there: like my other brothers." What words could I tell him?'

'This land used to yield. Rains used not to fail. What happened?' inquired Ruoro.

It was Muturi who answered.

'You forget that in those days the land was not for buying. It was for use. It was also plenty, you need not have beaten one yard over and over again. The land was also covered with forests. The trees called rain. They also cast a shadow on the land. But the forest was eaten by the railway. You remember they used to come for wood as far as here – to feed the iron thing. Aah, they only knew how to eat, how to take away everything. But then, those were Foreigners – white people.

'Now that we have an African Governor and African big chiefs, they will return some of the fat back to these parts . . .'

'You mean bring back our sons?' retorted Njuguna. Then he coughed, a cough with a meaning, and turned to Abdulla: 'Now about this, your donkey: don't you think it is eating too much grass in a season of drought?'

Munira stood up. He left them arguing about the donkey. For him Ilmorog without Wanja had been a land of drought. But he was strangely affected by their words. He remembered his strange conversation with Karega almost two years before and his own sudden thoughts about an unevenly cultivated garden.

❀

Every day they all waited for the rains, or a change in the sun. They all waited for something to happen. But every morning they woke to wind and dust and a dazzling sun.

As the days dragged on and there was no visible change, Abdulla's donkey became increasingly the centre of talk. Elders met and discussed what they could do about it.

Early another day Njuguna, Ruoro, Njogu and Muturi once again called on Abdulla and they refused to sit down. They also refused to drink anything. They would not even look Abdulla in the eye. Abdulla saw the shifty eyes in solemn faces.

'You appear burdened in the heart,' said Abdulla. 'Is it anything I can help?'

'Do you see how the sun shimmers? It almost blinds the eye to look,' Njuguna commented, vaguely pointing to the sun-baked land.

'It will rain,' said Abdulla without conviction.

'It is not that we are saying it will not rain!' said Ruoro. 'It is too early to tell about the vagaries of the weather.'

'Can't you see the dust and the wind?' added Ruoro.

'What do you want?'

'We are only messengers from the village,' said Njuguna.

'We come in peace and good heart.'

'But what do you want from me?' Just at that point, his donkey hee-hooed across Ilmorog. The elders looked at one another. Njuguna delivered what he called only a friendly message, a request.

Abdulla watched them walk away, the sun shimmering on their bare heads. Emissaries of evil, he hissed, and buried his face in his hands on the table: what could he do without his other leg?

'So it is a question of my one donkey or their cows and goats? No, I'll not have it killed or sent away. I would rather leave the village. Oh yes: they want to drive me from Ilmorog.'

Joseph looked at him. He feared that this would mean that he would not return to school for his second year. He wanted to weep. Perhaps if Wanja had not gone, he thought in his boyish, sad but grateful remembrance of her action.

2 ✿ When at long last school reopened, Munira found that he could not possibly deal with four classes all by himself. Now, looking back over the two years that had gone, it seemed a miracle that he had managed to carry on the school that long. If he could get even one extra teacher, he could perhaps manage it. Standards I and III could meet in the mornings and Standards II and IV in the afternoons.

He decided to cycle to Ruwa-ini to confront Mr Mzigo with the problem. It would also be good to get away from these constant talks about sun and dust. If Mzigo did not give him a teacher, Munira would have to abandon the school.

But just before he could leave for Ruwa-ini to see Mzigo about the school's problems, two things which Munira was later to remember happened in Ilmorog. At the time, however, they only seemed out of character with the sunny somnolence of the old Ilmorog as he had known it. First came the tax officer in a government Landrover accompanied by two gun-carrying Askaris. Before the officer could get out of the Landrover, word of his arrival had gone round: all the men somehow managed to vanish into the plains. The officer knocked at the door of every house: in each place he found only women and children. 'All our men have gone to your cities,' complained the women, 'look at the sun and the dust and tell us if you would stay here.' In the end, the officer went to Abdulla's place and over a drink of beer he talked incessantly about Ilmorog country. 'It seems to be getting more and more depopulated. Every year that I have come here, I have been met by fewer and fewer males. But this trip breaks all records.' Abdulla agreed with the officer without adding any details. 'Anyway you have all the women to yourself,' the officer continued, writing a tax receipt for Abdulla. He drove away. In the evening the men miraculously reappeared and they talked as if nothing had happened.

But soon after this episode came two men from 'out there'. They claimed that they were sent by Nderi wa Riera. People of Ilmorog gathered around them at the school compound and patiently waited to hear the news: perhaps Nderi wa Riera had remembered his old promise to bring piped water to the area. One was fat with a shiny bald head which he kept on touching and they called him Fat Stomach: the other was tall and thin and kept his hands in his pockets and never once said a word. They baptised him Insect. Insect told them of a new Kīama-Kamwene Cultural Organisation – which would bring unity between the rich and the poor and bring cultural harmony to all the regions. Fat Stomach declared that the people of Ilmorog were to ready themselves to go to Gatunda to sing and have tea. He explained that all the people from Central Province were going to sing and drink tea. Just like 1952, he hinted and talked vaguely but with suggestive variation of voice, of a new cultural movement: let he who had ears hear. He explained how their hard-won property and accumulation of sweat was threatened by another tribe.

Ruoro stood up to answer back: where was Gatundu? Why would anybody want Ilmorog people to go and drink tea? How come that they from out there were threatened by other tribes? Had they piled enough property as to excite envy from other tribes? Here, people were threatened by lack of water; lack of roads; lack of hospitals. But what really was expected of them?

Fat Stomach laughed rather uneasily, but when he talked he oozed a sense of infinite patience. They would get free transport: but each man and each woman was expected to take with him twelve shillings and fifty cents.

At this, the women, led by Nyakinyua, started making a noise: did he mean that they had to pay all that in order to go and sing and drink tea?

'Let him who has ears listen,' Fat Stomach repeated, a mixture of warning and menace in his voice. And now Nyakinyua seemed possessed: 'You too, if you have ears, listen: you are worse than a tax gatherer. Twelve shillings and fifty cents! From what hole are we to dig up the money? Why should we pay to sing? Go back and tell them this: here we need water, not songs. We need food. We need our sons back to help this land grow.'

Fat Stomach was sweating a little and now his voice carried anxiety. At the same time he did not want to show fear in front of these people. He tried to say the tribe's wealth was being threatened by the lake people and others deceived by the Indian communist who was recently removed from this earth.

'You mean some of you have already made enough wealth while we scratch the earth?'

'Is that the wealth they want to steal from you?'

'Good for them if they are as poor as we are.'

'Yes, yes. What can they steal from us?'

'One year's harvest.'

'Our drought and dust.'

'If somebody can steal away this dust and this drought – that would be a blessing.'

'Here we live with our neighbours, the herdsmen. What quarrels have you amongst yourselves out there?'

The women had taken over the whole show, and they seemed to be enjoying it. Some started making threatening loud cries. There was a slight commotion.

'Let us pull out their penises and see if they are really men,' one woman shouted.

Fat Stomach and his companion, Insect, backed a little, trying to keep dignity, but at the woman's words, they started running across the school compound toward their Landrover, the menacing voices of women behind them.

Munira briefly thought about these two incidents as later the same month he cycled to Ruwa-ini to fight for more teachers. What madness had seized the women? What was that sudden rumble of violence behind the sunny rural passivity? Maybe it was the sun and the dust he thought dismissing the whole matter from his mind. Fat Stomach and Insect were charlatans, probably thieves who wanted to make money on the side.

He started reviewing in advance his coming confrontation with Mzigo. He was tired of his monthly cycling to Ruwa-ini. He was tired of Ruwa-ini Town with its red tiled colonial houses; its golf course; its bougainvillaeas and its jacaranda trees lining the pavements.

Ruwa-ini, the capital of Chiri District was famous only because it was originally the centre of hides and skins trade and also of trade in wattle barks.

Baumann and Coy, Forrestals, and also Primchand Raichand and Coy, in their nineteen-twenties fearsome rivalry for the control of wattle bark trade and of tanning extract, had set rival offices and factories here. It was these foreign and local giants of capital, together with the Mombasa-Kisumu-Kampala charcoal and wood-eating railway engines which had depleted forests near and far. Ruwa-ini had had an air of prosperity and growth before the wattle extract was replaced by synthetic tanning materials and the char-coal-eating engines by those powered by diesel oil.

The tanning extract used to be railed to Limuru, in Kiambu District where a Czech-Canadian International shoe-making factory had been established just before the Second World War. Ruwa-ini was now no more than an administrative centre although its daily market and its golf course were widely known.

Mzigo's office was still the same specklessly tidy affair. He sat in the same place, in the same position, as he had always done.

'Aa, Mr Munira, good to see you again and again. How is the

school? But do sit down. I'm sorry I have not been to your school yet:
but I'll be coming shortly. Any good roads yet? I don't need to tell
you about these damned cars. Anything to wet my throat? By the
way, congratulations. You were before only an Acting Headmaster.
It's now confirmed. You are the new Headmaster of Ilmorog Full
Primary School. Congratulations again.'

'I am touched by the honour,' Munira said, actually thrilled
inside.

'It's nothing,' said Mzigo. 'Your own dedication!'

'But I could do with a few more teachers. At least one . . .'

'Teachers? But Mr Munira, I told you almost two years ago that
you could recruit any help you needed.'

'It is a bit difficult . . . that place . . . It is slightly out of the way. A
bit dry. Few people come that side.'

'I hear that it's been deserted by its men: is that true Mr Munira?
That only women remain? Lucky you, Mr Munira. I shall be coming
along to help you . . . Not a bad job eh? Meanwhile do attract one or
two teachers there. Tell them about the free women. Try, Mr
Munira, try. When I was at school, Mr Munira, my headmaster used
to tell us: Try and Try Again. He was a fat Scotsman in charge of
religion and he used to tell us a story of a Scottish king who was
driven out of his kingdom and he saw a spider try and try again to
climb up a wall until he succeeded. He too went back and this time
regained his kingdom. So, Mr Munira, try and people your kingdom
of Ilmorog with teachers . . .'

Munira was about to go out when Mzigo called him back.

'By the way, here is a letter to the Headmaster of Ilmorog School.'

Munira took the envelope and opened it. He could not believe it.
He read it over and over again. Kamwene Cultural Organisation
(Ilmorog Branch) invited the Headmaster of Ilmorog School and all
his staff to join Nderi wa Riera in a delegation that would go to tea
at Gatundu . . . He was trembling . . .

'Thank you . . .' he said.

'It's not me . . .'

Munira's heart was glowing with pride. And so he was making
something of himself after all. A headmaster. And now an invitation
to tea. To tea at Gatundu! Admittedly, the note was handwritten,
and came from the district office and it asked him to organise all his
teachers and their wives. He had never heard of KCO (Ilmorog
Branch). But it was something to remember. A headmaster. An invitation to tea. Tea at Gatundu. He thought of going back to tell Mr
Mzigo the story of a Mr Ironmonger who used to talk of heaven in
terms of tea, sausages and vanilla ice-cream. But now he had to

hurry home to tell his wife of the news. A headmaster! Invitation to tea! Ilmorog had given him greatness. Hoyee!

Before sunset he crossed into Limuru. Even if he had not known the features and the lie of the land – the ridges that gave way to deep valleys that rose up into more ridges and valleys – he would still have known it by the cold brisk air which suddenly hit him and made his body and mind alert, ready to leap and pounce. This land; these ridges, these valleys nearly always green through the year made Limuru a scion of God's favourite country: long rains in March, April and May; biting cold icy showers in misty June and July; windy sunshine on green peas and beans in August and September; a dazzling sun in harvest-tide in October and November and red plums and luscious pears ripening in December, January and February under a brilliantly clear blue sky. So different, he thought, from droughty Ilmorog.

But coming into the place he always felt in himself a strong tension between this vigour, this energy that was Limuru and that long night of unreality that was his past: between the call of life and involvement in living history and an escape into a family seclusion with a morality rooted in property and the Presbyterian Church; between an inexplicable fear of the people and an equally inexplicable fear of his father; between the desire for active creation and a passive acceptance of one's ordained fate. His father's face now loomed large in his mind . . .

❁

His father was an early convert to the Christian faith. We can imagine the fatal meeting between the native and the alien. The missionary had traversed the seas, the forests, armed with the desire for profit that was his faith and light and the gun that was his protection. He carried the Bible; the soldier carried the gun; the administrator and the settler carried the coin. Christianity, Commerce, Civilisation: the Bible, the Coin, the Gun: Holy Trinity. The native was grazing cattle, dreaming of warriorship, of making the soil yield to the power of his hands, slowly through a mixture of magic and work bending nature's laws to his collective will and intentions. In the evening he would dance, muthunguci, ndumo, mumburo in celebration or he would pray and sacrifice to propitiate nature. Yes: the native was still afraid of nature. But he revered man's life as much as he revered nature. Man's life was God's sacred fire that had to remain lit all the way from the ancestor to the child and the generations yet unborn.

Except that Waweru and his father had been driven from their family land in Muranga by even more powerful mbari lords and wealthy houses who could buy more potent magic and other protective powers. Here in Kiambu they had to start all over again with his grandfather having to work his way up from a ndungata on yet another powerful family's land to the time when he got a few goats to strike out on his own. Waweru had seen all that and he hoped that when he grew up he too would acquire even more potent magic and create an even more powerful house.

The native. The missionary. Driven by forces they could not always understand. The stage was set.

Waweru's father wakes up, the hour it is said Mara threw away his dying mother to the forest. He tells Waweru: my son, take these goats and cows to the grassland near Ikenia Forest. I have a meeting with the elders to discuss this thing prophesied long ago by the travelling seer – Mugo wa Kibiro. We and our fathers used not to believe him when he told us about red Foreigners and now indeed it has happened. And now the red stranger has started taking our lands in Tigoni and other places. You know how we have struggled to get this land and, even harder, this wealth. If he takes our land: where shall we cultivate miriyo? Where graze the cattle? So all the clans and mbaris and all the houses big and small must now close ranks and fight the stranger in our midst. Do not forget your calabash of sour milk. Also your spear and shield. We shall need them in the struggle to come. Gird your loins and always remember everything good and beautiful comes from the soil. Some clan-heads and mbari lords and some heads of the big houses are betraying the people and allying themselves with these Foreigners. But remember those who betrayed the nation to the Arab trader, Jumbe? The voice of the people haunted them to death. Waweru takes the cows and the goats and then he stands, watches the retreating figure of his father and spits on the ground. *Big houses: big families: more powerful than the work of my hand is the possession of magic: didn't the big houses drive us from our land in Muranga and we had to start all over again? I'll create my big house to beat all the big houses* ... Waweru has always passed by this new building where the daily peals of bells strike awe and curiosity into his heart. This magic and the one that comes from bamboo sticks is making the big houses and the big mbaris and clans afraid: they struggle against it or seek friendship with it. At least it is splitting houses, clans, and even ridges. Not even Kamiri's sorcery proved more powerful than this magic. Waweru knows one or two young men who have sought shelter inside. They were given lumps of sugar and a piece of white calico. Now it is morning: and it is cold. They see him and beckon him in. He has already made up his mind. Let his father resist alone. He, Waweru, will join Kamenyi and Kahati. Better than the warmth of cow-dung and urine and biting dew was the odour of the white man sweetened by sugar, with church bells and music stranger than that from the one-stringed wandindi and the mwariki flute – and, protected by gunpowder and tinkling coins, possessing life longer and stronger than that of cows and goats and sheep. This was a new world with a new magic. His father, trembling with anger, comes to fetch home the prodigal son: he can't speak, but helplessly points a walking stick at Waweru. Waweru feels a bit guilty: after all, he is shin of the shin, blood of the blood of the trembling old man. But above the voice of doubt, he hears another voice calling him into a higher glory: he who forsaketh his father and mother for my sake ... and he sees himself the fulfilment of the prophecy which is also the proof of the truth of it. At the behest of his new father and mother, Waweru, who now becomes Ezekieli – how sweet the name sounds in a new Christian's ear – divests himself of every robe from his heathen past.

Wash me, Redeemer, and I shall be whiter than snow: so they sang then, as Munira was later to sing in Siriana.

Rewards there were: a proof of God's nodding response. With a mixture of tinkling coins and trickery of the pen and the law he was able to buy whole lands from some of the declining mbari lords and clans and also from individuals who needed money to pay their expected dues to the new Caesar. Such were those who did not want to turn into workers on European settlers' lands, then the only means of securing the coins needed by Caesar. They sold their lands bit by bit to those like Waweru who could get the coins through bringing more souls to Christ. In the end they joined the very labouring clan they were trying to avoid by the sale of their land and property. For the Caesar kept on making more and more demands. There were other mbaris too, like that of Kagunda whose sons wanted only to drink and not look after their inherited wealth. So Kanjohi, elder son of Kagunda, sold all his family lands to Waweru and himself went to the Rift Valley. This and more: Waweru seized all the openings so that under the old colonial regime, he was a very powerful land-owner and churchman. Waweru was amongst the first Africans allowed to grow pyrethrum as a cash crop and to sell it to the white growers. This gave him a head-start over his more pagan neighbours, some of whom had been pacified to eternal sleep or to slave-labour camps in towns or farms by Frederick Lugard, Meinertzhagen, Grogan, Francis Hall and other hirelings of Her Imperial Majesty, Defender of the Faith, Elect of God. God save the Queen, they sang after every massacre and then went to church for blessings and cleansing: it had always fallen to the priest to ordain human sacrifice to appease every dominant God in history.

There was a photograph of his father taken between the wars which had always impressed Munira.

Waweru is standing by a gramophone on which is drawn a picture of a dog sitting on its hind legs barking out: HIS MASTER'S VOICE. He is dressed in a jacket and riding breeches and boots and a chain passes over the front of the waistcoat. He is wearing a sun-helmet and in his hands he is holding the Bible.

Munira had always felt a slight discomfort with this picture, but he could never tell what it was to which he was really objecting. In the same way he had married a girl from a pagan home, maybe as a prompting from the heart against what his father stood for. But the girl turned out a replica of his more obedient sisters. She could never get it out of her mind that she had married into a renowned Christian house, and she tried to be the ideal daughter-in-law. She broke his parents' initial resistance by her readiness to be moulded anew. Julia soon became his mother's special creation and as such his mother adored her. Munira could have forgiven her everything but those silent prayers before and after making love. But he had never lifted a finger to fight against the process.

Life for him had always been a strain. His father thought him a loss. And he, Munira, always felt a need to break loose. But he always hesitated. It was as if he would not have known what he was running away from and what he was running toward.

❁

But now as Munira approached his home, a headmastership and an Invitation to Tea all in one pocket, he felt happy. His first big initiative, occasioned by the general idealism that had gripped the country just before and for a little while after independence, had produced a fruit however small. Invitation and a promotion. He could now even stand up to the profile of his father looming large in Munira's imagination as he rode through the brisk air toward his home.

It turned out that most teachers and their wives had been invited to tea at Gatundu. They had also been asked to take twelve shillings and fifty cents for a self-help project. Munira's wife, despite attempts to cover it with a Christian grace, was also excited. For Munira the Saturday would remain tattooed in his mind so that he would pass it alive to his children: he, Munira, was going to tea with a living legend which had dominated the consciousness of a country for almost a century. What wouldn't one give for the honour! Once again Munira felt a little bit above the average.

The bus that took them came around six to the Ruwa-ini post office, and everybody was worried: someone even suggested that they should cancel the trip, but he was hushed by the others. It was better late than never: tea in such a place would mean a night's feast. The solemn-looking government official assured them that all was well.

The sudden reversal of fortune was the most painful Munira had experienced since the Siriana incident. They were taken past Gatundu, through some banana plantations where they found yet another crowd of people solemnly waiting for something. A funeral tea? Munira wondered, numbed to silence by the eerie sombreness of everything. He looked around: the government official had vanished. They were now ordered into lines – one for men, the other for women. A teacher asked loudly: is this the tea we came to have? He was hit with the flat of a panga by a man who emerged from nowhere and as suddenly disappeared into nowhere. How did Mzigo and the government official come into all this? It was dark: a small light came from a hut into which people disappeared in groups of ten or so. What is it all about? thudded Munira's heart. And then it was his turn!

On the way back, around midnight, Munira knew that Julia was silently weeping. He felt her withdrawal, the accusation of betrayal: but how could he answer her now, how could he tell her that he truly did not know? He was hungry and thirsty and all throughout the bus was this hush of a people conscious of having been taken in: of having participated in a rite that jarred with time and place and persons and people's post-Uhuru expectations! How could they as teachers face their children and tell them that Kenya was one?

Later Munira was to learn that a very important person in authority, with the tacit understanding and approval from other very important persons in authority like Nderi, some even from other national communities, was the brain behind this business. But the knowledge did not reconcile him to the act.

At home Julia looked at him and said: 'So you could not be man enough to tell your wife!'

For the first time in his life Munira felt that he must have a man-to-man talk with his father. He now saw his father in a new and more positive light. In the 1890s he had stood up to his grandfather and joined the mission. In 1952 he had defied the movement and stuck to the Church. He had even dared preach against the movement. For these efforts he had had his cattle boma broken into and his cows taken away. His left ear was cut off as a warning. It is true that he had ceased preaching against it, but at least he had not abandoned the faith and the side that he had chosen. Yes. He would talk to him man to man, face to face, and learn the true secret of his father's success.

He went to his parents' house early the following day. He found his father in prayer. Munira felt weak at the knees. He knelt on the floor, genuinely trembling before the Lord. If being saved would help him, he would be saved. If beating and tearing and baring his chest before the Lord would really help him to choose the right path once and for all, he would surely do that so as to be cleansed of terror and doubt and indecision for ever. How proud he now was of a father so serene, so sure and secure in both wealth and faith!

Ezekiel Waweru was still one of the most powerful landlords in the area, adding to his pyrethrum estates new tea estates he bought from the departing colonials. It was an irony of history, or, for him, a manifestation of the mysterious ways of the Lord, that the new tea estate was in Tigoni, the very area Waweru's father had cited as the one act of colonial theft which caused big and small houses of the period to join the people in armed resistance. His children except Mukami and Munira had done well.

If he was surprised to see Munira call on him so early on a Sunday, or puzzled by the man's contrite face and sudden involvement in prayer, he did not show it on the face. Maybe God had finally brought him home, he reasoned, suppressing the contempt he felt toward Munira.

Munira's fear and puzzled anger at yesterday's experience seemed to grow and increase with reflection and distance in time. But not wanting to shock his father – and now, Munira thought, he would descend to the lowest depths in his father's estimation of him – he trod gingerly, softly, though his bitterness at being tricked, he, of all people, a teacher, urged him to spill everything. His father listened rapt in thought and this encouraged Munira.

'What I could not understand ... what I shall never forget was this man ... he was so poorly dressed ... rags ... no shoes even ... and he stood there, when all of us were trembling, and he said: "I am a squatter – a working-man in a tea plantation owned by Milk Stream Tea Estates. I used to work there before 1952. During the movement I was in charge of spying and receiving guns and taking them to our fighters. I was later detained. Now I am working on the same estate owned by the same company. Only now some of our people have joined them. It is good that some of our people are eating. But I will not take another oath until the promises of the first one have been fulfilled." They beat him in front of us. They stepped on his neck and pressed it with their boots against the floor, and only when he made animal noises did they stop. He took the oath all right. But not with his heart. I shall never forget his screaming.'

Munira had never felt so close to his father. Even when Waweru started lecturing him about his failures, he took it as justified chastisement: and who was he to contradict a father who at least had stood by some principles?

'I don't need to tell you that you have been a disappointment to me. You are my eldest son and you know what that means. I sent you to Siriana: you got into bad company and you were sent home. If you look at some of the people you were in school with you can see where they are: you go to any ministry, go to any big company, they are there. Your first act of manhood was to impregnate a woman. We thank the Lord that Julia turned out to be a good woman. But instead of staying together with her, you ran away to a place whose name I can't even mouth. You have always run from opportunities. You have always run away from every chance to make yourself a man. I have all this property. I am ageing. You could at least look after it. Look at your brothers ... only the other day little children. Take a lesson from them. The banker one has bought houses all over Nairobi. He has a number of trading premises in Nairobi. He could set you up in one. He could get you a loan. And your brother in the oil company. Go to any petrol station between here and everywhere. He has some small thing there. Your sisters too ... Now it has been reported to me that you even drink. You will come to a bad end: just like your sister ...'

'Mukami?' Munira asked automatically. He deserved all this and more, and after today he would reform his ways. 'Tell me, father ... what really happened to Mukami? What drove Mukami to it?'

'Bad company ... bad company ... Mariamu ... bad woman ... Her sons have been my ruin.'

His father's voice broke at the memory. There was a minute of silence as he tried to regain his balance. Munira was sorry that he had raised the question and stirred painful memories. His father suddenly stood up, took his coat and beckoned Munira to follow him.

They walked to the top of the ridge looking down upon the vast estate. Waweru was always proud of this estate because it was the one he had acquired when he was beginning to accumulate, before the Second World War.

'Do you see all this?'

'Yes.'

'Flowers. Fruit trees. Tea ... cows ... everything.'

'Yes.'

'It has not come into being just because of the strength of my limbs alone. It is the Lord's doing. It is true that this land of the Agikuyu is blessed by the Lord. The prosperity has multiplied several times since independence. My son, trust in God and you'll never put your foot wrong. God chooses the time of planting and of harvesting. He chooses His vessel for His vast design. Now listen my son. The old man is truly God's vessel. He suffered. But when he came out, did he take a stick and beat his enemies? No! He only said: "Lord, forgive them, for they know not what they do." Now all that prosperity, all that hard-won freedom is threatened by Satan working through other tribes, arousing their envy and jealousy. That is why this oath is necessary. It is for peace and unity and it is in harmony with God's eternal design. Now you listen to me. I have been there. I used the Bible. I want your mother to go. She is refusing. But Christ will soon show her the light. Even highly educated people are going there, of their own accord. My son, the fear of the Lord is the beginning of wisdom. This KCO is not a bad thing . . . We shall even have a Church Branch. It's a cultural organisation to bring unity and harmony between all of us, the rich and the poor, and to end envy and greed. God helps those who help themselves. And He said that never again would He give free manna from heaven . . .'

Munira was not sure if he had heard his father correctly. He looked at his father, at his missing ear: he remembered his father's denunciation of the oath in earlier times: whence this change to the same thing? Was it the same thing? He was again confused:

'You mean that you . . .'

'Yes, yes,' he said quickly, almost impatiently. Munira for the first time tried to argue back with his father.

'But before God there are no tribes. We are all equal before the Lord.'

'My son,' he said, after considering his words for a few minutes. 'Go back and teach. And stop drinking. If you are tired of teaching, come back here. I have work for you. My estates are many. And I am ageing. Or join KCO. Get a bank loan. Start business.'

'Here on our farm, since I was a child, I've seen so many workers: Luo, Gusii, Embu, Kamba, Somali, Luhya, Kikuyu — and they have all worked together. I have seen them praise the Lord without any ill-feeling between them.'

'I don't know why you came. I did not know that you had come to preach to your father. But I will repeat this. Go back and teach. These things are deeper than you think.'

And he went away.

Munira watched him walk down the huge farm. No, he had never known his father, he would never understand him: what was this about? What was this new alliance of the Church and KCO. No, it was better not to wade more than knee-deep into affairs that did not concern him. And he felt some kind of relief. It was as if he had been pulled back from the brink. He had postponed a decision. And yet he felt as if a decision had been made for him, because when he took his bicycle from against the walls of his father's house, he did not cycle toward his home. He cycled toward Kamiritho Township – to have a drink. But he knew that later that day or night he would be returning to Ilmorog, to his waterless, rainless cloister, without the teachers he had set out to recruit.

❀

The Kamiritho he now came to had changed much. Yesterday, so to speak, it was only a huge village. Now it had sprawled into a fast-growing shopping centre with more than a fair share of beer-halls and teashops. Outside, artisans, self-employed or employed by the slightly more well-to-do, beat corrugated iron sheets into various objects: huge aluminium water-tanks, braziers, charcoal-powered water-heaters, iron troughs for chicken-feed. Higher and higher rose up two huge mounds of scrap metal and waste iron from abandoned lorries and buses. Unemployed motor-mechanics lay on the grass watching cars pass by, hoping that one would develop a mechanical problem or something.

He stood outside the petrol station and looked across the shops to where the lorries used to go for Murram, to where Amina and others had erected Swahili majengo-type houses, and recalled that past humiliation. So long ago.

Then he turned round and he saw several lorries pass. On the boards were scribbles of KANU PRIVATE. He knew where they were coming from. His last night's terror seized him. He cycled toward Safari, the nearest bar, and hid inside.

It was early but he ordered a drink, cleared the first bottle very quickly and asked for a second. He started admiring the murals on the walls to keep his mind away from the outside and soon he was completely engrossed in the fantasy world of the artist:

A Masai Moran, a simi sword tied to his barely covered loins, fearlessly spearing a roaring lion accurately through the mouth; a man with a hat leisurely stretching his feet along the ground by an acacia bush in the Weru-wilds of Australia and giving a banana to a kangaroo carrying a baby in its belly pouch; city gentlemen and ladies sitting on chairs in a desert sipping Tusker and Pilsner; monkeys jumping from branch to branch with amused human eyes

– what a yoking of far-flung elements which nevertheless seemed in harmony. On yet another wall was Bus No. 555 speeding along a road that led to a wide blue sea with baby-holding breasted mermaids rising from the sea. The surreal images flashed through his mind as he ordered yet another Tusker, remembering at the same time Abdulla's place and Abdulla's fears for his donkey … A surreal world … where he could be made a headmaster in a clean modern office one hour and be drinking tea of unity to protect a few people's property in dark banana groves later the same day … where beautiful women appeared suddenly and made you happy for one or two months and as suddenly disappeared. He started reading the names of the drinks on the shelves behind the counter: Tusker, Pilsner, Muratina, Vat 69, Johnnie Walker, born 1820 and still walking in Kamiritho on a Sunday morning … somebody was playing a record from the juke-box … he turned his head … He saw the woman in a green dress wriggle her hips in slow motion and he could not believe his eyes…'Wanja! Wanja!' he called out. 'What are you doing here?'

3 ✿ Thank you for this beer … it is strange that you should find me here today, this morning, or rather that I should find you here. I was coming back to Ilmorog. Maybe you don't believe it. But it is true. I made up my mind this morning. Or I should say it was decided for me. Let me begin … where shall I begin? Before this … I used to work … it sounds so long ago. Doesn't it? I am talking about last night, but it feels like many years ago to me … anyway before this morning I used to work at the Heavenly Bar near Bolibo Golf Club. It was quite an exciting place. All the big shots from the Bolibo Golf Club visiting the place to eat roasted goat's meat and to buy five minutes of love. They came in Mercedes Benzes, Daimlers, Jaguars, Alfas, Toyotas, Peugeots, Volvos, Fords, Volkswagens, Range Rovers, Mazdas, Datsuns, Bentleys. It was like a parade ground for all the cars made in the world. Big shots from all the communities in Kenya. They would talk about their businesses. They talked about their schools. Many things. Anyway, it was a good place. But this was so before I left for Ilmorog that first time! I wish I had stayed in Ilmorog. After Ilmorog – that is, after I left you and Abdulla in Ilmorog – I went back to the same place. I found a change there. Big shots from the different communities sat together and talked only in their own mother tongues. Sometimes in English or Swahili. The different groups didn't mind us bar girls. So I could catch one or two things. Every group talked about the danger of other groups. They were eating too much. They are grabbing everything. Or they are lazy … they only drink mnazi beer … or wear

suits or eat birds ... or they have taken all the white highlands. Then about a month ago the groups from other communities suddenly stopped coming to the place. So the cars were fewer. Now the talk changed a little. We shall fight: we have fought before ... the other communities want to reap where they never planted ... No free things in Kenya. So we knew that something was happening. We started seeing these Kanu private lorries. The bar girls were the first to be rounded up. But I somehow escaped the net. I was ill or something on the night the girls were taken to tea. When they came back they were angry. Some were laughing mockingly. For to us what did it matter who drove a Mercedes Benz? They were all of one tribe: the Mercedes family: whether they came from the coast or from Kisumu. One family. We were another tribe: another family. Take my regular. He was a tall Somali. He was a long-distance driver. He worked with Kenatco and he knew so many places: Zambia, Sudan, Ethiopia, Malawi. He had so many stories about each place. Anyway I liked him. I liked the stories of all these places which he could make me see. He was really funny – never wore underwear – said they were too heavy for a daily traveller – but he was really generous. Well, he came yesterday and stopped his lorry at the place, as was his custom. I was off duty. So he hired a taxi and we drank from place to place. We really drank. I tried every mixture ... whisky, cider, Tusker, Babycham, vodka ... but somehow I was not getting drunk. It was not the way it used to be. My staying in Ilmorog had affected me, and last night I kept on thinking about it. Or it may have been the way people were looking at us. Or it could have been ... I am at times very depressed. But it was not that even. Anyway I was not happy. He wanted to hire a room at Mucatha. But I told him, no, let us go back to my place. He was surprised because I had never before taken him to my room. It was a rule of mine never to take a man to my place. That way when your friendship with a person was over, he would not be coming to your place to trouble you. So he hired another taxi – I tell you long-distance drivers have got money – and we drove back, in silence. It may have been the drink or the moving from place to place or the whole atmosphere but we were silent all the way to my place. If something is going to happen to you, do you feel anything in your stomach, or in your hair, or any other part of you? The window of my room was smoking. I rushed to the door. A small fire had been started there but it had not caught the door. I tried to cry, to shout, but no sound would come out and no tears either. I just banged at the door as if waking up somebody inside ... then I remembered I had the key in my handbag. I opened the door, tried to go in, but I was hit back by the heavy smell of wood-smoke. They must have used paraffin or petrol and whoever had done it had obviously wanted us both to be trapped in the room. I ran back to my friend, who had stood as if gummed to one spot. Take me to a police station ... He said wait, let me pass water ... I went back to the place. It was a stone building with only one room at the back. The others were about to be completed. So only the window and the door were burnt. I was still shaking. A few minutes later, I heard the huge lorry drive away, pressing hard on stone and tar ... My friend had run away: but how could I blame him? Anyway I went to another girl's place in another building. She told me that she had heard it said that I was arrogant: that I was going with a shifta, and that I had even refused to go to tea. But she had not taken it seriously, and anyway it was difficult to tell who had done it or ordered it done, and whoever it is I don't really want to find out ... It is better not to know ... This morning I found that the bedding and my clothes were burnt: some petrol must have been thrown into the room. But it has made me think. Since I left Ilmorog this is the second serious thing to happen to me. I now want to go ... I must go back to Ilmorog. So I took a bus to this place. I was now only playing some music to try and forget a little, before continuing my journey back to Ilmorog.

4 ✿ The coincidence must have really impressed Munira, must have struck him as having a God-ordained significance, because years later, in the statement, he was to dwell at length on this strange encounter on a Sunday after a night of mutual baptism by fire and terror.

I was without words with which to respond to her story (he wrote years later). A kiruru and chang'aa* drinker drifted in from the rooms at the back and staggered to where we sat, demanding Tusker from me. I mechanically gave him a five-shilling note. He bowed several times and showered saliva in his hands, calling on heaven to bless me and save me from evil. I was wishing he would go away. I looked at the Masai Moran spearing through the jumping, roaring lion; at the kangaroo on the opposite wall; at the mermaids rising from the sea – breasts above the water, fishtails under the water – and all these suddenly appeared more real, more rooted to the earth and the paltry day-to-day happenings than Wanja, sitting over there, speaking in a small, low, lifeless voice in the same level tone. My heart beat and my stomach contracted, disgust and attraction alternated. Then, remembering my own ordeal in a hut hidden in a thick banana-grove, recalling too the lorries I had just seen earlier written Kanu Private, I relented a little and I felt that maybe we

*Kiruru and chang'aa are potent home-brewed liquors.

were all enmeshed in a surreal world. I wanted to drown all memories, all thinking, all attempts to understand, everything, in a pool of beer. Let's go to another bar, I said. Let's drink, drink, we shall go to Ilmorog tomorrow. I left my bicycle at the petrol station near Safari Bar. All day we drank. I did not now care even if my father or my wife found me.

We went to Mary's Bar, Young Farmers', Mount Kenya, Muchoru-i, Highlands, Mathare, drinking a beer in each place, hardly talking. Wanja watched everything, scouring every corner and every face as if for something lost, for a secret remembered. She had withdrawn into herself as if she was inwardly evaluating every face, every happening in the light of her recent encounter. Most bars were full: it was what they called a fortnightly pay-day for workers from a nearby factory. The huge smoking complex of machines and hides and skins and polluted air had come to dominate our lives, bringing even remoter villages within its money-protective orbit. Here and there, and especially at Kambi Bar, people recognised me and probably wondered how the Mwalimu they had known for his restrained habits and aloofness, a son of a prominent churchman and landowner, could be drinking like that, so openly with such a companion. Later in the evening, I suggested we go to Limuru Town proper. We hired a matatu from outside the Young Farmers' Bar and drove round Kimunya's corner to Limuru. Again we visited most of the drinking places, lingering longer at the New Alaska Bar, Paradise, Modern, and Corner Bars. By the time we got into the Friendly Bar, Night-club and Restaurant, I was really tipsy and full of stories.

I started telling Wanja about Limuru, mixing fact with fiction, and I was surprised that I knew so much about the place, jumping from the Tigoni lands stolen by Europeans from the people of Limuru and later becoming the storm-centre of Kenya's history, to what later was called the massacre at Lari. The factory once again loomed large in my memory. There was once a strike, soon after the big war, and I always remembered the screaming workers as they were beaten to blood by plate-helmeted black policemen led by two gum-chewing white khakied officers. Black on Black, I now thought, remembering her recent ordeal and my own. I was drunk, I told myself, and ordered more Tuskers. I was feeling good, a little bit fascinated with myself and my stories and my bits of philosophical reflections. But Wanja was not really interested: what seemed to draw her out was people: young men gyrating their bodies in front of the juke-box; young men in tight American jeans and huge belts studded with shiny metal stars, leaning against the walls by the juke-box or at the counter by the high stools, chewing gum or breaking matchsticks between their teeth with the abandoned nonchalance of cowboys in the American Wild West I once saw in a film; young men and bar girls trying out the latest step. To hell with singers and dancers. To hell with Wanja and her stories. To hell with Abdulla, Nyakinyua, my family, everybody. We were all strangers . . . in our land of birth. No more prayers. No more praying over me. The music from the juke-box was oddly mixed with organ sounds in my mind carried from my days in Siriana. And my head was still protesting . . . No more singing over me, oooover meeeeeee, and before I become a slave – aaa slaaave – to hell with – with – the spinning tops in my head – Siriana – school – faces – the strike – expulsion – my father's contorted face: you have brought shame to your family: you have disrobed your own father in public: do you think you are cleverer than the white man? Do you want to join the mikora* who go on singing Ka – 40! Ka forty! and challenging the white man to a duel? – mother's tears – my shame – teaching – Manguo – Ilmorog – Wanja! The warmth I now felt for her turned into fire, fire-tongues of desire. I wanted to make love to her there: on the Friendly floor: I wanted to hear her little screams and cries for help. Power. I had not a care in the world. Noooot a care in the—

And suddenly from a filmy-dimmy region in my mind I saw her eyes fixed on an object vaguely familiar. I looked harder. I saw him. He was gesticulating with an empty bottle of Tusker in his hand. His drunken voice rose above the others. They were arguing about the merits and demerits of Kamaru and D.K. He was shouting: Kamaru sings about our past: he looks to our past, he wants to awaken us to the wisdom of our forefathers. What good is that to the chaos that is today? Another was arguing: his is the tinkling of a broken cymbal. But D.K. sings true – about us – the young – here and now – a generation lost in urban chaos. Another interrupted: we are not a lost generation. Do you understand? Don't you go about abusing folk in a bar doing their thing. Geee – I gonna dance to Jim Reeves and Jim Brown and break a safe or two like some cowboys I saw in the Wild Bunch – Geee. Another came in, joined in the argument, putting as much venom and contempt in his voice as he could: look at our scholar, he could not manage to pass his exams, he was booted out, and here he comes to lecture us on things of a dead past.

Violence sickens me: I feel that now, I felt so then. But Wanja, who until then had been quiet, rapt in thought, could hardly sit still in her chair. I felt rather than saw her excitement. What I could not believe was the evidence of my eyes.

'Karega! Karega!' she called out. His raised bottle was arrested in the air. He turned his head away from the juke-box and his adversary.

*thugs

101

He stared in our direction: then he came to our table, trying with some difficulty to walk straight. He slumped into a chair opposite Wanja. 'Thank you,' he said to nobody in particular, 'I could have smashed his head, see? Like that, and for what gain?' He planted his elbows on the table and buried his head in his hands. Once he raised it and ejected a stream of saliva onto the cement floor. Then he resumed his sunken position.

Someone had put a shilling in the slot machine and music once more blared out. The singer's voice wafted sadness and regret into the whole room, advising, admonishing, gradually possessing the whole bar with the power of the voice. I listened, trying hard to make out the words.

Watumaniirwo, Nyukwa ni murwaru
> *You received a message that mother was ill*

Ui ugacokia, Kuu ndikinyaga
> *You said, I never go home*

Nanii ngakwira ugwati nduri Njamba
> *I am telling you, danger knows not the brave*

Ningi ngakwira, Mutino ni Muhiu
> *I again tell you, an accident knows not the quick of hand*

Ninguigua Uru-i, ukiruma aciari aku
> *I feel bad when you abuse your parents*

Ndaririkana ati ni makurerire
> *When I remember how they brought you up*

Wakuagwo na Ngoi ugithaithagwo
> *They carried you on their backs*

Ui ukiragwo, Mwana kira!
> *Pleading with you, our little one do not cry!*

I happened at that point to look at Wanja. Her face was pained. Seeing my eyes on her, she tried, not too successfully, to smile away the grotesque expression on her face. She said:

'Do you remember the night I told you how I went away from home?'

'Yes.'

'I told you that mother sent me to throw manure in the shamba?'

'Yes.'

'Well. There is something else I did not tell you. The reason she begged me to help her was because she was ill in bed. Later she was in fact taken to the hospital and her appendix was removed. She almost died. I learnt this while dancing in a bar, and do you know, I laughed? I laughed!'

The others had resumed their hip-gyrations, all facing the juke-box, almost as if they were fornicating with a woman hidden in the music box. What was in the words that could move the young so? For me there were no tender memories of my father and mother, only fear, a vague fear I had never quite learnt how to overcome. Karega snored through the song. Wanja watched him closely with that look I had once seen her bestow on Abdulla, as if they shared a common pain and common betrayal of hopes. My stomach tightened a little. I had that uncomfortable feeling of an intruder into a private act. I said to Wanja rather curtly: we can't leave him here. I staggered out and got a taxi. We dragged him into it and he immediately slept. Wanja was quiet. The tension in my stomach remained. Kamiritho, where earlier I had reserved a room for two, was only a mile and a half from Limuru Town. But I felt as if we had driven a whole night. I paid the driver his three shillings. I tried to get an extra room for Karega. But by now all the rooms had been taken. I had no alternative but to share what I had already secured until he woke up from his drunken stupor. Wanja and I supported him up the stairs to our room and sat him on one of the beds. Again, he immediately slumped into it and slept. I sat on the edge of the bed, reviewing vaguely my mission and the events of the last three days since I left Ilmorog. How had I become involved in all this? I was happy in my previous slumbering state. Wanja sat on the other bed and made no effort to get into it. I would walk over and join her, I thought, desire rising. I pulled a blanket over Karega and covered him, head, feet and all, and I was about to walk over to where Wanja was sitting when he suddenly woke and sat up and anxiously looked around him without taking in anything. I sat down on the only chair in the room. By now I had sobered up, or rather the crisis had sobered me a little. I was also a little sad and guilty. For how could I forget that this drunken wreck had only eighteen months or so back – though it felt like ages past – been at my hideout in Ilmorog and I had let him go? How, now, how could the young, the bright and the hopeful deteriorate so? Was there no way of using their energies and dreams to a purpose higher than the bottle, the juke-box and sickness on a cement floor?

'Where am I? Where am I?' he was asking.

'It is all right. It is only me – or don't you recognize me?'

'Aaah, so it is Mwalimu? I feel bad . . . this is – this is a real shame!'

'What happened, Karega?' I asked him. He looked about him, bewildered, without taking in much. Then he bent his head and he talked, staring at the floor most of the time.

'I do not understand it, the whole thing. The beginning so clear

... or was it an illusion? And the end so hazy that the beginning and the idea behind the beginning were buried in a mist of bitterness, the recrimination and cruel, blind vengeance. Massacres of hopes and dreams and beauty. The bright beginning ... the bitter end. For a time I was determined to make it. I had after all a good school certificate. I said: Chui and the school can eject me ... but the country: there is room for all of us at the meeting point of a victorious struggle. Fruits of Uhuru. You do my bit ... I do my bit ... we move a mountain ... why not? There was the big city. I walked from office to office and everywhere, it was the same. No Vacancy. Hakuna Kazi. Occasionally they would ask you: who sent you? My face became familiar to the door-keepers who sympathised and asked: don't you know anyone big? A big brother, somebody ... Mkono mtupu haulambwi, eh? Hakuna Kazi ... no vacancy ... and in one place ... For Vacancy Come Tomorrow ... how inventive! At times I thought of going back to Siriana, intending to burn Chui's place or something. For I would say to myself: why should he be sleeping comfortably when it was he who was in the wrong? Why should I suffer for mistakes made by another? Do you know what I did in the end? I started selling sheepskins, fruits, mushrooms, by the roadside. You should see us, the roadboys as they call us. We scramble for any car that might stop: buy mine, it is better, shines more, and mine, mine, mine. Sometimes they throw coins in the air to see us dive and scratch one another for them. They laugh. Mark you, you got to be smart, quick, and pretend not to see, or hear insults. Tourists ... watalii ... we love them. We pray for them to come by with their sliver coins and notes and curse them afterward. Please take this ... good ... am hungry, mister ... school fees, mister ... And they laugh to see us plead misery and plead for charity, harambee.

'It has been a difficult life,' he continued, staring at the floor. 'It has been hard, Mwalimu ... I have let my mother down. Utterly. Can you not see my mother? Old Mariamu they called her. You probably remember her. She was a squatter on your father's land, the oldest squatter. A devout woman. She has scratched and scratched the earth for her son's education and she is saying to herself, maybe muttering it in her prayers, all is well, all is well, for in my old age he will prop me up: for where is the house with a he-child where the head of a he-goat shall not be eaten? She was always the earliest traveller to tea and coffee plantations, to pull out thangari grass. And she is saying – in my old age is my joy. She once said to me: "It's good you want to go to school, Karega, look at the children of Koinange, look at the children of Elder Ezekieli Waweru, they all got education." And so I went to school, her voice and another with

me. Manguo, Kamandura, Siriana – glory? And now look at her son
... fighting ... extracting every ounce of juice from the juke-box. I
tell you, I have been unable to face her. She never would lash at me
with harsh words. She simply told me: "You have never disobeyed
me. How could you rise against your teachers?"

'I would picture her in my mind even as I sold sheepskin and pleaded for charity from watalii.* But after a while, I was tired of charity.

'Charity ... charity ... we are a nation that believes in charity ...
and I was fed up with charity. Why should I be the object of anybody's charity? Why should I continue an object of charity from
foreigners in my own land? Then I remembered you. You had gone
through a similar experience. So I came to Ilmorog to seek advice. I
thought ... I thought I was being childish, that you would only
laugh at me ... excuse me ... but that was what I thought you were
doing ... pleading ignorance and mock surprise in a matter that was
life and death to me. I asked myself: why should he treat me like a
child? Then there was the pale light in the woman's room. I was
alone. I just walked out into the night. Then the moon came out ...
a cold moon ... but it lit my way. I came back to my sheepskins and
fruits and watalii. I said one day: I will drink ... like other people ...
Do you despise me, Mwalimu? Do you? Ha ha ha. Wouldn't you
like to buy one of my sheepskins? Nice, shiny, fleecy rugs? Or some
oranges and pears? Oranges cheap today ... You pay me in advance
... I am a man of my word. Truth of God. Then maybe I can buy
you a drink ... to ... to thank you ... you see I try to sell sheepskins
and oranges wherever I am. God bless watalii. They help keep our
bones and skins together.'

What a day! What a night! Waweru's son: Mariamu's son:
Nyakinyua's granddaughter, now in the same hole! It was now the
hour of dawn! He had started quietly, soberly, his head lowered, but
at the end he was shouting at an invisible presence. He raised his
head and looked at me with a bitter sarcastic smile on the edges of
dry lips. He then turned away and the smile suddenly froze on his
half-open lips. He must have caught her big eyes resting on him; he
seemed to be aware of her for the first time. 'You ... you ...' he
whispered as if he was looking at a ghost of a familiar face from the
past. They looked at one another in silence.

The constriction in my stomach tightened, for in that instant, in
that minute, I knew that – but what? A strange thing. A burning
pool in my stomach. Fire-tongues of stinging nettles. Spilt bile.
Water. I was alone. A spectator.

'Come to Ilmorog,' she said with submissive authority.

'Yes!' Karega answered, hypnotised.

*tourists

105

Chapter Six

1 ❧ They returned to Ilmorog, this time driven neither by idealism nor the search for a personal cure but by an overriding necessity
to escape. They used Munira's bicycle. Sometimes all three would
walk, one person pushing the bicycle. Sometimes all three would ride
the bicycle with Munira on the saddle, Karega on the frame and
Wanja on the carrier. But mostly they rode in a kind of relay.
Karega would walk. Munira would take Wanja for a mile or so and
leave her to walk on. He would come back for Karega and take him a
mile or so past Wanja. Then Munira would walk. Karega would take
the bicycle and go back for Wanja. Soon they all looked like the
earth on which they trod, enveloped by an enormous sky of white
and blue.

As he walked, Munira was struck over and over by the oddity of
the present situation. He felt as if he had been away for three years
instead of only three days. So many things he did not understand:
his father's action and attitudes ... the mystery of Mukami's death
... his father's cryptic reference to Mariamu ... what was the connection? And here he was with Mariamu's son – the teacher he had
recruited from a bar – and Wanja, all going to seek a home in Ilmorog. It is the way of the world, he decided, and looked forward to
his new arrival in Ilmorog. He was convinced of some sort of hero's
welcome: eager questioning and grateful faces from at least Abdulla
and Nyakinyua.

But he remembered the two men in a Landrover and their suggestive hints and menacing faces and their talk of 12/50 and KCO and
all that. He suddenly saw the connection between the two men's
visit, the ordeal he had undergone, and the gigantic deception being
played on a whole people by a few who had made it, often in alliance
with foreigners. He was once again stabbed by a different kind of
guilt: he had himself actively participated in an oath of national betrayal. He had not shown the courage shown by Ilmorog women, or
by the worker who protested, or by all those men and women in the
country who were openly criticising the whole thing at the risk of
their lives. Then he thought: but what could he have done? And
thus he stilled the inner doubt that would have awakened him to
life. He turned to Wanja. He thought of telling her about his own
experience, then stopped.

Wanja had made a pact with herself. She would have a completely new beginning in Ilmorog. Since she left Ilmorog she had had two humiliating and shameful experiences. She would now break with that past and make something of herself in Ilmorog. As an evidence of her cleansed spirit, she resolved that she would not again obey the power of her body over men; that any involvement was out until she had defeated the past through a new flowering of self.

Karega was not sure what he really expected of the place and the people. He had responded to Wanja's call as if he were accepting his destiny. Yes, a covenant with fate, he thought, for the future seemed a yawning blank without a break or an opening, like the sky above them. But what was it that stirred, rippled dormant pools of blood at the sight of Wanja? Why this sudden pain at a presence that was really only a memory? Fate, he again decided, remembering Mukami, and he was seized with sadness and vague bitterness. But he was grateful to Munira that he had said he would hire him as a teacher. From a seller of sheepskins in Limuru to a teacher of children in Ilmorog: that anyway was a beginning.

Munira also explained to him why Ilmorog school was without teachers. During the colonial days African teachers could only teach in African schools. All the African schools were of much the same standard: poorly equipped, poor houses, and limited aids. But at least they got the best of the African teachers available.

But after internal self-government, the colour bar in schools admissions and the allocation of teachers was removed. The result was that while the former African schools remained equally poorly equipped, they now also lost the best of the African teachers. These were attracted to the former Asian and European schools which remained as high-cost schools with better houses, equipment, teaching aids. Some schools in remote places like Ilmorog were almost completely abandoned to their own rural fate.

Karega felt good: his teaching career would have added significance. Cambridge Fraudsham used to tell them that teaching was a calling, a vocation, and hence satisfying to the soul. Karega swore to give everything he had to the children in Ilmorog.

But the Ilmorog they now came to was one of sun, dust, and sand. Wanja and Karega were especially struck by the change in the face of Ilmorog countryside.

'So green in the past,' she said. 'So green and hopeful ... and now this.'

'A season of drought ... so soon ... so soon!' echoed Karega, remembering past flowers of promise.

'It is the way of the world,' said Munira as they stood by the bicycle, skins glazed dry, coughing and sneezing out dust from cracked throats and noses, watching specks of dry maize-stalk whirled to the sky.

They found Nyakinyua and Abdulla and Joseph standing outside the shop.

They evinced no surprise or curiosity at seeing them and Munira felt a slight deflation of the spirits. Not even a question!

'We were discussing Abdulla's donkey,' Nyakinyua explained by way of welcome.

'What has happened to it?' Wanja asked quickly, noticing the heaviness on Abdulla's face. Was this the place where she was hoping to make a new mark?

'The elders want it killed,' she continued. 'Some think they should beat it and then let it loose in the plains to carry this plague away.'

'A donkey? I thought that only a goat was used in the ritual?' Karega said.

'Who is this one?' Nyakinyua asked.

'He is Karega,' Wanja explained. 'He comes from Abdulla's place, Limuru, and he will help in the school.'

'Our new teacher,' added Munira.

'In this drought? God bless you,' she said.

They all sat down outside Abdulla's shop and Munira asked for a beer to wash down the dust in his throat.

'That donkey is my other leg,' Abdulla moaned. 'They want me to cut it off and throw it away. A second sacrifice.'

'But a donkey has no influence on the weather,' Karega commented, and he too asked for a drink.

'Joseph, bring another beer for your new teacher,' said Abdulla. 'I thought you didn't drink.'

'Things have changed,' Karega said thoughtfully, remembering their last encounter in Wanja's hut six months back. 'I should say times have changed,' he added.

'It is the drought . . .' Nyakinyua was explaining. 'Grass is scarce, only a few stems will soon be left. The question is this: to whom shall we give it, donkeys or goats?'

'The one carried on his mother's stomach: and the other carried on his mother's back: how can we choose between them? Aren't they all our children?' Abdulla countered.

What a homecoming! A second homecoming to an argument about droughts, Munira was thinking, and no questions about the drama they left behind.

'The drought will pass away. This is only March,' Munira said. 'We might drive away the rains by this talk.'

'Yes. It will rain in March and grass will grow,' echoed Wanja, hopefully, eagerly: it had to rain otherwise they were ruined; the whole community would be ruined. 'Abdulla,' she called out, 'aren't you glad to see your barmaid return?'

They laughed. They became a little relaxed.

'Go wash off the dust first. Else you'll drive away my customers. They will take you for a daughter of the drought.'

2   Karega worked as a UT – an untrained teacher – in Ilmorog Primary School under its new headmaster, Godfrey Munira. Munira had taken him to the HQ and Mzigo, after his usual inquiries and promises to visit the area, had agreed to hire him 'on the strength of Mr Munira's recommendation and assurance about your character and good behaviour. Mr Munira has set very high standards and I would like you to follow his example of selfless dedication to a noble profession.'

The school was now divided into four sections, Standards I to IV: two classes meeting in the morning and the other two in the afternoon. For Standard IV, which contained bigger and brighter boys who had been taught off and on by teachers who never stayed for long, Karega arranged extra classes after five to make up for lost time.

Standing in a classroom in front of those children released something in Karega. It was like continuing with the dialogue he had started with himself at Siriana and which had been interrupted by his expulsion and one year's slavery to watalii. He was concerned that the children knew no world outside Ilmorog: they thought of Kenya as a city or a large village somewhere outside Ilmorog. How could he enlarge their consciousness so that they could see themselves, Ilmorog and Kenya as part of a larger whole, a larger territory containing the history of African people and their struggles? In his mind he scanned the whole landscape where African people once trod to leave marks and monuments that were the marvel of ages, that not even the fatal encounter of black sweat and white imperialism could rub from the memory and recorded deeds of men. Egypt, Ethiopia, Monomotapata, Zimbabwe, Timbuctoo, Haiti, Malindi, Ghana, Mali, Songhai: the names were sweet to the ear and the children listened with eager enthusiastic wonder that was the measure of their deep-seated unbelief. He made them sing: I live in Ilmorog Division which is in Chiri District; Chiri which is in the Republic of Kenya; Kenya which is part of East Africa; East Africa which is part of Africa; Africa which is the land of African peoples; Africa from where other African people were scattered to other corners of the world. They sang it, but it seemed too abstract. And it was this struggle to believe him that he found so disquietening, that made him realise that there were questions they posed by their very struggle and enthusiasm, for it had to do with the doubt that was in him too, that had haunted him even in Siriana. The African experience was not always clear to him and he saw the inadequacy of the Siriana education now that he was face to face with his own kind, little children, who wanted to know. His one year as a seller of sheepskins and fruit to watalii seemed, in retrospect, less demanding, less frustrating than the present ordeal. For to confront Ilmorog, this poverty – and drought-stricken, depopulated wasteland; to confront the expectant eyes of those who tomorrow would run away to the cities whose cruelty he had experienced and where they would face a future which held the hope of a thousand mirages, was at once to confront himself in a way more profound and painful because the problem and the questions raised went beyond mere personal safety and salvation. It seemed to him, looking at the drought, at the tiny faces, at the lack of any development in the area – where, he wondered, were the benefits of modern science? – a collective fate to which they were all condemned.

It was hopeless: it was a gigantic deception. He and Munira were two ostriches burying their heads in the sand of a classroom, ignoring the howling winds and the sun outside. Was this not the same crime of which they had accused Chui in Siriana? How could they as teachers, albeit in a primary school, ignore the reality of the drought, the listless faces before them? What had education, history and geography and nature-study and maths, got to say to this drought?

He came out of the classroom late one day at the end of March and found a group at Abdulla's shop.

'Ruoro's goat died last night,' Nyakinyua explained. 'And he cried. We looked at one another because a grown man's tears can only portend ill. But we knew he could not help it, and we sat with him as at a wake.'

3 ✿ By the end of April it still had not rained. Cows and goats and sheep were skeletons: most herdsmen had anyway moved across the plains in search of fairer and kindlier climes wherein to shelter. They hoped that May would bring rain. But by mid-May which was the last hope for rains which would save them, two cows died; vultures and hawks circled high in the sky and then swooped in hordes, later leaving behind them white bones scattered on stunted and dry elephant grass.

Wanja waited for Karega and Munira outside the school.

'It has been decided. The elders went to see Mwathi wa Mugo: he said that the donkey must be taken across the plains although a sacrifice of a goat will still be necessary. We must help Abdulla. The donkey's death will also be his death.'

'Did they say when?' Munira asked.

'They will be meeting soon to decide on the day.'

'Did he say how they would take it across the plains?'

'No ... But there is talk of the whole village scourging it ... men, women, and children taking part.'

'But what can we do?' asked Munira and nobody answered the question.

4 🏵 Haunting memories from the past; the year of the locust; the year of the armyworms; the year of the famine of cassava: the Ngigi, Ngunga and Ngaragu ya Mwanga circumcision-groups still bore these names of woe, a witness that uncontrolled nature was always a threat to human endeavour. There was of course another lesson. In 1900, only six years after the year of locusts, the famine was so bad it put to a stop all circumcision rites for the year. No group now carried a name as memorial to the famine of England, so called, because it had weakened people's resistance to the European marauders of the people's land and sweat. The famine of cassava itself was a bitter funeral dirge for their sons lost in North Africa, the Middle East, Burma and India fighting against the Germans and the Japanese, thus prompting the young to sing:

> When I came from Japan
> Little did I know
> I would give birth
> To a stillborn child
> Flour of cassava.

Thus history and legend showed that Ilmorog had always been threatened by the twin cruelties of unprepared-for vagaries of nature and the uncontrolled actions of men.

These thoughts mocked at Karega as he was carried along by the grandeur of the people's past, the great cultures that spread from Malindi to Tripoli. He confided: The Earliest Man, father of all men on earth, is thought to have been born in Kenya... Lake Turkana... and he stood back and expected a gasp of disbelief or a few questions.

'Yes, Muriuki,' he pointed to a child whose hand seemed raised.

There was a great rustling of books, noise from the benches, children clambering from their desks. Muriuki had fallen down.

'Move away, move away,' Karega urged the children, pushing them aside. He felt the prostrate form of Muriuki. 'He is just hungry,' one boy said. 'I know, he told me he was hungry.' Karega got the hint: he took him to the house where he concocted something – a mixture of an egg and milk from a tin.

Just now, Karega thought, people in the city and other places were drinking and laughing and eating and making love out of excess of fullness, and here people were fainting with hunger and malnutrition.

He talked to Munira. Munira asked the same question:

'What can I do? It is not my fault. It is not anybody's fault. We can only close the school until better times.'

'Accepting. Even defeat?'

'It can't be helped. An act of God.'

'An act of God? Why should people accept any act of any God without resistance? God, it is said, helps those who help themselves.'

'How?'

'We can go to the city!' he said, as if he had already thought about it. But in fact it had just come into his mouth.

'The city?'

'Yes, and seek help.'

'No, Karega. I left those places. I don't really want to go back,' he said suddenly remembering the terror.

'Why?' Karega asked, astonished by Munira's prompt refusal.

'You talk as if you didn't go to tea.'

'Did you?' Karega asked.

'Yes. I was so ashamed. I was cheated into it and I cheated my wife into it, and now she can't believe that I didn't know,' he answered quietly ... 'But even if I had not been led into it, I wonder if I would have had the mettle and the stamina to refuse, and this frightens me even more.'

Karega thought for a little while. His voice was a little hard:

'I did not. But it is not that I would have been ashamed of it. As I sold sheepskins to watalii I asked myself, how could a whole community be taken in by a few greedy stomachs – greedy because they had eaten more than their fair share of that which was bought by the blood of the people? And they took a symbol from its original beautiful purpose ... and they think they can make it serve narrow selfish ends! Make poverty and stolen wealth shake hands in eternal peace and Friendship! And what do we do with people who are hungry and jobless, who can't pay school fees; shall we make them drink a tinful of oath and cry unity? How easy ... why, there should then be no problems in Ilmorog, and in all the other forgotten areas and places in Kenya.'

'I can see your point,' Munira said. 'You had better talk it over with Wanja and Abdulla. Why,' he added suddenly, enthusiastically, 'we can go and tell Nderi wa Riera that we are all members of KCO.'

The fact was that Karega's heated ridiculing of the whole thing had made Munira feel better and more calm inside. It had given form in words to thoughts in Munira's mind.

The more Karega thought about the idea which took form in the course of his talk with Munira, the more it seemed the right thing to do. He felt restless, eager to effect the plan. It was this very restlessness which had always driven him on, often bringing him into trouble, but he could not help the inner voices of discontent. He would have to face the drought as a challenge and also as a test. But whatever the decision, he would not be able to teach under these conditions where theory seemed a mockery of the reality.

He broached the plan to Munira, Wanja and Abdulla.

'It seems to me that we all have our reasons for coming to Ilmorog. But now we are here. There is a crisis facing the community. What shall we do about it? The elders are acting in the light of their knowledge. They believe that you can influence nature by sacrifice and loading all our sins on Abdulla's donkey. Why – I even heard Njuguna say that the sacrifice will also bribe God to shut his eyes to the Americans' attempts to walk in God's secret places. I believe we can save the donkey and save the community.'

Anything which would save his donkey was welcome to Abdulla. So he asked eagerly: how?

'This place has an MP. We, or rather they, elected him to Parliament to represent all the corners of his constituency, however remote. Let us send a strong delegation of men, women, and children to the big city. To the capital. We shall see the MP for this area. The government is bound to send us help. Or we can bring back help to the others. Otherwise the drought might swallow us all.'

'And the donkey?' asked Abdulla.

'We shall take him with us. We shall repair the cart. We shall bring back food and things in it.'

Wanja was stabbed with pain: Go back to the city, the scene of her other humiliation? She fought against the faintness at the remembrance of her double terror.

'Can't we send one person? You, for instance? You can go on Munira's bicycle,' she suggested wildly.

'Me? He would not listen to one person. He would think it a trick or something. But I am sure he can't ignore a people's delegation.'

Abdulla readily agreed with the idea. Wanja was thinking: that time last year I went to the city to seek sudden wealth for my own

113

self. Now I am going for the people. Maybe the city will now receive us more kindly.

Munira could not see what an MP would do for them. He was thinking: I seem unable to settle: I keep on moving, driven by other people's promptings: can I never will my own actions and decisions? But since Wanja and Abdulla had agreed, he also accepted. At the same time he saw a chance to finally still the occasional voices of guilt since his midnight tea at Gatundu. It would also be good to test if there was anything to this KCO and its call for unity and harmony of interests.

The next problem was the elders. They had called a meeting for the following day to announce the verdict on Abdulla's donkey and also announce the day for the sacrifice of a goat. Wanja would that night talk to Nyakinyua, who in turn would discuss it with a few more elders before the crucial meeting.

The meeting was well attended: Njuguna told the people what Mwathi wa Mugo had said:

'We send this donkey away. We sacrifice a goat. Nobody has the mouth to throw words back at Mwathi. You know he is the stick and the shade that God uses to defend our land. You know that since that fight for Ilmorog a long time ago we have not had many plagues in our midst. Nobody can throw words back at him. So we did not ask him how! He did not tell us how. He knows we are not children. If it was a goat we would beat it and then send it away and ask it to pass the plague to others. This animal is not a goat. But we are using it for the same illness: I say we shall beat it and when it is about to die we shall send it away into the plains to carry this plague away.' A few other elders spoke and agreed with the idea: a donkey was truly the stranger in their midst!

'But perhaps the teachers of our children might have a modern cure for an old illness,' another suggested.

Karega trembled a little. In school debates he had talked and argued. But he had never before talked to a gathering of elders. He could not now think of an appropriate proverb, riddle or story with which to drive home his points. So he made a plain speech.

'A donkey has no influence on the weather. No animal or man can change a law of nature. But people can use the laws of nature. The magic we should be getting is this: the one which will make this land so yield in times of rain that we can keep aside a few grains for when it shines. We want the magic that will make our cows yield so much milk that we shall have enough to drink and exchange the rest for things we cannot grow here. That magic is in our hands. Tomorrow when it rains: we should be asking the soil: what food, what offering does it need so that it will yield more? If we kill Abdulla's donkey we shall all be cutting our other leg in a season of drought. I come from Limuru where donkeys have proved to be motorcars that don't drink petrol. When the last grain in your stores is finished, will any of us be able to walk afar and fetch food and water on our backs? Let us rather look to ourselves to see what we can do to save us from the drought. The labour of our hands in the magic and the wealth that will change our world and end all droughts from our earth.'

He told them the idea of a delegation, singing a bit too glowingly the virtues and duties of an MP. 'We give him our votes so that he can carry our troubles. But if we do not show him that we have troubles so he can pass them to the government, can we blame him?'

They started talking and whispering among themselves ... Yes, that was right ... We should let those in authority know. Maybe if they knew ... Yes, yes, maybe if they knew of our plight they would not be sending men to only collect taxes and others to demand money for organisations the villages knew nothing about ... This your teacher ... Hardly been here two months ... Where did he get such words?

Njuguna stood up and opposed the idea of going to the city.

'My ears have heard strange words. That we should send a whole community to beg. Have you ever heard of a whole people abandoning their land and property to go and beg on strange highways? The young man has youthful blood: we shall send him to the city and he will tell the MP to come to us. Yes, it is the MP who should come to us instead of his sending us envoys and children as his spokesmen,' he added, glancing at Karega.

Njuguna's idea seemed simple, direct and it upheld the dignity of Ilmorog. There was renewed argument. Nyakinyua stood up:

'I think we should go. It is our turn to make things happen. There was a time when things happened the way we in Ilmorog wanted them to happen. We had power over the movement of our limbs. We made up our own words and sang them and we danced to them. But there came a time when this power was taken from us. We danced yes, but somebody else called out the words and the song. First the Wazungu. They would send trains here from out there. They ate our forests. What did they give us in return? Then they sent for our young men. They went on swallowing our youth. Ours is only to bear in order for the city to take. In the war against Wazungu we gave our share of blood. A sacrifice. Why? Because we wanted to be able to sing our song, and dance our words in fullness of head and stomach. But what happened? They have continued to entice our youth away. What do they send us in return? Except for these two teachers here, the others would come and go. Then they send us messengers who demand twelve shillings and fifty cents for what? They send others with strange objects and they tell us that they are measuring a big road. Where is the road? They send us others who come every now and then to take taxes: others to buy our produce except when there is drought and famine. The MP also came once and made us give two shillings each for Harambee water. Have we seen him since? Aca! That is why Ilmorog must now go there and see this Ndamathia that only takes but never gives back. We must surround the city and demand back our share. We must sing our tune and dance to it. Those out there can also, for a change, dance to the actions and words of us that sweat, of us that feel the pain of bearing ... But Ilmorog must go as one voice.'

She sat down to a thought-charged silence. They were all affected by her words. She had touched something which they all had felt: yes, it was *they* outside *there* who ought to dance to the needs of the people. But now it seemed that authority, power, everything, was outside Ilmorog ... out there ... in the big city. They must go and confront that which had been the cause of their empty granaries, that which had sapped their energies, and caused their weakness. After her, there was not much argument. They all talked of going to the city. Long ago when their cattle and goats were taken by hostile nations, the warriors went out, followed them, and would not return until they had recovered their stolen wealth. Now Ilmorog's own heart had been stolen. They would follow to recover it. It was a new kind of war ... but war all the same.

Muturi stood up and summed up the whole thing. He suggested that indeed this could be what Mwathi had meant: he had said we should send the donkey away: but he did not say where, or how: and he did not say that the donkey could not come back ...

It was then agreed that some elders would remain to sacrifice a goat. Others would form the delegation. Abdulla was the first to volunteer. Next stood up Nyakinyua, followed by Munira, Muriuki, Joseph, Njuguna, Ruoro, Njogu and others. Muturi and others would remain to do the other rites.

From that moment, they forged a community spirit, fragile at first, but becoming stronger as they strove and made preparations for the journey. Women cooked food for the journey, some draining their last grains. Others gave any money they might have saved. Munira, Karega and Ruoro worked on the donkey-cart to make it ready for the great trek of the village to the city.

Abdulla especially seemed to have gained new strength and new life. His transformation from a sour-faced cripple with endless curses at Joseph to somebody who laughed and told stories, a process which had started with his first contact with Wanja, was now complete. People seemed to accept him to their hearts. This could be seen in the children. They surrounded him and he told them stories:

'Once upon a time Ant and Louse had an argument. Each boasted that he could beat the other in dancing Kibata. They threw challenges at one another. They decided to name a day. The coming contest of dancing feet became the talk of the whole animal community and none was going to miss the occasion. Came the day and early in the morning Ant and Louse went to the river. They bathed and oiled themselves. They started decorating themselves with red and white ochre. Ant was the first to dress, and he wanted to kill all the ladies' hearts. He had a special sword which he now tied to his waist. He tied, and tied, and tied it so tight that his waist broke into two. When Louse saw the plight of his rival, he laughed and laughed and laughed until his nose split into two. And so because Ant had no waist and Louse had no nose, they never went to the arena and Kibata was enjoyed by others.'

He told them how Chameleon defeated Hare in a race; why Hyena limped; how Death came to the world; of the woman who was lured into marrying a wicked ogre – and the children were insatiable in their cries for more.

He also made them small gadgets like spinning tops and paper windmills and fans. But what they loved most was the catapults he made for them out of Y-twigged sticks and rubber straps. The boys were excited and they tried to bring down birds from the sky, but without much success.

'You'll take them with you on the journey,' he told them, 'and try them out there.'

They looked forward to adventures on the journey: but more so to their visit to the city that was a hundred times bigger than Ruwa-ini – a city whose buildings touched the sky and where people ate nothing but sweets and cakes.

Throughout the preparations people, especially the elderly ones talked of nothing but the Journey and this young man who had suggested it. God sometimes puts wisdom in the mouth of babes. Of a truth, wisdom could not be bought.

And then suddenly the day of the trek came: it was the first time that they had dared such a thing and they were all struck by the enormity of their undertaking!

❁

It was the journey, Munira was later to write, it was the exodus across the plains to the Big Big City that started me on that slow, almost ten-year, inward journey to a position where I can now see that man's estate is rotten at heart.

Even now, so many years after the event, he wrote, I can once again feel the dryness of the skin, the blazing sun, the dying animals that provided us with meat, and above us, soaring in the clear sky, the hawks and vultures which, satiated with meat of dead antelopes, wart-hogs and elands, waited for time and sun to deliver them human skins and blood.

The journey. The exodus toward the kingdom of knowledge . . .

Part Two: Toward Bethlehem

But most thro' midnight streets I hear
How the youthful Harlot's curse
Blasts the new born Infant's tear
And blights with plagues the Marriage hearse.
— William Blake

Pity would be no more
If we did not make somebody Poor.
— William Blake

The Journey

1 ❀ Ilmorog, the scene of the unfolding of this drama, had not always been a small cluster of mud huts lived in only by old men and women and children with occasional visits from wandering herdsmen. It had had its days of glory: thriving villages with a huge population of sturdy peasants who had tamed nature's forests and, breaking the soil between their fingers, had brought forth every type of crop to nourish the sons and daughters of men. How they toiled together, clearing the wilderness, cultivating, planting: how they all fervently prayed for rain and deliverance in times of drought and pestilence! And at harvest-time they would gather in groups, according to ages, and dance from village to village, spilling into Ilmorog plains, hymning praises to their founders. In those days, there were no vultures in the sky waiting for the carcasses of dead workers, and no insect-flies feeding on the fat and blood of unsuspecting toilers. Only, so they say in song and dance, only the feeble in age and the younglings were exempt from the common labour: these anyway were carriers of wisdom and innocence. Sitting round the family tree in the front yard the aged would sip honey beer and tell the children, with voices taut with prideful authority and nostalgia, about the founding patriarch.

He was a herdsman who, tired of wandering and roaming all over the plains, merely adapting to nature and its changing fortunes, tired too of whistling songs of praise only to the cow with the long horns and the one rich with milk, had broken with the others. At first they pleaded with him: whoever heard of life away from the udder, dung and urine of cows on the long trail across plains and mountains, life away from the bull with bells around its neck leading the others to the salt-lick and the waters? They also pleaded: was he not their best magician in words, making the steps of cattle and men rise and fall with the cadence of his voice? They failed. So they turned to laughing at him and mocking his talk of taming the high ground and the forest that was really the seat of evil genii; how dare the son of man wrestle with gods?

Ndemi: he fashioned a tool with which he cut some of the trees and cleared the undergrowth. The beasts of the earth with their forked tongues spat out poison at him, but he was also learned in the ways of herbs and medicines made from the roots and bark of trees. The fame of his experiments with different types of plants spread and no herdsman would pass Ilmorog without calling on him, at first to see the outcome of man's wrestling with God, later for advice on this or that herb, or simply for a taste of domestic honey and sugar-cane. They would give him a goat or two, in gratitude, and trek further to spread Ndemi's name to the four corners of the wind. He had made the earth yield to the touch of his fingers and the wisdom of his head, and he now had more wealth in cows and goats on top of his numerous crops!

In no time, his lone courage had attracted Nyangendo of the famous gap in her upper teeth and Nyaguthii of the black gums and breasts that were the talk of herdsmen wherever they met. Your gods of the forest will now be our gods and we shall be the mothers of your children. Other women, tired of the unsettled life, pitched their shelters of poles, ferns, mud and grass so that they could suckle the young in peace and await the return of their men and cattle following the sun. Ilmorog forest became a series of cultivated fields and a breed of tamed cows and goats. They sang of Ndemi:

He who tamed the forest,
He who tamed the evil genii,
He who wrestled with God.

Ilmorog continued to prosper even after Ndemi, father of many sons and daughters and grandchildren, had departed to the secret land of the kindly spirits. It became a great centre of trade: its market days were known from Gulu to Ukambani, to the land of the Kalenjin people and even beyond. People came from all over with their different wares and took others in exchange. Soon a settlement of skilled workers in metal, pottery and stonework grew side by side with the community of tillers. Their knowledge of metal became legendary, reaching the ears of the Arab and Portuguese marauders from the coast.

Here the first European Foreigner pitched his tent and sought supplies for his journey across the plains. See what naked creatures our market days have brought from the land of the sea, they said, and gave him maize and beans, sweet potatoes and yams in exchange for calico and shiny beads. Later another came with a collar around his neck and a Bible, and he too sought supplies and guides, for he wanted to reach the court of the great King of Uganda. They showed him the way. But they called a war council: shall we let evil walk across our lands and not do anything? May he not be a scout from Mutesa's court disguised as Mzungu, a spirit? For whoever saw or heard of a human being without a skin? The elders cautioned them against haste. But a section of the more youthful warriors were not satisfied and whispered together, ending with a battle cry. The Foreigners were never seen again except that for years, late at night, you could see the whiteness of a ghost wailing to its kind for blood and vengeance. Other European Foreigners came and pitched their tents, and this time stayed a little longer, exchanging more cloths for maize and beans and Ilmorog metal while urgently seeking news of gold and elephant tusks and asking less loudly about a collared white man.

The day they dreaded finally came. The peaceful traders now suddenly surrounded the market. They all carried bamboo sticks that vomited fire and venom. They demanded that those responsible for the lone Mzungu's death should give themselves up. Nobody came forward. The warriors scrambled for their spears and shields. But it was too late. They fired at the women and men and children, and afterward sang God save the King. The warriors fought back the way they knew how; but what could they do to a people, mizungu hasa, who whistled death across nothingness? But tomorrow ... tomorrow ... the survivors swore, sharpening their spears in readiness!

Later the Foreigner introduced a strange kind of metal possessed of an evil power: it actually walked on the ground.

It is said that the first black man in Chiri to ride a metal horse came from Ilmorog.

A prosperous farmer Munoru was then. But the walking metal bewitched him. His hands were for ever numb at the sight of hoes and pangas. He only wanted to walk on the new metal to the acclaim of crowds. For a time he lived off demonstrating his skill on the machine. Women especially would look at him with awe, they sang of him as a hero and followed his movements with expectant ecstasy. Similar metals later came to the villages, more young men were able to ride and control them, and people anyway were tired of paying for idleness and idol worship. But no longer could Munoru return to any work which might dirty his hands: he just longed for the white Foreigner's things which might enable him to recover the lost glory.

He was again the first among the very few who actually volunteered their services in the carrier corps of guns and food supplies to the warring Europeans. Ilmorog was a recruiting centre, and most young men were driven into the war with the butt end of the gun. Across the Ilmorog plains they went, clearing roads, toward the Tanganyikan border to ferret out the Germans. Wonder of wonders: Wazungu were actually killing one another, over what the natives could not quite understand: how could they tell that they and the division of their land and labour were the object of the war? Munoru came back, a wreck, and he talked of Voi, Darasalama, Mozambika, Morogoro, Warusha, Moshi, and other places sweetly distant to the ear. But he was a corpse, living on memories of what he thought had been. Even some of the others, when they came back, were not interested now in making the land yield to their fingers as the founders had done. A metal more deadly than the one which walked on legs had bitten them. In search of it, to pay their taxes, but also to buy useless things of the Foreigners, they went to work on farms stolen from Kenyan people and on the network of roads connecting the farms to the capital and the sea.

Ilmorog, the once thriving community of a people who were not afraid to live on the sweat of their hands, started its decline and depopulation. The railway line to Mutesa's court had in any case bypassed Ilmorog. The second European war saw more youth flee Ilmorog to the cities of metallic promises and what was once the centre of trade and farming became just another village, a pale shadow of what it was yesterday ...

Thus Nyakinyua talked to them, keeping up their spirits with stories of the past. They had lit a huge fire and sat in groups around it. The trek to the city had attracted many people carried on the waves of hope and promises, and had awoken a feeling that the crisis was a community crisis needing a communal response. Nyakinyua was the spirit that guided and held them together. And she talked as if she had been everywhere, as if she had actually participated in the war against the Germans, as if the rhythm of the historic rise and fall of Ilmorog flowed in her veins. She was dressed in black, there were deep lines in her face, but she was beautiful even in age. She abruptly stopped and stared at the fire before them. The journey might take many days and she feared for the children, her children.

'Tell us, tell us what they saw!' Karega asked, anxious to know the rest.

'There is nothing to tell ... nothing,' Nyakinyua said, still looking at the fire. Her eyes were alive, intense, a concentration of light more intense than the moon-glow above them. Nyakinyua, mother of men: there was sad gaiety in her voice, she was celebrating rainbow memories of gain and loss, triumph and failure, but above all of suffering and knowledge in struggle.

'Nothing more to tell,' she repeated in a voice that was distant from them, that probably had gone a-walking to those other lands. And Karega, troubled inside, anxious for a glimpse and insight into the past, what indeed made history move, wanted to know what it was she was holding back, what it was that had suddenly made her retreat into silence and gloom amidst the noise of the children. Wanja, Abdulla and Karega looked to the old woman and back again and waited.

'It has been a hard day,' said Njuguna to the whole group. 'We should all sleep and be ready for tomorrow. We must set out early. We are still a long way from the city.'

❀

Karega could not sleep. He took a walk in the plains, thinking about the woman's story. He lived it: for a second, he was Ndemi felling trees in the forest, building a nascent industry ... but his mind, as if being challenged by the vastness of the space, went beyond Ndemi, beyond Ilmorog. It was to a past he could not know but which he felt he knew: was it a hundred years, three hundred years, or was it more? What he had tried to teach the children, what he had tried to work out in Siriana was only a series of logical affirmations and refutations, a set of intellectual convictions. But now the past he had tried to affirm seemed to have a living, glowing ambience in the mouth of the woman on this journey to save a village, a community. He went over it ... images on images ... and he was, for a time, carried away: the knowledge in metal and stone ... the careful piecing of things together ... and the stories, the songs and the disputations of an evening ... and beyond the site where they tried to capture the power of metal and stone were the settlements of those who tried to do the same with the land. Then came the ship and the smoke from the mouth of a bamboo and the equation of power was altered: now it was the African who had to flee from his settled agriculture, from his wrestling match with the god of metal and stone, for security in the depths of the forest. Karega, now transported, saw the bitterness and the fear in the ones who fled, diving deeper into the forest to establish new homes in new climes ... and lord, the fire burnt the villages, and the fire of greed for the red dust and black ivory burnt the accumulated wisdom of many seasons ... so that those unable to flee were clamped and chained together and were made to walk to the sea and beyond to contend with new worlds. Yes, he could see it now, and he confronted his earlier doubt with what he thought an irrefutable rejoinder. The voice had said: if so and so was true, how then explain the virtual dominance of nature over man? Didn't you hear, did you not listen to Nyakinyua's story? If sixty years could so destroy the work of Ndemi that no trace of his industry and knowledge was left, how much more the four hundred years of slavery and carnage, the blood-sucking serpent changing only the colours of the poison?

He suddenly stopped in his track and abruptly broke off the intense, ceaseless flow of his thoughts. Beyond, at the very heart of the plains, was a cone-shaped hill, firm but seeming vulnerable in its utter solitude. He looked back, startled by the breathing presence of another.

'It is only me,' Wanja said. 'Did I scare you?'

'No, not quite. But I have a deep-seated fear of snakes, and I have always associated the poisonous things with dry plains.'

'Sssch! You should not call them by their names at night. Call them Nyamu cia Thi. I fear them too.'

'Oh, I don't believe that superstition. A leopard is called spotted one, or the shy one. Why? If their spirits can hear, they can still hear even if you call them animals of the earth or snakes or by any other name.'

'I remember that once in my hut you declared that you did not believe in names. You said something about a flower being a flower. Ritwa ni mbukio.'

And she laughed a little. This slightly irritated him and he tried to explain.

'It is not that I don't believe in names. For what could be a more ridiculous caricature of self than those of our African brothers and sisters proudly calling themselves James Phillipson, Rispa, Hottensiah, Ron Rodgerson, Richard Glucose, Charity, Honey Moonsnow, Ezekiel, Shiprah, Winterbottomson – all the collection of names and non-names from the Western world? What more evidence of self-hate than their throwing a tea-party for family and friends to bribe them never to call them by their African names? It is rather that I believe in the reality of what's being named more than in the name itself.'

'Is that what you were thinking about just now? I followed you for quite a distance and you did not seem to be aware of being stalked. Or are you now worried about the journey to the city?'

'Not that. I was thinking about Nyakinyua's story.'

'About Ndemi?'

'Yes.'

'Why. Do you believe it?'

'It must be true. Why not? If not the details, then at least the idea.'

'What idea?'

'Of a past. A great past. A past when Ilmorog, or all Africa, controlled its own earth.'

'You are a funny young man,' she said, and laughed a little, a bit guiltily, remembering the night Karega ran away from the hut.

'Why?'

'Well, the things you do and say. One day you say you don't touch drinks. You drink milk or water. Yet the very next time, you are drunk and fighting in a bar.'

He felt a little embarrassed by this. He fidgeted on his feet. He looked at the hill in the distance.

'I don't know how I succumbed to it. I think I just wanted to lose myself. So many things hitting at you on every side. You want to forget.'

'Forget? Then look at this journey. You said you suffered in the city. I think I know what you meant. I felt with you. The city can be a cruel place. But what made you think it will now be different? I fear for you. The past few days my heart bled because so many men and women and children were willing to join us. I was even more touched by the songs of hope that we sang. Don't you think they will sing with bitterness against you should the city slap them in the face the way it did you?'

'I must confess I never thought about that. We can but try. Why should we fail, though? We are now going as a community. The voice of the people is truly the voice of God. And who is an MP? Isn't he the people's voice in the ruling house? He cannot ignore us. He cannot refuse to see us.'

'You have a touching faith in people. This is maybe a good thing. But I wonder ... I wonder.'

They both paused and for a time withdrew into their separate and private thoughts. The moon shone over them. The moon shone over the plains. Wanja was turning over in her mind words she had once heard from a Nairobi lawyer. Karega gazed at the solitary hill but his mind was on the journey and the doubts that Wanja had raised.

'Let us sit down,' he suggested, suddenly feeling weary. 'Isn't it strange that that hill should have stood when all else collapsed?'

'That! It is called the hill of the uncircumcised boys. It is said that if a boy runs right round it, he will turn into a girl and a girl will turn into a boy. Do you believe that too?'

'No, I don't. We should have heard of cases of some who had tried and were changed into their opposites.'

'I wish it were true!' she said rather fiercely, almost bitterly.

Wanja had sworn that she would really make something of herself in Ilmorog. And as a measure of her determination, she would not, she would never again sleep with another man, until she had achieved something. Love-play, love-making would then only be in celebration of her victory and success. What it is she wanted to achieve was vague in her mind. The very sight of Ilmorog threatened

by thirst, hunger and the drought was enough to discourage anyone. Where in that Ilmorog was she to begin? At Abdulla's village
bar and shop? One might well run round the hill and be changed
into a man, like Karega she thought, and wondered about her vow.

Karega was thinking of another hill, in another plain. Manguo
marshes flashed across his vision and he felt a thrill of pleasure and
bitterness at the memory. Triumph and defeat; success and miserable
failure . . . which was which? He had tried not to think of Mukami
who had so dominated his life, but in so trying he had only admitted
her absolute hold on him, his total being even after her death. He
had involved himself in books, in literature, in history, in philo-
osophy, desperately looking for the meaning of the riddle at the
meeting-point of the ironies of history, appearance and reality, expectation and actual achievement. He had thrown his weight into
one cause after another, one work-activity after another, seeking, in
the process, a rebirth of something he could never quite define –
innocence? Hope? At times, he missed her: and he would worship
her memory, celebrating in his mind the dawn of innocence and
hope before succumbing to gloom as, in his mind, he stood at the
top of the hill, facing Manguo marshes, and watched with a sinking,
sickening feeling, the failure of purity and innocence. Once, in Siriana, falling into such a mood, he sat down to write: but he captured
not the bitterness he felt, but a strange unsettled nervousness,
the pessimism at the bottom, at the remembrance of Mukami's
suicide.

My heart is heavy. There is ulcerous pain in my belly. How is it
that small things, the screech of a cricket, the touch of a grass-
hopper, make me suddenly start and look about me? Why do I look
at her, my soul-image of truth, and become frightened for
tomorrow? Why, why, why should I not be secure in the knowledge that once on the hippo hump of Manguo marshes two hearts
refused to hate and beat each to each?

That was just before he left Siriana, a bitter fulfilment, as he
thought later, as he thought now, still looking at the solitary hill
under the immensity of the moon, of what at the time of writing was
only a premonition. Chui came to the school. The rest was history.

Wanja asked him:

'Tell me, Karega, do you always think about the past?'

The question startled him and he now stared at her: was she reading his mind? In some ways Wanja reminded him so much about
Mukami: He stirred himself to answer.

'To understand the present . . . you must understand the past. To know where you are, you must know where you came from, don't you think?'

'How? I look at it this way. Drought and thirst and hunger are hanging over Ilmorog! What use is Ndemi's story? I am drowning: what use would be my looking back to the shore from which I fell?'

'The fact that they did things, that they refused to drown: shouldn't that give us hope and pride?'

'No, I would feel better if a rope was thrown at me. Something I can catch on to . . .' she was silent for a few seconds. Then she said in a changed tone of voice. 'Sometimes there is no greatness in the past. Sometimes one would like to hide the past even from oneself.'

Karega suddenly realised that she was not talking about an abstract past.

'What do you mean?'

She did not answer him at once. She made as if to move and she nestled close to him. He felt her near warmth in his lungs, warm against his ribs. Life quickened in an unwilled expectation. She sniffed once and he realised that she was crying.

'Why are you crying?' he asked, puzzled.

'I don't know . . . I don't know . . . Please don't mind me,' she said, trying unsuccessfully to smile between her tears. 'My past is full of evil. Today, now, when I look back, I only see the wasted years . . .'

'Was it . . . was it hard, then?' he asked, concerned, but felt, at the same time, the triteness of the question. What did he know about her? What could he know about a woman who kept on metamorphosing into different shapes and beings before one's very eyes? When he first had met her in the hut, she was master of the men around her. She had seemed so sure in her movements and glances. Once or twice she had sought his eyes above the heads of Abdulla and Munira, but he had instinctively recoiled from the light in her own eyes. When they next met in Limuru it was he who had sunk into the lower depths of falsity, the attempt to escape from oneself, and she had thrown him a lifeline. Her voice, as she called him out of the depths, sounded genuine, concerned, softened with the pity and sympathy of recognition. Over the last few weeks, he had witnessed the gradual withering away of her earlier calculated smoothness, the practised light in the eyes, and the slow birth of a broken-nailed, lean beauty. And here she was now, crying! But even amidst these thoughts he noticed her slight hesitation at his question, as if she did not know how to respond to it or how to approach the answer.

Which was true?

For somehow she could not, she realised suddenly as she was about to say something, bring herself to tell him of her involvement with Kimeria the man who had ruined her life.

But she briefly told him about her work in the many bars which had mushroomed everywhere since independence.

'We barmaids never settle in one place. Sometimes you are dismissed because you refused to sleep with your boss. Or your face may become too well known in one place. You want a new territory. Do you know, it is so funny that when you go to a new place the men treat you as if you were a virgin. They will outdo one another to buy you beers. Each wants to be the first. So you will find us, barmaids, wherever there is a bar in Kenya. Even in Ilmorog.'

She laughed. Somebody coughed behind them. They were both relieved to see that it was only Munira.

'You came to hide here. And we all thought that you had been eaten up by wild animals,' he called out in a jovial voice, slightly exaggerated.

'It is difficult to sleep early in such a vast wilderness,' Karega said.

'Wanja is telling you about her life in the bar wilderness?' he asked as he sat down so that Wanja was between them.

'She had only started,' Karega said.

Karega had had glimpses of this world when he was as a seller of sheepskins and mushrooms by the roadside. He knew of many boys who after a hard day's labour would later empty all their earnings on the waiting laps of a barmaid who probably had two or three children to feed.

'It is not a very beautiful wilderness,' Wanja said. 'But it is not all bad. For a woman, anyway, it is a good feeling when a thousand eyes turn toward you and you feel that it is your body that is giving orders to all those hearts. Sometimes you see what is wrong. You want to get out: you also want to remain. You keep on saying to yourself: tomorrow ... tomorrow. I know some who tried. One became a housemaid. She did all the work in the house. She woke up at five ... She helped in milking the cows. She cooked breakfast. She cleaned the house. She went to the shop or to the field to fetch food to cook lunch. She also looked after the little children. She made afternoon tea; she made supper, washed the children ... and when the wife was away the man wanted to share her bed. And all for what? Seventy shillings a month! She ran away. Another tried picking tea leaves and coffee beans for the new African landlords. And for what amount of pay? And so in the end they all return to the world where they have friends and where they know the rules: where they know what is honest and what is not honest; what is truth and what is not truth; what is good and what is not good. For example. It was not good and it was not honest not to make a man spend his money on you. A girl was once beaten because she was careless about this: why did she have to spoil the market for the others? Me? I too have tried to get out. Once I went home. My father said: "I do not want a prostitute in the house!" It hurt me coming from a father. A barmaid does not take herself to be a prostitute. We are girls in search of work and men. I returned to bar life. I have been lucky. I have had good friendships. I like people's faces: I like new places: and I even find counting figures, arranging things in certain patterns, enjoyable. Sitting behind a counter I say to myself: if that face was put on those shoulders ... if that nose was on that head ... if that ... if that ... and people and places do look suddenly funny and very interesting. Other girls would say: Wanja, what are you always thinking about? It was difficult to explain. But at the same time, I was lonely. I liked people, yes. I liked the noise and the music and the fights – oh yes, even the fights – and unexpected happenings, but I was lonely. I travelled from place to place. I was looking for something. I came to Ilmorog. I did not find what I was looking for. After a few months I felt I wanted to go away. I did not know where. I did not want to return to the life of a barmaid. One gets tired of being everybody's barmaid. I said: I will not go back to the same job. I said to myself: Ilmorog is a good place. Why don't I make some money very quickly and go back, build a house there and live there for all time! I wanted to return to the village – but a rich woman. I don't know where this thought came from. As I said, I depended more on friendships, and I never had cared much for tomorrow. To live ... to live ... I liked buying clothes ... colours move me ... I try to attach a meaning to every dress that I buy. But now I said: No more friendships. I'll never marry anyway. So why not become rich? How? And the answer came. Nairobi. Europeans. Now this thought surprised me ... because I could never bring myself to go with a white man. Once I went with a Kalasingh. He was a police inspector. He arrested us because we were selling beer late at a bar in Kikuyu town, and when he searched the boys he found they had bhang. I was frightened. He put the boys in jail. He took me to his house. Well, I saved myself that way. The boys were locked up for five years. That was the first and the only time. There was this woman. She was very rich. She had a farm in the settled area. She also had houses in Nairobi. But she was lonely for friendship. She would come to where I used to work in Lower Kabete. She would say: Wanja, I can get you a European boy friend. She herself had been a teacher and then a secretary. But she made money after office hours. Anyway she had married a very old European ... over seventy years ... people said that after she had made him make a will, she had thrown him down the steps in the house. She got all his wealth. When she told me that, I would only laugh. I could not tell her that I thought of Europeans as naked bodies like the skin of pigs ... or that of frogs that had lain buried in the ground for a long time ... But now I said: this is going to be business. In a business you don't say who your customers are going to be. It would anyway only be for a month or two months. For Europeans only. So when I left Ilmorog I haunted all the doors of the big hotels. Hilton. Ambassador. New Stanley. Serena. Norfolk. Inter-Continental. Fair View. Six Eighty. May Fair. Grosvenor. Pan-Africa, plums. I had never thought there could be so many big hotels in one place. But I was trembling and without the knowledge. I didn't have the right sort of dresses I saw the other girls in: and I could not paint my lips red and my eyelids mercury green and wear wigs. And with Europeans I did not know how to use my eyes. In a bar, especially when I was behind the counter, I could have talked to all the men in the bar without once moving my lips. But Nairobi ... For two nights following I ended up with Africans. At the College Inn, I met a girl I once worked with in a bar in Eldoret. She it was who told me about Starlight and Hallian's Night Clubs. There you can make even a thousand shillings if it is your week. I went to Starlight. There were such changing colours of blue and red and green I could not see anything clearly. My heart had sunk low. I could not jump to the music. I know you are surprised about this, but bar life is slightly different. But one thing I would say for Starlight: it was full of Europeans. I sat in a corner, and I was feeling now I would like to jump over the enclosing bamboo walls and run all the way back to Bolibo. Anyway I saw this one throwing me many eyes. I returned a smile. He was tall, with a pipe in his mouth, and he did not look as old as the others whose face-skins fell into many folds. He spoke Swahili well, but in a funny way, and would add one or two English words. He was a Mtalii from Germany and he had come to the country on a special mission. He was looking for a certain girl from Kabete. She had been taken to Germany by another German with promises of marriage. But she found that she had been tricked and he had wanted her to start a trade with her, for he and others had figured that if watalii could pay all that money for aeroplanes and for hotels at Malindi on account of having seen an advertisement of an aged white man with a young African woman with the words: For only so much you can have this: they would pay even more willingly if Malindi was instead brought to Germany. Did I know of her? I said: how could I know of her? Why did he want her anyway, was she not in Germany?

Because, he told me, the man who had brought her had treated her badly, he had beaten her and such things and this might cause bad feelings between Germany and Africa. She had managed to run away and returned to Kenya and she had left a baby behind. The man was refusing to take care of the baby, and this group who cared about black people and feelings between Germany and Africa had come together and collected money to send him to Africa to find the girl and collect evidence which could be used against the man in a court of law. Did I know her? Anyway, I said again: how could I know her, there being so many girls in the country? He said exactly; that was why he was going round most of the bars and night spots to see if he could trace her. Would I like to be his companion in the search? He would pay me well, and if we were successful in finding her I would be flown to Germany as a witness in the trial. It was a strange story, and at first I thought he was wrong in the head, but he looked all right and he talked all right, and I had heard that some Europeans were stealing girls so they could trade with them in Italy and Germany. Well, you can see how busy my mind was counting this, counting that and I said to myself: yesterday I was a barmaid without pay at Abdulla's place. And now? By the time we finished the search I would be a rich woman and I would buy a guitar and a flute. You don't maybe believe me, but I like music and I can see blue waves of the sea when music is being played and sometimes I am riding on orange and blue and red clouds: on acres of green fields when certain flutes are played. Choral voices of birds can also lift me from a depression, and you know sometimes in my head I can hear a solitary orange tune later joined by many tunes like streams of colours from nowhere ... anyway it's rather childish of me and I am ashamed of it ... but I am running away from the story. Just now I was telling you about the counting in my head as he drove me to his home for the night. Really I didn't mind Europeans any more.

'I have never been in a house like that before. A wide road with tall jacarandas led to a yard of flowers of every kind. He took me round the house ... a gentle person he was, and he showed me the various rooms ... really, Europeans were not bad, not bad at all ... he would stop at a picture and he would explain something about grapes or vines hanging from a window – all that. He took me to another room. Ooh, I cried out in sudden fear. There were two figures of men clad in strange armour and swords as if ready for a war fight or something. And on the walls were swords of various lengths and shapes ... He touched the blades of a few of them and explained something about his hobby. I did not understand all this and anyway I was afraid of the swords and the armoured figures and I was wondering: how did he come to own this house and this collection if he only had just come from Germany? But before I could even ask him, he led me to his bedroom. There were mirrors on the wall, so many and so arranged that you became many many people scattered in endless lines. My heartbeat of fear returned. He must be very rich to have been able to hire such a house although he was only here on a search for a girl. Or I thought it could mean that he was going to stay here for some time, in which case ... my head started counting again and I was lost in my dreams about money when, suddenly, beside me I saw or rather felt the presence of a dog staring at me with huge green eyes. I gasped in fear and stepped back. I was frightened and felt weak at the knees. I looked about me and I saw we were many many with many many dogs in endless space. I sat on the bed, or rather several of me sat on several beds in a dream. The man came over, or several men came over, and sat beside us on many beds and it was as if he or they were enjoying our fright. He told me not to worry ... it was all right ... and the animals came toward us, roaring a little, their green eyes fixed on us. I tried to control my trembling with difficulty. It stood there as if waiting for more orders from the master. And the master was now panting besides me, letting out a nasty smell and I could see by the movement of his fingers and his dilating eyes and his trembling lower lip that he was excited. I had grown roots to the bed of terror. Strength was ebbing out of me, it was as if the green-red glow of the dog's eyes was sapping my energy and strength to resist. I was hanging in space ... nothing. But behind the terror, behind this inexplicable thing that was affecting my nerves to a tingling something and the slow death-ness, was another feeling of watchfulness. And the man was now fumbling with my clothes and the animal was growling and wagging its tail and the man was trembling. The watchful feeling became stronger and stronger, struggling with the deathness, and the animal was about to lick my fingers when somewhere inside me I heard my own voice exclaim: "Oh, but you know I left my handbag in your car." The moment I heard my voice I knew that the deathness was defeated and I was returning to life. He said: "Don't worry, I will get it for you." I said: "No, a woman's bag contains secrets, so could he take me to the car?" It was my voice all right but commanded by I didn't know who inside me ... I stood up. He led the way to the door. The animal followed behind. And now I was silently praying: give me more strength, give me more strength. He went out first and I quickly shut the door so that the animal was shut in. Even now I can't tell where I got wings from. I flew and flew through the trees and the grass undergrowth and I only looked back once when I reached the main tarmac road ...

'A car screeched and stopped beside me. I jumped to the side, fearing it might be him. My friends ... I have never been so grateful for the sight of another black skin. I was now crying and in between my sobbing, I must have told bits and pieces about my terror. He took me to a house in Nairobi West. He made me some coffee and gave me some tablets and showed me a place to sleep. I must have slept through the night and through the following day. He let me stay for another night and I told him my story and he asked me a few questions: would I know the house? Would I recognise him? Then he looked at one place and said: It is no use. This is what happens when you turn tourism into a national religion and build it shrines of worship all over the country. I did not ask him what he meant, but I know he sounded angry. The following day he took me to Machakos bus stop and I felt like crying now with gratitude because he had not so much as tried anything on me, and had treated me without any contempt. Now he gave me some money and he simply said: "Why don't you return home to your parents? This city is no place for you ... well ... it is not a place for any of us ... yet!" He told me where he worked and he gave me a card and he said that should I ever be in difficulties – but not like those of the other night, for he hoped that I would return home – I should not hesitate to go there, and he drove away without waiting for me to finish the words of gratitude I had started.

'I would go home, I told myself, I should go home ...

'But when the bus I had taken stopped near my place I did not get off. I asked myself: how can I go home just like that, as if I have not been working all these years? I returned to Bolibo and to the life of a barmaid ...'

2 ✿ Abdulla became the hero of the journey. He seemed to continue revealing newer and richer aspects of his personality. For a start people were now grateful for his donkey. They kept on making comparisons between the donkey-pulled carriage and the bull-pulled wagons that the colonial settlers used to own. They too were on a mission of conquest – of the city.

Then, despite his crippled leg, Abdulla would not accept a ride in the cart. Let the children take their turns, was all he said. His stoic endurance infused strength and purpose into the enterprise. The sun persistently hit at them and the short stems of the elephant grass pricked their bare soles. Abdulla was very good with the children. He told them stories, especially in the evening when the moon was up:

'Moon and sun are enemies. That is why one appears in the day and the other at night. But they were not always enemies. This is how it happened. Sun and moon went to bathe in a river. Scrub my back and then I shall scrub yours, said sun to moon. So moon carefully scrubbed sun to a brilliant shine. Moon said: Now it is your turn. Sun mixed spittle with soil and rubbed moon with it.'

In the daytime he told them the names of the various shrubs and grass: if the shrubs had not been dry, he would have shown them the uses of the different parts. He showed them tricks with a knife. Once he threw the knife and it split a thin stick into two. He acted as a judge in their competitions to see who was the most accurate with the catapults Abdulla had made for them. The boys were happy and they went on arguing as to who could bring down a bird from the sky. Indeed they seemed to gain from Abdulla's reserve of strength, and for the first two days they too refused a lift and walked beside Abdulla.

Somewhere in the procession somebody started a hymn. They fumbled with the words, and after a few trials they were all singing it.

> They say that there's famine,
> But they don't say there's famine
> Only for those who
> Would not eat the bread of Jesus.
>
> Many houses, much land and property,
> Money in banks, much education,
> These will not fill hungry hearts unless
> People eat the bread of Jesus.
>
> Look at the wealthy, the poor and the children:
> Aren't they all staggering on a highway?
> It's because of the hunger in their hearts,
> It's because they would not eat the bread of Jesus.

The words and the pallid Christian message seemed a mockery of their present plight. But the voices in unison moved Abdulla: the spirit behind the singing awakened memories of other voices in the past.

Abdulla once again walked those other journeys and flights across the plains. Ole Masai, the tall half-Indian, led them. Then they too used to sing, reminding themselves of promises they had made at the taking of Batuni oaths in earlier times:

When Jomo of the black people was arrested in the night
He left us a message and a mission.
I will hold the donkey's head, he told us:
Will you, my children, endure the kicks?
Yes, yes, I said, and reached for my sword,
And I linked hands with all the children of the land.
And I vowed, tongue on a burning spear,
I will never turn my back on the cries of black people,
I will never let this soil go to the red stranger.
I will never betray this piece of earth to foreigners.

He had indeed endured thirst and hunger, briars and thorns in scaly flesh in the service of that vision which first opened out to him the day he had taken both the oath of unity and later the Batuni oath.

He was then a worker at a shoe-factory near his home, where strike after strike for higher wages and better housing had always been broken by helmeted policemen. He had asked himself several times: how was it that a boss who never once lifted a load, who never once dirtied his hands in the smelly water and air in the tannery or in any other part of the complex, could still live in a big house and own a car and employ a driver and more than four people only to cut grass in the compound?

How he had trembled as the vision opened out, embracing new thoughts, new desires, new possibilities! To redeem the land: to fight so that the industries like the shoe-factory which had swallowed his sweat could belong to the people: so that his children could one day have enough to eat and to wear under adequate shelter from rain: so that they would say in pride, my father died that I might live: this had transformed him from a slave before a boss into a man. That was the day of his true circumcision into a man.

Abdulla walked, or rather hobbled on his one leg: but they saw this glitter in his eyes, chin held high, face fixed on the distant mountains and they were again surprised, for in this hostile terrain and wilderness it was he who knew and led the way.

But images on images crowded in his mind, so that though he set the pace and kept his place at the head of the procession, he was not with them. Ole Masai ... strange that it should be happening again in Ilmorog ... happening again ... an illusion? A bean fell to the ground and we split it amongst ourselves ... how good it was that Karega had come to Ilmorog ... a later messenger from God ... Old Muturi said it ... God puts wisdom in the mouth of babes ... true ... true ... the conversation in his shop had changed since Karega's arrival. For the last five months they would ocacsionally touch on names which were sweet to the ear ... Chaka ... Toussaint ... Samoei ... Nat Turner ... Arap Manyei ... Laibon Turugat ... Dessalines ... Mondhlane ... Owalo ... Siotune and Kiamba ... Nkrumah ... Cabral ... and despite the sun and the drought and his anxiety over the fate of his donkey he would feel that Mau Mau was only a link in the chain in the long struggle of African people through different times at different places ... Aaa! New horizons ... again ... like that time in the forest ... with Ole Masai. They called him Muhindi, but now he did not mind that. He would often tell them how he had hated himself, his mother, his father, his divided self, how indeed at times he had wanted to kill himself, he who did not belong anywhere. It was not that he was poor ... They lived in the better parts of Eastleigh ... his Indian father often came and left them money and was paying for his education and had promised him a bit of his wealth ... indeed had already opened a bank account in his name ... but he still hated himself. He ran away from school, from home into the streets ... Kariokoo ... Pumwani ... Shauri Moyo ... playing dice and stealing a bit ... fighting a bit ... but he also had picked things from talks ... and read a bit ... Lal Vidyardhi's papers, especially *Habari za Dunia* and *Colonial Times.* The arrest of Markhan Singh for identifying with African workers had cleared a bit of the mist in his eyes ... He now sought ways of getting into the city underground. They had played a cruel joke on him ... casually told him to take a parcel to a certain person standing at the corner of Khoja Mosque ... He told them how he tripped over in River Road ... how the parcel fell and he discovered, oh, he was carrying a revolver ... he had trembled, excited, but he had also been afraid ... he had guarded the revolver carefully until he came to the man ... he was about to hand him the badly wrapped parcel when two European policemen in plain clothes laid hands on the man ... Ole Masai whipped out the revolver and pointed it at the policemen ... he was so excited he shouted for all the people to come and see him kill policemen ... whose hands were up ... but the man pulled him by the shoulder and they both disappeared among the Nairobi crowds ... He was never to forget that moment, the moment of his rebirth as a complete man, when he humiliated the two European oppressors and irrevocably sided with the people. He had rejected what his father stood for, rejected the promises of wealth, and was born again as a fighter in the forest, a Kenyan, and his doubts were stilled by new calls and new needs. He had told them how later he had sent a letter to his father, ordering him off African people's property ... a remarkable man, Ole Masai was, Abdulla sighed. He had indeed read a bit, because they had talked of other lands, other peoples ... China ... Korea ... Russia ... and how the working people and the peasant farmers had arisen against their foreign and native overlords ... Then suddenly Ole Masai was killed and he Abdulla, was shot in the leg. He would ever remember that day ... they had carefully planned to capture a garrison in the heart of Nakuru Town, and free the prisoners in the adjoining prison, as earlier in the struggle Kihika had done at Mahee and Kimathi's guerrillas at Naivasha. They had freed the prisoners. The garrison was about to surrender, when Ole Masai was shot and only ... how fate could play tricks on a people's destiny? ... only because his gun was jammed ... There was pandemonium everywhere ... people were shouting ... catch ... catch ... and for a second Abdulla had the illusion of a double vision.

For indeed, around him, the children were shouting catch, catch, meat, meat ... then he too saw what they had seen. The procession had surprised a herd of antelopes which were now leap-leaping across the plains. Abdulla's mind worked very fast.

'Wait!' he shouted at the children, and they obeyed the sudden authority in his voice. 'Bring the catapult, and quick, get me some stones.'

They gave him the catapult he had helped to make earlier in the day, and also some stones. They stood aside, hushed with excited curiosity, but also sceptical about his power. He put a sharp-edged stone in the catapult and the rest in his pockets. He picked a bit of soil and threw it up in the air to see the strength and direction of the wind. He adjusted his support-walking stick and placed its seat more firmly under his right armpit. And all this time his eyes had not let go the antelopes, which had stopped and stood at a distance from them. He took out the stones in his pockets and asked Muriuki to hold them, on open palms. He held his lower lip and let out some sounds, made the animals suddenly turn and move toward them. But as soon as they saw the procession near, they again turned as if undecided on the next step, so that the sides of their bodies and necks faced the people. Abdulla set his arms, shut one eye, and pulled back the rubber string, before letting it go. Everything was happening so fast, a magic act in a dream. They never even saw the stones nor how he managed to put one and then another and yet another into the catapult and pull and let go. They only heard the sounds of the stones whistling through the air. Then they saw two antelopes jump high in the air, one after the other, and then land still for a second, before falling writhing to the ground. They could not believe it. Munira, Karega, Njuguna and the children ran to the scene. The two animals had been maimed in the legs. The rest was easy.

Abdulla stood in the same position, now transformed in their eyes into a very extraordinary being whom they had never really known. Immobile, like a god of the plains, Abdulla still rested his eyes on the distant hills which for years had been a home to him. He still dwelt on Ole Masai and their group's desperate and fatal attempt to capture that soldiers' garrison in Nakuru, to regain the initiative temporarily lost after Kimathi's capture. Even the enemy papers admitted that it was a well planned and ambitious attempt. The glitter in his eyes became more intense. He brushed them off with the back of his hand and threw the catapult to the ground.

They had a feast that night. Even long afterwards they were to remember it and talk about it as the highest point in their journey to the city. The children played around the fire and the elderly people sat in groups talking and reminiscing over old times and places. Njuguna teased Nyakinyua about antelopes, supposed to have been women's goats which had run wild because the women could not look after them. Munira lay on his back counting stars, and felt for a time freed from that overwhelming sense of always being on the outside of things. There were still many questions in his head: about Karega for instance. He always felt ill at ease with him, but he had not yet defined his attitude to him. Maybe in the journey they would talk. He also would have liked to have a heart-to-heart talk with Wanja. He had thought that he and Wanja would take up the thread where they had left it, especially now that they had gone through almost identical baptisms by fire and terror. Wasn't there some kind of destiny in the coincidence of their suffering? But instead he had felt her slipping away from him: where was she going? He watched her moves, but she obviously was not developing a relationship with anyone else. She always surprised him with her moods and the changing aspects of her character. What struck him most, listening to her the other night, was the way her experiences took the form of stories, a kind of ballad of woes with a voice that demanded and compelled a hearing, and which ended by binding the listener even more to her life and fate. He now listened to Abdulla and Nyakinyua talking. How could he have not seen this side of Abdulla? Munira, like the others, had witnessed an extraordinary feat of human skill and it had united them all, as if each could see a bit of himself in Abdulla. Wanja, sitting just behind Nyakinyua and Adbulla, was particularly happy: she had always felt that Abdulla had had a history to that stump of a leg. Now it was no longer a stump, but a badge of courage indelibly imprinted on his body. She listened to Abdulla telling the story of Ole Masai and their fatal attempt to capture the Nakuru garrison. Njogu's heart glowed with pride. He had always felt ashamed of the fact that his daughter should have borne children to an Indian. They had heard of one Ole Masai but not from one who had worked with him. Njogu felt it was the blood from the black side which had asserted itself. A truly great night of revelations, even for Abdulla, who had not known that fate would later turn him into a shopkeeper on the premises once occupied by Ole Masai's father. He now understood Njogu's cryptic statements when he had first inquired about the shop. Wanja tried to picture this Indian, who at least had half-acknowledged his African woman and his son by her. She thought that maybe under different times and conditions it would not matter who married who or who slept with whom, but suddenly, remembering her ordeal in the city, she started wondering. Her attention was now taken up by the turn of the conversation. It was not her alone. Even the children stopped playing and sat down to hear their new hero answer Karega's question about Kimathi. At long last he was going to tell the story he had once refused to tell. Silence gripped the whole group, hanging on Abdulla's lips. He did not hesitate for long and his voice was subdued, the tone matter-of-fact, almost drained of emotion.

'Actually, some of us had not seen Dedan although we acted in his name. Our group operated all the way from Limuru, through Kijabe, Longonot, Nare Ngare, right to Ilmorog, these very plains. For four years our Limuru group, which had joined hands with the Ole Masai group, had, although diminishing in numbers, through hunger, forest weariness, enemy guns, fought with all the skills of survival we could muster. Our food supplies were cut when moats with death spikes planted in them were dug around many villages. You have heard of Kamiritho, Githima and other places. Now and then an old man, an old woman or even a boy might avoid the evil eyes of our brothers who through ignorance, bribery, torture, or promises of wealth and individual safety, had sold themselves as Home Guards – spear-bearers for the Foreigners – and would bring us food and news of what people were saying and doing. But such contacts were becoming rare. I confess that there were moments of quarrels, of doubt and of flagging of faith. But such acts of courage or the memory of them would make us know that our people had not forgotten us: how could they? We were their very arms, armed. This knowledge, that we were really our people, kept us going. We raided the settlers' own homes, we burnt their houses, we cut their animals to pieces and almost wept because this, in truth, was our property. All the same, new recruits to swell our numbers were becoming difficult to find, for most of the youth had been taken to concentration camps and at one point we were reduced to twenty or so in our group.

'It was at this time that news reached us of a great meeting of an All Kenya Parliament in Mount Kenya Forest. All the fighting groups or their representatives were expected to attend, for Dedan had new plans for the next phase of the war. He wanted us reorganised into different zones, and he wanted us to elect a military high command and a separate political and education high command to prepare us to seize and administer power. He also wanted us to make greater efforts in linking with other forces opposed to the British occupation in Ukambani, Kalenjin, Luo, Luhya and Giriama areas and all over Kenya. He also wanted us to spread our cause to the court of Haile Selassie and to Cairo, where Gamal Abdel Nasser had taken the Suez Canal and later fought the British and the French. I have told you we were without food. But we were determined to make the long journey through Olkalou, the Nyandarwa mountain ridge, across Nyeri plains to Mount Kenya. I wanted to see this man who was but a voice, a black power, and whose military genius was recognised even by our enemy. Look at it this way. He had fought and he had defeated generals like Lt.-General Sir Erskine, General Hinde, General Ladbury and their armies brought from England: the Buffs, Lancashire Fusiliers, the Devons, the Royal Air Force, the K.A.R. and other forces that had seen action in the Canal Zone, Palestine, Hong Kong, Malaya, wherever the British had once reigned. We spoke of him with awe and his favourite places had become important shrines in our lives. We knew him as Knight Commander of the African Empire, our Prime Minister, one who could move for fourteen days and nights without food or water, who could move for seven miles and more on his belly, and we all tried to emulate him. There was also Mathenge, Karari wa Njama, Kimbo, Kago, Waruingi, Kimemia and others whose letters and messages we had often read but whom we had never seen. What united us was our cause.

'And what a journey, my friends! Our ammunition was scarce. We had tried to make more bullets by splitting open one and sharing the powder into smaller shells, but it did not work. For meat, we often relied on traps, but what use was this on a journey? Sometimes we ate raw maize, bamboo shoots, anything: once we found some wild millet, and we rubbed it in our hands and carried the flour in our deerskin bags. Ole Masai would enliven us with stories of old Nairobi. He tried to tell us again the story he had told us a thousand times: how he had pulled a gun on European policemen, and how they had trembled against the walls of Khoja Mosque while Muslims prayed in the house, and it did not really excite us as much as it used to do in happier days. Now our animal skin clothes were tattered, but we pressed on, through the thick undergrowth, our skins torn by wild thorns, often running away from poisonous snakes. Sometimes, too, tempers would flare amongst us: and still we moved on toward the mountain, to hear words from his own mouth. Soon we reached the mighty mountain and the meeting-ground. My friends! What do they say in the good book? That to everything there is a season, and a time to every purpose in heaven ... a time to love, and a time to hate. For us, that was a time to do both: hate and love. A great gathering I found there: not a tree, not a bush for a mile was without a man or woman leaning against it. They sang in defiant tones and their one voice was like a roll of thunder:

> And you, traitors to your people,
> Where will you run to
> When the brave of the lands gather?
> For Kenya is black people's country.

'My heart fell, my eyes were dry although I felt tears pressing. I went to the nearest bush and diarrhoea and urine came out of their own accord. Still sang the voices around me:

> Where will traitors run to
> When the clouds roll away
> And the brave return?
> For Kenya is an African people's country.

'Dedan had been caught, delivered to our enemies by our own brothers, lovers of their own stomachs, Wakamatimo. May their names, like that of Judas, ever be cursed, an example to our children of what never to be! We were now awaiting the outcome of the mockery they had called a trial. Plans and attempts to rescue him had failed. The hospital where he lay was heavily guarded, with armoured vehicles, troops on horses, soldiers on foot and on motorcycles patrolling the streets and jet fighters circling in the sky. Scared indeed they were that somehow Africa's God might intervene from above! They say that in every European settler's home that week was held a party in celebration of the Temporary victory of Colonialism over liberation struggle. But in the mountain we sat and waited for our own spies sent to Nyeri. They were expected any day, any minute.

'And when they finally came, early on the morning of the fourth day, we needed no words from their mouth: how shall I tell it? You know when there is an important death. It is hot and it is not hot. It is cold and it is not cold. A lone bird flies in the sky, you don't know where it is going because it is going nowhere. We all returned to our places determined to continue fighting and the struggle but things were no longer the same! My friends . . . no longer the same.'

3 ❀ They did not know it, but that night was to be the peak of their epic journey across the plains. It was true that Abdulla's feast, as they called it, had leased them new life and determination, and the following day, despite the sun which had struck earlier and more fiercely than in the other days, as if to test their capacity for endurance to the very end, despite indeed the evidence of the acacia bush, the ashy-furred leleshwa bush, the prickly pears, all of which seemed to have given in to the bitter sun, they walked with brisk steps as if they too knew this secret desire of the sun and were resolved to come out on top. Abdulla's story had made them aware of a new relationship to the ground on which they trod: the ground, the murram grass, the agapanthas, the cactus, everything in the plains, had been hallowed by the feet of those who had fought and died that Kenya might be free: wasn't there something, a spirit of those people in them too? Now even they of Ilmorog had a voice in the houses of power and privilege. Soon, tonight, tomorrow, some day, at the journey's end, they would meet him, face to face. It would be the first time that they would be demanding anything from him and they, in their different ways, felt awed at the novelty and daring of their action. During the last election campaign, some recalled doubtfully, he had promised them many things including water and better roads. It would take time, he had warned them. Maybe, they thought, taking heart, maybe he was still involved in intractable negotiations with Kenyatta's government. Recalling, too, Abdulla's heroism in the past and also yesterday – how good, how fortunate, that God had brought them Abdulla, Wanja, Munira and Karega – they walked with eyes fixed on a possibility of a different life in Ilmorog, if not for them, at least for their children. They even made up a song in praise of Abdulla, Munira, Wanja and Karega, but also touching on their new hopes and visions.

But in the next three days, they increasingly became quiet, listless. Some, led by Njuguna, once or twice let words edged with contempt and derision at a hasty journey, undertaken at the advice of children, drop from their mouths. Karega remembered Wanja's warning of a few nights before and avoided her eyes. They were now without food and without water. At one stage their thirst became so intolerable it almost threatened their will to proceed: Abdulla led them to a place where once flowed a stream and they dug up some stones, turned over some rocks and put their tongues on the sides hidden from the sun to cool the fire in their tongues. No herds of antelopes came their way: only a carcass of an eland newly dead. The children clambered back to the cart – how fortunate, every one thought again, that they had brought the donkey, so that the children need not feel the teeth of the sand and the needle stems of the grass – and they continued their journey, with hawks and vultures flying high above them, maybe hoping ... Nyakinyua, was encouraging them. 'Don't despair when you have already done over half the journey. It is said that once in Muranga a child who had bravely put up with hunger a whole day fatally gave up just when his mother was throwing the last mwiko into the pot to mash the irio.'

And then suddenly one morning they came to the bottom of the hills and valleys of the escarpment and the beginning of a green belt of spotted bush and forest trees.

They rested at the foot, exhausted, but not without pride at the many miles they had covered to put the vast plains behind them. One heave, one more heave and the rock will be moved, Nyakinyua encouraged them after they had rested a bit, pointing out that they were bound to find water and wild fruits further up the slopes. Where did she get the strength, this old woman who, like Abdulla, had refused a ride in the cart?

A surveyors' team had cleared some kind of road that zigzagged through the bush and trees on the side of the slopes. And on either side of the road, the forest department had cleared off wide avenues, treeless belts to arrest the unmitigated spread of bush fires. They resumed their journey along this highway, their hope and faith renewed. A mile or so on, they came to a valley and Abdulla said there was water down there. They went down the shallow valley and indeed there was water. They all knelt to drink, and others, especially the children, stripped to bathe. The elderly people chose more hidden spots. They also found gooseberries, guavas and other wild fruits.

Karega saw to the donkey which drank and ate wildly. Wanja sat with the children. At the voices of children, Wanja often felt a wound inside her smart so sharply that tears would press against her eyelids. She felt an excruciating love for them and she would have liked, at such moments, to embrace and give milk to all the little ones of the earth. Lord forgive us our sins, Lord forgive us our trespasses, and let the children come unto me. She brushed aside the voices of prayer murmuring in the heart and looked more closely at Joseph, the only one who had not bathed.

His face had fallen, he was breathing with difficulty and he was obviously trying to hide his pain from her. She rose and felt his chest and it was hot.

'How long has he been ill?' she asked them. Some turned their faces away, and she had to ask again.

'Since yesterday and through the night,' one said. 'But he told us not to tell on him. I mean, he did not want to add to your worry and hardship.'

The naïveté – well, the selfless fortitude – touched her and she hurried to where Munira, Karega and Abdulla were talking.

'Joseph is ill,' she announced without ceremony.

They went to where Joseph was. They were joined by Njuguna and Nyakinyua and soon the whole procession knew of it. Abdulla and Njuguna went into the bush and came back with roots and some green leaves. They gave some to Joseph to chew. But what was needed, Abdulla explained, was for the leaves and the roots to be boiled and Joseph covered together with the pot under a heavy blanket to sweat out the fever and the illness from the joints. So the best thing was for them to move on and go to the nearest farmhouse and seek aid in medicine or a place they could sit and treat Joseph themselves.

They led the donkey back to the road and reharnessed it to the cart. Although the highway ran along the slopes, it was still steep and the donkey's hooves kept on slipping. Munira, Karega and Wanja helped push the cart, and this way, panting and sweating, they eventually came to the top and joined the tarmac road.

But for Joseph's illness, they would all have felt immeasurable happiness at the sight. For they could now see the city below them. Wanja could even recognise the Hilton and the Kenyatta Conference Centre dominating the city centre.

They hurried down the road and it was almost dark by the time they finally reached the first farmhouse. Karega and Munira were about to open the iron gates when a European woman came toward them, told them that there were no vacancies, hakuna kazi, and ordered them off the premises without waiting for an explanation. Karega and Munira could not help laughing as they continued down the road. 'Why did she think we would go to her house in the evening to seek employment?' Karega wondered, and he was going to say something about white people when he remembered his own struggle in the city and kept quiet.

At the next iron gate they took care to first read the signpost. Their hearts beat with hope and indecision. Rev. Jerrod Brown, Karega read again. They would have preferred an African but then a man of God under whatever skin was a soul of goodness and mercy and kindness. They sent Karega and Munira and Abdulla. Abdulla's bad leg would be evidence of their good intentions.

The driveway leading to the house had a very neatly trimmed cypress hedge on either side. Beyond the hedges spread very neatly mowed grass lawns. Here and there on the lawns stood single cypress trees whose leaves and branches had again been nicely trimmed and brought together into beautiful cones as if in perpetual supplication to heaven. A well finished application of sweat, art and craftsmanship over a number of years, so much energy and brains wasted on beautifying trees, Karega reflected. The house itself was a huge bungalow with red tiles and steep gables, so imposing.

Suddenly two dogs came rushing toward them. The volume of their combined barking was enough to make one halt and take to his heels. But a man emerged from behind a pine tree and ordered them to halt. A watchman, they thought: he had a blue uniform and a white cap on which the words *Securicor Guards* were written. Another man, with a green kanzu, a red fez on his head, and a red band to match, around his waist, emerged from the big house and joined the Securicor guardsman who was now holding the two Alsatians by their collars.

'Who are you and what do you want?' asked the man with the red band who was obviously the Bwana's cook. The Securicor guardsman was patting the fat panting animals, at the same time raising his eyes as if he would only be too glad to let them loose on the vagabonds.

'We have come from afar and we would like to see the owner of the house. We are in a little trouble.'

'You look it,' said the Securicor guardsman, 'and you may be in more trouble unless you can state your business quickly.'

'But what is it that you want?' insisted the man with the red band. 'You see, Reverend Brown is praying and after prayers he generally retires to his study to prepare a sermon or something. He is a very busy man and he hates to be disturbed.'

'We are in difficulties,' reiterated Munira. 'There are more of us at the gate. We have a sick child. We certainly do not mind waiting until the Reverend Bwana has done with prayers.'

'You can come and wait in the verandah,' he said, once again, giving each one of them a thorough look-over. And really it occurred to Karega that they must indeed be a sight to see: what without a proper bath and without a change of clothes, for so many days.

They stood in the verandah. From there Karega could just manage to see the workers' houses of mud-walls and grass thatch in two lines. And all along Abdulla was thinking: and we fought to end red fezes and red bands on our bodies. Munira was imagining his own father in fervent prayers of devotion.

Soon the Reverend came out and stood just outside the door, and they could hardly believe their eyes. Rev. Jerrod Brown was a black man. Munira's heart missed a beat. He recognised the man: he had, once or twice, seen him at his father's house. But at home he was known as Rev. Kamau. Jerrod Brown were his Christian names. He was one of the most respected men in the Anglican hierarchy: he was even considered a possible candidate for a bishopric.

'How are you?' he asked them in a squeaky voice.

'We are well,' they chorused, hopes rising.

'It is only that we are in difficulties,' continued Munira.

'We have come a long way,' explained Karega.

'We are thirsty and hungry and we have a sick child at the gate,' added Abdulla.

'Where do you come from?'

'Ilmorog,' they again chorused.

'Ilmorog! Ilmorog!' he repeated slowly, looking them up and down, from one to the other. If they had asked for work, he could have understood: but such big and obviously very fit, able-bodied men begging for food? He sighed more in pity than in anger.

'Come into the house!'

His voice was filled with pity and understanding. As a Christian he knew wherein lay his duty. And Munira, full of happiness, was thinking: maybe I should tell him who I am.

The sitting-room was very huge. The wife, a huge matron, very much like his own mother, Munira observed, sat on a sofa by the fireside knitting. She gave them a quick glance, asked them if they were well, and continued with her work. Near her, against the wall, was a glass-cased bookshelf full of gold-lettered Children's Encyclopedias and Bibles of various sizes and colours. Above the mantelpiece hung a wood-framed slogan behind a face of glass: Christ is the head of this house, the Silent Listener to every conversation at every meal. On another wall was a framed picture of King Nebuchadnezzar naked, hairy, on all fours like an animal, with words of warning printed below the picture. Otherwise on the walls mostly hung group photographs of the Reverend with various dignitaries.

Munira coughed in readiness to introduce himself, but the Reverend after fetching a Bible from the shelf had already asked them to join him in prayers. He prayed for the poor in spirit; the crippled in soul; for jobless wanderers, and all those who were hungry and thirsty because they had never eaten the bread and drunk the water from the well of Jesus. He prayed for everything and everyone under the sun and his voice touched something, a softness in their hearts.

He ended the prayer.

Munira coughed, cleared his throat to start the self-introduction. But the Reverend had already opened the Bible.

Now Peter and John were going up to the temple at the hour of prayer, at the ninth hour. And a man lame from birth was being carried, whom they laid daily at that gate of the temple which is called Beautiful to ask alms of those who entered the Temple. Seeing Peter and John about to go into the temple, he asked for alms. And Peter directed his gaze at him, with John, and said, 'Look at us.' And he fixed his attention upon them, expecting to receive something. But Peter said, I have no silver and gold, but I give you what I have: in the name of Jesus Christ of Nazareth, walk.

They sat patiently through the reading and the sermon that followed, thinking that it was only a necessary preliminary, though a rather long one: but what else would they have expected from a Church minister?

'What the Bible is talking about is not so much a physical illness as a spiritual condition. For note that the man never went inside the Temple until he was cured of his spiritual lameness. He never begged again. The Bible is then clearly against a life of idleness and begging. This is what's wrong with this country. Most of us seem to prefer a life of wandering and begging to a life of hard work and sweat. From the moment man ate the fruit of knowledge in complete disregard and defiance of God's express command and wishes, he was told by God that henceforth he was to work and sweat, that never again was he to get free things, manna provided by the Lord. Even my own children, when they come from boarding schools at Lenana, Nairobi, Kenya High School and Limuru Girls School, I make them work: cut grass and trim up the hedges and feed chicken for their pocket money. As for the child who is ill (and why indeed did you not bring him in?) I have already offered prayers for him. Go ye now in peace and trust in the Lord.'

'But Reverend Sir ...' Karega tried to say something, and could not proceed.

'We need ... we only need ...' Abdulla also tried and something blocked his throat.

Munira was so stunned he could hardly speak. Inwardly he was so glad that he had not made himself known to Rev. Jerrod. They stood up to go, but at the door Karega could not help it and turned round and quoted a passage he knew.

And when it grew late, his disciples came to him and said, This is a lonely place, and the hour is now late; send them away, to go into the country and villages round about and buy themselves something to eat. But he answered them, you give them something to eat . . . and taking their five loaves and fishes he looked up to heaven, and blessed and brake it and gave to his disciples to give the people. And they all ate and were satisfied.

'That is it my son,' said the Reverend gravely . . . 'the bread and fish of Jesus!'

Bitter and empty-handed, the recalcitrant three went back to the group waiting at the gate. They did not know how to break the news but their very faces and silence told them everything. Abdulla said: 'Let's try another house. This time we must avoid Europeans and clergymen.'

Wanja joined Karega and asked him what had happened. Karega suddenly burst out with laughter. 'Do you remember the hymn we were singing at the beginning of the journey?' He recited the words. 'They are hungry and thirsty, those who have not eaten the loaf of Jesus. Do you know the Reverend holy bastard could only offer us the food of the spirit, the bread and fish of Jesus?'

❀

They passed several houses not knowing which they should choose to enter. Most had Asian and European names, for this was one of the most fashionable farming and residential districts around the city. For Wanja the whole area brought back unpleasant memories of that experience in the city, and she did not want to venture into any. Munira abruptly stopped and his heart gave several beats. He read the name again before calling Karega. 'Raymond Chui,' Karega read, and looked up at Munira.

'I will not accompany you,' Karega told him, 'I will stay back with the others and wait for you.'

'It's all right, it's all right,' said Munira happily. 'Don't you know, he was a classmate . . . a great player . . . oh, my friend . . . you know . . . you and I have a lot to talk about . . . we were expelled from Siriana together . . . a comrade-in-protest, you know.'

He went alone. There many cars in the compound. Through the window Muniar could see several ladies in long dresses holding glasses, talking in high animated voices. A group started singing a few native cultural songs. They were female voices.

Waru wa ngirigaca
Red potatoes.

Uthigagirwko ku?
    At whose place are they peeled?

Uthigagirwo kwa Ngina
    They are peeled at Ngina's place.

Twetereire oe Kihinguro
    We waiting for her to pick the key.

Ciana citu ciaragie Githungu
    Our children speak English.

Harambee! Tuoe Madaraka
    Harambee! We take up high offices.

The men took over and sang the juicy sections of songs normally sung at circumcision.

Ngwirwo ni utuku
    They say it's dark.

Ngwirwo ni utuku
    They say it's dark.

Ngionaga Irima
    But I can still see.

Cia Tumutumu
    Tumu Tumu hills.

Hui, Wainaga
    Oh yes, Wainaga.

Njuguma nduku
    A big club.

Njuguma nduku
    A big club.

Ya gukura k—ru kabucu
    For pulling out a jaw of cunt.

Hui, Wainaga
    Oh yes, Wainaga.

K—na igoto
    Cunt with banana leaves.

K—na igoto
    Cunt with banana leaves.

Githi k—ni unyuaga mbaki
    So cunt! you take snuff.

Hui, Wainaga
    Oh yes, Wainaga.

And they would burst out laughing and clapping at the daring of their voices. There were also a few Swahili and English ones. It was a truly culturally integrated party and Munira lost courage. He merely stood at the door, eaten by indecision, for now he was suddenly conscious of his stinking body, his uncombed hair, his creased, muddy, dirty clothes. At the same time he was thinking about the social gathering of so many top representatives of the various communities: but only the other day, hardly six months ago, ordinary working people were being given an oath to protect: what? The singing voices?

The door was opened from the inside and Munira stood floodlit, face to face with a red-lipsticked lady with a huge Afro-wig and bracelets and bangles all over her neck and hands. He had no time to see the rest. For the lady, at first flabbergasted by the apparition, now found her voice and screamed, a loud blood-curdling scream, before she fainted on the floor. For a second he was chilled to the ground. He heard the scuffling of feet and the sound of broken glass. Chui and his friends were coming to the lady's rescue, some voice told him, and he might be manhandled before he could explain. Courage completely deserted him. He would not, he dared not wait for the consequences. He slipped into the shadows and ran as fast as he could make his legs carry him. He jumped over the outer hedge; Munira could never tell how or where he got the strength. He joined the others and urged them to move, to hurry on down the road. Behind them, they heard a gunshot in the sky and all knew without being told that Munira was involved in yet another disaster.

'Let us go straight to the city,' Munira suggested. 'There's no point in entering any of these houses, they are all the same.' Abdulla agreed: 'It is getting late anyway.'

But Joseph's fever worsened and his groans and sighs were now audible to all. They crowded around him. He was now talking to himself, recalling scenes and things in his own past that only Abdulla seemed to understand. He would cry and laugh and shout and complain. 'It's mine ... it's mine ... that ... that ... bone ... I'm hungry ... truth of God, I didn't eat anything last night ... Don't beat me ... please don't beat me.' He stopped. He was now obviously talking to somebody answering questions about himself. 'I'll sleep in a ndebe tonight ... sometimes I sleep in wrecked abandoned cars ... Yes, yes ... in a bush too.' He gasped for breath and once or twice he called out to his mother for help. But she was not there. Wanja could not bear it. The groans ate straight into her unfulfilled motherhood. It was she who suggested that she enter the very next house. Nyakinyua offered to accompany her, but the others protested in case of another disaster that might involve a hasty exit. Karega and Abdulla offered to go with her, but it was suggested that it was better for Abdulla to stay by Joseph's side. But Njuguna was now urged to join them, for as an elder he would be good evidence that they were not ill-intentioned. Munira had not sufficiently recovered from his three previous shocks and he decided to stay behind and await the outcome of Wanja's last mission.

But the mission met misfortune even before it got anywhere near the first building. Several men noiselessly surrounded them on all sides, grabbing their arms and tying them together behind. Karega protested but the men who arrested them did not even bother to answer. They just shone torches onto their faces. 'They even have a woman among them,' one said, and pushed them forward. They were taken to a room in the big house and locked up in darkness. The whole thing was so mysterious they felt as if they were in a foreign territory. And indeed that was what Njuguna was thinking: I was happy in Ilmorog. Aloud he said: 'What does this mean? How dare they arrest an old man, their own father? Is this what has happened to our children, is this what they turned into after leaving Ilmorog?'

Before either Karega or Wanja could answer him or say anything in commiseration, the lights were suddenly put on. For a second their eyes were blinded by the light, but after blinking they looked around and could see no one apart from their own shamed faces. A few minutes of silence elapsed. They heard somebody try the handle of the door. They looked at it expectantly. The door opened and a gentleman in a dark suit and a flowered tie stood before them.

Wanja's eyes and his met and for a few seconds they surveyed one another in silence. Karega and Njuguna did not notice the little drama. The gentleman now looked at Njuguna and Karega before again turning to Wanja who was now staring ahead of her as if looking past the man, past the door, to a distant place, another location.

'I am sorry I had to invite you to my home in this manner,' he said with contrived politeness. 'But as you may perhaps understand there has been an increase in incidents of robbery and violence in these parts. One must take the necessary precautions. Prevention is better than cure. Do you know even the Masai Moran occasionally wake up loyal peaceful citizens as they come to claim *their* cows? No, we all have to be careful and no harm is intended. Now, what can I do for you?'

'How dare you treat an old man like this? Is this how you would treat your father, a man with grey hairs?' Njuguna protested.

'My father, were he alive, would know better than to disturb people's peace on such a night. Anyway, you should thank your grey hairs and this lady that you were not shot.'

Karega explained the situation as best as he could. He even mentioned the purpose of their visit to the city.

'The Hon. member for Ilmorog? Mr Nderi wa Riera? I know him. A friend of mine. You see how things change, old man, and hence don't you speak ill of anyone. You never know where we shall meet tomorrow. Now, Mr Nderi wa Riera. We used to have our little differences. He was what you might call a, eh, a freedom fighter, that is, he was a member of the party and was taken to detention. And I was, well, shall we say we didn't see eye to eye? Now, we are friends. Why? Because we all realise that whether we were on that side of the fence or this side of the fence or merely sitting astride the fence, we were all fighting for the same ends. Not so? We were all freedom fighters. Anyway, Mr Nderi and I, we are quite good friends. We have one or two businesses together. Did you people go to tea? I'll tell you something. Some of it was held here. We are all members of KCO. Some of us have even been able to borrow a little – shall we say thousands – from the money collected from this tea ceremony. I am a life member of KCO. So is Nderi. I'm telling you this to show you that Nderi is no stranger to me. But he has not told me of a drought, let alone a famine, in Ilmorog! I am sure he would have organised a Harambee there – you know, self-help – he has many friends – and they all would have contributed something. Charity begins at home, ha! ha! ha!'

'Can't you show some charity and have these ropes cut?' Njuguna interrupted his laughter. Karega was surprised at the man's love of talk. It was as if he was striving to impress them. But why should he want to show off in front of them, prisoners? Why?

'A spirited old man. I will send somebody.' And without another word he left the room.

Karega looked at both Wanja and Njuguna. They had been turned into statues. He crept to the door and tried it with his foot. It was so strange, a scene in a melodramatic film or a novel, a thriller. The door was locked, and the experience was not particularly thrilling.

After a few minutes the man who had locked them in came. His face seemed mellower, he looked as if he was going to say something to them all and then changed his mind. He cut off the ropes and said the gentleman wanted to see the lady. Karega moved as if to accompany her. But the man said: only the lady.

Wanja, woken from her statuesque posture, bit her lower lip and followed him out, with a heart that trembled and a mind that tried to arrive at a decision. They went through so many corridors: a huge mansion, it was. She was shown into the man's room, which looked like an office.

He stood up at her entrance, shut the door behind her. He showed her a seat but she refused to take it.

'Do you mind if I sit down? At long last, Wanja, at long last,' he said, in a tone halfway between a question and a statement.

'Why are you doing this? To us, to an old man, to a child who is desperately ill?'

'Do you think I believed your little story, Wanja? I sent two of my men to the gate to bring the others in. For your sake, I was willing to help them all. But they were not there.'

'It is not true. You are lying. They are there and with a donkey-cart.'

'I don't want your little lies, Wanja. Maybe you thought this was somebody else's house. Maybe you were coming to visit a friend. Because I could see you were rather surprised to see me. Tell me — but why won't you sit down? I will not bite you. I will not harm you — tell me, why did you run away from me?'

'Can't we talk of something else? You ruined my life once. Is that not enough?'

'How? It was you who ran way. I only teased you about your being pregnant. I just wanted to test you and see if you were telling the truth. Tell me, what happened to the child? Where is he? Was he a boy or a girl? You see, I married a woman who has been bearing only female rabbits.'

She looked at him and there was cruelty in her eyes. There was cruelty in her heart. One day you'll pay for this, she said inside her, one day you'll pay for this. Aloud she only pleaded:

'Why don't you let me, us, go in peace? What harm have we done to you? We were only seeking for a little help because a child was ill.'

He stood up and walked to where she stood. She moved to one side. The man never seemed to grow old, Wanja thought, and hated herself for thinking even that much about him. He moved nearer her, she moved further back. She tripped over the sofa. He pressed a button and the sofa settee spread into a bed.

'Kimeria! If you come near me, I shall scream, and your wife will hear,' she warned him, eyeing something like a knife on the desk.

He stopped. She sat up and moved to the far end of the bed. He stood and rested his eyes on her. Then he suddenly knelt on one knee, edging toward her as he spoke.

'My wife is not here tonight, but that is not the point. You are a witch, do you know that? My witch. Will you, will you come back to me? I can give you a nice little flat in the city centre. Muindi Mbingu Street. Or in Haile Selassie Avenue. Anywhere you choose. I shall pay the rent. You need not do anything. Just paint your nails or something. Or wait. You can join a Secretarial College. There are so many in the city. You need only know how to bang! bang! the typewriter. Then I can find you a job. I know a few people. Kenya is a black man's country, you know. What are you really doing with these funny-looking fellows? What are you doing in Ilmorog? I love you, Wanja. The years, the hardships, seem not to have impaired your beauty.'

He sat beside her and placed one arm tentatively around her.

'Stop that, Kimeria,' she said and pushed him away with all her might, at the same time feeling a kind of weakness through her intense hatred. 'Why can't you leave me alone? How can't you – but you were always like that – without feelings – you only cared about your thing. And the power of instant conquest.'

Then suddenly she sprung up and grabbed the knife. Then he looked at her, malice on his frowning face. His voice was now gritty, hard, cruel.

'Is that all you can say and do? When I have offered you everything? Listen to me, then. You will not leave this place until I say so. I could lift that telephone and have you all arrested and charged with the offence of trespassing in Blue Hills. You could be remanded in custody for over six months. All we need, for the sake of a semblance of justice, is to keep on making you appear in court for mention. We are law-abiding citizens. No woman ever treated me the way you did. Running and hiding from me. Am I a monster? And you dare lift a knife at me? Now that fate has brought you to my house, I shall not let you go until you have lain, legs spread, on that bed. Remember you are no longer a virgin. Think about it. The choice is yours to make, and freedom is mine to withhold or to give. Go.'

He rang a bell and she was taken back to the others. She went to a corner and just sat facing the wall, unable to talk or even cry. Karega and Njuguna asked her what the man had wanted. She simply shrugged her shoulders.

The door opened and Njuguna was called outside by one of the many hands about the house. Outside Njuguna listened to the message from the chief: Wanja was a former wife of the gentleman. She had run away to Ilmorog and now she was refusing the man's bed. Njuguna came back looking reproachfully at Wanja.

Njuguna explained the situation as tactfully as he could, presenting them with the harsh prospects before them.

155

'No!' Karega shouted as soon as he got the gist of the man's demands.

'Will a child die ... will Joseph die just because ... because ... Besides she is ... in a way the man's wife,' insisted Njuguna.

'But she does not know the man! She has, we all have, met him tonight for the first time!' Karega protested incredulously.

'Let her deny it,' said Njuguna with a tone of triumphant finality.

'Is it true? Wanja, is it true?' Karega asked, and waited for her to answer.

But she sat in the same position as if she had not heard his question. What pained her was not so much the man's lies, not so much Njuguna's attitude, not even Karega's question, but what Njuguna had said about Joseph dying. She would be responsible for a death of another who did not even belong to her. She looked back to the origin of the journey. Maybe she was to blame. If she had not suggested, indeed insisted on their coming into this place when others had opted for a continuation of the journey ... if she had not slipped in her youth ... If ... if ... so many ifs and they all weighed heavily on her. What was she to do? Give in to a man she hated, and hardly six months since she had vowed to herself? If she didn't ... and Joseph died ... and Nyakinyua and the others ... in the cold ... hungry .. thirsty ... the drought in Ilmorog ... failed mission ... no rescue ... more deaths .. what shall I do? What shall I do? Face another humiliation? She wished she had told Karega the whole truth about her past ... then he might have helped her solve her dilemma ... she raised her head and looked Karega full in the eyes.

'Yes! yes!' she whispered and stood up, reaching for the door.

For a second, Karega sat completely still, immobile, and gazed at the same spot: what did one believe? What really could one believe now? He stirred himself. He stood up and saw himself walk toward her and hold her by the hand just as she was about to open the door. She felt one thrilling shivering in the flesh, and raised her eyes to him in weakness and appeal, and then turned her eyes away, aside, waiting for judgment from him. Anything, anything but this dilemma which was also her shame.

'I do not know anything,' he said, a little put out by the pregnant silence in the room, 'but ... but ... must you go?' he ended rather pathetically.

She looked at him again, briefly, saw the dancing intensity in his eyes, and almost hated him for his youth and his innocence. She was in that second conscious of the moral gulf of knowledge and experience between them and she steeled herself against crying. A bit impatiently, irritably in fact, she disengaged her hand, opened the door and walked out, banging the door so hard behind her that it left a tremor in the room and inside her. He must die, a voice thudded within, he must die. It was simple. It was bitterly sweet. It restored her calm and peace.

Behind, in the room, Karega, who suddenly diminished further into his corner, groaned once. He should die, he said as if answering a question somebody had asked. If I had a light I would burn up the whole place, he said. Njuguna, startled by the unexpected groan and more by the utterance, looked at him, saw him huddled together in a statuesque position, and then looked at the wall. Youth, youth, Njuguna muttered to himself. Now eerie silence and ill-foreboding gloom surrounded them both.

4 🏵 Finally on Monday morning the delegation reached the city. They joked and laughed at their new anxieties and constant amazement at everything: the streets, the buildings so tall, the heavy traffic and even the various dresses worn by men and women in the city. Crossing the streets was their most major undertaking. Once or twice, as they ran full speed across the streets, two or three cars screeched to a sudden stop with the drivers swearing: who are these Masai? These Dorobo and their donkey-carts should be banned from the city! But they were glad that after so much hardship they had arrived in the famous city. There is no night so long that it will not give way to the light of day.

The offices of the Hon. Nderi wa Riera, MP for Ilmorog and Southern Ruwa-ini, were situated in the second floor of Iqbal Iqlood Buildings in the then Market Street within a walking distance of Camay Restaurant and Jeevanjee Gardens. The main delegation waited in the gardens while Karega and Munira went to the offices to see if their honourable member would receive the delegation.

The secretary, a heavily lipsticked and wigged lady, whom they found manicuring her nails, looked the two men up and down, and then froze their expectant hearts: the MP was not in, he had gone to Mombasa and was expected back any day. She saw the sudden drop of their faces and the dullness in their eyes and for some reason she felt pity: would they try the afternoon of the following day? With despondent faces and hearts, Karega and Munira went back to the others: where would they sleep tonight? Why, oh why had they not thought of such a possibility? But what would they have done even if they had known it?

Karega and Munira found the others in another crisis: Abdulla's donkey and cart had been detained by the police, for holding up the traffic and shitting in one of the streets and in Jeevanjee Gardens.

But Abdulla explained the circumstances of their journey. The police said they would hold the donkey until the group was ready to leave.

Karega was not particularly religious: but even he felt a devil had been trailing them and their mission. They had endured lashes of hunger and thirst and the cruelty of their fellow men. Now fortune had decided to strike at the already fallen. People looked up at him, the author of the journey, expecting him to solve the riddle. But what can I do, he asked himself bitterly, unable to tell them the most obvious truth: that they would have to stay and spend the night in Jeevanjee Gardens.

It was Wanja who again rescued them.

Sitting alone, as if set apart from the others, she nevertheless saw the agony on Karega's face and a thought, not unconnected with the soul-searching turbulence and turmoil in her heart, came to her.

'Listen, Karega. I told you about a man, a lawyer, in this city. He is ... he is ... somewhat different from most people.'

Karega gratefully clutched at the straw without any questions.

The two went across the Gardens to an Indian restaurant near Khoja Mosque. At any other time Karega would have liked to look at the building and try to imagine at which corner Ole Masai had once so dramatically held up the two colonial policemen. But now the same question was in their minds: suppose the lawyer too was not in? Wanja dialled the number: his voice was to her like yet another hand reaching out to her after a night of terror and now she felt she would cry. She tried to explain her problem but he cut her short: why didn't she go to his office instead? He gave her the directions and told her the bus she should take.

Karega had never been to a lawyer's place, and as the bus took them along Mboya Street, Ngala Street, River Road, Kariokor, and then Pumwani, he kept on picturing awe-inspiring corridors of gruff power and privilege. But they ended by going into a rundown part of the city with endless lines of cardboard and tin roofs. A long queue of clients waited outside the tiny room of an office. He received them cordially and did not show any surprise at seeing Wanja again.

'Aah, the young lady,' was all he said, and told them to sit on the bench. Karega expected to see an old man with heavy-rimmed glasses or something and grey hairs with striped trousers, a waistcoat, a hat, and an umbrella by his side. But he saw a man, maybe in his forties, but with a white short-sleeved shirt and a simple tie, looking too young to be a lawyer and to have that crowd waiting to see him. On a closer look, Karega noticed that his face had a touch of weariness, and his eyes were restless as if troubled by an inner light, an inner consciousness, weighed down, it seemed, by a burden of abundant knowledge.

'You did not go home,' he said, but there was no blame in the tone of his voice, there was no accusation, it was as if he genuinely wanted to know.

'No . . . I could not,' she answered in a whisper.

'And how can I help you?' he asked, including Karega in the conversation with a glance. Again he had a way of seeming interested, receptive, and he made it easy for someone to talk, as if what he said could never be used against him in censure, blame or ridicule, or in any adverse judgment. So Karega told him about the drought in Ilmorog, the decision to send a delegation to the city, and the journey, up to their present predicament. He omitted a description of the actual hardships. All they now wanted was a place in which they could stay for the night while they waited for an audience with their Member of Parliament. The lawyer's face clouded a little: he tapped the table twice with his fingers and said:

'As you can see, I have these people waiting outside. Most of them come from the villages: they need advice on everything, from their lands threatened by banks to how they can acquire this or that kiosk . . . or about money taken from them by a big fellow after promising to buy them a farm in the Highlands . . . all that! Can you remember my place?'

'Yes . . . if you tell me the bus to take or the road to follow.'

'You take them there. There's a garden at the back of the house. In any case there is no other house behind mine. I will see you later.'

Karega felt tremendous relief. He would not now have to sit out a night of reproachful eyes. But what a strange man . . . so there are such people left in this country, he thought, feeling grateful to Wanja.

In the bus he tried to say this to Wanja, then he changed his mind and simply looked out at the slums, the naked children playing in the narrow streets, and he wondered: who was better off, the peasant in a forgotten village or the city dweller thrown onto these rubbish heaps they called locations?

Wanja noticed his hesitation and it pained her, it touched her barely healed wounds, but she tried to understand. He would always judge her in the light of the ordeal at the house. How could she have known that fate would bring her face to face with a past from which she was running? Suddenly she felt hatred well up inside her: she hated his innocence: she hated the moral weight he made her carry even in his very silence. So what if she had given in, she hissed inside to prevent tears, so what? Had she not suffered enough for them? She had not even wanted to come on this journey!

The lawyer's place in Nairobi West was one of those areas formerly and exclusively reserved for Indians. The house had a wide cobblestoned front yard enclosed by stone walls and a small garden, again enclosed by stone walls, at the back. Some sat in the front yard, others in the garden. It was good that Abdulla's roots and eucalyptus leaves had worked: the roots and the leaves had been boiled and Joseph had been covered with a blanket until he had sweated out the illness. Now he was playing with the other boys. They were happy to be in Nairobi. Wanja had mixed feelings and attitudes to this place: a reminder of salvation and shame. Then she remembered her latest moment of shame and humiliation only two nights back when after ten minutes or so she had joined Karega and Njuguna. Karega, Njuguna and Wanja had walked to the gate in silence and to their dismay found that the others had gone. But a man suddenly emerged from the darkness and told them to follow him. It was then that the mystery was solved:

It was true that the owner of the house had sent the two men to the gate to check on Wanja and Karega's story. The two, after listening to the people's wretched story, had put their heads together. They knew how cruel their boss, whom they only knew as Mr Hawkins, could be: he had once locked up a man who had called to simply ask directions for a whole week with only water for food. They decided not to disclose these people's presence. One had led them to the workers' quarters: the other had returned to tell a lie. And that was where they had all spent the Sunday and the Sunday night to resume their journey that morning. And throughout the Sunday and the night Karega and Wanja had somehow avoided each other. Even Njuguna was withdrawn and sad.

Karega too was thinking about the experience of the two nights before and the mystery of Wanja's past. What was the true connection between her and that Mr Hawkins? He dismissed the thought. Everybody had his own secret past. He looked at Abdulla who sat and leaned against the wall. He had withdrawn into a shell, into a seemingly impenetrable world of gloom and silence. To Karega it was painful: the change from the godlike hunter in the plains, the master of guns and knives and herbs and elements of the weather, so confident in his knowledge of and intimacy with a heroic past, to this old man shrinking into himself. Then Karega remembered that the donkey was under police care and he understood. He saw Wanja slip out of the house and he followed her into the street. He alone understood how much they owed to her. He caught up with her.

They walked together in silence along a narrow tarmac road at the back of the house.

'Go away, go away from me,' she suddenly said, almost savagely. But he did not. They walked on, along Muhoho Road, through Gadhi Avenue, to Langata Road, toward Langata Barracks. She stopped by a fence and looked to the plains of Nairobi Park. He also stood beside her and looked at the Ngong Hills in the distance silhouetted against a misty sky. Then they saw a small aeroplane fly low, low ... 'It's going to fall, it's going to fall,' Wanja said. They saw another and yet another and Karega remembered that they were near Wilson Airport. It was the place where tourists came to hire private planes for a quick venture into the interior to see the wild game parks and return to the city before dark.

'I wanted, I wanted to thank you for all you have done,' he said, confused, hoping she would not mistake the meaning.

'I am sorry about my outburst. I feel so ashamed ...'

He thought for a while.

'No,' he said ... 'it was not you alone ... It was a collective humiliation ...' He did not know how to proceed, so he tried to make it general. 'Whenever any of us is degraded and humiliated, even the smallest child, we are all humiliated and degraded because it has got to do with human beings.'

The lawyer came home after six bringing them welcome packets of Jogoo flour and milk and cabbages. He invited them into the sitting-room, a huge oblong space. Nyakinyua exclaimed that a hut could easily fit into it: what waste! and they all laughed. Some of the children were still playing outside and watching aeroplanes fly toward Embakasi. But a few sat with the grown-ups. The walls were decorated with the pictures of Che Guevara with his Christlike locks of hair and saintly eyes; of Dedan Kimathi, sitting calmly and arrogantly defiant; and a painting by Mugalula of a beggar in a street. At one corner was a wood sculpture of a freedom fighter by Wanjau. Abdulla stood a few seconds in front of Kimathi's picture and then he abruptly hobbled across the room and out into the garden. The others surrounded the sculpture and commented on the fighter's hair, the heavy lips and tongue in open laughter, and the sword around the waist. But why did he possess breasts, somebody asked: it was as if it was a man and a woman in one: how could that be?

They started arguing about it until Nyakinyua almost silenced them with her simple logic.

'A man cannot have a child without a woman. A woman cannot bear a child without a man. And was it not a man and a woman who fought to redeem this country?'

'But a man is more important than a woman,' Njuguna said. 'Is it not a man who sleeps, hmmm! hmmm! You know where?'

'Where is the wife of the house?' Nyakinyua asked the lawyer, to change the conversation.

'She has gone to another country for some months to train as a midwife. But I am going to write to her and tell her that she had better hurry back now that I have suddenly got myself another wife and all these children.' He looked with conspiratorial eyes to the kitchen where Wanja was making ugali and vegetable soup.

They all laughed and an argument ensued about polygamy.

'It was not just anybody who could marry more than one wife. You had to pay goats, and goats were wealth in those days. Often only the big houses could do this,' Nyakinyua explained.

He looks so different away from the office, Karega was thinking. The weariness seemed to have gone. Karega wanted to ask him questions but somehow could not find an opening.

After the meal, the lawyer took Karega and Munira into his library where they were soon joined by Wanja and Abdulla. There were many books – heaps on heaps – and he was fingering each with obvious care and love. Munira was ashamed of his almost empty shelves. They sat down on the floor and the lawyer suddenly started questioning them very closely about Ilmorog, its history, their MP, the conditions, and what they had hoped to achieve by this visit. Karega tried to explain and in the process became acutely aware of the vagueness behind the whole venture. He noticed too that the weariness had come back to the man's face and a sadness crept into his voice as he now said:

'I suppose he will receive you. Why, he might even organise a Harambee meeting to buy peace for an uneasy conscience. A little charity ...'

'We do not mind a little charity,' explained Munira, 'except that we have hardly met any in this city.' He told of his experiences at the priest's house and at Chui's place. 'What I could not understand was their obvious competition to say the most shocking words. In the old days, I am told, the songs and the words and everything were in their place – singers talked to one another, abused one another, even, but there was dignity in the whole thing. When I was young I used to hide from home to attend circumcision festivals.'

He stopped and wondered: maybe one or all his other brothers were there, while his father sat at home singing their praises. Karega and Wanja were each thinking of the ordeal in the house. But they didn't say much about it. The lawyer started talking. It was as if he was holding a dialogue with an inner self and they were only spectators at this naked wrestling with his own doubts and fears. 'It is sad, it hurts, at times I am angry, looking at the black zombies, black animated cartoons dancing the master's dance to the master's voice. That they will do to perfection. But when they are tired of that, or shall I say, when we are tired of that we turn to our people's culture and abuse it ... just for fun, after a bottle of champagne. But I ask myself: what other fruit do I expect that what we sowed would produce? All the same I look back on the wasted chances, on the missed opportunities: on the hour, the day, the period, when, at the crossroads, we took the wrong turning. Aaah, that was a time to remember, when the whole world, motivated by different reasons and expectations, waited, saying: they who showed Africa and the world the path of manliness and of black redemption, what are they going to do with the beast? They who washed the warriors' spears in the blood of the white profiteers, of all those who had enslaved them to the ministry of the molten beast of silver and gold, what dance are they now going to dance in the arena? We could have done anything, then, because our people were behind us. But we, the leaders, chose to flirt with the molten god, a blind, deaf monster who has plagued us for hundreds of years. We reasoned: what's wrong is the skin-colour of the people who ministered to this god: under our own care and tutelage we shall tame the monster-god and make it do our will. We forgot that it has always been deaf and blind to human woes. So we go on building the monster and it grows and waits for more, and now we are all slaves to it. At its shrine we kneel and pray and hope. Now see the outcome ... dwellers in Blue Hills, those who have taken on themselves the priesthood of the ministry to the blind god ... a thousand acres of land ... a million acres in the two hands of a priest, while the congregation moans for an acre! and they are told: it is only a collection from your sweat ... let us be honest slaves to the monster-god, let us give him our souls ... and the ten per cent that goes with it ... for his priests must eat too ... and we shall take it to his vassal, the bank ... meanwhile let's all pray and the god may notice our honesty and fervour, and we shall get a few crumbs. Meanwhile, the god grows big and fat and shines even brighter and whets the appetites of his priests, for the monster has, through the priesthood, decreed only one ethical code: Greed and accumulation. I ask myself: is it fair, is it fair for our children?

'I am a lawyer ... what does this mean? I also earn my living by ministering to the monster. I am an expert in those laws meant to protect the sanctity of the monster-god and his angels and the whole hierarchy of the priesthood. Only I have chosen to defend those who have broken the laws and who might be excommunicated. For remember, only a few, the chosen few, can find favourable positions in the hierarchy. And mark you, and this is where it pains, it's their sweat and that feeds the catechists, the wardens, the deacons, the ministers, the bishops, the angels ... the whole hierarchy. Still they are condemned ... damned.

'I am a priest, a father-confessor, and looking through the tiny window, I am really looking at the soul of a nation ... the scars, the wounds, the clotting blood ... it is all on their faces and in their eyes, so bewildered. Tell us, tell us before we confess our sins: who makes these laws? For whom? To help whom? I cannot answer the questions ... but as I said, they open a window for me to see the world.

'I ask myself: what happened? What happened? I take all these books ... I read, trying to find wisdom and the key to the many questions. Our people had said: Let's not be slaves to the monster: let us only pray and wrestle with the true god within us. We want to control all this land, all these industries, to serve the one god within us. They fought ... shed blood, not that a few might live in Blue Hills and minister to the molten god, the god outside us, but that many might live fully wherever they live. The white ministers, seeing defeat, now turned to sneering and jeering at the new priests. Look at these destroyers: we are going, yes, but these people will surely destroy all the canon laws ... and we, who were educated in their schools, beat our breasts: we destroyers? We break the canon law? We are as civilised as you, we shall not be the ones to dismantle the monster god, and we shall prove it to you. You'll be ashamed that you once had all these doubts about us.

'It's an old story. You say that you were in Siriana with Chui. I was also there, but much later, years later. We used to hear of Chui ... but he was then described as a destroyer. My ambition was to become a priest: a highly educated priest. So I hated Chui. The very name brought images of the night-prowlers of the jungle ... Then Peter Pooles shot dead an African who had thrown a stone at his dogs. The trial raised a lot of interest in Siriana. We were all happy when he was condemned to death. But do you know? Fraudsham called a school assembly. He argued about the need to be sensitive to animals. The measure of a civilisation was how far a people had learnt to care for animals. Did we want to be merciless like those Russians who, in the face of world protest, sent a dog, poor Laika, into space to die? Pooles had been a little excessive, maybe. But he had been prompted by the highest and most noble impulse; to care for and defend the defenceless. And he read us a letter he had sent to the

Governor appealing for clemency, ending with a very moving quotation from Shakespeare.

> The quality of mercy is not strain'd;
> It droppeth as the gentle rain from heaven
> Upon the place beneath: it is twice bless'd;
> It blesseth him that gives and him that takes.

We left the assembly with guilty, downcast eyes. A few of us wept. Can you believe it? We wept with Fraudsham. But still there were doubts, and I did not understand the whole thing. How could I? The education we got had not prepared me to understand those things: it was meant to obscure racism and other forms of oppression. It was meant to make us accept our inferiority so as to accept their superiority and their rule over us. Then I went to America. I had read in a history book that it was a place where they believed in the equality and freedom of man. While I was at a black college in Baton Rouge, Louisiana, I saw with my own eyes a black man hanging from a tree outside a church. His crime? He had earlier fought a white man who had manhandled his sister. There was so much tension in that town. Aa! America, land of the Free and the Brave!'

He stopped and it seemed as if his eyes were fixed on a distant past. Then he started humming a blues song by Josh White:

> Southern trees
> Bear strange fruits
> Blood around the leaves
> And blood at the roots
> Black body swaying
> In a Southern breeze
> Strange fruit
> Hanging from poplar trees.

He again stopped ... Although they did not understand all the allusions, they caught the feeling behind it. He continued:

'Is this not what has been happening in Kenya since 1896? So I said to myself: a black man is not safe at home; a black man is not safe abroad. What then is the meaning of it all? Then I saw in the cities of America white people also begging ... I saw white women selling their bodies for a few dollars. In America vice is a selling commodity. I worked alongside white and black workers in a Detroit factory. We worked overtime to make a meagre living. I saw a lot of unemployment in Chicago and other cities. I was confused. So I said: let me return to my home, now that the black man has come to power. And suddenly as in a flash of lightning I saw that we were serving the same monster-god as they were in America . . . I saw the same signs, the same symptoms, and even the sickness . . . and I was so frightened . . . I was so frightened . . . I cried to myself: how many Kimathis must die, how many motherless children must weep, how long shall our people continue to sweat so that a few, a given few, might keep a thousand dollars in the bank of the one monster-god that for four hundred years had ravished a continent? And now I saw in the clear light of day the role that the Fraudshams of the colonial world played to create all of us black zombies dancing pornography in Blue Hills while our people are dying of hunger, while our people cannot afford decent shelter and decent schools for their children. And we are happy, we are happy that we are called stable and civilised and intelligent!'

He had spoken in a level tone except at the end when he spat out the words stability, civilisation, and intelligence with obvious disgust. They were all captivated by the parable, although they did not always understand it. But each caught different aspects of it. For Abdulla it was the idea of a blood that was shed because the question had always troubled him, looking at the lands in Tigoni and other places: is it right that that which had been bought by the collective blood of a people should go to a few hands just because they had money and bank loans? Was it banks and money that had fought for it? But he had never found an answer because it was true that black hands were owning it. And he would have liked to own one of those farms himself. For Wanja it was the idea of white prostitutes in a white country: could this really be true? Munira was bored with the image of the monster, but he was directly hit by the coincidence: the lawyer had been to Siriana? And Karega had been to Siriana, and the two had now come into his house! What was the meaning? What was it? Karega felt that the man was not telling all. But the talk had aroused in him a curiosity, an excitement, as if his mind was about to reach, grasp, grapple with, an elusive idea, as if indeed a coherent structure of outlook was forming in the bewildered universe and chaos of his own experience and history.

'What really happened to you in Siriana, Karega?' Munira suddenly burst into their different thoughts and they were startled by the violence of his concern.

'Were you also educated at Siriana?' asked the lawyer, surprised, turning to Karega.

'Yes,' Karega said. It now occurred to him that he might have been unfair to Munira: the three had seen different Sirianas and different Fraudshams and maybe they were not moved by the same things: why should he have expected Munira to keep up with every happening at Siriana?

'When was this?'

'I left there ... I was expelled ... about a year and half back ... about two years ... almost three years. Time flies.'

'Because of the strike? Were you involved?' The lawyer was excited. Karega felt his heart quicken at the sympathetic curiosity of one who at least had heard about the strike.

'I suppose you can say ...'

'It was a – how shall I – it was –' the lawyer interrupted and fumbled for words. 'You see, when I came back from America and saw that we were really worshipping the same monster, I was very depressed. Where did one begin, I asked myself? So I started my practice in the poor areas of the city. I would charge a small fee: but was I not also making money out of them? And was my training and my job, the fact that I practised, not in itself a justification for those very laws in the service of the monster – was I not, in a sense, making a living out of the very system that I abhorred? Then came that strike in Siriana and, reading between the lines, I thought I saw a new youth emerging, a youth freed from the direct shame and humiliation of the past and hence not so spiritually wounded as those who had gone before. So different from our time; so different shall I say, from those who had seen their strong fathers and elder brothers fold a kofia behind them in the presence of a white boy. I said to myself: here is our hope ... in the new children, who have nothing to prove to the white man ... who do not find it necessary to prove that they can eat with knife and fork; that they can speak English through the nose; that they can serve the monster as efficiently as the white ministers; and therefore can see the collective humiliation clearly and hence are ready to strike out for the true kingdom of the black god within us all: Mugikuyu, Mmasai, Mjaluo, Mgiriama, Msomali, Mkamba, Kalenjin, Masai, Luhya, all of us ... the total energy, the spirit of the people, the collective we, working for us ... sisi kwa sisi ... Maybe I read too much into it, but it lifted me from my depression. I saw a glimmer that could be a light, and I said: Fraudsham, and all the black Fraudshams, you have had it.'

His every mood seemed to carry them with him and Karega succumbed to that encouragement.

'There were actually two strikes, but most people know about the first one because it involved a European, I suppose. The second was equally serious and we were angry that it was so little publicised. But they were two in one, because the dominating figures in both were Cambridge Fraudsham and Chui Rimui – and I am not,' he turned to Munira, 'referring to that early one in which you and Chui were the actors.'

'Were you, Mr Munira, also expelled?' asked the lawyer.

'Yes,' said Munira.

'How strange . . . when?'

'During the first strike . . . the Chui strike.'

'With Chui? There was a man . . . a legend . . . we talked about him . . . told stories about him. It was because he had gone to America that we all wanted to go there. Fraudsham did not like America . . . said Americans spoke bad English . . . But because Chui had chosen America . . . it had to be good . . .' The lawyer shook his head at his reminiscences.

'He had promise,' Munira agreed and turned to Karega.

Karega coughed, cleared his throat and started:

❀

'Well, as you know Cambridge Fraudsham was great in his own way: he could unsettle a face, however calm and sure. Whenever he went to the city to see the men in the Ministry, the other teachers would lounge about the yard, slow measured strides, or they would perch on the table cross-legged, smoke, talk, joke and laugh with us boys. But let them spy Fraudsham or his VW from a distance: they would tense up, quickly put out their cigarettes and throw the stubs out of the window or grind them to a pulp on the floor. But these people were white; how could Fraudsham make them piss into their calves? How could he so put the fear of the Lord into them? We would talk about this, lying on our Vono-beds in the dormitories: we would puzzle it out as we scrubbed the floor in the morning. We would discuss with heated voices the inner mettle of whiteness as we cold-showered our bodies at five in the morning. "Fraudsham is tough"; we all agreed. He would have been made a governor or something bigger than a headmaster, but he had refused, or so some knowing boys claimed. This increased our awe of the man. You should have heard us unravel the mystery around his life. We spun yarns and legends involving his life and love, though how anyone knew them was itself a bigger mystery. But he was the cleverest man of his time at Cambridge, this we knew, and even how he used to correct the other lecturers. He was among the bravest, and he had fought in Turkey and Palestine and Burma and had held up a German tank all by himself: for this he had received a medal or something from the King. In Burma a shrapnel shell caught him in the thigh and he was given leave. What was he thinking as he went back home alive and a hero? We could picture him taking out his wallet and gazing in an ecstasy of unbelief at the image of her who had given him strength through all those campaigns in the Saharan sands, through the dense Eastern jungles, through the roar of guns, shells, bombs and rockets. The train clanged along the rails: his heart throbbed: his imagination flew ahead. She was in his arms, his arms, but ... when he finally arrived, he only sat and wept. Then he went to church and prayed. He prayed until he heard an answering voice. He would go to Africa to serve God and die there, leaving maybe a tiny trail of spiritual heroism and glory. But he could never forgive the woman who had run away with another returning soldier: no, nor any woman. His true love was for dogs. The one he had in our time was a little dog called Lizzy. She was his constant companion to classes, to the chapel, to Nairobi, anywhere. The dog often dictated his moods. If she was ill, he became difficult and irritable and looked so alone and abandoned. Lizzy, the VW and Fraudsham: we called them the school's three musketeers, because they seemed inseparable:

'Lizzy died.

'Something in Fraudsham snapped. He could not teach; he could not preach. The lines on his face suddenly deepened, his eyes greyed, he would talk or not talk as if his mind was elsewhere. He was really so alone that we felt a certain pity. But we could not understand this. Dogs had died in our villages: dogs had died on the roads: we had chased dogs across fields and terraces and whenever you hit one with a stone and it yelped you laughed to tears. Good dogs were those for hunting rabbits and antelopes: brave dogs were those that guarded cattle and homes from marauding hyenas and thieves. But Lizzy was not any of these: how could she make a man lose himself so?

'He assembled the school. We thought it would be another session during which he would lecture us on scouting, England, Cambridge and the history of the world from the Celtic times to the birth of the new nations in Africa and Asia. But what he said made us want to laugh: my ribs pained me as I tried to hold in my laughter. He talked of the place of pets in human life: that in all civilised countries learning to care for pets and animals enriched one's appreciation of human life and God's love. Then suddenly the whole school was one thunderous laughter. Fraudsham swore and fumed and said that Africans had no feelings. But we went on laughing through his fury because how could we understand it, how could we believe our ears? I mean who ever heard of a dog being given human burial?

'He asked the school captain to select four boys from each class who would get jembes to dig a pit and make a coffin for Lizzy. He also wanted pall-bearers. The captain asked for volunteers. There was another outburst, with our heads bent down in fear of being selected. No volunteers and the captain named a few. They refused to go. We all refused to go. Fraudsham woke up to the present rebellion.

'He expelled the boys selected.

'We all went on strike.

'The whole school shivered with unbelief. There had been one strike in the history of the school and Fraudsham had won. Now he stormed and shouted and threatened. He claimed that we had refused to obey orders. In any civilised society there were those who were to formulate orders and others to obey: there had to be leaders and the led: if you refused to obey, to be led, then how could you hope to lead and demand obedience? Look at heaven: there was God on a throne and the angels in their varying subordinate roles: yet all was harmony. But he had opened our eyes.

'Yesterday he had been white and big and strong; but it was no longer the same. Yesterday he had been white and strong and invincible, a rock that could not be moved, but now, it was no longer the same. And all the things, all the cracks, all the contradictions that we had often whispered about but which had never been part of our conscious minds came to the fore. He tried to compromise: only one would be expelled. We still refused to go back to our classes. O.K., only a simple punishment: four canes each and cutting grass for a day. We saw his unease. We made new demands.

'We wanted to be taught African literature, African history, for we wanted to know ourselves better. Why should ourselves be reflected in white snows, spring flowers fluttering by on icy lakes? Then somebody shouted: We wanted an African headmaster and African teachers. We denounced the prefect system, the knightly order of masters and menials. That did it. And imagine. The newspapers took up this aspect of the crisis and denounced us. Since when did students, a mob, tell their teachers what they ought to teach? If the students were so clever and already knew what they ought to be taught and who was fit to teach them, why had they bothered to enrol in the school? And a school with such a record! A headmaster whom even the very best school in England, like Eton, would have been proud to have in their midst? They counted the money spent on a student and compared it with the income of the poor peasants.

'But we were adamant, despite the divisive hate campaign. Chui, Chui, somebody cried. Chui, the name had been alive, a legend. We wanted him to come and lead the school. Down with Fraudsham: down with the prefect system: down with whites: Uuuuuuup with Chui, shake them ... Black Power!

'Well ... the people in the ministry came. One was an old boy of the school. They appealed to us to go back to our classes. Our demands and our grievances would be looked into: the four boys would accept a simple punishment of cutting grass for a day and having their heads shaven clean.

'We went back to our classes. But something had happened: the rules of the game had been questioned and everything had been altered. We knew this, Fraudsham knew this, and almost a month later he resigned and soon afterward followed Lizzy. We were proud and thrilled and saw ourselves anew. We vowed that should we get an African headmaster we would give him the utmost obedience; we would work even harder, so as not to shame him and ourselves. No more prefects. We would elect our own leaders. We called ourselves African Populists and we wanted a populist headmaster.

'It was Chui – it was Chui. We waited for him with bated breath. None of us had ever seen him or knew anything about him outside the school's legend and folklore. But we sang with hope: a new school, a new beginning, a new people. But among the white teachers, there was only gloom and uncertainty: one or two did in fact resign. Apprehension and jubilation; despair and hope; sullen lips and radiant smiles: these battled in the air as we waited for Chui's arrival.

'Well, he did come, finally: we lined up the route from the gate to the office. He waved at us once and we replied with a heart-rending cry: Chuuuuuui!

'The first assembly ... we went to the hall almost one hour before the time. We sang and clapped and made a few speeches. The white-teachers stood outside and talked nervously.

'Chui arrived. Deathly, sepulchral silence. He climbed the steps ... up ... up ... to the foyer. Our eyes were glued to the scene before us. He had khaki shorts and shirt and a sun helmet: a black replica of Fraudsham. We waited for words that would somehow still the doubt and the fear. He spoke and announced a set of rules. He thanked the teachers for the high standards and world-wide reputation of the school. It was his desire, nay his fervent prayer, that all the teachers should stay, knowing that he had not come to wreck but to build on what was already there: there would be no hasty programme of Africanisation, reckless speed invariably being the undoing of so many a fine school. There had been a recent breakdown in discipline and he vowed that with the help of all he would resolve it. Far from destroying the prefect system, he would inject it with new blood. Obedience was the royal road to order and stability, the only basis of sound education. A school was like a body: there had to be the head, arms, feet, all performing their ordained functions without complaints for the benefit of the whole body. He read a passage from William Shakespeare.

> The heavens themselves, the planets, and this centre
> Observe degree, priority, and place,
> Insisture, course, proportion, season, form,
> Office, and custom, in all line of order:
> And therefore is the glorious planet Sol
> In noble eminence enthron'd and spher'd
> Amidst the other; whose med'cinable eye
> Corrects the ill aspects of planets evil,
> And posts like the comamndment of a king,
> Sans check to good and bad: but when the planets
> In evil mixture to disorder wander,
> What plagues and what portents, what mutiny,
> What raging of the sea, shaking of earth,
> Commotion in the winds! Frights, changes, horrors,
> Divert and crack, rend and deracinate
> The unity and married calm of states
> Quite from their fixture! O, when degree is shak'd,
> Which is the ladder to all high designs,
> The enterprise is sick! How could communities,
> Degrees in schools and brotherhoods in cities,
> Peaceful commérce from dividable shores,
> The primogenity and due of birth,
> Prerogative of age, crowns, sceptres, laurels,
> But by degree, stand in authentic place?
> Take but degree away, untune that string,
> And, hark, what discord follows!

'Those are words of a great writer – greater even than Maillu and Hadley Chase. The school's traditions, which had stood the test of time, had to be maintained. He did not therefore want to hear any more nonsense about African teachers, African history, African literature, African this and that: whoever heard of African, Chinese, or Greek mathematics and science? What mattered were good teachers and sound content: history was history: literature was literature, and had nothing to do with the colour of one's skin. The school had to strive for what a famous educator had described as the best that had been thought and written in the world. Racism had been the ruin of many a school, many a state, many a nation: Siriana believed in peace and the brotherhood of man. He would never have a school run by rebels and gangsters and the European Foreigners should have nothing to fear.

'We listened in silence, unbelief struggling with belief: was this the Chui who had once led a strike in this same same school?

'We debated his words for almost a term. The new prefects were even more pampered than those of yesterday. The new headmaster gave orders through a very tight and rigid chain of command from the school captain, the senior prefects, the junior prefects, down to the rest of us. Privileges were also graded according to the seniority of the classes, Form VI for instance being allowed to wear trousers and jackets and ties while the Form I was not allowed to wear shoes except on the day of worship. Chaucer, Shakespeare, Napoleon, Livingstone, Western conquerors, Western inventors and discoverers were drummed into our heads with even greater fury. Where, we asked, was the African dream?

'He complained about the falling standards of spoken and written English. At one Assembly he turned to the European teachers and said:

' "I don't of course want to look a gift horse in the mouth. I don't want to tell you how you should approach your jobs. I don't want to be like the enthusiastic American salesman who went to sell refrigerators to the Eskimo. But I am the headmaster, and it is the piper who calls the tune.

' "Teach them good idiomatic English."

'We went on strike and again refused the divide-and-rule control tactics. Down with Chui: up with African populism: down with expatriates and foreign advisers: up with black power.

'Well, the rest is common knowledge. Chui called in the riot squad which came to our school, and would you believe it, led by a European officer. We were all dispersed, with a few broken bones and skulls. The school was closed and when it reopened I was among the ten or so not allowed to sign for re-admission.'

There was a slightly pathetic note in Karega's narration, something between despair and dumb incomprehension. A certain gloom encircled the room and they each tried to struggle against it. Munira was the first to speak, echoing the words of the lawyer.

'I do not understand – so different from our time – I mean the demands. Was it because of independence? I mean what did you really want?'

'I don't really know ... when the lawyer spoke, I seemed to get it ... an inkling ... but it eludes the mind ... an idea ... I mean, we were men ... a communal struggle ... after all, we were the school, weren't we? We imagined new horizons ... new beginnings ... a school run on the basis of our sweat ... our collective brains, our ambitions, our fears, our hopes ... the right to define ourselves ... a new image of self ... all this and more ... but it was not clear ... only that the phrase African populism seemed to sum it all!'

5 🌼 There was a time when Nderi wa Riera was truly a man of the people. He used to play darts and draughts in small and big places, punctuating his playing with witty lighthearted comments and threats to unnerve his opponents: you will know me today ... You think I was in Manyani for nothing! It used to be said that he had chosen his offices in the Market Street to be near Camay which was then a renowned centre for darts and draughts and roasted goat meat and beer. Camay had in fact thrown up first-rate African darts players like Waiguru and Parsalli who, on reaching the thrilling finals staged at the Brilliant Night Club in what used to be an exclusively Asian and European pastime, had become household names in dart-playing circles all over Nairobi. He was in those days also one of the most vocal and outspoken advocates of reform in and outside Parliament. He would champion such populist causes as putting a ceiling on land ownership; nationalisation of the major industries and commercial enterprises; abolition of illiteracy and unemployment and the East African Federation as a step to Pan-African Unity.

Then he was flooded with offers of directorships in foreign-owned companies. 'Mr Riera, you need not do anything: we do not want to take too much of your busy and valuable time. It is only that we believe in white and black partnership for real progress.' The money he had collected from his constituents for a water project was not enough for piped water. But it was adequate as a security for further loans until he bought shares in companies and invested in land, in housing and in small business. He suddenly dropped out of circulation in small places. Now he could only be found in special clubs for members only, or in newspapers – photographed while attending this or that cocktail party. As if to reinforce his new social standing, he took a huge farm in the Rift Valley. But his most lucrative connection was with the tourist industry. He owned a number of plots and premises in Mombasa, Malindi and Watamu and had been given shares in several tourist resorts all along the coast. Soon he began talking of 'the need for people to grow up and face reality. Africa needed capital and investment for real growth – not socialist slogans'. But he remained a strong advocate of African culture, African personality, Black authenticity: 'If you must wear wigs, why not natural African or Black wigs?' He insisted on most of the companies of which he was chairman or director dropping their European names and taking names like Uhuru, Wananchi, Taifa,

Harambee, Afro, Pan-African, which would give the enterprises a touch of the soil.

Nderi wa Riera was the envy of most of his parliamentary peers. His area was so remote from the city that he was hardly ever troubled by endless complaints from his constituents. A happy contented lot your people are, they would tell him, and he would receive the compliment with a beaming smile. An MP's political freedom! And it was true that the chairs and the carpets in his office would have gathered dust had their cleanliness depended on visits from Ilmorog. The arrival of the delegation from his area became instant news among his parliamentary friends. They eagerly waited for him in his night haunts to find out the outcome of this unexpected confrontation.

As it was they all had to wait for Tuesday: Riera had gone to Mombasa for a business inspection and on-the-spot investigation of two tourist resorts which had been mentioned in a foreign newspaper as 'special places where even an ageing European could buy an authentic African virgin girl of fourteen to fifteen for the price of a ticket to a cheap cinema show'. This had raised one or two awkward questions in the newspapers.

He came back on Monday night and after a quick visit to his home and family in Lavington Green went to places to find out the latest gossip. He went to Tumbo's in Adam's Arcade, saw nobody he knew, and after swallowing a cold Tusker drove further down Ngong Road to the Gaylord Inn.

It was there, at the Farewell Bar, that he was quickly surrounded by friends who all wanted to know about the delegation. For a second he thought they were asking him about the affair of the authentic virgins. He laughed it off: there was nothing to it ... Europeans cannot tell the ages of Africans, and to them any woman with breasts that have not fallen – even if they are cotton-wool – is a virgin. It was only when they had mentioned Ilmorog that he looked at them rather sharply as if somebody was playing him an unpleasant practical joke. It was his friend Kimeria who confirmed the truth of it and mentioned something about a drought. Riera shrugged off the importance of the delegation and continued drinking. But inwardly he was slightly apprehensive: could they really have come all that way because of a drought about which there had not been even a column-inch in the newspapers? How anyway could they have managed to organise themselves? It was more likely, he thought, that somebody wanted to unseat him.

He was in the office by eight o'clock. His secretary showed him the appointments for the day. He was visibly impatient for two o'clock to come: he was ready and expectant for a fight: he was old and experienced at political manoeuvering: he would show those who were plotting against him that he was the same Nderi son of Riera and he never ate nyeni cia terere sukuma wiki at anybody's mother's house!

The delegation was a little late because they had all overslept and it took them time to cook and eat porridge. How lucky they all had been to find the lawyer! It was a sign of good luck, Karega thought, as they approached the Jeevanjee Gardens. The talk with the lawyer had gone on to the small hours of the night. It had opened so many avenues of thought for Karega that he wished Ilmorog was next to Nairobi so that they could continue the discussion daily. The lawyer had been careful not to discourage them in their quest for an audience with their MP. 'We must stretch the resources and processes of democracy to their utmost limits,' he had said. 'But should anything adverse happen, you are always welcome to the floor space. I would anyway like to know the outcome of your call.'

As they did yesterday, the main delegation sat in the Gardens. But this time, Wanja, Abdulla and Njuguna accompanied Karega and Munira to Iqbal Iqlood Buildings. Their creased, greasy, dirty clothes made them the strangest group of scarecrows ever to face an MP in offices that previously had only known men and women in impeccable business suits.

But Nderi wa Riera, in a three-piece grey suit, did not show any surprise as he stood to welcome them and even personally pushed chairs toward them. This was a good beginning, Karega thought, easing into the chair with a sigh of inward relief. And Riera was thinking – people can be malicious – only five, and his friends had talked of a multitude – but at the same time he was disappointed, for a politician lives by crowds.

'Is it well with you?' he asked them politely, and shook hands with each of them.

'It is well,' they chorused.

The MP sat back on his chair, his eyes all the time trying to assess and place them

'Have you come a long way?' he asked, not letting it out that he knew about them.

'Ilmorog,' said Munira. 'We were here yesterday. Didn't your secretary tell you?'

'Of course she did,' and he laughed. 'It is part of our language, remember. You find somebody digging or felling a tree, and you ask them: what are you doing?'

'True, true,' Munira said, and they all laughed.

'But you must be tired, coming all that way. Did you take a bus?' he asked and pressed a button.

'No,' said Wanja. 'We walked.'

'Really?'

The secretary's head peeped through the door.

'Please, can you make coffee – five coffees, for these gentlemen and lady ... Really?' he asked again, looking at them. 'But I am asking too many questions. We have not even introduced ourselves. My name is Nderi wa Riera.'

'We know you,' they all said.

'I used to be called David Samuel. But I asked myself: why should we abandon our names for these foreign ones? Ha! ha! ha! I know a friend, black as the soot on a cooking pot, who calls himself Winterbottom. Ha! ha! ha!'

'These Europeans made us give up many beautiful customs. And I am not talking only of circumcision,' said Njuguna. This was indeed a sensible man in Parliament, he thought, 'I am Njuguna and I am a farmer in Ilmorog.'

'I am sorry Parliament work has been so heavy, I have not had a minute to myself, but I was planning to come for a whole week or so and tour the constituency and get to know the people. I have wanted to acquaint myself with the farming problems in the area. Kenya is an agricultural country and our survival depends on farmers like you.'

The secretary came in with a tray. They each took a cup and a biscuit and started drinking.

'And you?' he asked, pointing at Wanja.

'I am Wanja ... a sort of a visitor to Ilmorog.'

'Good. And you joined them in this journey? Mgeni siku mbili, ya tatu umpatie njembe! Not so?' he asked and turned to Munira. 'You are also a farmer?'

'No. I am the Headmaster of Ilmorog Full Primary School, and my name is Munira, Godfrey Munira. I am afraid I have not yet shed the foreign name. After all, if we can wear their shirts and live in their houses ... but we have been over this before,' he said turning toward Karega and Wanja.

'You should have been in Parliament,' said the MP. 'I am glad to meet you, Mr Munira. What's in a name? What's more crucial is the quality of what one is doing for the country. Take teachers for instance. Without good teachers there is no nation. Teachers are the true men of the people. We here are only messengers. Do you come from Ilmorog?'

'Not quite. I hail from Limuru.'

'The Minister is your representative. I know him very well. Do you also come from Limuru?' he asked Karega.

'Yes. But I teach in the same school as Mr Munira here.'

'You look too young to be a teacher,' he said laughingly, but thinking, I must be careful now, why is it there is only one true Ilmorogian? 'It is good to see a young man with sense these days. Most of the others want to be clerks – white-collar jobs – and they don't even know how to type.'

'I don't agree with you there, sir,' Karega replied, recalling his own experience in these same offices. 'I am sure that many of the school leavers would be glad to accept a job which gave them a decent salary.'

I knew I had to be careful, thought the MP, noting the passion behind Karega's words. As a politician, Nderi had learnt that no enemy was too small, and no incident was too insignificant to be careless about and ignored, unless with calculated deliberation.

'I quite agree with you. Unemployment is an acute problem in this country. But it is the same all over the world. Even in England and America you read of millions laid off and begging for bread. It is the population explosion. Family planning and population control is the only cure.'

'Again, I am not so sure that I agree with you. Don't you think that family planning is a deliberate trick of Western powers to keep our population low? Britain is a tiny island, yet it has over fifty million people: why don't they curb their population growth? And after all, China is able to feed and clothe her millions.'

Strange, that he should be talking the way I used to talk, thought the MP, seeing a bit of himself in this earnest youth.

'But at what price has China been able to do that? No individual freedom ... no freedom of the press ... no freedom of worship or assembly and people wearing drab uniform clothes. Would you wish that for your country? You know when I was young I thought I could solve the problems of the world by shouting a slogan. But as I grow older I have learnt to be more realistic, and to face facts in the face. And we black people must learn not to fly against hard truths even if this means revising our dearly held theories. Take this population problem—!'

'Are you saying that women should not have more children?' asked Wanja in a strangely pained voice.

'No. But it should be paced to keep up with our abilities to feed the mouths. Unless something drastic is done we shall soon be like India, with a thousand hungry mouths reaching out for our throats. Don't you agree with me?' he said, turning to Abdulla. 'You have not yet told us your name, and here Karega and I are solving the problems of the world.'

'So people are now the enemy,' thought Karega.

Abdulla did not respond at once. He coughed a little, and then spoke in a dull lifeless tone of voice.

'Hare and Antelope once fell into a hole. Let me climb on your back first, then I shall pull you out, said Hare. So Hare climbed on Antelope's back and out he jumped onto dry sunny ground. He dusted himself up and started walking away. Heh, you are forgetting me, shouted Antelope. Hare lectured Antelope. Let me advise you, my friend. I fell into the same hole with you by mistake. The trouble with you, Mr Antelope, is that you go jump-jumping leap-leaping in the air instead of firmly walking on the ground and looking to see where you are going. I am sorry but you have only yourself to blame.'

And Abdulla stood up and walked out, leaving a pall of awkward heaviness in the room.

'Who is he?' asked the MP.

'He is Abdulla ... a businessman ... a shopkeeper at Ilmorog,' Munira explained.

'And a good storyteller too, ha! ha! ha! Business good in those parts?'

'Not bad ... he manages,' continued Munira, obviously at pains to undo any harm that might have been caused by Abdulla's abrupt departure.

'That is the spirit, self-reliance. You know, before independence business was all in Indian hands. But now we have Africans managing the same dukas, and doing very well, sometimes making even bigger profits than the Indians. Good profit-making is not a monopoly of any one race. Is he a native of Ilmorog?'

'Not quite. He too I am afraid is a newcomer to the place.'

The MP sat back in his chair, leaning it back. His fears were now confirmed. There must be a plot to smear his good name. His political enemies were sending strangers to Ilmorog to unsettle a peaceful people. He had not yet forgotten what had happened to the two messengers whom he had sent to Ilmorog to arrange for a bit of tea. He himself had been very busy arranging for the smooth running of tea drinking as a whole. After all the idea of a cultural movement had been his and that of a few friends. They had sold the idea to a very important persons. The tension in the country after the assassination of the Indian Communist had shaken Nderi and a few others, and the tea drinking on a mass scale to pledge eternal loyalty seemed ideal. But his constituents had let him down.

'And now my friends, in what ways can I help you? We are all your servants, you know, no matter what constituency you come from.'

'Sir, we have others waiting in the Jeevanjee Gardens. They only sent us to see if you were in.'

'Why didn't you bring them in?' He pressed a button, slightly more relieved, and the secretary came in. 'Can you go to the Jeevanjee Gardens and ask the others to come to the office? This is their office, their home, and they should not fear.'

'Wait a minute ... They are too many to fit in this office and it would be better if you went and talked to them out there,' Munira explained.

'All right, secretary ... I am really so sorry I was not here yesterday. I had gone to Mombasa. Government work. Aah, too much. But we have sworn to serve the public. No elephant is ever unable to carry his tusks, however big and weightful. So maybe you could tell me what has brought you this way before I meet the others.'

He had at first wanted to go right out and meet the crowd, but suddenly thought it more prudent to learn about the mission beforehand so he could prepare himself.

'We have come,' said Njuguna, 'because we know you are our son. There is no house with a male child where the head of a he-goat shall not be eaten. For the last six months we have been without rains in Ilmorog. Our cattle and goats have started dying. We have eaten the last grains of maize from the last harvest season. So we put our heads together and said: we have a son whose mouth is close to the ears of our government.'

As he listened, Nderi became more and more grave. As an MP for the area he ought to have known about this. If it became general knowledge, his opponents would make political capital out of the whole mess. It might in fact be too late. It might be his enemies who had learned about the drought and engineered the whole thing to see what he would do about it, certainly to embarrass him.

'Why didn't you come earlier?' he asked, with a frown of concern, at the same time racking his brain for a dramatic escape route.

'We knew you are a busy man. We knew that government work was keeping you away, else, you would have come back to see us. But we had elected you for that: so why should we complain? And we thought it would still rain. But they say that God above does not eat ugali. He brought us this woman and these teachers who know more about these things than we do. They told us that you would be glad to see us.'

'Of course, of course. They were right and I am most grateful,' he said, turning appreciative eyes toward Munira and Karega. But inwardly he was seething with anger at this obvious trick. My enemies think they are clever, working through teachers, or maybe this Munira here has ambitions, ingratiating himself with my constituents. Ha! 'It is a good thing that you went to teach in Ilmorog. Is – eeh, I have forgotten his name – who is the Education Officer at Ruwa-ini?'

'Mr Mzigo.'

'How long have you been – eeh – at—'

'We are strangers there, really. But I have been there for over two years, and Mr Karega only the last few months.'

Ha! That Mzigo. Bribed. Make trouble for me. Create disaffection. His fighting instinct was now fully aroused.

'You have had a long and difficult journey. Right! Let us go out now and meet the others. Then I can give you an answer together.'

They trooped to the Jeevanjee Gardens and, as they approached the others, the women ululated the Five Ngemi usually sung for a male child and a returning victorious hero. Within seconds, this had attracted a crowd of hangers-on, the hordes of the jobless, who normally slept off their hunger at the Gardens and were grateful for any distracting drama, religious, political or criminal. The reception pleased Nderi but did not quite allay his fears. Njuguna introduced him to the crowd as 'our prodigal son we sent to bring us back our share from the city', and repeated their call for help in face of the drought. Karega could not quite analyse his attitude to the MP but he, like the others, was hopeful and hung on the MP's lips, closely followed his movements and gestures, and eagerly waited for a dramatic solution to their problems. As for Nderi, he had not yet worked out a coherent plan. But a politician was a politician and the sight of the growing crowd excited him, inspired him, and even reminded him of the thrilling days of the Lancaster House Conference, trips to London, other waiting crowds at the airport and the speeches at Kamukunji which were always greeted with heart-rending cries, ululations of hope and glory.

'Uhuru!'

'Uhuru!'

'Uhuru na Kanu!'

'Uhuru na Kanu!'

'Down with the enemies of our hard-won freedom!'

'Down with our enemies!'

'Down with rumour-mongers and trouble-makers!'

'Down with rumour-mongers and trouble-makers!'

'Harambee!'

'Harambee!'

'Thank you, my friends. Thank you. My people of Ilmorog. This is the happiest day of my life since you gave me your votes and told me to go forward and forever fight as your servant in Parliament.'

He paused and waited for the encouraging applause to die.

'I have heard of your tribulations in Ilmorog. It is not of any man's making or doing ... but I am glad that you brought the problem to your servant. Kamuingi Koyaga Ndiri. That is the meaning of Harambee. Do you want us to work together so we can fight against joblessness and other maladies?'

'Yees!'

'You are talking!' the crowd of job-seekers shouted.

'Toboa! Toboa!' others added.

He paused for the riotous applause to die away. And suddenly, as if inspired by the crowd and the applause, he saw clearly how he could confound his enemies and turn their machinations to his own advantage. The idea was so simple and direct that he wondered why he had not thought of it earlier and ended the whole business.

'Thank you, my friends. So now I have a few suggestions to make and I want you to listen carefully, for it will mean a sacrifice from each one of us – big or small, teachers or pupils – for the common good and the glory of Ilmorog.'

The women ululated for three continuous minutes, which brought in more people walking along Market Street, Muindi Mbingu Street and Government Road, from their places of work. It also brought in a few University students.

'Now, I want you to go back to Ilmorog. Get yourselves together. Subscribe money. You can even sell some of the cows and goats instead of letting them die. Dive deep into your pockets. Your businessmen, your shopkeepers, instead of telling stories, should contribute generously. Get also a group of singers and dancers – those who know traditional songs. Gitiro, Muthuu, Ndumo, Mumburo, Muthungucu, Mwomboko – things like that. Our culture, our African culture and spiritual values, should form the true foundation for this nation. We shall, we must send a strong representative delegation to Gatundu!'

He was so excited at the prospects of such a mission that he took the hushed silence for attentive assent and this spurred him to even higher imaginative realms.

'To drink more tea – Gachai!' somebody shouted.

'But—' a few voices tried to get to him, but he was already off to more details.

'We must show that we are playing our part in self-help schemes in the Harambee spirit to put an end once and for all to all future droughts in the land.'

'But – but – we are starving,' more voices tried to interrupt the flow of his rhetoric in vain.

'Very important. And you, Munira and Karega, play your parts. Prepare the children. Let them form a choir. Teach them a few patriotic songs.'

The man is mad, it painfully occurred to Karega, sensing a general unease and unrest in the crowd.

'Mr Nderi,' he shouted and stood up to speak, but Nderi waved him to silence.

'Get a few elders. Sensible ones like Njuguna – you know, those who can colour their speeches with a proverb or two. Get true Ilmorogians as your spokesmen, not foreigners – and I shall definitely lead the delegation. I will present your prayers and petitions. We must put the name of Ilmorog on the national map. Uhuuuru! Harambeeee!'

He paused to gather breath and to bask in the applause. Somebody in the crowd shouted: 'These are the people who are misusing our freedom,' and this was greeted with a general murmur of protesting assent. Suddenly a stone flew and hit Nderi on the nose. This was followed by a hailstorm of orange-peels, stones, sticks, anything. For a few seconds Nderi tried to maintain his dignity and ignore the miscellaneous missiles which flew about him. Then a bit of mud hit him full on the mouth. It was too late to make a dignified exit. He suddenly took to his heels, wondering what had gone wrong, whether he had underestimated the desperation of his political enemies. He ran across Jeevanjee Gardens toward the Central Police Station with a few people pursuing him and shouting 'Mshike! mshike! Huyuu!' and he wishing he could truly fly in the air above the staring passersby.

'The mission has failed,' Karega bitterly muttered. He felt hot tears pressing. He avoided people's eyes. Abandoned by their MP, abandoned by the crowd of townspeople, who had all quickly dispersed to the surrounding streets, the delegation from Ilmorog sat on the grass, feeling as if the whole world was against them.

A riot squad and sirened police car came to the scene. But the officer-in-charge was surprised to find a dignified though puzzled group of old men, women, children. Nderi sat beside the officer in the car and pointed at Munira, Abdulla and Karega.

'You are wanted at the police station to answer a few questions,' the police officer told the three men as he led them to the waiting police car.

Nyakinyua watched them drive away. She turned to the stunned delegation. 'Let us follow them and demand their release,' she said, firmly. 'They have done no wrong, no wrong!'

6 ❧ Munira, Karega and Abdulla were detained at the city's Central Police Station for a night. The following morning they were taken to court where they pleaded not guilty to acting in a manner likely to cause a breach of the peace.

It was the lawyer who saved them. He successfully applied not only for the case to be heard the next day but also for their release on bond, whereas the prosecutor had wanted the case postponed to a fortnight hence and for the three to be remanded in custody while investigations continued. And on the day of the trial they witnessed a different face of the lawyer: not the jovial host, not the concerned social analyst but a hard fierce defence lawyer, ruthless and totally contemptuous when it came to cross-examining prosecution witnesses and especially the MP. From the questions and side comments the lawyer somehow managed to tell a story with a coherent pattern which highlighted the plight of those threatened by the drought and the general conditions in the area. He described Ilmorog with such phrases as a 'deserted homestead', 'a forgotten village', an island of underdevelopment which after being sucked thin and dry was itself left standing, static, a grotesque distorted image of what peasant life was and could be. He castigated the negligence of those entrusted with the task of representing the people. If the people's representatives did their duty, would such a journey have been necessary? He summed up by describing their epic journey in such detail that the people in court, even the magistrate, were visibly moved. Then he dramatically asked the court to go outside to see the donkey and the cart which he had only that morning managed to have released from custody.

In acquitting them, the magistrate agreed with the lawyer's description of the three men as the Good Samaritans and this thrilled and warmed their hearts.

Thrilling too, was the sight of themselves, their pictures and names in the newspapers. *Three Good Samaritans acquitted*, one daily had headlined it. There was also the feature editor who, sensing a news drama behind the headlines, had followed the group, taken several pictures and asked interminable questions. The day after, their story was splashed across the centre pages under three catching captions: DEATH IN DESERT: HUNGER IN ILMOROG: DONKEY ON A RESCUE MISSION. Dominating the story was a photograph of Abdulla's donkey pulling behind it an empty cart and the group looking a little surprised by fear, a little lost in the city jungle of vehicles and buildings and people busy about the streets.

It was this, ironically, which in turn saved their mission. Donations poured in from every quarter. Within three hours of the newspaper's story, the lawyer's place was flooded with donations of food and soon the donkey-cart was filled to the top. One company offered to provide free transport for the group, their donkey and cart, and the gifts. Rev. Jerrod called on an alliance of churches to send a team to the area to see how the church could help. A government spokesman promised to despatch experts to see how Ilmorog fitted into the government long-term rural development schemes; to see if plans could be speeded up so that in future Ilmorog and similar areas could be self-sufficient to meet threatening droughts.

For a whole month after the group's triumphant return *they* came: church leaders who conducted prayers for rain and promised a church for the area; government officials who said the area clearly needed a District Officer of its own – it was too far from Ruwa-ini for effective administration – and who promised to write a report to recommend a high-powered commission of inquiry into the development needs of the area; charity organisations which promised to sell more raffle-tickets in the area – Jaribu Bahati – and a group of university students who later wrote a paper relating droughts and uneven development to neo-colonialism, called for the immediate abolition of capitalism and signed themselves as the committee for students against neo-colonialism.

❁

The only person who was decidedly not happy at the way things had turned out was Nderi wa Riera. He retreated to his social clubs hiding his temporary defeat in beer and whisky. But his planning mind was busy. The more he thought about the whole thing the more he became convinced that his political enemies and indeed the enemies of the country's prosperity and stability had engineered the whole thing. There was a pattern to the orchestration of events leading to the court appearance.

He again recalled the humiliation of his two emissaries; he still felt a personal hurt at having to suppress the story, for fear that he, one of the top brains behind the whole tea drinking culture, was not in control of his constituency. But his enemies must have mistaken his silence for weakness. He would prove them wrong. Because of his business connections with many at the top. Nderi wa Riera pulled more weight than even a minister. He would now use all his connections to defeat his enemies. He had also worked out details to make KCO grow into the most feared instrument of selective but coercive terror in the land.

KCO had originally been a vague thing in his mind. It had grown out of his belief in cultural authenticity which he had used with positive results in his business partnership with foreigners and foreign companies. Why not use culture as a basis of ethnic unity? He had read somewhere that some prominent leaders in some West African countries were members of secret societies, that used witchcraft and other remnants of pre-colonial cults and parties to keep their followers in fear and obedience. Yes! Why not! He himself had recently been sent a secret invitation to join the Free Masons in Nairobi – a secret European business fraternity. Why not an African based counterpart to control Central Province where peasants and workers seemed very restive and this was dangerous because these people had had a history of anti-colonial violent resistance, a spirit of struggle, which could be misused by the enemies of progress and Economic Prosperity. Later the idea could be sold to other leaders of the other communities.

He had discussed it with top directors of companies, big landlords, and other men of status. A few had opposed it saying such practices and revivals were too primitive; that there was always the Police, the Army and the Law Courts to put down any resistance from below.

But his arguments had been given substance by the unexpected effect of the assassination of the Indian and later of a top African politician. Suddenly even those top few who opposed it were for the idea.

The Mass Tea Party had almost been a hundred per cent successful but for the outcry from a few misguided voices in Parliament, the Church, and the students of the University. There was also the foreign press which in their naivety thought this Tea Party was another Mau Mau. Under the emotions of the period it would have been very difficult to explain to the western press that this was a different thing all together – that it was not against progressive co-operation and active economic partnership with imperialism. He, Nderi wa Riera, was convinced that Africa could only be respected when it had had its own Rockefellers, its Hughes, Fords, Krupps, Mitsubishis ... KCO would serve the interests of the wealthy locals and their foreign partners to create similar economic giants!

But KCO had survived the recent denunciation of the Mass Tea Party and he was quite convinced that the organisation could be made to grow using other means. Even the foreign press and the leaders of the other communities would not oppose it once they realised the kind of economic and social interests it really stood for.

At the thought of KCO he suddenly felt peaceful, calm inside. He knew how to go about paying back his enemies. For a start he admitted that he had neglected Ilmorog. He would now work to strengthen the Ilmorog Branch of KCO of which he was the Chairman, General Secretary and Treasurer. He would in time probably give two of the jobs to dependable fellows from the area. Then he would institute Ilmorog (KCO) Holding Ltd. Capital could always be raised from the people. Sell shares to all the sons of Ilmorog be they in or outside Ilmorog. He might even use his share of the millions collected during the Mass Tea Drinking. He could borrow additional funds from banks. Ilmorog (KCO) Holding Ltd through the control of other companies would tap and develop Ilmorog's tourist potential ... but the roads!

Then he remembered his enemies. Would they not expose his motives? Who were they? Could it be that boy Karega and that teacher and the crippled fellow? No, these were only front men: they were working for somebody else. Who could it be?

And suddenly he knew. The lawyer of course. Nderi bought drinks for everybody in the club. Why had he not seen it earlier? Why? The lawyer was the brain behind it all. The lawyer was the Enemy. He was the Enemy of KCO and Progress. Even if it took him ten years, Nderi would surely have the lawyer eliminated. He would ask his henchmen to open 'file' for the lawyer in their minds.

Long live Ilmorog. Long live KCO, his heart sang joyfully. And that night he went to the Casino to try his new luck.

The following day he issued a statement promising to explore the possibilities of opening up the area for tourism; and of securing loans for people in Ilmorog – but only for true Ilmorogians, not outsiders sent there by his political enemies to make capital out of natural disasters – to develop their shambas. He would soon launch a giant financial project – Ilmorog (KCO) Investment and Holdings Ltd – as a quick means of developing the area. Ilmorog would never be the same ...

Part Three: To Be Born

The morning blush'd fiery red:
Mary was found in Adulterous bed;
Earth groan'd beneath, and Heaven above
Trembled at discovery of love.
                              — William Blake

Your two breasts are like two fawns,
    twins of a gazelle,
    that feed among the lilies ...
                              — Song of Solomon

The voice of my beloved!
    Behold he comes,
leaping upon the mountains,
    bouncing over the hills.
                              — Song of Solomon

Chapter Seven

1 ✿ 'Yes, Ilmorog was never quite the same after the journey ...' wrote Munira years later, echoing Nderi's words. His was a mixture of an autobiographical confessional and some kind of prison notes.

At night, pacing about the cold cement floor, feeling the unfriendliness of the cell's bare walls and the barren darkness creep through the flesh to the bones, he would mutter to himself ... 'things were never quite the same'. He sat in a corner and leaned against the walls and stretched his legs along the floor. He started scratching himself, his ribs, his waist, his behind, his everywhere, and for a second he almost enjoyed this cruel distraction from heavy thoughts and memories. From his hair he dug out a fat louse which he killed by pressing it between his thumbnails. The tiny sound of death so sharp in the cold darkness startled him. He cleaned the lousy mess against the sides of his trousers and muttered: 'After the journey ... after that journey ... a devil came into our midst and things were never quite the same.'

Munira had now been held at the New Ilmorog Police Station for eight days. He had expected that Inspector Godfrey would call on him daily for questions and discussions. Every evening one of the policemen on guard – either the short or the tall one – would collect the day's instalment and take it away. And Munira would hold himself ready; he felt an incandescence of the spirit, a glow of the intellect, the pride of an inventor or a discoverer, and he was eager to communicate this to any listener. He felt even more than before that he now held the key which opened up, once and for all time, the true universal connection between things, events, persons, places, time. What caused things to happen? The New Ilmorog of one or two flickering neon-lights; of bars, lodgings, groceries, permanent sales, and bottled Theng'eta; of robberies, strikes, lockouts, murders and attempted murders; of prowling prostitutes in cheap night clubs; of police stations, police raids, police cells: what brought about this Ilmorog from the old one of sleepy children with mucus-infested noses, climbing up and down miariki trees? And why did things happen the way they did at the time they did and no other? How was it that the puny acts of men, arising from a thousand promptings and numerous motives, could change history and for ever condemn and damn souls to eternal torment and loss, guilt and cruelty, but also to love – yes – love that passeth all understanding? No there was a design, a law, and it was this that he would have liked to impress on Inspector Godfrey.

But when by the ninth day the Inspector had not yet called him, Munira felt a little alarmed. He was beginning to get slightly weary of the daily routine: porridge in the morning; the writing-desk; lunch of ugali and boiled sukuma wiki; the writing-desk; supper of maize and mbuca-infested beans: and finally the cement floor. An uncontrollable anxiety gnawed at his sleep at night and in the morning it made him restless. For relief he tried walking about the exercise yard. It was during the night of the fifth day that he suddenly felt the effects of his isolation. Time was a vast blankness without a beginning, middle and end, no tick-tock-tick-tock divisions, no constant lengthening and shortening of shadows, no human altercations of laughter and the to-and-fro activity which ordinarily made him aware of time's measure and passage. Suppose ... suppose ... well ... suppose it was not ...! And alone in the dark without a human voice to argue with he felt his assurance desert him, he panicked – and tried to reach out for the law, only to find that it was not as palpable as when he was arguing with or trying to persuade an avowed adversary. Inspector Godfrey was playing with him. He was laughing at him. He was probably amusing himself the way a cat let a rat run a little with illusions of freedom and near-escape before joyously pouncing on him. In the morning Munira walked to the tall policeman on guard and found himself pleading and demanding at the same time:

'I want to talk to the officer in charge. I demand to see the highest authority at the New Ilmorog Police Station. Why, Mr Policeman, even you can see that this is becoming ridiculous. I, a grown-up, a teacher, guarded and scribbling fiction on paper. For what are recollections but fiction, products of a heated imagination? I mean, how can one truly vouch for the truth of a past sequence of events? I have my rights too. I know their sly ways: the officer protesting his readiness to accede to my wishes: *Mr Munira, all we want is a simple statement* ... Why then has he kept me here for eight days? Today is the ninth day. *Mr Munira, we shall give you pen and paper* ... I don't want their paper: I don't want their pen. Listen to me, Mr Policeman ... It is not a statement they want ... They want a confession, an accusation. Tell them that I am not accusing anybody. No, Mr Policeman. That is not true. Please go and tell him, them, anybody, even the first officer, the youth I mean, that I am ready to answer any questions. Only they must take me away from this, er, this prison . . .'

The tall policeman looked at him, unable to follow the logic of his argument. But he was still afraid of Munira, as indeed he was of anybody who claimed to hear voices from God. He would in fact have preferred to guard another: he tried to be reasonable and very polite.

'But you are not in prison, Mr Munira!' he said. Munira was startled by the mention of his name.

'What's this, then? Open that gate and let me out.'

The policeman was really alarmed. He feared something might happen. Ever since childhood, he had always been afraid of Christ's second coming and he kept himself on guard ready to jump to the right side. With these things one could never really be sure. He now spoke quickly, almost nervously.

'Be reasonable, now, Mr Munira. Here you have a cell, well, a room to yourself. You have an open courtyard. You can walk about or sleep or write. Nobody interferes with you. Look at the other side of this partition. All those newly arrested, all those remanded are put there. They share cells, sometimes four or five or ten in one cell. Not even as big as yours. Last night two young fellows, totos I would say, well, thugs. They were brought in. Would you have liked that kind of company? I am not suggesting that you are in prison, arrested, or remanded. Only . . . well . . . Chui, Kimeria and Mzigo were such important people. VIPs. It will take us years before we can get their likes. So wealthy. Millionaires. Imagine. African Delameres. Did you ever visit the scene of the arson? Of course you couldn't have. It was terrible . . . terrible . . . Mr Munira, between you and me it was not a case of robbery or attempted robbery. There's more to it than meets the eye. The police must leave no stone unturned. And this Inspector Godfrey . . . so famous . . . a bit odd . . . I mean his methods . . . like now . . . He never leaves the office . . . reads . . . reads. . . .'

'I don't want your theories. I just want to speak to Inspector Godfrey. You are only a jailer. Both you and I are in prison. Well, everybody is in prison . . .'

'Mr Munira. But you chose to be confined here! You wanted to write down truth. You are a big man yourself. A teacher. A man of God. You ought to be sympathetic. Imagine. It might have been you. Well, it might be you next time. Mr Munira, prevention is better than cure.'

Munira laughed. Uneasily.

'You are too talkative. But look. I don't even have clothes into which I can change. You came for me in the morning. You said: *It's nothing much, Mr Munira, just routine questioning: we have nothing against you*. Now you don't even give me a newspaper...'

'A newspaper, Mr Munira? But you have not asked for it. I am under instruction from Inspector Godfrey himself to supply you with whatever you need. Ask and it shall be given, that kind of thing. I will go just now and get you one, Mr Munira. Only I must lock this gate. But don't take it ill. I am not your jailer. I am only waiting on you.'

Munira watched him lock the heavy iron gate. He had felt better talking with him. But now the panic of the night returned. He almost called him back. For it was as if, now, his last human contact had deserted him, and he was alone with the unresolved question ... suppose ... suppose this law is not there ... He walked away from the gate and sat by the barbed wire that divided his yard from the others. He felt sleep steal on him. He readied himself to submit, hopefully. Suddenly he heard voices coming from the other side and his heart leapt a bit with pleasure. At first the voices were a little distant and a little vague, but after a while he could follow the conversation. He looked in that direction. Their backs were turned to him. So he just listened.

They were telling their story, maybe to a third person, probably their warder, or they were simply reliving their experience, uncaring, daring the warder or the listener to reveal it outside those walls. In court they would certainly deny it. They laughed at one another, laughed at their earlier declaration of innocence before the resident magistrate at Ilmorog. The two had been arrested trying to rob the Ilmorog branch of the African Economic Bank. They seemed proud of this as of their other exploits and their hide and hope-not-to-be found games with the law.

The voices were vaguely familiar to Munira. But he could not place them. He wished they would turn their faces toward him. They went on talking and laughing as if they had not a care in the world, as if the whole thing was a game with certain rules, and except for the 'traitor' they were not bitter with anybody or anything else.

The policeman came back and brought him a copy of the *Sunday Mouthpiece*. Munira simply looked at him: he was not any longer interested in reading. What did it matter whether one read or not? But he took the paper all the same and idly flipped through the pages. He sat up and stared at banner headlines on the fourth page. *Murder in Ilmorog. Foul play suspected. Political motivation?* The headline, as it turned out, was more dramatic than the story which followed. The news aspects of the incident would of course have been exhausted by the national dailies, especially the more sensational *Daily Mouthpiece*, Munira reflected, and hence the speculation without evidence. So that was the source of the policeman's theories. He quickly glanced up at the policeman who was eyeing him from the gate, and resumed his reading. The feature column was more interesting. The writer, after giving brief life histories of Chui, Mzigo and Kimeria, described them as three well-known nationalist fighters for political, educational, and above all, economic freedom for Africans. Their ownership and management of *Theng'eta Brewcries & Enterprises Ltd*, which had brought happiness and prosperity to every home in the area as well as international fame for the country, was cited as an example of their joint entrepreneurial genius, unmatched even by the famed founders of the industrial revolution in Europe. Our Krupps, our Rockefellers, our Fords! And now their lives were brutally ended when they were engaged in a bitter struggle for the total African ownership and control of the same Theng'eta factories and their subsidiaries in other parts of the country. Negotiations for them to buy out the remaining shares held by foreigners were soon to start. Whom then did their untimely deaths benefit? All true nationalists should pause and think!

Below this were more tributes and denunciations.

But the one that most held Munira's interest was another news item captioned: *MP to lead a Delegation of Protest.* 'The MP for Ilmorog and Southern Ruwa-ini, The Hon. Nderi wa Riera, yesterday told a press conference that he would be leading a strong delegation to all cabinet ministers and to even higher authorities if necessary to demand a mandatory death sentence for all cases of theft, with or without violence. He would also seek the same mandatory death sentence for all crimes that were politically and economically motivated.

'Speaking over a wide range of subjects, the MP called for a total and permanent ban on strikes. Strikes generated an atmosphere of tension which could only lead to instability and periodic violence. Strikes should be regarded as deliberate anti-national acts of economic sabotage.

'Calling on Trade Union leaders to be unselfish, he asked them to refrain from demanding higher and higher wages without proper regard for the lower income groups or the jobless, who would be the sole beneficiaries of a more equitable reallocation of what would have gone into unregulated wage increases. It was time that Trade Unions were told in no uncertain terms that they could no longer hold the country to ransom.

'Referring to the proposed delegation, the MP called upon teachers, employers, Churchmen, and all men of goodwill to join it to demonstrate their unity of purpose in abhorring recent dastardly acts which would only scare away tourists and potential investors. Even local investors, he warned, might find it necessary to invest their capital abroad if the situation were left to deteriorate.'

The MP was fond of press statements and government by delegations and petitions, Munira thought. He recalled the picture of the MP ten years back pontificating in a solemn suit and tie and then dashing across Jeevanjee Gardens, abandoning all pretences to dignity, with a group of the city's unemployed in hot pursuit, and he probably praying for a miraculous intervention. Munira started laughing. He laughed until the newspaper fell from his hands. He turned his eyes to the other side and he caught the three youths also laughing and looking in his direction. Their eyes met. He stopped laughing. He had recognised Muriuki. And so he, Munira, had educated Muriuki to make him ready for robbery and jails?

'Why my sudden doubt?' he wrote, answering back the temptation of the night before. 'Everything is ordained by God. The vanity of man's actions divorced from a total surrender to the will of the Lord! We went on a journey to the city to save Ilmorog from the drought. We brought back spiritual drought from the city!'

There was an element of truth in Munira's interpretation of events that followed their journey to the city. An administrative office for a government chief and a police post were the first things to be set up in the area. Next had come the church built by an Alliance of Missions as part of their missionary evangelical thrust into heathenish interiors. Only that, for him, so many years later, this irony of history was just the manner in which God manifested himself.

2 ❧ Even the rain that fell a month after all the charitable individuals and organisations had packed their bags and returned to the city was, later for Munira, the way God chose to reveal himself in all his thunderous and flaming glory. It was this way of showing that men's efforts could only come to nought and could never influence God's will. Only total surrender . . . But for Nyakinyua, Njuguna, Njogu, Ruoro, and the others who knew about Mwathi's powers, the rain had clearly been God's response to the sacrifice and it signalled the end of a year of drought. They heard Afric's God wrestling with the Gods of other lands. They heard and listened in wonder to the gods' fearful roar and the clashing of their swords which emitted fire from heaven.

The whole school came out and in supplication to the heavens, sang with expectant voices:

Mbura Ura	Rain pour down
Nguthinjire	So I'll slaughter you
Gategwa	A young bull
Na kangi	And another
Kari Iguku	With a hump
Guku Guku	Hump, Hump!

The rain seemed to hear them. The earth swallowed thirstily, swallowed the first few drops and gradually the ground relaxed its hardness and became soft and sloshy. The children splashed their feet in muddy pools and slid smoothly on slopes and hills.

Wanja was possessed of the rain-spirit. She walked through it, clothes drenched, skirt-hem tight against her thighs, revelling in the waters from heaven. She would at times sit or stand still on her hut's verandah and look, wonder-gaze, at her life in droplets of rain falling from the roof. What was the meaning of her life? Where was the continuity of purpose? Why should she go through life an unfulfilled woman? She wanted to cry for ... she knew not what. She and Nyakinyua were now close, very close, mother and daughter more than grandmother and granddaughter, and when the rain subsided they would wander about Ilmorog, would go to the shamba to break the clods of earth and of course plant together.

In the evening people would crowd Abdulla's place and talk about the rain blessings. Baada ya dhiki faraja; and Abdulla wished he could truly believe this. The older folk told stories of how Rain, Sun and Wind went a-wooing Earth, Sister of Moon, and it was Rain who carried the day, and that was why Earth grew a swollen belly after being touched by Rain. Others said no, the raindrops were really the sperms of God and that even human beings sprang from the womb on mother earth soon after the original passionate downpour, torrential waters of the beginning.

This waiting earth: its readiness powered Wanja's wings of expectation and numerous desires. Feverishly, she looked out for tomorrow, waiting, like the other women, for earth to crack, earth to be thrust open by the naked shoots of life.

And indeed came the sunshine, and the rain stopped, the earth steamed, the earth opened, and the seeds germinated, bean ears flapping free in the breeze, maize-blades pointing skywards, green potato leaves spreading out and wide in the sun.

Karega, Abdulla, Munira often met at Abdulla's store. They sat outside, basked in the sunset beams over the new growth, warm bellies, drowsy heads, dreams over a Tusker beer, and their hearts would beat suddenly at the sight of Wanja coming toward them from the fields.

But brooding not too far below their tranquil existence was their consciousness of the journey and the experiences which spoke of another less sure, more troubled world which could, any time, descend upon them, breaking asunder their rain-filled sun-warmed calm. They did not talk about it: but they knew, in their different ways, that things would never again be the same. For the journey had presented each with a set of questions for which there were no ready answers; had, because of what they had seen and experienced, thrown up challenges that could neither be forgotten nor put on one side, for they touched on things deep in the psyche, in their separate conceptions of what it meant to be human, a man, alive and free.

Karega said to Abdulla: Joseph will get far. He is doing extremely well in school and we have asked for him to join Standard IV.

❁

School had resumed almost as soon as the city crowd dispensing charity and promises had gone, almost as suddenly as it had appeared, leaving behind the kind of restless silence that is felt after an abrupt cessation of numerous high-pitched voices. Karega once again threw his weight into teaching, to avoid answering anything to himself, but the same questions came back, with greater unsureness than before: where, he asked himself was the unity of African people?

There was a time when he used to be sure of things: there was a time for instance when he thought that contact with a loved one could solve everything, was the key to the world. And indeed in those days when his heart beat in rhythm with Mukami's, he had seen a world without knots and riddles opening out, a world which, bathed in the floodtide and light of their innocence, promised eternal beauty and truth. He was soon to know, shockingly so, that there were those who waited in shadowy corners to suffocate growth with their foul breaths with the fart and shit of their hypocrisy and religious double-dealing. But even after Mukami had gone from his life he had retained some kind of expectation, an irresistible need to have faith in at least the decency of those who had known suffering in the past, those who had heroically stood up to oppressive forces. The existence of people like Chui, even though only in the school's popular lore, had strengthened his faith in deeds of heroes. Hero-worship of those he thought could clear the air of suffocating man-made foul smells had gradually replaced his earlier faith in the universal healing power of love and innocence. But in Siriana he had watched the transformation of Chui from a popular hero into a tyrant who thought that his power came from God and foreigners. Karega had gone through all these experiences including his fruitless search for jobs in the city and his even more humiliating venture of selling fruits and sheepskins to tourists. Why then had he not learnt from these? Why had he urged a whole community to undertake a journey which he should have known would end in futility and added humiliation? Yes, Njuguna had been right: they had all gone begging in the streets!

Alone, in his one-bedroomed house a few yards from Munira's, he could not readily fall asleep. In class, he did not feel that glow he had felt before the journey to the city. The same thought would buzz in his head: so it was not he, alone, as an individual: so a whole community and region could be condemned to only giving! And when their store was exhausted, through philanthropy to cities and idle classes, or through the fatigue of the soil, or poor tools, or drought, they had nothing and nowhere to turn to! A whole community of direct producers reduced to beggary and malnutrition and death in their country! He would recall Nyakinyua's words before the journey and she too was right. Wanja too was right. Everybody had been right except himself with his enthusiasm and idealism: where now the solidarity and unity of blackness?

Amidst this chaos and whirlwind of thought, the figure of the lawyer would suddenly stand out, clean, splendid in his dedication and understanding.

He one day sat down and wrote to him. Send me books, he appealed, for somewhere in the high seats of learning in the city somebody was bound to know. For two weeks he waited not so much for the books as a word which would restore his faith and his belief. But the lawyer did not say anything. He just sent him books and a list of other titles written by professors of learning at the University. 'See what you can make out of these,' the lawyer had scribbled. Karega did not know what it was that he really wanted to get, but he vaguely hoped for a vision of the future rooted in a critical awareness of the past. So he first tried the history books. It had seemed to him that history should provide the key to the present, that a study of history should help us to answer certain questions: where are we now? How did we come to be where we are? How did it come about that 75 per cent of those that produce food and wealth were poor and that a small group – part of the non-producing part of the population – were wealthy? History after all should be about those whose actions, whose labour, had changed nature over the years. But how come that parasites – lice, bedbugs and jiggers – who did no useful work lived in comfort and those that worked for twenty-four hours went hungry and without clothes? How could there be unemployment in a country that needed every ounce of labour? So how did people produce and organise their wealth before colonialism? What lessons could be learnt from that?

But instead of answering these, instead of giving him the key he so badly needed, the professors took him to pre-colonial times and made him wander purposelessly from Egypt, or Ethiopia, or Sudan, only to be checked in his pastoral wanderings by the arrival of Europeans. There, they would make him come to a sudden full stop. To the learned minds of the historians, the history of Kenya before colonialism was one of the wanderlust and pointless warfare between peoples. The learned ones never wanted to confront the meaning of colonialism and of imperialism. When they touched on it, it was only to describe acts of violent resistance as grisly murders; some even demanded the rehabilitation of those who had sold out to the enemy during the years of struggle. One even approvingly quoted Governor Mitchell on the primitivity of Kenyan peoples and went ahead to show the historical origins of this primitivity, or what he called undercivilisation. Nature had been too kind to the African, he had concluded. Karega asked himself: so the African, then, deserved the brutality of the coloniser to boot him into our civilisation? There was no pride in this history: the professors delighted in abusing and denigrating the efforts of the people and their struggles in the past.

He turned away in despair: maybe it was his ignorance and his lack of university learning. What of the resistance of African peoples? What of all the heroes traversing the whole world of black peoples? Was that only in his imagination?

He tried political science. But here he plunged into an even greater maze. Here professors delighted in balancing weighty rounded phrases on a thin decaying line of thought, or else dwelt on statistics and mathematics of power equation. They talked about politics of poverty versus inequality of politics; traditional modernisation versus modernising traditions; or else merely gave a catalogue of how local governments and central bureaucracies worked, or what this or that politician said versus what another one said. And to support all this, they quoted from several books and articles all carefully footnoted. Karega looked in vain for anything about colonialism and imperialism: occasionally there were abstract phrases about inequality of opportunities or the ethnic balancing act of modern governments.

Imaginative literature was not much different: the authors described the conditions correctly: they seemed able to reflect accurately the contemporary situation of fear, oppressions and deprivation: but thereafter they led him down the paths of pessimism, obscurity and mysticism: was there no way out except cynicism? Were people helpless victims?

He put the books in packets and posted them back to the lawyer with a note: why had he sent him books which did not speak to him about the history and the political struggles of people of Kenya? And now ironically he got a rather long letter from the lawyer:

'You had asked me for books written by Black Professors. I wanted you to judge for yourself. Educators, men of letters, intellectuals: these are only voices – not neutral, disembodied voices – but belonging to bodies of persons, of groups, of interests. You, who will seek the truth about words emitted by a voice, look first for the body behind the voice. The voice merely rationalises the needs, whims, caprices, of its owner, the master. Better therefore to know the master in whose service the intellect is and you'll be able to properly evaluate the import and imagery of his utterances. You serve the people who struggle; or you serve those who rob the people. In a situation of the robber and the robbed, in a situation in which the old man of the sea is sitting on Sindbad, there can be no neutral history and politics. If you would learn look about you: choose your side.'

What did he mean look about you? Choose your side? He did not want any more masters – he just wanted to know the truth. But what truth? Weren't they all, shouldn't they all be on the side of blackness against whiteness?

He looked out of the window and saw the green crops, the new growth: crops will flower and later we shall harvest, he muttered to himself but his questions remained unanswered: was that the kind of African studies he and others had gone on strike about?

❁

Munira could not understand the new motion of things, the new mood of the village after the journey. Wanja and the other women on the ridge had formed what they called Ndemi-Nyakinyua Group to cultivate and weed the land and earth the crops, working in common, on one another's fields in turn. Munira and Karega were busy teaching, but on certain selected days the whole school joined in the collective enterprise. At first some were suspicious, but on seeing how much a Kamuingi could accomplish within only a few weeks, they joined the group.

They all felt the stirrings of a new birth, an unknown power riding wings of fear and hope. The previous certainty had deserted the village. They now knew that forces other than droughts posed new types of threats but nobody wanted to quite voice their new fears.

He looked at Wanja, at her face, and marvelled at her ready involvement in practical labour. He looked at her hands, now cracked, nails broken, and he could hardly believe any of the stories she had told about the city and about her wanderings. He wanted her now, to possess her, and it pained him that she kept him at a distance. But then she seemed equally distant to everybody and this consoled him and made him bide his time. He himself was possessed of a new thirst to find out about things. His desire to read had gradually come back and whenever he and Karega went to Ruwa-ini to collect their salary they would pass by a bookshop to buy books. He was on the verge of being inside things and he felt good and generally grateful.

Alone in the shop, Abdulla would keep alive memories of hope and bitterness. He wondered what mood he could now trust, seeing that one so quickly and frequently, without any warning, changed into the other. But he was glad that Joseph had started school: how, he asked himself over and over again in his repentant moods, how could he have kept Joseph from school? He eagerly waited their fatigued return in the evening from school and from the fields, for only then, lost in their talk and their drinking, could he be sure that the calmness in him would not suddenly be rent asunder by his remembrance of things past. He looked at Wanja's utter transformation, a kindred spirit, and he felt that maybe with the rains and the crop and the harvest to be, something new was happening.

The herdsmen also returned. They talked of the cattle they had lost to the sun. They talked about the journeys they had made across the plains. Now they hoped that the drought would never return. Not after so much sacrifice. Things would soon follow their normal rhythm.

But the previous flow and pattern of the seasons was obviously broken by the late rains. This irregular season, for instance, ran from December to March which under the old rhythm should have been the beginning of the major Njahi season. Their first harvest since the journey to the city was not big but it would keep bones and skins together.

They adjusted to the new pattern and once again after the harvest they cultivated the fields, readying the earth for new rains and new planting whenever this would come to be.

And so once again the peasants of Ilmorog waited for rains, their hearts alternating between fear and hope. Nothing seemed to have changed in Ilmorog. The journey to the city seemed a thing of the past.

Then suddenly two lorries came almost at the same time and brought men who started erecting a church building and a police post. What was all this about, they wondered? Was this the promised-for development? The post would be occupied by a chief, they were told.

The builders who lived in tents would occasionally come to Abdulla's place. Their very voices and their presence marked them as different, as outsiders, and this made the people of Ilmorog feel a solidarity and an intimacy among themselves that was a way of rejecting the strangers. It was as if the men had been sent by the forces that had earlier humiliated them in the city. Even Wanja, Abdulla, Munira and Karega took the side of Ilmorog against the new intruders.

But suddenly, soon, the church and the post were forgotten under a new flurry of activity.

June had brought rains.

It fell day and night for two weeks so that nobody could really leave their huts.

The builders packed their tents and tools and drove away.

Children sat at the doors and went on with singing:

Mbura Ura	Rain, rain
Nguthinjire	I slaughter for you
Gategwa	A young bull
Na Kangi	And another
Kari Mbugi	With bells, around the neck
Kara, Kara	Ding-Ding-Ding-Dong.

After two weeks it changed the rhythm: it would pour only at night to be followed by a day or two of sunshine. Rain, sunshine. That was always the classical pattern heralding a big crop and a big harvest. And this balance remained so until the whole land was one luscious green growth with crowds of flowers of many colours.

So that even when toward the end of the season the builders returned and resumed their twin structures of the post and the church, the fears of Ilmorog were drowned by two big expectations.

The second harvest since their return from the city was going to be one of the biggest in the history of Ilmorog. It was a total reversal of previous years when Njahi season that started in March produced the most. This now was more or less the Mwere season at the end of the year and it had all the signs of a major event. Munira and Karega offered the school's help in the harvesting.

There was also going to be a circumcision ceremony after the harvest. Some of the herd-boys were going to be initiated into men. As a boy Munira used to hide from home to listen to the singing which accompanied the ceremony. And even as a young teacher, after Siriana, he once or twice stole to the ceremonies. That was before the dances were banned during the Emergency. It was during one of the ceremonies that he had met Julia. She was then Wanjiru. Her voice, her dancing, her total involvement had attracted him and he had decided that here at last was what would bring fulfilment to his life. But she had become Julia and the temporary dream of an escape into sensuality had vanished on the marriage bed.

Maybe it was the memory of the dream: but Munira was thinking of possessing Wanja again during the harvest or after it and he felt a thrill course through his blood at the prospect.

3   There was something about harvesting, whether it was maize or beans or peas, which always released a youthful spirit in everyone. Children ran about the fields to the voices of women raised to various pitches of despairing admonition about the trails of waste. Sometimes the children surprised a hare or an antelope in a lair among the ripened crops: they would quickly abandon whatever they were carrying and run after the animal the whole length of Ilmorog, shouting: Ḳaau ... Kaaau ... catch ... catch it ... catch meat. Even old men looked like little children, in their eyes turned to the fields: only they tried to hide their trembling excitement as they carried token sheaves of beans to the threshing-ground. But as they sat and sipped beer or merely talked about this and that they were still thrilled by the sight of children competing in threshing the mass of pea-and beanstalks with thin poles: a purring rustling sound issued forth as the bare grains of beans or peas jumped from the beaten dry sheaves and coursed through the dry stalks to the ground. Women winnowing beans in the wind was itself a sight to see: sometimes the breeze would stop and women would curse and wait holding their wicker trays ready to catch the breeze when it returned. It was as if the wind was teasing the women and was only being playful with their hopes and desires and expectation of clearing off the chaff before darkness fell and put an end to the working day. Later it was the turn of the cows: they were left loose to roam through the harvested fields of maize: they would run about, tails held up to the sky, kicking up dust with their hind legs, their tongues reaching out for the standing feed of maize. Sometimes the male would run

after a young female, giving it no rest or time to eat, expecting another kind of harvest.

❀

Munira and Abdulla were one evening resting from the last stages of the busy harvest, talking about the coming ceremony of circumcision. Karega was teaching Joseph some algebraic sums. Munira was telling Abdulla how he had always felt a little incomplete because he had been circumcised in hospital under a pain killer, so that he never really felt that he truly belonged to his age-group: Gicina Bangi. Wanja suddenly sprang among them, micege and grass and maramata sticking to her skirt. Abdulla gave her a beer. Munira playfully admonished her: where has our proprietor been? Karega continued with his teaching. Wanja sat quietly on a low stool, her legs parted a little, her hands pressing down her skirt between her thighs. She looked at them all as if she was in deep meditation. Maiden from the fields, Munira thought, and now he remembered the bruises on their skins, sustained when gathering beanstalks into sheaves. They were all caught up in that atmosphere of indolence and relaxation from a fatiguing session of breaking maize in the sun which only needed a beer and a fire to send them to sleep. 'Like she had come from another world,' Munira continued with his line of thought. Was there anything she would do which could possibly make her less attractive? There was a fever-excitement in her eyes which would not go even when she laughed off the male concern in Munira's eyes. Then she started talking almost to herself: 'I've got it now, now I've got it. And you won't believe it when I tell you of it. But I shall tell you, for you see – must we not redeem this village, bribe the troubling ghosts of those that went before us? Sometimes it pains, the memory. Must we not lure new blood to a forgotten village? Theng'eta is the plant that only the old will talk about. Why? It is simple. It is only they who will have heard of it or know about it. It grows wild, in the plains, the herdsmen know it and where it grows, but they will not tell you. Nyakinyua says that they used to brew it before Europeans came. And they would drink it only when work was finished, and especially after the ceremony of circumcision or marriage or itwika, and after a harvest. It was when they were drinking Theng'eta that poets and singers composed their words for a season of Gichandi, and the seer voiced his prophecy. It was outlawed by the colonialists. He said: These people are lazy. They drink Theng'eta the whole day. That is why they will not work on the railway line. That's why they will not work on our tea and coffee and sisal farms. That's why they will not be slaves. That, says

Nyakinyua, was after the battle of Ilmorog, and they said that these warriors must have been drunk: for how dared they put out their tongues and flex their muscles at the colonialists when they already knew what had happened to others who had resisted? So only the less potent stuff. Muratina, was now allowed. Even this was only licensed to the headmen and chiefs who had shown that they could secure more people to work on European farms – for according to her, people kept on running away. For how could a whole people leave their land to go and work for strangers? So that's why the art of making Theng'eta was lost, except to a few. But it is a Gichandi player's spirit: it is also used in fertility rites.'

Karega, who had stopped the teaching to listen to her monologue, asked:

'This battle of Ilmorog. What did she say about it?'

'Aah! she is always evasive. She will tell you a story without your asking and when you become curious she suddenly cuts it off. You had better ask her yourself.'

'And Theng'eta,' asked Abdulla. 'Did she tell you how to make it?'

'She said she would show us how to make it. Theng'eta ... just a little spirit to bless the work of our hands.'

'When?' Munira asked.

'Soon. It must be ready on the day of circumcision. When the elders are having their Njohi we too can join them with our Theng'eta.'

'Why not? To celebrate! To say farewell to a season of drought,' said Karega with boyish enthusiasm. 'To celebrate a big harvest.'

'Farewell to the drought in our lives,' added Abdulla.

'And for more sperms of God to fertilise the earth,' Munira said.

'A Village Festival,' Abdulla agreed.

'Time too, before the police post and the church are occupied,' added Karega.

❁

They started work on the idea with a playful religious fervour. Nyakinyua's hut was the centre of action. The old woman took out some millet seeds, soaked them in water, and put them in a sisal bag. Everyday at about five they all would pass by the woman's hut to see if the seeds had started to germinate. On the third day they found Nyakinyua standing at the door, beckoning them to hurry up. She had sighted little shoots, she told them, with the eagerness of a child. It was true: as if peeping through numerous holes in the bag were yellowish greenish naked things. Lord watch over us. Wanja poured out the seedlings onto a tray and they all joined hands in spreading them out to dry. Munira's fingers were trembling at the nearness of Wanja. Lord, breathe strength into our hands. Another three days of anxious waiting. The old woman supervised the grinding but it was Wanja on her knees, a cloth tied just above her breasts so that her shoulders were bare, who did it. This in itself was a kind of festival and children and even men came and sat around and watched the grinding with stone and mortar. She would put some seeds on a large, hard, flattened granite stone, inoro, and she used a smaller one, thio, to crunch-crunch the millet. The spectators stood or sat and moved their eyes with the forward-backward motion of her beautiful body, until the seedlings were one stringy velvet mass. She was sweating by the time she finished but her eyes were shining with suppressed elation.

The old woman now set to work. She mixed the crunched millet seedlings with fried maize flour and put the mixture in a clay pot, slowly adding water and stirring. She covered its mouth with the mouth of yet another pot through which she had bored a hole. A bamboo pipe was fixed into the hole and its other end put in a sealed jar over which she placed a small basin of cold water. Then she sealed every possible opening with cowdung and when she had finished she stood back to survey her work of art and science. Karega exclaimed: 'But this is chemistry. A distillation process.' She now placed the pot near the fireplace.

After this it was simply a matter of waiting for the brew to get ready. It would take a number of days, she told them. But their attention was now taken by the preparations for the ceremony. People were already beginning to sing and dance in groups in rehearsal for the eve of the ceremony. It would also be the eve of Theng'eta drinking and celebration.

Karega could hardly wait for Saturday. He had always liked the dances connected with the ritual of circumcision and the singing, especially when two or more good singers happened to be present and faced one another in a kind of poetry contest. Then his heart would be lifted to lands far and beautiful where people were held together by a common spirit.

The main venue was at Njogu's house because Njenga, one of his sons, was going to be circumcised. Muriuki too, and a few others were going to face the knife, as they would say.

The dances on the eve of circumcision attracted people from ridges near and far. Even the builders came to participate so that both the hut and the compound of Njogu's place were full. Karega took part in some of the more general dances like Mumburo. But he, like Munira, did not know how to do the mock fight. At times it really looked as if somebody would really throw another into the fire, and Karega's stomach tingled with fear of expectation. But all the same, he was soon drawn into the dance, and after a while, he was sweating.

Wanja was amused to see Karega laughing and jumping about, completely absorbed in the atmosphere. He was normally so serious that at times Wanja wanted to tickle him under the armpit just to see him laugh or relax that earnest face.

Munira liked the dances: but it always made him sad that he could not take part, that he did not really know the words, and his body was so stiff. So he only watched, feeling slightly left out, an outsider at the gate of somebody else's house.

And the house tonight belonged to Karega and Abdulla and Nyakinyua. Nyakinyua especially. She was good at singing and she threw erotic abuse, compliments, or straight cerebratory words with ease. She would make up words referring to anybody, any event, without breaking the tune or the rhythm. Most of the dance songs had a refrain and everybody could join in the chorus. But it was Njuguna and Nyakinyua who provided the dramatic tension in the opera of eros. They all, young and old, women and men, had formed a circle, and they moved round, feet raising a little dust, in rhythm with the songs:

Njuguna is now a visitor, standing at the gate of the homestead. He pays compliments to the house but demands to know who the owner is so that with his permission Njuguna can throw himself to the ground and bathe in the dust like the young bull of a rhinoceros. Nyakinyua answers him and says he is welcome so should feel himself at home:

> Njuguna: And show me the bride!
> And show me the bride!
> Chorus: I'll pass through Ilmorog –
> Njuguna: For whom our goats
> Came crying in daylight
> Chorus: I'll pass through Ilmorog –
> Greeting Muturi and the young braves.

Wanja is pulled to the centre of the circle. All fingers point at her as Nyakinyua replies that this is the bride, 'truly ours and not the other one, belonging to a different neighbourhood, for whom I was being abused.'

Njuguna's tone suddenly changes. He puts contempt on his face:

> Njuguna: Is this the bride?
> Is this the bride?

Chorus:	I'll pass through Ilmorog –
Njuguna:	So dark, so beautiful
	But with a broken cunt?
Chorus:	I'll pass through Ilmorog –
	Greeting Muturi and the young braves.

Nyakinyua's voice comes in strong accepting the challenge and swearing to abuse him and even extend the abuse to his clan:

Nyakinyua:	But can you do it?
	But can you do it?
Chorus:	I'll pass through Ilmorog –
Nyakinyua:	You are the one that roars threats
	But keeps a bride wakeful for nothing!

Njuguna is not at a loss for words but comes back to the attack with the prideful authority of a choosy lover:

Njuguna:	I saw cunt holding tobacco wrapped in banana leaves,
	I saw cunt holding tobacco wrapped in banana leaves
Chorus:	I'll pass through Ilmorog –
Njuguna:	I didn't know that cunt
	You took so much snuff.
Chorus:	I'll pass through Ilmorog
	Greeting Muturi and the young braves.

It is now a full battle in an erotic war of words and gestures and tones suggestive of many meanings and situations. The crowd of dancers is getting more and more excited, waiting to see who will be the first to give way, to crack under the weight of the other's abuses and allusions. Nyakinyua is now on top and she presses home her advantage:

Nyakinyua:	I was not even giving it to you
	I was not even giving it to you
Chorus:	I'll pass through Ilmorog –
Nyakinyua:	It's only that I found you
	Fucking a crack
Chorus:	I'll pass through Ilmorog –
	Greeting Muturi and young braves.

Njuguna gives way. Why, he asks, should children from the same womb fight one another, with the enemy at the gate? He is now pleading to his mother. He is really her warrior returning weary but victorious from wars:

208

Mother ululate for me!
Mother ululate for me!
Or do you leave it to strangers and foreigners
To ululate for your son's homecoming?

All the women now ululate the five Ngemi for a boy newly born or one returning from wars against the enemy of the people.

Under the emotion of the hour, Munira suddenly tried a verse he thought he knew. Njuguna and Nyakinyua were making it sound so easy and effortless. But in the middle he got confused. Njuguna and Nyakinyua now teamed up against him:

You now break harmony of voices
You now break harmony of voices
It's the way you'll surely break our harmony
When the time of initiation comes.

But Abdulla came to the rescue:

I was not breaking up soft voices
I was not breaking up soft voices
I only paused to straighten up
The singers' and dancers' robes.

Nyakinyua's voice now drifted in, conciliatory, but signalling the end of this particular dance. She asked in song: if a thread was broken, to whom were the pieces thrown to mend them into a new thread? Njuguna replied, turning to Karega: it was thrown to Karega for he was a big warrior, Njamba Nene.

All looked to Karega to take up the broken thread. The school children laughed not only at his inability to take up the challenge, but also because of the reference to Njamba Nene. It was Abdulla who helped him out. He sang that when the old thread was broken, it was time for the whole people to change to another tune altogether, and spin a new and stronger thread.

In response as it were to Abdulla's call for a change of threads, they now sat down. They listened to Nyakinyua as she sang Gitiro. At first it was good-humoured, light-hearted, as she commented on those present to a chorus of laughter.

But suddenly they were caught by the slight tremor in her voice. She was singing their recent history. She sang of two years of failing rains; of the arrival of daughters and teachers; of the exodus to the city. She talked of how she had earlier imagined the city as containing only wealth. But she found poverty; she found crippled beggars; she saw men, many men, sons of women, vomited out of a smoking tunnel – a big, big house – and she was afraid. Who had swallowed all the wealth of the land? Who?

And now it was no longer the drought of a year ago that she was singing about. It was all the droughts of the centuries and the journey was the many journeys travelled by people even in the mythical lands of two-mouthed Marimus and struggling humans. She sang of other struggles, of other wars – the arrival of colonialism and the fierce struggles waged against it by newly circumcised youth. Yes, it was always the duty of youth to drive out foreigners and enemies lodged amongst the people: it was always the duty of youth to fight all the Marimus, all the two-mouthed Ogres, and that was the meaning of the blood shed at circumcision.

She stopped at the dramatic call and challenge. Then the women applauded with four ululations. Nyakinyua had made them relive their history.

And so it went on to the small hours. It was really very beautiful. But at the end of the evening Karega felt very sad. It was like beholding a relic of beauty that had suddenly surfaced, or like listening to a solitary beautiful tune straying, for a time, from a dying world.

❈

Later after the ceremony of the Ilmorog river, Karega and Munira went to Abdulla's place to wait for Wanja and the old woman and for the mysterious plant. Wanja came for them late in the afternoon. They all went to Nyakinyua's place.

'We looked for it all over and at last we found out where it grew abundantly,' Wanja was explaining.

'Didn't you go to the ceremony?' Abdulla asked.

'We went. They all bravely went through it. None showed cowardice and so we didn't get a chance of beating anyone.'

The plant was very small with a pattern of four tiny red petals. It had no scent.

Theng'eta. The spirit.

Nyakinyua dismantled the distillery. The pot-jar was full of a clear white liquid.

'This is only ... this is nothing yet.' Nyakinyua explained. 'This can only poison your heads and intestines. Squeeze Theng'eta into it and you get your spirit. Theng'eta. It is a dream. It is a wish. It gives you sight, and for those favoured by God it can make them cross the river of time and talk with their ancestors. It has given seers their tongues; poets and Gichandi players their words; and it has made barren women mothers of many children. Only you must take it with faith and purity in your hearts.'

They crowded around as she squeezed drops of a greenish liquid into the jar. There was a small hiss, then the whole thing became a very clear light green.

'We can try it later in the evening. Wanja will call a few elders, for this is not a stuff for children.'

They came back later in the evening. Under the mood of the frank atmosphere of the circumcision ceremony, they all felt together – a community sharing a secret. They sat in a circle according to their ages. Munira found himself sitting next to Njuguna. Wanja sat between Abdulla and Karega. They all removed their ties, their shoes, anything which might prevent their bodies from being loose and at ease. She commanded them to remove all the money in the pockets, the metal bug that split up homes and drove men to the city. She took all the money and put it away on the floor outside the ritual circle. She sat down.

Millet, power of God.

She poured a few drops on the floor and chanted: for those that went before us and those coming after us, tene na tene, tene wa tene.

Then she put some in a small horn, and continued her admonitions, looking at them, fixing them with her eyes.

'And now, my children,' she intoned, holding the tiny horn in her hands, 'you must always drink from the common measure. Always the correct measure, starting with the eldest amongst you. You may then dream your wishes and wish your dreams. Who knows? If you are the lucky one, the one most ready to receive, it may be given to you. Not for me today. But I will sniff a little.'

She brought it to her nose and seemed to inhale something. Then she tasted a drop or two.

'Aaaaah. I am old. I have no more dreams. And what are my wishes? There is only one. To join my man in the other world. Do you know we wooed in a millet field while chasing away birds? He was good with herbs, my man was. He showed me how to make this holy water as we lay wakeful to the noise and movement of the birds. Every night of our watch, we would sniff and sip a drop and there was peace around us. The millet fingers caressed our bodies and – and – here, Njuguna, why don't you take this and start the round?'

Her voice had stilled their hearts and they already felt a oneness even as each waited his turn. When it came to Munira, he sniffed and the slightly acid fumes raced up his nose to his head. You must also sip, he heard some voice say. He felt its burning down his throat – something like the eucalyptus leaves that cured Joseph – right down to the seat of his stomach. For a few seconds he felt only this burning in his belly and in his head. But gradually the fire became less and less as his body and mind relaxed, becoming warmer and warmer, lighter and lighter. Oh, the twilight stillness within. His eyes were a little heavy and drowsy but he could see clearly to the smallest detail. Oh, the clarity of the light. Oh, Lord, the colour of thy light. Changing colours of a rainbow dream. He was now a bird and he flew up and up in the air, and at the same time he saw heaven and earth, past and present open out to him. The old woman, strong sinews forged by earth and sun and rain, was the link binding past and present and future. And he saw her in black robes of celebration-in-work, saw her way, way back in the past and in the future, one continuous sweep of time, how immense, saw her beside Ndemi fell-ing the forests, harnessing the elements and secrets of nature for use by her children. He longed to be there. There past – present – future were one and his children were schooling to some national purpose, also felling trees, clearing virgin grounds, new horizons for the glory of man and his creative genius. Gradually he heard a distant voice calling: tell us your dreams and wishes. He halted, in his flight: what did he wish for in life? What did he want? His parents had always played it safe and he, Munira, had always stood at the shore and watched streams and brooks flow over pebbles and rocks. He was an outsider, he had always been an outsider, a spectator of life, history. He wanted to say: Wanja! give me another night of the big moon in a hut and through you, buried in you, I will be reborn into his-tory, a player, an actor, a creator, not this, this disconnection. But when he spoke, his voice was strangely calm: I don't really know my wishes and my dreams are few. But this thing I now see – what is it? What is the meaning of this motion about me? I seem to see Nya-kinyua yesterday and tomorrow! I see her beside Ndemi, but how can this be since he lived a long time ago? I also see her beside these people marching to war: tell us, Nyakinyua, tell us, since you started it during our journey to the city. What did they see? What did they see that seems suddenly hidden from my sight?

❁

Why, my children ... you ask too many questions, even after I have told you that there is nothing more to tell. You have been to school. You and this small one here are the teachers of our children. What do you tell them? That we were always like this, will always be like this? And you, my daughter, have you not seen more than you dare tell? What about Abdulla here? What other secrets does he hide in that stump of a leg? Going-away generation ... but they will one day return to a knowledge of themselves and then the kingdom of

God and of man will be theirs. Ndemi left a curse. His children were never to abandon this land: they were to defend it with blood, it and all that it produces. Not that I understand the meaning of it all, why despite the spear, despite our numbers they beat us and scattered us to the four corners of the wind ... how can I understand this alternation of fertility and barrenness, drought and rain, night and day, destruction and creation, birth and death? No, there are many things that I too do not understand.

There was my man too, remember. He was among the batch that carried food and guns for the white people to fight it out amongst themselves. He did not choose to be a slave like Munoru. The chief who had been appointed watchman for the colonialist demanded the fat of ten sheep and goats. My man was proud. He refused and spat his contempt for a slave. So he was listed together with the poor who in their poverty could not also produce the required fat. My man was wealthy: but proud. Some were taken to work on European farms while the white men went to war. Imagine that: taken to keep the white man's shambas alive while theirs fell into neglect and waste! For a woman alone can never do all the work on the farm. How could she grow sugar cane, yams, sweet potatoes which used to be man's domain? How break new ground? And how could she smith, make chains, pull wires, make beehives, wicker work for barns? All that and do her own share of the work? The others in single file, loads on their heads, went toward the coast, cutting paths in the forest, sometimes following the tracks made earlier by Swahili and Arab raiders from the coast. And then – it was before they reached Kibwezi – they saw this animal of the earth. It was so long, they had never seen anything like it before, it was a sight more terrifying than the Ndamathia of the sea from whom we all get our shadows. Its eyes spat out light, its forked tongue fire and hisses, and they, circumcised though they were, stood witch-rooted to the ground. A voice said to them: don't touch this strange creature that walks on its belly. Study it carefully and learn the gifts of God to all his children, world without end. They were tired. They had walked miles, day in, day out, fighting sleep and even desire for the more permanent sleep. And now the animal was blocking the way. A man took a stone and hit it. It raised its head once, briefly, it vomited out a fire and light tenfold more intense than lightning, and with one huge hiss that shook the ground it moved away, belly on the earth. Blood-lust caught some of the others. They hurled stones and curses at it and even laughed at their easy deliverance! Listen, my children, listen, and fear the ways of the Lord. None who touched that animal ever returned. Some fell to the German fire, others to malaria, yet others to strange and violent vomiting. Only a few of all those who went returned from the war.

And your man, somebody asked?

He came back. He came back all right, but not the same man with whom I had earlier coiled together thighs and bodies made smooth by mbariki oil and sweat.

She was again silent. She stirred the Theng'eta pot once then let her hand just touch the stirring stick. She was not with them now, she had, just as when she had told them the story in the plains, descended into a private gloom of memories and uncertainties. She remained thus, hand on the stirring stick, head inclined to one side, eyes on the floor, answering none of the questions on their silent faces.

❁

Karega glanced at her figure, bent so, and repeated to himself: no longer the same. He turned the phrase over and over again in his mind as if this alone explained all the agony, all the hidden meanings in her unfinished – well, in their unfinished – story. It was how he had felt after Mukami's departure: it was how he had felt on leaving Siriana; it was how he felt after the recent journey. Indeed, he thought now, things could never really be the same even in viewing that past of his people, the past he had tried to grapple with in Siriana, and at Ilmorog school. Which past was one talking about? Of Ndemi and the creators from Malindi to Songhai; from the cape of storms, to the Mediterranean Sea? The past of a broken civilisation, retarded growth, black people scattered over the globe to feed the ever-demanding god of profit that the lawyer talked about? The past of houses and crops burnt and destroyed and diseases pumped into a continent? Or was it the past of L'Ouverture, Turner, Chaka, Abdulla, Koitalel, Ole Masai, Kimathi, Mathenge and others? Was it of chiefs who sold the others, of the ones who carried Livingstone and Stanley on their backs, deluded into believing that a service to a white man was really a service to God? The past of Kinyanjui, Mumia, Lenana, Chui, Jerrod, Nderi wa Riera? Africa, after all, did not have one but several pasts which were in perpetual struggle. Images pressed on images. He tried to wrestle with each, fix it, study it, make it yield the secret that had thus far eluded him. And suddenly as the past unfolded before him, he saw, or he imagined he saw, the face of his brother! But how could this be, seeing that he had never met him? Still the face was there, it persisted in its elusive suggestion of many seasons! He remembered the story Abdulla had told them in the plains and he wondered if Abdulla could have known him. Abdulla, after all, came from Limuru. Then he thought of Munira: he had known him, and he wondered why he had not asked him more about Nding'uri. But then, despite their almost two years together, sharing the same compound, it was surprising how little they knew of each other's lives. Thinking of Munira brought back the face of Mukami. Was it Theng'eta in his head? But then Mukami's face had haunted him all his life.

Many a time had he tried to give what he felt a captive form in words – cupped hands raised to the heart in prayer. Under the power of Theng'eta, he seemed to feel the words. But suddenly, and despite the face that now stood vividly before him – had he crossed the river of time? – he wanted to laugh. He had just remembered Fraudsham telling them that writing was akin to religion: 'My boys, a sublime act, a cleansing rite'. and Jesus and Shakespeare had changed the English language. Before they did an essay, he would lecture them, so serious: My boys, it is what you truly feel that you must put down on paper. Not that they believed him and his talk of writing as an act of confession of heated passions and anguish. He, Karega, for instance, would often weave incredible heroic deeds and tuck in a little Christian message around the simplest topics. Like that visit to his aunt. That imaginary aunt, he now thought: she had followed him in every class in every school and he could never understand why teachers, black, white, red, or yellow, were always obsessed with people's aunts, people's last holidays, people's first visits to a city. Anguish and passion. What nonsense, he thought. Anything he truly felt, anything that had really happened to him in life was banned from his pen. There were things that one could not say on paper, there were things that belonged to oneself alone: how then could he have spoken his heart to another, to a teacher, for the award of a mark or two? And would they have believed him if he had written that he had not gone to visit any aunts or any cities, that with every sunset he would simply walk up the hill overlooking Manguo and wait for her, hoping that she would come his way? And he would pray, Karega would truly pray, that Christ, God, Lord, anybody in that high sky should let her come out of the big house for just a little walk across the fields or command her to walk up the mountain or go to Manguo to wash clothes or something, anything!

'Millet, power of God!' he started, and at their hushed silence even as the horn of the spirit was passing round he knew that he would tell it. It was, after all, what many times he had written over and over again in his exercise books, in his mind, in his thoughts.

'Whatever I did, wherever I went, she was always inside me,

fluttering at the edges of my dreams and desires, between sleeping and waking. It was, God knows, as if I had met her in another world before this one and she had left me a sign by which I would later recognise her.

'I first really met her when I found her sitting at the edge of the Manguo quarry on a hill we called ha-Mutabuki, near the household of Njinju wa Nducu and that of Omari Juma, but whom we called Umari wa Juma. She was sitting on the edge of the quarry, resting back on her hands planted to the earth, her legs swinging in the menacing caved hollow. Further down the hill was the tarmac road said to have been carved out of the hill by the Italian prisoners of war. It always seemed to me that motor-cars, bicycles and men were suddenly vomited out, or suddenly swallowed by the earth, so sharp was the road at the place we called Kimunya's bend, facing Kieya's ridge on which stood Manguo school. I was struck by her daring, for I always felt dizzy even at the thought of standing at the edge of any precipice. I walked toward her nevertheless and she looked up and saw me and invited me, well, challenged me to join her. Just like that. I hesitated. Come on, it is nothing to fear, she said. Who told you I am afraid? I said, pretending anger. I walked on because of her challenge and because I did not want her to see my fear. Still I was scared. My heart gave one huge beat: my legs seemed to lose strength at the knees. I was scared. I was scared. But the fear also fascinated and thrilled me. It was strange: I was walking toward life and death, my legs were really giving way, and yet something between pain and joy coursed through my fear-warmed blood and this became intense. I wanted to cry but I went on, magnet pulled by that face and the smile and the slight gap in the upper teeth – all of which I had seen before but never been really aware of.

'We sat there and talked and watched the thabiri birds fly away with the sun. I knew her, of course, because my mother had lived as a squatter on her father's other farm on the other side of the hill facing Limuru Town and the settled area.

'She asked me why I didn't go to school. I said I always wanted to, which was not quite true. She said she went to school at Kamandura. I there and then swore that I would go to school.

'The following week I was daily at her father's pyrethrum field picking the yellow daisies.

'I was adept at it anyway, but now there was a new personal involvement in the job and my mother wondered what had come over me. I want to go to school, I said. I want to earn money to pay fees.

'Sometimes she came to help me and she would tell me more

stories about her school. She would also bring me ripe red plums and later juicy luscious pears.

'Well, I earned enough money to pay for a term. When mother saw my determination, she offered to help with the rest.

'She taught me what she knew, and I made quick progress. The teachers allowed me to skip a class or two so that within two years I was only a class behind her.

'My mother was God-fearing, murmuring prayers at every opportunity. But she had never managed to make me pray or to know the meaning of prayer.

'It was Mukami who taught me prayer. My first prayer – she had told me that God would do anything that one asked for – was on the road to school, under a cedar tree, a place we called Kamutarakwa-ini.

'She was not with me that day. I think she was ill or something. Anyway, an emotion I had not previously experienced suddenly seized me: I bent my head, and shut my eyes, and I asked the Lord to cure her: and Lord, if it is true that you can do anything let me, let me, let Mukami be mine.

'On weekends and during school vacations, I worked on her father's farms, and again she would come and help me.

'Oh, and we often waded through the green reeds in Manguo lake chasing away thabiri and collecting thabiri eggs.

'And sometimes in the pyrethrum fields, or out by the lake, we wrestled. She would fall to the ground and I would fall atop of her and she would cry and I would get off and she would stand up and rub off dust or grass from her skirt, and then she would laugh at me saying: you coward. Then I would chase her, we would wrestle again, she would suddenly become limp and I would fell her to the ground and there was the strange song in my blood and she would cry and call me sinful and wicked. I would go away again and she would laugh at me and I hated her for all those things in me that I could not quite explain.

'She went to Kanjeru High School, and I thought our worlds had parted. A year after, I followed and went to Siriana High School. The two schools, as you know, are next to one another, separated only by a valley between. There we continued meeting on Saturdays and we talked about our schools, our teacher, our homes, Uhuru and everything was good.

'We saw one another during the school vacations – this time not too often – but once or twice in church.

'It was during her fourth year and my third year in high school that I started noticing changes in her attitude. She was more irritable, it was as if she was angry at seeing me, and yet if I missed a meeting with her she would become even more angry. I could never do anything right and I thought, well, I thought it was because of exam fever.

'One day during a school vacation she passed by our place, our hut in Kamiritho village, and told me, let's go to church. We followed the same dusty road we used to follow as children going to primary school. We recalled many friends and incidents. There was that tall lanky fellow called Igogo: boys used to tease him to tears by calling him hawk, hawk. There was that daughter of Kimunya, reputedly one of the most beautiful women in all the land. We got into church: and were glad that Rev. Joshua Matenjwa, then the most popular preacher with the youth, was in the pulpit. All throughout she was very playful and where before she had been careful about being seen with me or any boy by her parents, this time she did not seem to care. After church we walked the tarmac road, through Ngenia, to Nguirubi. We lay on the grass and dreamed big dreams: of finishing school, going to University, getting married, children, and all that, even quarrelling about which should come first: a boy or a girl. She wanted a boy and I wanted a girl, we argued, and did not notice the time passing. We ran through Gitogothi, and near Mbira's place she suddenly said: let's do like we used to do when we were children: pick thabiri eggs from the lake. It was mad, it was crazy, dusk was coming, but really it was good. We waded through the water, birds flew in the sky, and the green reeds and the tall grass entangled our feet and slowed our progress to the centre. We picked some eggs as we went along.

'In the middle of Manguo lake were two humps which were never covered by water no matter how much it rained, they always seemed to float above the water. Later I learnt that these were sides of a dam built by the young men of Kihiu Mwiri generation at the insistence of Mukoma Wa Njiriri, then a chief, as a condition of his giving them licence for initiation. But ... legend among us boys had it that they were the humps of two giant shark-like animals that used to dwell in the lake, and the reeds were supposed to be their puberty hair. On one of them we went and sat down. It was still. So still, and we watched the thabiri birds fly away following the sun. We counted the eggs. We had collected about ten. Between us. Then suddenly she broke into the stillness with a little piercing cry – uuu! and I saw that a leech had bitten her chin and was now sucking her blood. I pulled it off and blood flowed. I rubbed it and told her not to worry and she told me to stop it, she was not a child or something. I got angry and she got angry and I really wanted to slap her for calling me a big baby but she held my hand and we started wrestling. We wrestled one another and I was really very angry with her. I threw her to the ground and I fell on to her. I felt warm all over and blood coursed through every vein and artery of my being and she held me, dusk was over us and the world was still, so still in its gentle motion.

'When later I awoke, I saw that night had descended and a small moon had appeared.

'Mukami was sitting down. She had broken all the eggs and the shells scattered on the ground beside her.

' "What have you done?" I asked. "Why did you do it?" '

'It was then that I saw that she was crying. I held her and told her not to worry, that nothing would happen to her, and that I would anyway marry her, should anything happen.

'She looked up at me, sadly I imagined, and she said:

' "It is not that. It is not that at all."

' "What's wrong, then?" I asked, concerned, fearing I would never fathom her or any woman.

'Her next question really shook me, so unexpected it was:

' "Had you a brother who died or something?"

'I always had vague feelings about my brother. I even had vague misty feelings that I might have seen him way, way back when I was a tiny child. But no, it could not be, and yet something must have happened because we moved from our place on her father's farm and went to a village. The whole thing was mixed up in my mind. I once or twice asked my mother — I think I must have heard a whispering from our neighbours — but she waved off my questions and said something about his having gone to my father in the Rift Valley, and since I had also never seen my father I did not follow up her answer with more questions.

' "I don't know," I said. "Maybe ... no, I don't think so. I mean, the one I know went to the Rift Valley. But why do you ask?"

' "You see, my father has discovered our love. He knows that you are the son of Mariamu. He says that your brother used to be a Mau Mau ... and that it was he who must have led a gang into our home and who cut off his right ear after accusing him of helping white men or preaching against Mau Mau in Church. Uhuru or not Uhuru, he would never forgive that indecency, and he would never let his daughter marry into such a family, so poor, and with such a history of crime. For a whole term he has been telling me to break it off. And now he has finally asked me to choose between him and you. I give you up or else I look for another father and another home."

'We waded back through cold water and the reeds, through the moon silence and the gloom. I took her to near her home and I went back to Kamiritho. I asked my mother about my brother.

' "Please tell me the truth," I told her.

' "Nding'uri. He carried bullets for fighters and he was hanged. Don't ask me any more. I am not a judge over the actions of men. We are all in the hands of God."

'Well, I never saw Mukami again.

'Mukami, my life, later jumped off the quarry where I first met her. She died before they could get her to Aga Khan Hospital in Nairobi.'

4 ❀ The effect of this extraordinary confession on those present was great. The old woman remained staring in the same place. But her hand mechanically stirred the Theng'eta pot faster and faster. Wanja moved closer to him. Munira sighed, something between a cough and a choked cry. He then stood up and went out. He was unable to understand the hatred that had suddenly seized him. Mukami was his sister, the only one who had taken his side, and between his father and Karega he now did not know whom to blame. He stayed out until, slightly composed, he came back to find an even more eerie spectacle.

Abdulla had grabbed Karega by the shoulders and was shaking him almost violently, all the time asking him, repeating the same same thing: 'You, you, Nding'uri's brother?' And his tone was something like the cry of a strangled animal.

In his mind – but how could they know? – seethed memories of a childhood lived together with a friend, haunting the butcheries and tea shops in Limuru, scrambling for rotten bread thrown on the rubbish heaps from Manubhai's bakery at Limuru; bitter, sweet, bitter dreams of an education he was never to have in colonial Kenya; crowded memories of the search for a decent job or trade: the years of toil at the shoe factory: the years of awakening, with more dreams of black David with only a sling, a spear and a stolen gun triumphing over white Goliath with his fat cheques and machine-guns; dreams of a total liberation so that a black man could lift high his head secure in his land, secure in his school, secure in his culture – all this and more ... and below it all ... the loss ... the unavenged loss.

He could not spill this out at once. He only asked: 'You? You? Nding'uri's brother?'

They all waited to see what he would do next, waited for an explanation.

Abdulla sat back on his stool and quickly swallowed one or two

Theng'eta drops. Their puzzled eyes were now on him, for his dramatic act had temporarily taken them from Karega's story. He seemed to be savouring the Theng'eta effect, then he looked at them all. He struck a fly buzzing near his right ear and then rested his eyes on Karega. Amid their silence of unuttered questions, he now started in a pathetic, chanting voice.

'Millet, power of God!

'Nding'uri, son of Mariamu. Nding'uri, my childhood. Nding'uri, the bravest of them all. Unwept, unavenged he lies somewhere in a common grave. In a mass grave. The unknown unsung soldier of Kenya's freedom . . .'

They all felt uncomfortable, embarrassed even.

Then he shook himself, composed himself, and his voice was now slightly tired, neutral, almost without emotion.

'Millet, power of God,' he repeated.

'Nding'uri, son of Mariamu. He had come early to my mother's hut and together we drank the millet porridge she had cooked. In a day or two it would be his turn to enter the forest. I had not yet taken the batuni oath, but I was to join the fighters as soon as I had successfully undergone the ritual. After the porridge we went out into the yard, leaned against the mud-walls to capture the morning sunshine. There was the sun, there was no wind, but it was still cold. We took a turn around the one-acre shamba, aimlessly pulling out a weed here, a weed there, from among the peas and bean flowers. We threw stones at the pear tree in the middle of the shamba to see who would be the first to bring down a pear. But the game and even the fruit were a little tasteless. Later at ten we sauntered toward the Indian shopping centre. We passed by the house of Kimuchu wa Ndung'u, a wealthy supporter of Mau Mau who was later shot by the white people: we stopped by the house, it was newly built, a stone house, the only stone house owned by a black man in the area, and we asked ourselves: will there come a day when all Kenyans can afford such a decent house? Nding'uri said: That is why I am going to join Kimathi and Mathenge. At the Indian-owned shopping centre we were going to meet a man, our man, who had some shadowy conections with the colonial police and used to get bullets from them and in exchange, according to him, he would bring them juicy women. At least that was the story he had told us. His sister, anyway, was Nding'uri's girl – they came from Ngecha – or Kabuku or somewhere in that direction – probably Wangigi – yes – I think it was Wangigi, but he was often to be found in Limuru. And indeed on one or two occasions he had sold us some bullets which we had promptly passed to our brothers in the forest according to our oath of unity. Today he was going to bring us some more and possibly a gun. Nding'uri, son of Mariamu. He was so excited about handling a gun, I knew it, I could see it on his face, although he tried to hide it. I joked about his prospects as a fighter. "Once upon a time, a warrior went to fight in enemy territory," I was telling him. "He came back home and started describing the battle to his father ... 'And this enemy came toward me and hit me one in the ribs. I fell. Another came and his spear just missed my neck. Another threw his club and it hit me right on the nose...' "he went on and on and did not see that his father was getting angry. "My son, I did not send you there to be beaten and to enjoy defeat. Such stories ... tell them to your mother." We laughed. Suddenly he stopped in the middle of the road, and thrust his fingers shaped like a revolver, toward me. "Stop, halt, you drinkers of blood! Halt, come here! Lie down. Flat. Arms stretched. You, you, get those hands out of your pockets ... Why do you oppress black people? Why do you take our land? Why do you take our sweat and ruin our women? Johnnie boys, red men, say your last prayers to your gods ... No answer? Guilty ... Trrro-Trrro-Trrroooo ..." the pistol was now a machine gun in his eager hands, and he was actually sweating. It is all right, I told him, shaking him by the shoulder. He laughed, I laughed, uneasily. And now we re-called the night he and I had done it to the same girl in my grand-mother's hut, where goats and sheep were kept, way back in the past. I did it to her, standing her against the wall and she holding up her skirt. The goats and sheep were bleating, some stampeding. She was crying, not true crying, it was a mixture of sighing and whimper-ing and sucking in juices of inward pains and it was good. When it was Nding'uri's turn, she protested a little, no ma Ngaikai inyui muri aganu-i, and then begged for a little rest. But Nding'uri would not hear of it and went straight at her. He found it difficult to enter her in that standing position and she tried to help him, not there, below, that's too far down, there, and suddenly both fell to the ground, lit-tered with dung and urine, but Nding'uri would not hold back. We recalled her words and laughed. She stood up, when it was all over, and angrily said: See, now, you have ruined my skirt and my calico, and ran out of the hut. We wondered if she, now a happily married mother of two, even remembered that night. Our talk somehow drifted to Nding'uri's present woman. As I told you, she was our friend's sister, in fact we had met him through her. At first he did not like their friendship, she told us, but Nding'uri and I dismissed this as the usual protective jealousy of a brother. And indeed he had later become friendly, he was really a talker, and it was he who had cas-ually broached the possibility of his supplying us with "grains of maize", as we called the deadly things. I told Nding'uri that he should have married the woman and he said it was all right, she had promised to wait for him until after the struggle, and in any case he wanted somebody for whom he would really be fighting. In this manner we soon reached the place, the back street next to a shop belonging to an Indian called Govnji-Ngunji. He was waiting for us. We shook hands and each handshake was a passage of the grains. It was so smooth and easy and it lasted hardly a minute and he was gone. The gun, he forgot to give us the gun, I told Nding'uri, and he tried to follow him. But then we decided we had better wait until the evening or another day. Two men came, emerged from nowhere, and tapped us on the shoulders. Something cold and hot flushed in my stomach. I knew and I think Nding'uri knew that we had been betrayed. The rat, Nding'uri hissed between his teeth, and was jerked forward with a sudden kick. A police van was parked near a kei-apple hedge near the Indian shops. The two plain-clothes men were laughing and cracking jokes and calling us Field-Marshals and Generals. Torn-trousered Generals. I felt bitter at my own impotence and accepted their jibes in bitter silence. One searched me. Then he suddenly stopped and he looked puzzled. Where are the things? he shouted at me. I too was puzzled. Suddenly there was a shout of triumph from the one who was searching Nding'uri. We all looked in that direction. He was holding high the deadly things found in Nding'uri's pockets. Then it occurred to me that my man had not searched the inner pocket of my jacket where I had put the grains. It was a split second. I didn't think about it. The decision as it were decided itself. I only followed it, and made a desperate leap for freedom. They were stunned at first. Then they cocked their guns. I heard the sounds. But this was not really me: how could I be so cool inside? I mixed with Indian children and all the police could do was to shoot in the air and shout to the Indians to help. But the traders were probably frightened by the gunsmoke and the children probably thought it was a joke because they were shouting and clapping and hollering, hurry up, hurry up! which brought more of them into the streets, thus further complicating the issue and so sheltering me from harm. I went through the back lanes, onto the fields near Gwa-Karabu toward Rongai, the African shops. Now they shot at me. I fell. I rose. They shot again. I fell and rose, over ditches and hillocks, through fields of grass, through Rongai market-place, across the railway line and on to the workers' quarters at Bata Factory. By this time, word had reached Bata. They hid me, passing me from door to door onto a secret path that led to the tea bush, to the forest and to friends.

'Nding'uri, son of my aunt. I never saw him again. A week later, they hanged him at Githunguri.

'Millet, power of God. I prayed: "Spare me, spare me, oh Lord, so that I can one day get that louse."

'And what did I do when I came out? I, Abdulla, forgot my vow to the Lord . . . I was busy looking for money . . . and even came to hide in Ilmorog.'

He broke off, choked, and for a few seconds he was lost to them. Karega's eyes were fixed on Abdulla. Nyakinyua raised her head and looked at all of them in turn as if she alone could see things hidden from them, as if she alone could read signs in the enigmatic gloom in the hut.

5 ❀ For years, Munira was to remember that night of Theng'eta drinking. Later in his statement he tried to sketch the scene, just the outline, of those puzzled faces, to capture in words Wanja's troubled voice, as she broke into their thoughts with the question that lay beneath the confessions, the memories, the inner wrestling with contradictory impulses, of that first night of contact with the Theng'eta, the spirit, in its purest form. Was she, he had then wondered, trying to save the occasion by changing the subject? And yet it was appropriate, directed at the only person who could show them the light out of their darkness.

'Tell us, mother, tell us this: what did your man see that changed him? What made him no longer the same? Did he tell you the meaning of what he saw?'

'In the glare of that light?' she had asked as if she had all along expected the question and had readied herself for it. 'What he saw in the glare of that light, he tried to tell me many times. But something always blocked him, his throat, in the beginning of telling it, and he could not continue. But then came the second big war, and once again our children, our sons, your father among them, were taken away and we heard strange names when they came back: Abithinia, Bama, India, Boboi, Njiovani, Njirimani, and others. And this time our sons were actually holding the guns and helping, unwillingly, in the general slaughter of human lives. My man would whisper all these things to me late at night and the fever would seize him and he would tremble so and I would hold him to still him. And one night he told it to me in words that were then strange and lacked meaning. Even this, even this slaughter is not what I saw. I tried him again: tell me what you saw, what is it that has troubled you these many years? Is it your son? Then he trembled again and I could see there were tears in his eyes and I held him to reassure him. He told me this: You see, woman mine ... when the animal, bigger it was than the famed Ndamathia remember, when it spat out the light, I thought I saw sons and daughters of black people of the centuries rise up as one to harness the power of that light, and the white man who was with us was frightened by what would happen when that power was in the hands of these black gods. He turned his wiles on us: he turned his poison tongue at us: do you remember Wakarwigi, the white man we called the hawk? He would run to Agikuyu and tell them: The Masai are coming to steal your cows and they are armed to the teeth: and he would would then run to the Masai and tell them: Wagikuyu are coming to steal your cows and your daughters and they are armed to the teeth. Do you remember how we almost slaughtered one another, with Wakarwigi coming in at the last minute as peacemaker? And when that finally failed, he turned his guns to the black children, who, having grown wiser, retreated to the forests and to the mountains, to reform their broken lines. They came back no longer trembling slaves, but itungati warriors armed with pangas, and spears and guns and faith. Yes, woman, and faith which was another kind of light. There were a few traitors among them, those who wanted to remain porters at the gate, collectors of the fallout from the white man's control of that power and of the human energies which worked it. But in the main they remained together ... and there was much blood, many motherless, many maimed legs, many broken homes and all because a few hungry souls sick with greed wanted everything for themselves. They took the virtues that arise from that as true virtues of the human heart. They practised charity, pity; they even made laws and rules of good conduct for those they had made motherless, for those they had driven into the streets. Tell me, woman: would we need pity, charity, generosity, kindness if there were no poor and miserable to pity and be kind to? And did they think that we would continue to be the receivers of their kindness and charity, when the power worked by us was enough to feed and clothe us all with the strength and infinite wisdom and love of a human being? And so there was this groaning, woman, this groaning in the fiery fury of the struggle. That, woman, was a terrible sight and sound to see and to hear, and it has kept me awake or in restless sleep this many a night, and I feared to tell you ...'

Abdulla was actually groaning and it was this that interrupted her narrative of the vision passed to her by her man, whose meaning they thought they understood: for had it not already happened? But Abdulla continued groaning and shouting obscenities at faces only he could see, and they thought that it was probably the memory of it that moved him so. Wanja rested her hand on his shoulders and he stopped writhing and groaning with pain and looked up into her eyes; then he turned away with a strange incomprehensible expression on his face. She too had a slightly contorted look of pain on her face and she bit her lower lip as if holding back further tears.

The old woman got off her stool by the Theng'eta pot. She looked at them all and Munira had the impression of tremendous compassion and gentleness and eagerness to heal on her emaciated face. 'Go home, children. Go home and sleep. You have all read the good God's own book ... vengeance is mine, and I say, is it any man's job to do God's justice and vengeance? Sleep, and let it be, let it be, for there are still so many karwigis in our midst. Sleep.'

❀

I keep on asking myself, now that it has happened, what it was she was trying to tell us that night, Munira scribbled with the inner fury of trying to understand. Would it have stopped what has now happened if it, whatever it was, had been heeded? By whom? Abdulla was the first to go out, he remembered, followed by Wanja and Karega. Wanja walked with Abdulla for a little distance and then came back and joined Karega where he was standing. And Munira could still recall distinctly the feeling he then had of being excluded from something that bound the others together. He would anyway have liked to be alone, with his thoughts, but Wanja's action somehow increased his smouldering wrath at his own uncertainties. He called her and she came to him. He thought he should hold back his words, but they were out, speaking his bitterness and the frustration of the many months she had kept him at a distance, playing with his emotions, memories, and expectations.

'Why did you come to Ilmorog? There was more peace before you came here.'

'The peace of nothing happening?' she retorted, and he, Munira, waited for her to continue, to say more, but she had already danced to Karega's side.

❀

I left them standing together and I walked home, alone, wrestling with my own thoughts and inner anxieties. Theng'eta ... Ilmorog ... Karega's story. During his telling it, my past had flashed across the dark abyss of my present. It was as if before tonight I had never known my family, my past. I remembered my only too recent conversation with my father and his apparent change in attitude. I remembered his missing ear. I had never, I confessed to myself, cared much for my father although I was slightly scared of him. I had never really known any of my sisters or brothers most of whom had married into wealth or had acquired wealth. Others had even gone to England for training as nurses, doctors and engineers. I had been an outsider, a distant spectator, who could only guess what was happening through hastily dropped hints, through earnest conversations that were abruptly stopped on my arrival at the scene. Why, my father had even run my home for me, and my wife had looked up to him for orders and approval. What now pained me, I don't know how to put it, was a feeling that Karega was more of an insider even in my family. Had he not already affected the course of its history? Mukami, although I had never known her beyond the fact that she was my sister and pupil, was of my blood: had he come all this way to throw her death in my face? Was this why he had come to Ilmorog, hiding the real motive behind past pupilship and desire for advice and help? Was there not a note of triumph at the edges of his narrative?

I argued with myself: my father was after all my father. What I felt was a strange feeling, an uncomfortable eerie sensation, disagreeably sitting in my stomach, of a son who had wined and dined with those who had deformed his father, blood of his blood, and brought death to the family. It was this I could not now justify in my own mind. I remembered Abdulla's words calling on the Lord to bring him face to face one day with Nding'uri's real murderer. How short a time it took me to forget Nyakinyua's words of wisdom and compassion! I cried in my heart: Give me the strength, Lord, give me a steadfast will. I felt, may the Lord forgive us all, that I had to take a drastic step that would restore me to my usurped history, my usurped inheritance, that would reconnect me with my history. Something to enable me to claim my father. And Karega loomed large in the way.

To say the truth, I did not know, I was not quite sure, whom I wanted to avenge: myself, Mukami, my father: but I only felt driven to do something to give me a sense of belonging. I was tired of being a spectator, an outsider.

Chapter Eight

1 ☘ Karega walked ahead, in the dark, as if he would be happy, alone, with just his thoughts for a shadowy companion. But Wanja followed him without a word. Karega's head was ablaze with what had gone on in Nyakinyua's hut. Tonight, tonight he had lived more

conflicting experiences than ever before in his life. He had lost Mukami and he found, in telling the story, that the pain and the self-accusation had not lessened with the years. But he had also discovered his brother, who had been only a silhouette buried deep in his childhood's earliest memories. He now reclaimed him in pride and gratitude: had he not handled live bullets, ready to die, which was the ultimate measure of one's commitment to the cause of a people's liberation? He felt, at the same time, a little awed by the man and also by Abdulla: from whence that courage and inner assurance, when a whole world laughed at the threats of a peasant armed with only a rusty panga and a home-made gun? From where did that faith and that belief in justice come so close to absolute certainty? Abdulla had now become in Karega's eyes the best self of the community, symbol of Kenya's truest courage. And the history he had tried to teach as romantic adventures, the essence of black struggle apprehended in the imagination at the level of mere possibilities, had tonight acquired immediate flesh and blood.

The dark night about them was filled with the power of a blood-nearness. He stopped as if to let her catch up, but the path was too narrow for two abreast, and he continued in front. He did not know what he wanted to tell her, but he felt all the same that there were thoughts and feelings elusively clear in his head and heart which would not take the shape of words. They went toward Ilmorog hill and Wanja was inwardly struck by this repetition of an earlier experience. She also had a vague feeling inside of an inevitability, as if all the numerous accidents, coincidences, and vicissitudes of the past were leading to this: to what? What was the animal within, stretching and struggling to be born? They stood side by side, looking onto the plains they could no longer see clearly. Karega sat down on the grass and she followed. She too had many things she wanted to tell, to say, to ask, and yet none would come.

'You must have the blood of rebels in your family,' she said, without knowing that she had touched the very chord of his thoughts.

'Why?'

'Your brother, to begin with. Did he look like you? But of course you could not have known him. And then you. At Siriana you twice organised a strike.'

'So did Munira,' he said, rather absent-mindedly, for he was thinking of his brother and of Abdulla and what it meant to fight in the forest.

'Yes. But in his case it was different. He says that he was only a spectator, a bystander, who happened to be thrown into the stampede and the mêlée.'

228

'How do you know? You were not there.'

'He told us.'

She told the story of Munira and Chui as Munira had once told it.

'He talked as if he had become frozen with the memory of that event. By the road, you tried to organise the sellers of sheepskins and fruits. In Ilmorog you suggested and organised the journey to the city and saved us from famine. Is that not something?'

He liked the cooing vibrancy of her voice. Her fingers which occasionally brushed against his filled him with warmth of blood at his fingertips. But his mind was in quick turns on Abdulla, Nyakinyua, Mukami, everything else but schools and strikes and his own part in them, for they now looked so trivial and irrelevant placed against the larger theatre of events that had created the true undying spirit of Kenya.

'Do you think he told us everything?' he asked, again mostly for the sake of saying something.

'Who?'

'Abdulla.'

'As Nyakinyua said: there is a lot more hidden in that stump of a leg. But then who does not have something to hide?'

'Do you have anything to hide?'

'Yes,' she said quietly.

'Why? Haven't you told me everything?'

'I suppose I should tell how I too came to leave school.'

And she told him about her first love: her search for vengeance; and the subsequent seduction from school.

He listened and then he asked her: 'Is he – is he the same one we met on our way to the city?'

'Yes. Yes . . . But I try not to think too hard about it. It's nothing.'

'Nothing? Wanja, nothing? No. Nothing is nothing.'

'But why should I become a prisoner of a past defeat? Why should it always be held against me?'

She had raised her voice a little, protesting against what she thought was an accusation in his voice. He was taken aback, startled by the vehemence of her protest: who was he, a victim, to pass judgment on another victim?

'It is not that,' he said. 'It is not that at all. After all, you have tried, you have struggled.' He instinctively sought her hand as if to reassure her.

She nestled closer to him, wanting to assuage him, to fight the enemy of life in that voice. Her warmth gradually powered his lungs, ribs: life quickened in him. He felt this sharp pain of death-birth-death-birth and he tightened his left hand round her right-hand fingers. He felt the prolonged shivering of her body thrilling into him, and now it was he who wanted to cry as he remembered Mukami. This was somehow mixed up with a consciousness of Wanja's past anguish and suffering, and this in turn was mixed up with his own internal turmoil. Where was the power of words, that Fraudsham had once talked about? Now when words were in flight it was only the knowledge, the consciousness of past suffering and loss, that brought them together, giving birth to their mutual need of each other. Karega's heart seethed with a hopeless rage: he bit his lips trying to hold himself together, hold back the impulse toward recognition of their mutual nakedness. But the rage, the impulse, urged him toward her, made him hold her closer to him, gradually laying her on the grass, surely and methodically removing her clothes with her hands making impotent gestures of protest, oh please Karega don't do that, and he hearing that genuine fear of need and desire in the voice, felt hot blood rush up and suffuse his whole system as his body sought out hers in a locked struggle on the ground. He felt the tip of his blood-warmth touch her moistness and for a second he was suspended in physical inertia. Then she cried once, oh, as he descended, sinking into her who now received him in tender readiness. Then they started slowly, almost uncertainly, groping toward one another, gradually working together in rhythmic search for a lost kingdom, for a lost innocence and hope, exploring deeper and deeper, his whole body aflame and tight with painful desire or of belonging. And she clung to him, she too desiring the memories washed away in the deluge of a new beginning, and he now felt this power in him, power to heal, power over death, power, power ... and suddenly it was she who carried him high on ocean waves of new horizons and possibilities in a single moment of lightning illumination, oh the power of united flesh, before exploding and swooning into darkness and sleep without words.

They woke up in the morning, dew on their hair, dew on their clothes, dew on the grass, dew on the hill and the plains, with the earth aglow with a mellowing amber light before sunrise.

'Wake up, Wanja,' Karega called out to her.

She heard his voice and she felt cold but she kept her eyes closed.

'Wake up and see signs of dawn over Ilmorog,' he continued. They left the hill and walked to their separate places bathed in the cold glow of the morning.

2 ❀ Dawn over Ilmorog. Happy New Year. Alone in bed. She is lying flat, completely relaxed in the hips. How strange. Relaxation in exhaustion. She is enjoying an inner peace and an inner lightness

she has never felt before. Her other affairs were always accompanied by anxiety, bitterness, an overriding need for a palliative, a temporary victory, a tormenting need for blood and vengeance, for gain. This is different. This is peace. This holiness. Her eyelids are heavy, languid. She is sinking into a no man's land but holding on to his face and eyes. Theng'eta ... the spirit ... millet power of God ... millet fingers of God. Harvest. Prickly pains from prickly hairs on maize stalks. Sheaves of maize stalks. Leaves of grass. Micege and maramata on skirts. Clods of clay on feet and hands putting seeds into the earth. The journey. Journeys over the earth, on air, flight. Karima Ka ihii. Meeting in Limuru in her hut. In her mother's hut. And strange. It is not his face she is looking at. It is that of an awkward youth offering her a gift of a pencil and an indiarubber eaten at the edges. She is angry. Throws away the gifts. She wants a letter ... do you hear, she screams, if you love me, write me a letter and say you worship me ... you know no other arms. He runs for the pencil and the indiarubber. He writes her a letter with trembling hands ... uncountable as sands of the sea, stars and clouds moving in heaven ... she in glittering robes of weekend glory ... she snatches the letter from him. She starts reading it to her cousin just arrived from the city ... Eastleigh ... She glances over her shoulder at the pleading eyes and she disdainfully starts reading aloud ... But her cousin is not there ... she is sitting on her father's knees, trying to spell out and pronounce some words ... Kaana Gaka ni kau Ni Ga tata tata ena kaana kega Kamau etemete kuguru-i, etemete? etema na ithanwa ria cucu cucu ena hang'i matu ... she trips over some of the alliterative words and she raises her puzzled face to her father. But her father is in an army uniform and he sings to her in a rough vigorous voice ... When I was a big boy soldier fighting for the king, silver boy silver girl remember me ... a soldier fighting for the king.

'Where have you been?' she asks him, trying to remove the KAR hat pin-folded on one side from his head.

'Burma ... India ... Japan ... lands far away, soldier fighting for the king.'

'Whom were you fighting?'

'Italians, Germans, Japanese.'

'You had a quarrel with them? Oh, you must have been angry.'

'Nop.'

'Why then were you fighting them?'

'A soldier does not ask questions ... he obeys orders and dies, dies fighting for the king.'

'Which king? Does he also fight?'

'Oh, stop it, little girl. You ask too many questions. Let's go play in the yard ... soldier fighting for the king.'

They go out and into his workshop and there are many iron pipes of different sizes and lengths. He is heating some over a fire. He beats them into all sorts of shapes. He is so skilful and nimble with his hands, so clever he can make any pipe of the hardest possible steel bend to his every whim and shape in his head.

'Oh, father, where did you learn all this?'

'In the war, my daughter ... a terrible waste of life ... the bombs ... the planes ... these white men, my daughter, it is only human lives they cannot create. But I was only a soldier fighting for the king.'

He starts singing. This time, a hymn. He is joined in the singing by her mother. Mother ... mother, who always says that she taught herself to read and write in order to read the book of God and avoid the shame of having her letters written or read for her. The singing voices alternate with the noise of iron on iron. Father explains the intricacies of plumbing. Wanja is laughing because she is happy and her father has brought her things from Nairobi. Sweets, cakes. But now he is no longer in the army. He wears a dirty long coat and he carries the heavy tools of his trade and is always counting the amount of money he has made, always ticking crosses against those who owe him money and ticks against the names of those who have paid. Suddenly the scene changes. She is a little bit bigger and mother and father no longer sing together and when they do it is liable to change into intense whispering and quarrelling.

'Let's move away from Kabete, away from nearness to the wicked city,' she pleads.

'Where do you want to go, woman?'

'To Ilmorog ... to your mother and father ... our parents. You have only seen them once or twice since you came back from the war.'

'Go back to ignorance and backwardness?'

'Are you scared of what he told you? What he saw in the light?'

'Woman. Shut your mouth.'

Her father is trembling – and pleading at the same time. He reasons with her mother.

'Listen, woman. I have been to war. I know how strong the white man is. What does father know about the Englishman? Only that he carried the guns in 1914. And that there he had heard of Maji Maji and Africans standing up to the white man. What happens? They were wiped out as they waited for bullets to turn to water. I was in India. Indians are cleverer than we are. They were ruled by the

British for four hundred years. Has father ever seen a bomb? I have. I will tell you about the true secret of the white man's power: money. Money moves the world. Money is time. Money is beauty. Money is elegance. Money is power. Why, with money I can even buy the princess of England. The one who recently came here. Money is freedom. With money I can buy freedom for all our people. Instead of this suicidal talk of guns and pistols and oaths of black unity to drive out the white man, we should learn from him how to make money. With money we can bring light into darkness. With money we can get rid of our fears and our superstitions. No more stories about Ndamathia giving us shadows: no more superstitions about animals of the earth that vomit out light. Money, woman, money. Give me money and I can buy holiness and kindness and charity, indeed buy my way to heaven, and the sacred gates will open at my approach. That is the power we want.'

'What money will you make as a traitor in this war?'

Her mother is crying now . . . no, they are both in church praying and asking God forgiveness for past sins and the sins of those who had taken the law into their hands and were challenging God's divine message to all mankind . . . Aamen . . . But still the tension in the home increases, the nightly quarrels multiply. For her mother would not refuse to visit her sister next door in the new village of lined huts along trodden pathways and roads. Her sister is reputed to have links with men in the forest.

'You would bring God's wrath into this house.'

'You mean the white man's wrath?'

'Your sister is helping the Mau Mau. Can't you tell her, can't you remind her what happened to her husband when he was caught with home-made guns?'

'At least he put his skill in plumbing to better use. He was not a coward. And my sister is not a coward, like me, because I know the truth and I cannot face it. I have seen injustice and I can't speak out. I can't take the oath and yet I don't see anything wrong in it. So I take refuge in God's church and pray for deliverance, but I am not willing to be the vessel of this deliverance.'

'Remember the good book. Thou shalt not bow to idols. Thou shalt not murder. Thou shalt not . . .' her father warns her mother.

'Yet you worship golden coins: it is God's image which is imprinted on the coins? A white God called George? And you killed. You murdered for white men,' her mother says.

'That was different,' says her father.

'Different! Different! Is killing not killing? You were brave and strong to kill for the race of white people: didn't you retain a little courage, a little strength to lift a finger for your people, your clansmen? What did your father tell you? In his line were no cowards: in his line there had never been traitors against the people. His words frightened you. Is this not really why you never went back? Not even to see him hanged like a dog by the same white man you faithfully served in the war?' Wanja has never seen her mother like this.

'Woooman . . .' Her father shouts and hits her mother once, twice, then he loses his head and beats her, hits her, claws her, foams with bitter rage and . . . and mother is crying helplessly and she, Wanja, is speechless with terror and her mother suddenly lets out a piercing cry for help . . . 'Heeelp . . . Heeelp . . . Fire! Fire! House burning . . . oh, oh, oh, oh, my sister, my only sister . . .'

And her father is glaring at her mother saying:

'I told you. It's punishment from the Lord.'

And it is her mother's turn to be speechless with terror and hatred of his father because of the words. And the hut is still burning. Wanja now finds her voice and joins her cousin newly arrived from the city in a terror-filled voice: 'Help! Heelp! Heeelp! Karega! Karega! Heeeelp!'

She woke up still crying to Karega for rescue from the fire. She was frightened and looked about terrified by the red flames in her mind. Nyakinyua was standing by the bed.

'What is it, my daughter? What is it?' Wanja was at first without words. Gradually she recalled her minutes of glory on a hill. She laughed uneasily. She asked:

'Tell me, please, tell me: why is it my father never came back? What really happened to my grandfather, how did he die? I want to know.'

3 ❀ So many experiences, so many discoveries in a night and a half. Harvest-time for seeds planted in time past. The exhaustion of the body. But he is light, buoyant within. He feels in himself the power of an immense dewy dawn over Ilmorog. How is it that a certain contact with a woman can give one so much peace, so much harmony with all things, can open up this sense of immense promises and a thousand possibilities? He tries to sleep. His body is ready. But the mind races on, sailing swiftly but gently on low waves of memories of flesh in flesh. He is aware that he has only uncovered the first layer of a great, infinite unknown and unknowable, and yet he feels that he has known Wanja all his life, that what has gone before has a logic and a rhythm inevitably leading him to that moment of candour in the flesh. He tries to fathom out this link, this inner con-

tinuity, but the thread is lost in a distant mist surrounding his childhood. But silhouettes of certain scenes and events and figures begin to form out of the mist and gradually one stands out and refuses to go. He is a little child playing with sand near his mother. Oh, you wicked child, you have thrown sand into my eyes, she cries. Then women with pangas and folded mikwa-straps in their hands come into the compound and say: Mariamu, let's go and get firewood. Mariamu, his mother, turns to him: Go over to Njeri's place and play with the others till I return. He howls with fury. Tears of felt betrayal gush out of his tiny eyes. The other women laugh at him. They say: What a baby you are, and then they soothe him by calling him a man: Now, now, our man, go and play with the girls, they are all waiting for you, oh, oh, he is a sly one, a devil with women, eh? He is not easily soothed. He lets them walk a little distance. He trots behind them down into Mukuru-ini wa Kamiritho up another hill and down to Ngenia. They reach a bend and turn toward Kinenie and then maybe into the bush, because he cannot now see them any more. He goes into the bush. He runs this way. He runs that way. He suddenly finds himself in a green mubage bush. Fear grips him. He shouts out her name. He hears a mocking almost endless repetition of his voice thinning into the distant heart of the forest. He is desperate. He is scared of this total silence made more silent by the noises of insects and birds. To be alone, so alone in a world without human voices. He cries in protest against this total isolation, as if to say: He feels he will die, he is dead, and he cries out for help, for a hand to rescue him, for a chance to play one, one more game with the other children. He has probably cried himself to sleep for when he wakes up he finds himself in bed, his mother sitting beside the bed, and he can see the pity and tenderness in her eyes. But is she sitting by the bed or is his memory playing him false? It is another scene at another time, for she is not really sitting but bending over a bush of pyrethrum daisy flowers as if in prayer and devotion. So still. He is busy moulding balls from mud made from soil mixed with his urine. The field of pyrethrum daisies belongs to Mukami's father. Tired of making balls, he looks up, is frightened by this cessation of motion-activity in his mother. He shouts out her name with a strength amounting to panic and desperation. She raises her bent back and attempts a smile on dry lips. My head went round and round ... let's go home ... it is nothing, she says. But with a child's sure instinct he suspects that it is not nothing...she is hungry and tired under the baking sun. They reach their hut in the village – when did they cease living as ahoi-squatters on Mukami's father's land? In the evening women visit her and he is sent to bed, but he listens. They whisper long into the night and he falls asleep and wakes up to find them whispering and the only words he can make out are Githunguri and bullets and freedom. Anyway they look at him with strange eyes, with tearful eyes, and Mariamu tells them to kneel down and they pray and sing a hymn, Kuu iguru gutiri mathina, and then pray again in a low monotone and this makes him sink back to sleep ... he sinks deeper and deeper into a slumbrous land of hazy mist ... encountering more familiar faces and scenes. For it is Mukami who is really praying, and afterward he and she stand on a hill and watch thabiri birds soar high over Manguo Marshes and then fly away with the beautiful sunset of a thousand smouldering fires ... They are sitting on the hippo humps at the centre of Manguo and he stretches his hand to touch her ... But she floats away from him, and he is amazed: how can she float so easily, without wings, over the reeds they call huyo cia Nguu? Then he realises that she is flying with the thabiri birds and he is so sad: how can he lose her at the very moment of reach? Aah, it is not her at all ... it is Wanja ... but where has she suddenly come from? She had eaten more salt than he had because she is really Nyakinyua and Nyakinyua knew Ndemi and Ndemi ... but there must be something wrong with him? How can he mistake his pupils for Wanja and Mukami and Nyakinyua? He is in a classroom. Today, children, I am going to tell you about the history of Mr Blackman in three sentences. In the beginning he had the land and the mind and the soul together. On the second day, they took the body away to barter it for silver coins. On the third day, seeing that he was still fighting back, they brought priests and educators to bind his mind and soul so that these foreigners could more easily take his land and its produce. And now I shall ask you a question: what has Mr Blackman done to attain the true kingdom of his earth? To bring back his mind and soul and body together on his piece of earth? They are actually — how strange — on a raft of banana stems drifting across oceans of time and space. And he is no longer Mwalimu but Chaka leading induna after induna against the Foreign invader. He is L'Ouverture, discarding the comfort and the wealth and the false security of a house slave to throw his intellect and muscles at the feet of the field slaves ready for a united people's struggle against the drinkers of human sweat, eaters of human flesh. Children, he calls out: see this new African without chains on his legs, without chains on his mind, without chains in his soul, a proud warrior-producer in three continents. And they see him over and over in new guises Koitalel, Waiyaki, Nat Turner, Cinque, Kimathi, Cabral, Nkrumah, Nasser, Mondhlane, Mathenge — radiating the same message, the same possibilities, the same cry and hope of a million Africans ... And look: who is that unknown soldier following behind carrying three live bullets in the hand? That ... look children ... do you know my brother ... tireless toiler, tireless worker, do you know him? Nding'uri ... Heh, Nding'uri. He stops.

'Don't you know me?' Karega asks, anxiously.

'I do ... why else am I here?'

'That is strange. Did you know that we were coming? Did you really know of our journey?'

'Yes.'

'That is even more strange.'

'Why?'

'Imagine. I would never have thought—'

'Thought what?'

'That you would know me. I mean I was so small ... I must have been ... I may not even have been born!'

'Does it matter?'

'Seedlings from the same womb. Kinsmen. Mumbi's children. Nyumba ya Mumbi. It does matter, or is it not so?'

'Why are you adrift on a raft?'

'I wanted to find you ... to show you that I have grown big ... And ... and ... that I know your secret ... I know Abdulla.'

'But who are you?'

'I thought you said you knew me and of our journey.'

'Yes. I know of your journey. I know the journey of search and exploration undertaken by all my brothers and sisters. For have we not travelled this road together? Tell me one black man who is not adrift even in the land of his birth. But you? For a second I thought I knew you. Listen, my brothers, the true house of Mumbi, Mumbi the mother creator, is all the black toiling masses carrying a jembe in one hand and three bullets in the other, struggling against centuries of drifting, sole witnesses of their own homecoming. That is why in 1952 we took the oath.'

'Why did you?'

'Our land ... our sweat ... our bodies ... our minds ... our black souls,' he says, and carries on following the other soldier-toilers of the continent.

Karega shouts behind him: 'I want to follow you! Do you hear me? Let us journey together.'

Nding'uri stops and he is now both weary and angry.

'What kind of teacher are you? Leave your children adrift? The struggle, brother, starts where you are.'

He dissolves into the mist of time. And Karega feels the full

impact of that last rebuke. How foolish of me ... how foolish ...
Foolish Africans Never Take Alcohol ... FANTA ... Teachers'
Union Says Karega Evades Responsibility ... TUSKER ... what
foolish answers. He sees that more children have raised their hands
to ask questions.

'Yes, Joseph.'

'You have told us about black history. You have been telling us
about our heroes and our glorious victories. But most seem to end in
defeat. Now I want to ask my question ... If what you say is true,
why then was it possible for a handful of Europeans to conquer a
continent and to lord it over us for four hundred years? How was it
possible, unless it is because they have bigger brains, and that we are
the children of Ham, as they say in the Christian Bible?'

He suddenly starts fuming with anger. He knows that a teacher
should not erupt into anger but he feels his defeat in that question.
Maybe the journey has been long and they have wandered over too
many continents and over too large a canvas of time.

'Look, Joseph. You have been reading eeh, American children's
encyclopedia and the Bible. They used the Bible to steal the souls and
minds of ever-grinning Africans, caps folded at the back, saying
prayers of gratitude for small crumbs labelled aid, loans, famine
relief while big companys are busy collecting gold and silver and
diamonds, and while we fight among ourselves saying I am a Kuke, I
am a Luo, I am a Luhyia, I am a Somali ... and ... and ... There are
times, Joseph, when victory is defeat and defeat is victory.'

He is trembling with anger with his inability to reach them and
he shouts a few obscenities at Nderi and all the followers, all the
gun-bearers, of Goode and Livingstone and Rhodes and Gordon and
Meinertzgahen and Henderson and Johnson and Nixon. If he could
get at them, he shouts and suddenly wakes up, sweating.

He sat up and looked about him and was relieved to find that it
was only Munira standing beside him.

'I did not mean to wake you ... but you have slept a whole day
yesterday and a whole night. And now it's about ten o'clock.'

'Have I? Is it so?' he asked, yawning.

'Yes. You did not even bolt your door.'

'There are no thieves yet, else the policemen and the churchmen
would already have occupied the buildings they have just completed.'

Munira paced about the room and then stopped. He tried to say
something and then seemed to hold back the words.

Karega was puzzled by Munira's behaviour. He looked at him
more closely. Munira had resumed his pacing about the room, hands
folded at the back, clenching and unclenching his fingers. Even

238

through the fatigue that comes from oversleeping, Karega could sense that Munira was troubled by something and he felt concerned.

'What is it, Mwalimu?' He yawned again. 'Aah, my sleep. Do excuse me my yawning. It is an aftermath of that illusion-inducing Theng'eta stuff. You don't think it is dangerous? I feel fine and clear in the head, clear in the body. But I had such a terrible nightmare.'

'It is nothing. Nothing. I also feel fine. Strong, clear. No hangover even. Oh, no, I don't think it is dangerous. It is only that in your what you call nightmare, you kept on shouting names. Some were rather incomprehensible. But some were clear.'

'I hope I did not give away any secrets.'

'No, no, no secrets. You whispered Mukami and Wanja ... that kind of thing ...'

Munira suddenly halted his nervous walkabout. He leaned against the wall. Then he went to the bookshelf, picked out a book, *Facing Mount Kenya*, opened a few pages and put it back. He picked out, *Not Yet Uhuru*, again opened a few more pages and returned it to the shelf without reading it. Composed, he turned to Karega and cleared his throat.

'Mr Karega!' he said, rather abruptly. The tone made Karega look up, rather sharply. Munira seemed to be summoning enough courage to proceed. 'Mr Karega, I don't know how to put this, but – eh – you have now been here for about two years. But we could say that you came as a refugee and I did my best to welcome you. We have lived in the same compound and a few things, some pleasant, others not so pleasant, have happened to us. But after what has happened ... I mean ... after your own confessions about my sister, my family and all that, don't you think it is time, eh, don't you think it will be a little difficult our staying in the same place?'

'Are you, Mr Munira, suggesting that ... but I can't understand what has brought this into your head ... are you suggesting that I leave my job?'

'You are putting it rather strongly. But you will agree that your confession has made things rather awkward. We cannot after all escape from our separate though linked pasts. I mean one has memories ... responsibilities even though only to one's own self-respect. Now, in a manner of speaking, it could be said, couldn't it, that you drove Mukami to her suicide.'

'Munira!'

'Alas, it is you who after all had eaten more salt than she had. And one thing more, Mr Karega. It is not very flattering to me, even though it may only be in a nightmare, to have my own dear sister

239

compared to ... well ... mentioned in the same breath with a prostitute, even though a Very Important Prostitute!'

Karega sprang out of the bed and rushed at Munira. Munira moved a step to the side and Karega almost hit into the wall. As suddenly, Karega's hands became limp in the air, and then he let them fall by his side. But his eyes were still red with intense anger and loathing. He weakened with pain, with his own impotence for instant vengeance: this man had been his teacher, he was certainly older than he was, and even for that alone he deserved his respect. But he had welcomed him here, had even found him a job, and besides, did he but know, had touched a sensitive guilty core at the heart of Karega's being. So he only stood and fought to hold back hot tears threatening at the edges.

'If you had not once been ... if you had not been, if you ...'

He could not finish the sentence. He sat back on the bed for a time choked into silence by a mixture of guilt, bitterness, inward rage and incomprehension. He just stared past Munira, through the door, to the schoolyard and beyond, as if he would seek an answer out there where life, real life, was being played out, and not in this wretched corner of idleness and dreams and memories. He now spoke as if to a world outside Ilmorog.

'Only two nights ago we all drank Theng'eta together to celebrate a harvest and the successful ending of what was certainly a difficult year in Ilmorog. It was a good harvest and you'll agree with me that such sense of a common destiny, a collective spirit, is rare. That is why the old woman rightly called it a drink of peace. Now it has turned out to be a drink of strife. I suppose this had to be, though I still don't understand it. You had your reasons for coming here, I had mine. You say that we cannot after all escape from our pasts and with that I agree. But we do not have to heap insults on others. We are all prostitutes, for in a world of grab and take, in a world built on a structure of inequality and injustice, in a world where some can eat while others can only toil, some can send their children to schools and others cannot, in a world where a prince, a monarch, a businessman can sit on billions while people starve or hit their heads against church walls for divine deliverance from hunger, yes, in a world where a man who has never set foot on this land can sit in a New York or London office and determine what I shall eat, read, think, do, only because he sits on a heap of billions taken from the world's poor, in such a world, we are all prostituted. For as long as there's a man in prison, I am also in prison: for as long as there is a man who goes hungry and without clothes, I am also hungry and without clothes. Why then need a victim hurl insults at another victim?

Least of all need we pour vileness and meanness on the memory of those who were once dear to us, those rare few who rejected the class snobbery of their group, those who had faith and love and truth and beauty and only wanted free unfettered human contact and growth.'

There followed another moment of silence embarrassing to Munira because once again he felt on trial, that he had been placed on a moral balance and had been found wanting.

'My father is a church elder and so you can imagine that one can grow a little tired of sermons and moral platitudes,' Munira said, and felt slightly pleased with that rejoinder.

'I know he is – and more—' Karega said, and now he sharply looked at Munira, who winced a little at the piercing eyes. 'But I was not trying to preach. I was only thinking of those who chose and preferred to die for their chosen cause. But I shall not resign from this school. It will be hard, our working together, but I don't intend to go away.'

'We shall see, we shall see,' Munira said, ominously.

'About one thing, you are right, though,' Karega continued. 'I feel like I have been hiding from something. Do you know why I first came to look for you? You were her brother. You taught her. You taught me. And quite apart from needing help, I honestly thought you could unravel the Siriana mystery and make me understand the root cause of Chui's behaviour and actions. But during the journey, I saw many more Chuis and I am not sure if I want to understand it any more. One must grow. History after all is not a gallery of dashing heroes. But I intend to stay here and look about me. I want to choose my side in the struggle to come,' he added, remembering the lawyer's letter.

'We shall see,' Munira added with greater menace, 'but if I were you I would start thinking of employment elsewhere! or better still how to get a place at a Teacher Training College.'

Chapter Nine

1 ❄ Happy New Year. Grass was full. The wandering herdsmen had once again come back to the plains. Rain will rain. More grass will grow. More crops will grow. We shall eat our fill and forget the drought of the year before. But we shall not forget Munira and Karega and Abdulla and Wanja and the donkey – yes, Abdulla's donkey. They saved us. Their knowledge of the city, their contacts in

the city, their unselfish involvement in our lives: all this saved us. Abdulla's donkey wandered everywhere and women and children competed in giving it maize to eat from their own hands. This time nobody – not even Njuguna – complained about its eating habits. We often hired it to transport our things and foods and wares to and from the big markets at Ruwa-ini. So for a small fee it had become our donkey. People said that Abdulla was a good man. May the Lord bless him. Look at what he had done to Joseph. Sent him to school. And he, the unsung hero of our fight for freedom, is doing all the work in the shop on one leg and he never complains. He was at times withdrawn into himself, and we understood. In his relaxed moods, when in a good humour, he more than made up for it by his stories which were becoming part of Ilmorog lore.

Yes, it will rain. Crops will grow. We shall always remember the heroes in our midst. We shall always sing about the journey in the plains. May the Lord bless the old woman. But the drought will soon be a faint dream in a distant landscape. We say that the hunger of a thousand years is satisfied with one day's cooking. May ill thoughts and frightening memories go with the drought! Only the epic journey. That would always be a thing to remember, and our MP had never come to explain, even. So let it be, we said in the opening months of the new year: we did not then know that within a year the journey, like a God who cannot let his generosity be forgotten, would send its emissaries from the past, to transform Ilmorog and change our lives utterly, Ilmorog and us utterly changed.

That was yet to come. But at the time, well, at the beginning of the momentous period, we talked and whispered and gossiped about the chief and the policemen who would come and stay at the post for a week or so and then would go away. We also laughed at the churchmen who came all the way from the city or beyond to preach a sermon to empty benches. For nobody from Ilmorog would agree to go inside the new building.

2 ✿ Godfrey Munira, who for a long time had abandoned his iron horse, was one day seen on it galloping furiously across Ilmorog, his shirt untucked at the back, flowing stiffly behind him, like a bird's broken wing in the winds. He kept to himself mostly and was rarely seen even at Abdulla's place.

These days Karega was to be seen mostly with Wanja: what had happened between him and the teacher? It was strange, very strange, we said without understanding fully what was the matter.

But we were soon intrigued, fascinated, moved by the entwinement and flowering of youthful love and life and we whispered: see the wonder-gift of God. Crops will sprout luxuriant and green. We shall eat our fill and drink Theng'eta at harvest-time.

3 ❀ Later, years later, in Ilmorog Police Station, Munira was to try and recreate the feel of this period in Ilmorog which was completely dominated by the involvement of Wanja and Karega. And he used the same phrase, almost answering the question that underlay their waiting and watching as the drama unfolded before their eyes, making even the old relive the past of their youth, making love under leleshwa bush or under the millet fingers.

'Yes, I could have tried to save him,' he scribbled on, trying to interpret the facts in the light of the intervening time and events.

'I could maybe have saved him. It is this feeling that most pains me. That I might have saved him, he who only sought for peace and truthful connection between things. Instead, I threw him even more firmly into that fatal embrace that has been the ruin of many a great man across the centuries. I should know. For was I not later caught in the same heart-perfumed embrace?

'I tried, I struggled to extricate myself but I could not. I had, remember, watched her gradually receding from me into a neutral territory, standing, for a long time, distant to all our suits and seeking eyes, ever since Karega arrived in Ilmorog. It did not matter, I had reassured myself. It could never matter to me, for was I not really past these things? I was God's watchman in a twilight gloom somewhere between sleeping and waking, and should I not rest there, and not trouble the twilight stillness with passionate insistence? At first I thought that I was only fascinated by her transformation. She was no longer restless, savouring people with wide assessing eyes that hid maybe bitterness behind their dilating surface softness. Within a short time of her contact with the soil and the preparations for the journey to the city, her eyes had become less exaggeratedly bright, more subdued, with a different kind of softness, no longer caressing people in the first hour of contact. She had become a less fully fleshed beauty, more of an angular beauty of a peasant woman. It had pained me that when once or twice I wanted her again as on the night of the big moon she refused or somehow put me off. But I then thought that I understood. For had I not been the recipient of her stories of her past and recent suffering in the city? She needed time to recover, I consoled myself, and thought that I would get my chance during the journey to the city. I waited ... waited only to get the great slap on the face, the shock, during the night of Theng'eta drinking. For a day and a half, as Karega slept in his house as if drugged, I thought over the whole affair and I decided that I had really been too timid, hesitant. It was time that I took the initiative, took a step, however small, to start things in motion. I gradually worked myself into a rage and I really felt wronged over Mukami and over my father. But what was I to do about it? Could I resurrect the past and connect myself to it, graft myself on the stem of history even if it was only my family's history outside of which I had grown? And would the stem really grow, sprouting branches with me as part of the great resurgence of life? But I also knew that I did not want to admit to myself that I could be seriously affected by Wanja's defection. After all, I argued, I had never wanted to have more than a carnal link with her. I knew too much about her past to be feel free and uninhibited with her. Yet, yet I wanted to have it out with Karega and my action had now driven her further away from me.

I watched her after the night of Theng'eta drinking, after my quarrel with Karega, I watched her undergo yet another change. It was a new youthful, life-full, luscious growth after the rains.

It pained me that the luscious growth was beyond my reach, that I could not eat it, my share even.

The further she moved away from me, the more she drew me to her, until with months she had wrapped my soul in twists and knots around her. The security and the defences around my lifelong twilight slumber were being cut at the roots and I felt the pain of blood-sap trickling through heart's veins and arteries awaking from years of numbness.

I could not help it. I spied on them, watching them through the corner of my eyes, and what I saw would make me regret the more that I had hastily thrown him out of my orbit.

Of an evening I saw them together running across the fields, stumbling over mikengeria creepers, over yellow merry-golden flowers, over the tall thangari stem grass, bringing back thistles on the back and the front and the sides of their clothes. Often, they would walk across Ilmorog ridge, two distant shadows against the golden glow of the setting sun, and disappear behind the hill to come back in the darkness or in the moonlight.

Their love seemed to grow with the new crops of the year.

This thing that I cannot describe, that I thought could never possess me, now grew roots and shoots and alas began to flower.

The very movement of her skirt was a razor-sharp knife in my inside. And yet the knife seemed to cut deeper and sharper when I did not see the skirt. But still coming suddenly across it, or seeing it flit by in the sunlight or against the evening cool skies, I would feel, no longer the knife, but a thousand tiny needles in my belly, in my flesh. I sought her very shadow. Her steps in the sand agitated me, her presence occasioned thunderous palpitations of hope for the unattainable. Torturous angels.

To see her became a need. Yet seeing her was a quick act of torment. I hated it that I could not control myself. I would attempt a level voice when speaking to her or to Karega to convince myself that I could still hold myself together. Why had she come to Ilmorog? Why had Karega come to Ilmorog? Could Ilmorog contain the three of us?

I cycled to Limuru to recruit more teachers. This time I was lucky and got two with EACE passes from Kinyogori Harambee School and one who had failed his school certificate but had had his junior certificate at Ngenia High School. Three new teachers at a go!

I rushed back to my watch, now not so alone.

They were still a-wandering across Ilmorog country, always together in the fields, on the mountain-top, in the plains, their love blossoming in the wind, as if both were re-enacting broken possibilities in their pasts. A second chance. A second chance for him to get at me. First it was Mukami. Now it was Wanja.

I started finding faults in his teaching, with the level of his preparations, with the content of his lessons, with the kind of literature he introduced to the tender minds. But really, there was little to criticise.

I even started moralising, to myself of course, about the effect of their unmarried liaison on the children.

Crops ripened: came new harvests.

One afternoon, I invited all the teachers for a drink at Abdulla's place. It was in the middle of the third term.

I steered the conversation to the school and the teaching of certain subjects like history and civics.

'You see, the children have very impressionable minds. They like to copy. They take the opinion of their teachers as a Bible-sanctioned truth. That is why we should be careful, don't you think?' I asked, turning to Karega. They were all listening and I felt the power of my own argument.

'Careful about what?' Karega asked and his manner of asking, affecting not to know what I was talking about, irritated me.

'About our teaching. What we teach them. Politics for instance. Propaganda. I agree of course that it has more bite and juice in it and needs little preparation.'

He did not answer. I became more enthusiastic and drove home my points with mounting authority and sureness.

'You see. What they need to know are facts. Simple facts. Information, just so they can pass their CPE. Yes, information, not interpretation. Later when they go to High School, and I am sure these gentlemen will bear me out in this, they can start learning the more complicated stuff. By that time they will have learnt how to think and can start interpreting. I say let's teach them facts, facts, and not propaganda about blackness, African peoples, all that, because that is politics, and they know the tribe they belong to. That's a fact – not propaganda.'

I sat back and swallowed a glass of beer, rather satisfied with myself. Some of the things I had of course read from a circular sent to all schools by an English inspector of language and history at the Ministry, who had described himself as a scientist in language, literature and history, but what did it matter?

'I do not agree with that approach,' Karega started and I could see that he was having difficulties. 'I cannot accept that there is a stage in our growth as human beings when all we need are so-called facts and information. Man is a thinking being from the time he is born to the time he dies. He looks, he hears, he touches, he smells, he tastes and he sifts all these impressions in his mind to arrive at a certain outlook in his direct experience of life. Are there pure facts? When I am looking at you, how much I see of you is conditioned by where I stand or sit; by the amount of light in this room; by the power of my eyes; by whether my mind is occupied with other thoughts and what thoughts. Surely the story we teach about the seven blind men who had never seen an elephant is instructive. Looking and touching, then, do involve interpretation. Even assuming that there were pure facts, what about their selection? Does this not involve interpretation? What is the propaganda we are accused of teaching? When you talked just now, it was so funny, I was thinking of Chui. But that's another story. Now let's look at this propaganda which is Not Facts. The oppression of black people is a fact. The scattering of Africans into the four corners of the earth is a fact. That there are Africans in U.S.A., Canada, Latin America, the West Indies, Europe, India, everywhere – this is a fact. That Africa is one of the richest continents with infinite possibilities for renewal and growth is a fact. What mineral, from copper, gold, diamonds, cobalt to uranium, is not found in Africa? What crop? That our people fought against the Arab slave raiders is a fact: that the Akamba people built formidable defences against them even while trading with them in ivory is a fact. That our people resisted European intrusion is a fact: we fought inch by inch, ridge by ridge, and it was only through the superiority of their arms and the traitorous actions of some of us that we were

defeated. That Kenya people have had a history of fighting and resistance is therefore a fact. Our children must look at the things that
deformed us yesterday, that are deforming us today. They must also
look at the things which formed us yesterday, that will creatively
form us into a new breed of men and women who will not be afraid
to link hands with children from other lands on the basis of an
unashamed immersion in the struggle against those things that
dwarf us.

'Liberation: no child is ever too young to think about this: it is the
only way he can truly experience himself as he collects, breaks,
collects, rejects, assimilates and cries to discover himself. We must
teach our children to hate all those things which prevent them from
loving and to love all those things that make it possible for them to
love freely.'

I had never clearly thought about these things. I could see that the
others were captivated by the novelty and the purity of conviction
behind the utterances. I felt uncomfortable. I braced myself to hit
back, only I did not know how. At that moment Wanja hodi-ed and
stood at the door.

Her eyes sought out his. My tension-filled body felt rather than
saw their eyebeams entwine a second, two seconds, before she
greeted the rest of us.

I could not bear the pain.

I could not resist the evil thought.

I cycled to the headquarters.

Chapter Ten

1   It was the end of yet another year. School had closed and
Munira was in the office writing the annual report and drawing up
estimates for the following year. He was astonished that he had now
been here for five years. Next year the school would have six classes
learning all day. Joseph had made the most impressive progress. His
mind was clearly above the average. Even if Ilmorog did not send
any child to a secondary school on the first attempt at CPE, he was
sure that on the school's second attempt, Joseph would make it to
higher realms and thus finally put Ilmorog Full Primary School on
the national map.

He closed the office and stood outside. Ilmorog countryside was
clear, for it was after yet another harvest. The drought and the
journey to the city seemed like events in a legend. None of the

promises had yet materialised. Ilmorog was still a kind of neglected outpost of the republic. Even the churchmen and the chief and the policemen only came once every so many months. But Mzigo did visit the school once or twice, he would quickly wet his throat at Abdulla's place and then would curse the road and disappear. But some of the improvements, especially in equipment and buildings, were a direct result of those visits. He had brought him one other teacher so that they were five altogether.

'Come to Tea' also seemed like something which had happened in another country, long ago, and Munira thought he might visit his home: but how would he look at his father, he wondered, now that he knew how Mukami had met her death? Idle speculation, he thought, since his relations to his father and to his past and the discomfiture he felt had never had anything to do with Mukami's death. He took his bicycle: he wanted to run to Abdulla's place for a quick one.

He was whistling gaily when he saw her in the middle of the narrow path, almost the same spot where five years back she had accosted him and asked funny but hostile questions. 'Oh, it is you, mother of men,' he called out cheerfully, braking to a stop. He was feeling good, because but for Wanja's movement away from him he had almost regained his position as a hero, the bringer of new teachers for the children. He had for a time lost the position to Karega, soon after the return from the city, but now ... he only needed Wanja to complete his happiness. Nyakinyua looked to the ground but her voice reached him clearly.

'The three new teachers: they have now been here for many months. Is it not so?'

'Yes, yes,' he answered, puzzled.

'They have been doing well.'

'Yes. But why? Have the children been complaining?'

'No. They say that the new teachers are also good. Just like the two before them. Who has given them to us?'

'Serikali. How else can we pay them?'

'Mwalimu. Why, why have they given us with the right hand only to take away with the left? Is that fair for the children?'

'I do – I do not understand,' he said.

'You do: you know more than you dare to tell us.'

'I really – I do not understand the meaning behind your words.'

As he said this, he coughed and turned his head away. Ilmorog was quiet, very quiet. He sighted two children playing 'football' with two yellow mitura apples, competing to see who could kick furthest backwards. When again he looked to the road, the woman had vanished. 'Just like that other time,' he mused, going over her words in his mind. He suddenly lost the heart and the stomach for Abdulla's place. He didn't want more talk and gossip. He leaned the bicycle against the walls of the house. He stood at the door and once again looked at where the woman had been. He was a little scared of her because she was highly respected in the community and her hostility could mean somebody's ignominy and downfall.

He started. The repetition of past patterns had always frightened him. It was the tyranny of the past that he had always tried to escape. First it was Nyakinyua: now it was Wanja. Then he understood, and the first flush of fear was replaced by an elation at his new-found power.

'You have never learnt manners,' she said, also echoing the past. She looked at him evenly and he could not tell her attitude toward him. 'Won't you invite me into your house?'

'Come in, come in,' he said with awkward joviality. But inwardly he sunned himself against a nice warm glow.

She took a folding chair from against the wall and sat on it. She was barefoot with a simple flower-patterned frock. She had no jewellery. She seemed more mature in body: her eyes were firm, clear, and no longer dancing with devilish invitation. But they were alive and her direct look, though not hostile, made him slightly uncomfortable.

'Would you like a cup of tea?'

'I don't want any tea,' she said, 'but I could drink water.'

'Water is now plentiful,' he tried to joke as he fetched her a mug of water. He now had an aluminium water tank into which he collected the rainwater from the roof. His house had also improved over the years: there were now more chairs – including a sofa set – and more utensils and more books on the shelves. She drank a bit and then carefully, almost too carefully, put the mug on the floor.

'Do you remember the night of Theng'eta drinking?' she suddenly asked.

'Yes. I do. Why? It's a long time. A year ago.'

'I remember you asking me: why did I really come to Ilmorog?'

'Well, one gets curious ... but we all have our reasons for doing things. Our secret lives.'

'But the second time: you must have known ... I told you ... the fire ... and the tea.'

'Why do you want to rake up the past?' he asked, feeling even more uncomfortable. Then he added: 'I don't know if I told you that I myself had just come back from the same tea-party.'

'Is that so? Anyway, you did not tell me. But it does not matter.

Why did you want to know why I had come here? I suppose you meant the first time.'

'Listen, Wanja. You don't have to tell me anything you don't want. I must have been under the influence of Theng'eta. Strong stuff it was, and it rather loosened all our tongues.'

'But I want to tell you,' she said with an ironic smile. 'I have come all the way to tell you, so I must. I have told you many things. I have not tried to hide from you what I am and what I have been. But there is one thing which I did not really speak to you about. I have always feared that I am barren: that I am incapable of having a child. The knowledge has been a weight, a heavy weight to carry. For children, no matter how we neglect them, are what makes many a barmaid feel human. You are a mother and nobody can take that from you. I have tried. I have even been to Barabana's place in Thigio. He is famous with herbs, especially those to do with women's illnesses and with child-bearing—'

'Excuse me,' Munira interrupted – 'I thought you told me, you told us that you had a child, you were pregnant once.'

'That's so.' She looked at the ground for a long time and bit her lower lip as if to steel herself a little.

'It died,' she said, and continued: 'but it was really much afterward that I discovered this need in me. I must say that even as a girl in school, I always had felt a quickening of the heart, a kind of aching pleasure, at the sight of children, and I wanted to do things for them. The need became great. That's why I came here. To see my grandmother. First to know really well where my father was born and to seek advice. She took me to Mwathi's place—'

'But they say he does not see people below a certain age.'

'It's true. I was left outside. It's a big yard surrounded by a hedge of stinging nettles and matura. When I went in, I only heard his voice. He asked me a few questions. I don't want to go into that now. But he advised on a certain day under a new moon in the open fields. I didn't follow his instructions. I don't anyway quite believe in the moon business. The rest you know. It has been my life. It has been my misfortune. I accept it.'

'Why do you tell me this?' he asked, a little pained: so she was only using him, for a witchdoctor's experiment?

'Because I want you to understand what Ilmorog has meant to me, what Karega means to me. Please don't get hurt when I tell you that with most men I have gone to them with a purpose. I like friendships all right. But I know that at first it was to forget my earlier involvement. The scar. Later it was mostly with the hope ... sometimes I would make friends only with married men, those with children. Believe me, it has been lonely. Even with you, I was hoping, but it did not work out. With him it has been different. I want him. I really want him. For himself. For the first time, I feel wanted ... a human being ... no longer humiliated ... degraded ... foot-trodden ... do you understand? It is not given to many: a second chance to be a woman, to be human without this or that "except", "except" ... without shame. He has reawakened my smothered woman-ness, my girlhood, and I feel I am about to flower ...'

She paused and fixed him with a steadfast gaze. Her eyes were dancing. He felt even more uncomfortable under her naked, mad, challenging eyes. There was a kind of terrible beauty in them ... the beauty of a lioness.

'I tell you all this, Munira, because I know it is you who is behind Karega's downfall. Behind his dismissal from his job.'

He was about to say something, to make a weak protest, to blame it on Mzigo, but she continued, her voice raised.

'I want him back in this school. I want him back, we all want him back as a teacher of our children. Whatever you do, he must not leave Ilmorog. Either that or else ... Munira ... I am a hard woman ... and somebody, either now or later, will have to pay. I want you to understand that: that it will be ... I don't know how ... but should he go, either you or Mzigo or both ...'

She stood up and hurried out of the room as if she feared the effort and the words would choke her or weaken her at the knees. But for Godfrey Munira the words lingered in the air ominously and for a long time he was never to forget the power of that voice, the beauty of her body, the purity of the commitment in her heart, the moonlit brilliance of her angry eyes, all of which at that moment finally and dangerously bound him to her for ever. 'I am lost ... we are all lost ... but she is ... She must be ... my wild-eyed lioness.'

He knew she had conquered him. But he knew that there was nothing he could do now about Karega's dismissal. What was done was done ... and it was for you, my moonlight lioness, he murmured to himself.

2 ❀ So now help me God that he does not go, Wanja murmured to herself, gazing across the plains to the distant Donyo Hills. Just above the hills, the moving clouds had formed two shapes, the likeness of scraggy-mouthed caves, belching out mist and light. The mouths became smaller and smaller until the caves finally dissolved into a floating black-bluish wool. She followed the slow wool motion, trying to locate where the fingerprints of God had been. She

thus kept her mind off their present mission. But the thought persisted: if he left Ilmorog ... if he left Ilmorog ... she would also leave. She shuddered: she was now really scared of what she might encounter in the world beyond these rural boundaries. She had left her past behind her: let it stay there, outside these Ilmorog walls. But here in Ilmorog, without him, what was she to do? Follow him ... and once again she shivered at the thought of the world beyond the present cloister. My scars ... stay you without ...

'You can work in my shop,' Abdulla again offered to Karega. 'We shall be full partners.' He felt the inadequacy of this outlet: could the shop really contain them all? But it was all he had.

Wanja looked at Abdulla and she remembered his similar offer to her five years back. In the encircling silence, against the solemnity of the occasion, the words reaching her as she held herself together because of the slight breeze over Ilmorog Hill, the suggestion was comic and she wanted to laugh. It sounded odd, frivolous even, but she knew the feelings behind it.

Karega heard the words without taking in the meaning. For he knew and he thought they all could see that there was nothing more for him to do in Ilmorog, nothing. The bitterness and the rancour at what Munira and the schools inspectorate had done to him still dominated his responses to whatever was now around him. He could not understand it, the motive-spring behind this unceremonious ouster from what had started to give him life and meaning. In teaching the children, he had sensed a possible vocation, a daily dialogue with his deepest self, as he tried to understand the children and the world which shaped their future and their chances in life. He had already started to doubt the value of formal education as a tool of a people's total liberation, but he was not yet ready to leave, he was not yet ready for the world outside Ilmorog school. His first venture had after all landed him in jail. But what now? Go back to the road and sell sheepskins and plums and pears to watalii? Would his life merely be one long trail of thwarted desires and dreams, broken only by accidental escapades into places like Ilmorog? Searching for, only wanting truth and beauty and understanding, how was it that he had interfered with another's peace and comfort? How could Munira do this to him? For Karega did not accept Munira's avowed concern for a sister's death and a father's missing ear. He was ignorant of Munira's attachment to Wanja. And even if he had known, he would not have understood. He was too young. He was innocent. He did not as yet know of those doubts that needed affirmations of passion to silence them and which, unsilenced, could drive the middle-aged to murder even as an act of self-affirmation and assurance that one had not really failed. Had Lord Freeze-Kilby not followed his goodly lady with gun and powder originally meant for natives and animals? So Karega could only see motiveless paltriness in Munira's act of vengeance. He could not anyway think straight where Munira was concerned: behind his thinking, ill or good, just or unjust, he still felt an embarrassment, an empty deflation of expectations much like what he had felt when Chui, their hero, came to Siriana and tried to outdo Fraudsham. O.K. . . . actors . . . heroes . . . what was the point in believing in people? He had been looking up to the wrong heroes, or he had been looking for actors and heroes where they could not possibly be found. And so in that moment of despair, he came very close to the fatal mistake of losing faith in people and in the possibilities of truth and beauty and ideals in a world where people were daily struggling for bread and water. But he heard the voices of Wanja and Abdulla calling him from a sudden irrevocable plunge into the slough. He was touched by the evident concern in Abdulla's tone as he made the offer of partnership in trade. He turned to Abdulla:

'Why, really, did you come to Ilmorog?' he asked him.

Abdulla winced at the question: and yet it was not so unexpected: had he not asked himself that question several times? He watched the sun going behind the distant Donyo hills. He struck at a fly buzzing around his ears.

'After I was arrested, I was taken to Manyani detention camp. I was among the very last batch to be released. It was on the eve of independence and so you can imagine that for me it was full of emotion and memories and hope. I said to myself: If only Nding'uri and Ole Masai and all the others were here to see this! The flowering of faith . . . the crowning glory to a collective struggle and endurance. This would now change. No longer would I see the face of the white man laughing at our efforts. And the Indian trader with his obscenities . . . Kumanyoko mwivi . . . he too would go. Factories, tea and coffee estates would belong to us. Kenyan people. I remembered all those who had daily thwarted our struggle. I remembered the traitors: those who worked with Henderson. Vengeance is mine, saith the Lord: but I did not care: I would not have minded helping him a bit in the vengeance: at least weed out the parasites . . . collaborators. I could not help singing, this time, in triumphant expectation.

> You black traitors, spear-bearers,
> Where will you run to
> When the braves of the land return
> Trumpeting the glory and the victory of our struggle?

We did not fear rain
We did not fear death
We did not fear the dread lion
We did not fear naked colds and wind
We did not fear imperialists
For we knew
Kenya is a black man's country.

'For weeks and months after I kept on singing the song in antici-
pation.

'I waited for land reforms and redistribution.

'I waited for a job.

'I waited for a statue to Kimathi as a memorial to the fallen.

'I waited.

'I said to myself: let me sell half an acre of my one acre. I did: I
bought myself a donkey and a cart. I became a transporter of
people's goods in the market. A donkey does not drink petrol or
kerosene.

'Still I waited.

'I heard that they were giving loans for people to buy out
European farms. I did not see why I should buy lands already bought
by the blood of the people. Still I went there. They told me: this is
New Kenya. No free things. Without money you cannot buy
land: and without land and property you cannot get a bank loan
to start business or buy land. It did not make sense. For when
we were fighting, did we ask that only those with property should
fight?

'I said, maybe, maybe ... a master plan ...

'I waited.

'I thought O.K., I will become dumb. I will become deaf. I watched
things unfold. Happenings. I saw the mounting tensions between
black people. This and that community. Between regions. Ridges
even. Between homes. And I remembered our struggle, our fight, our
songs: for didn't I carry the memory on my leg? I said: why this and
that and this between our peoples? The white man: won't he now
laugh and laugh until his nose splits into two like the louse in the
story?

'I said: why this silence about the dead? Why this silence about
the movement?

'I said: let me go from office to office. I will go back to the factory
where I used to work. All I wanted was a job.

'I went to the office.

'Well, I said: I only wanted a job.

'They said: a cripple?
'I said: a cripple: must he not eat?
'They looked at one another.
'They said: he who has ears should hear: he who has eyes should see.
'This is New Kenya.
'No Free Things.
'Mkono mtupu haulambwi!
'If you want free things, go to Tanzania or China.
'I laughed bitterly. For even to go to Tanzania or to China one would need money for a bus fare.
'I stood outside the office perplexed. I was drinking my full measure of bitter gall when a man in a black suit came out of a Mercedes Benz and entered the office. All the clerks promptly stood up and put on their best smiles...'
Abdulla paused reflectively. He tried to hit at the fly again buzzing around his left ear. Then he seemed to forget it as he continued gazing across the plains, into nothingness.
'My friends ... Today nothing shocks me. Munira was once your teacher. He himself was expelled from Siriana. Just like you. Now he can have you kicked out for a private grief and you are puzzled to near despair. Do you think that surprises me? Tomorrow, my friends, tomorrow you too will turn against me. I shall not cry. Even Joseph will abuse me, maybe, and I'll not cry. But on that day? What shall I say to you? That I was not moved? What indeed can I tell you except ... except that all stomach waters that breed shock were drained out of me?
'The man who came to the office was the one who betrayed me and Nding'uri. He had, as I later gathered, a contract with the company to transport the company's goods all over. The clerks were saying after he had gone inside: Uhuru has really come. Before independence no African was allowed to touch the company's goods except as a labourer. Now Mr Kimeria handles millions!
'I remained rooted to the ground. So Kimeria wa Kamianja was eating the fruits of Uhuru!
'I went back to the village, sold the other half acre. I collected my few blankets and my donkey and journeyed, following the sun. I wanted to go deep deep into the country where I would have no reminder of so bitter a betrayal.
'Escape you might call it.
'But I had died a death of the spirit: only recently has blood started flowing in my veins. Ah, this fly again!'
He suddenly started hitting at the fly, missed it and smacked

himself on the face and muttered something inaudible. Then he turned to Karega and said:

'That is why I ask you not to go away. For where will you go to? Stay a muhoi here. Get a strip of land. Grow a crop, like Wanja here. Perchance one or two will germinate and bear a fruit or two!'

They heard Wanja sob once. They turned to look.

'What is it? What is the matter?' Abdulla asked. Then he remembered that Karega was going and maybe . . .

'Did you say Kimeria?'

'Yes.'

'He betrayed you—?'

'Yes.'

'Does he carry a small scar on his forehead?'

'Yes.'

'Then he is the one.'

'Who? What are you talking about?' asked Karega.

'He is the one who seduced me away from home,' she said. 'He called himself: Hawkins Kimeria.'

They all looked at one another. Something blocked Karega's throat.

'He – he is also the one!' he struggled to say, also remembering his own brother betrayed.

'Yes. Yes. It's only that the workers called him Mr Hawkins,' Wanja said recalling her last ordeal with Kimeria during the journey to the city.

Karega felt another kind of pain: so he had been sleeping with the woman of his brother's murderer?

Abdulla was slightly puzzled by their references. Then Wanja told him that the man who had detained her and Njuguna and Karega at Blue Hills was the same Kimeria!

But before Wanja and Karega could answer more questions from a startled Abdulla, they suddenly heard a rumbling in the sky. They thought it was thunder. It was distant at first but it came louder and louder. It was an aeroplane. It flew low above them, going round in circles as if it was looking for something lost in the sky. It would come near them and then it would move to the far end of the plains before describing yet another curve in the sky. Then they heard the droning stop abruptly. It would come back and then as quickly it would trail off. Purrs, whines, drones and then a final cessation of all sound as it came toward them. The plane was in trouble. They stood up. The plane was momentarily held up in the sky above them, before it started nosing toward them, and now they realised that it was going to crash on them. They were mesmerised with fear, with

Wanja holding onto Karega, moaning. God, God. Abdulla shouted: Down! Lie down! Flat.

They lay flat on the ground and heard the plane hurtling through the air, just missing them. It made a forced landing in a field half a mile away.

'A close one, it would have chopped off our heads,' Karega said as they scrambled back onto their feet and started for the plane.

It had landed safely. A European in khaki shirt and khaki trousers and three Africans similarly dressed stood a few yards away, hands akimbo, surveying the plane and also their luck.

'Why, it is a baby aeroplane,' exclaimed Wanja, 'just like the ones we saw at Wilson's airport.'

They went round the plane. A few yards away Abdulla let out a groan of pain 'My other leg, my other leg,' he said. Karega and Wanja went to his side. They looked at one another. But neither knew what to say.

Within an hour news of the plane's forced landing spread to ridges and villages near and far. People flocked there in hundreds. Even when later darkness fell, people still trekked to the plane carrying lamps and torches.

They took the plane captive and formed a huge dense circle around it, surveying and commenting on every part, feeling as if it was somehow their own power which had brought the plane down.

It became a day's, two days', a couple of weeks' festival with curious parties of school children brought in hired lorries to see the winged horse. Two policemen recently arrived at the post came to guard the plane.

It was Wanja who shook Abdulla from his sorrow.

'I have thought about it. But actually the idea came to me last night. Let us not kneel down to sorrow and to despair. This festival, it seems, will continue for a number of days. A few weeks even. These people will need food. Let us cook food for sale. And a bit of Theng'eta to drown the food ... and ... our separate griefs.'

It was simple: it was beautiful and Abdulla was struck by the novelty of the idea, the inspired suggestion. If Tusker, why not Theng'eta which would be cheaper and easier to make? If clubs all over the republic could sell Chang'aa, Kiruru, Busaa, why not Theng'eta in Ilmorog?

It was another immediate success. Toward the end of the week people were coming there as much to taste Theng'eta as to see the plane. Theng'eta was soon rumoured to possess all qualities from giving fertility to barren women to restoring potency to ageing men.

Dancing groups formed; drinking parties came over: Ilmorog had overnight become famous well beyond the walls of the ridge and the plains where once only shepherds and aged peasants roamed and sang to the soil and to the elephant grass, looking to the sky for sun and rain.

Ilmorog was once more in the national news. Nderi wa Riera was appointed a member of a commission of Government officials and aviation experts to report on the cause of the crash. A news item on the composition of the commission appeared in all the dailies and also on the radio. One newspaper carried a feature article with pictures of the plane and the crowds:

'A four-seater plane carrying a team of surveyors and photometrists which last week crashed in the tiny pastoral village of Ilmorog in Chiri District is now not only the subject of a Government commission of inquiry but also of a strange cult in the area. The plane was on a photo-surveying mission because of the new Trans-Africa Road project which is scheduled to soon pass through the area. This in turn is likely to affect the proposed wheat and ranching development schemes for the whole area.

'Acceleration of development along these lines was the main feature of a secret report prepared by a team of experts sent to Ilmorog two years ago as a result of the drought and the famine which had threatened thousands. Ilmorog is also seen as a high potential area for tourism, thanks to the untiring efforts of the energetic MP for the area, the Hon. Mr Nderi wa Riera, the great advocate for African personality and Black authenticity, and one of the national leaders of KCO.

'Well, I have got good news for the member.

'Tourists have already started flocking to the area.

'They may not have American dollars. But they carry their ten-cent pieces from the surrounding districts. And all because of the plane. The unprecedented crowd of visitors is likely to continue even after the plane has been removed.

'For it is now the subject of a cult. The cult is connected with a rumoured mythological animal of the earth. The animal, it is said, will bring power and light to the area. It was the animal, they say, which really brought down the plane.

'The crowds dance around it in Kanyeki-ini Garage. They sing and drink a strange mixture called Theng'eta which is reported to make barren women fertile, and not so strong men, potent. Theng'eta for Power. Some become tranced: some say they see visions of planes and other objects being driven by the strange animal of the earth, vomiting out fire and light . . .'

But for Wanja, Abdulla, Ruoro, Njuguna, Nyakinyua, and the children in Ilmorog Full Primary School the biggest talking point was not so much the plane, or the crowds of visitors, or the sudden boost in the sales of food and drinks – but the death of Abdulla's donkey, the sole victim of the plane crash, and the departure of Karega from Ilmorog.

Part Four: Again...La Luta Continua!

Those corpses of young men,
Those martyrs that hang from the gibbets – those
    hearts pierc'd by the gray lead,
Cold and motionless as they seem, live
    elsewhere with unslaughter'd vitality.

They live in other young men, O kings!
They live in brothers, again ready to defy you!
                — Walt Whitman

If we are brothers, it is not our fault or responsibility
But if we are comrades, it is a political engagement.
...It is better to be a brother and comrade.
                — Amilcar Cabral

Chapter Eleven

1 ❀ The Trans-Africa road linking Nairobi and Ilmorog to the many cities of our continent is justly one of the most famous highways in all the African lands, past and present. It is symbolic tribute, although an unintended one, to those who, witnessing the dread ravages of crime and treachery and greed which passed for civilisation, witnessing too the resistance waged and carried out with cracked hands and broken nails and bleeding hearts, voiced visionary dreams amidst sneers and suspicions and accusations of madness or of seeking pathways to immortality and the eternal self-glory of tyrants. They had seen that the weakness of the resistance lay not in the lack of will or determination or weapons but in the African people's toleration of being divided into regions and tongues and dialects according to the wishes of former masters, and they cried: Africa must unite.

Live Noliwe's Chaka. Live Toussaint L'Ouverture. Live Kwame of the eagles eyes. And thaai ... thaai to Kimathi son of wa Chiuri.

Some were scared of the searing vision, of course, and they felt more sure parroting out words from the mouth of the master: roads first, family planning, such practical needs, achievable goals, trade – the rest are dream-wishes of a Theng'eta addict. And so the road was built, not to give content and reality to the vision of a continent, but to show our readiness and faith in the practical recommendations of a realist from abroad. The master, wily architect of a myriad divisions, jealous God against the unity of a continent, now clapped his hands and nodded his head and willingly loaned out the money to pay for imported expertise and equipment. And so, abstracted from the vision of oneness, of a collective struggle of the African peoples, the road brought only the unity of earth's surface: every corner of the continent was now within easy reach of international capitalist robbery and exploitation.

That was practical unity.

Well, well ... we are all of the road now, part of the beauty of the partial achievement of the vision which gave rise to it and also of the hollowness and failed promises of which the road is a monument.

People, dwellers in the New Ilmorog, often sit on banks of the road to watch cars whining and horning their way across the seven cities of Central Africa in an oil company-sponsored race, and they muse: how man will play with death in mechanised suicide squads for a few silver dollars! They watch too the heavy tankers squelching tar on a long trail across the plains to feed a thousand arteries of thirsty machines and motors, and they mutter: before the road, before this animal of the earth, did we live in the New Jerusalem? They shake their heads from side to side, knowing the answer but keeping it close to their hearts: unless a miracle happened, they all waited to go the way Nyakinyua went:

> Maybe it was as well
> But
> The little ones!

Untroubled by memories and doubts, puzzlement and despair in the eyes of the elders, little boys and girls prance about the banks, trying to spell out LONRHO, SHELL, ESSO, TOTAL, AGIP beside the word DANGER on the sidebelly of the tankers. They sing, in shrill voices, of the road which will surely carry them to all the cities of Africa, their Africa, to link hands with children of other lands:

> Over the mud
> Over the tar
> Over the air
> From Luanda to Nairobi
> From Msumbiji to Cairo
> From Dar to Libya
> We all help one another

And so they would go on, varying only the names of the cities of Africa, their Africa!

Well there is the dream still taken up by the voices of children. It is the dream of visionaries and believers, all the seekers who retain their faith.

Such will always be.

Ni wega. It is good so.

We of Ilmorog: the road gave us a new town and catapulted us into modern times. New Ilmorog. New Jerusalem. Does it matter? We shall all, we are all about to go the way Nyakinyua went.

But what of the children?

Oh, yes, the voices of children. Our children!

❀

How Ilmorog rose from a deserted village into a sprawling town of stone, iron, concrete and glass and one or two neon-lights is already a

legend in our times. It has already been put into song: fact and
fiction mixed in fertile imaginations. You should anyway hear Abdulla sing of it, after a drink or two, or when he is selling oranges,
how Ilmorog almost magically and suddenly sprang up on Kanyeki-
ini Garage after the plane had been repaired and flown away:

> I will sing you a song of a town
> And of Wanja who started it:
> How she turned a bedbug of a village
> Into a town, Theng'eta town.
> I remember when she first came to Ilmorog
> I said: Who is that damsel come to sink my heart,
>   My village?
> Now you wagging tongues
> Cast eyes around you,
> See the work wrought by her industry.
> We greet you, Wanja Kahii,
> We greet you with ululations.
> Who said that only in a home with a male child
> Will the head of a he-goat be roasted in feast?
> Didn't your beauty bring down an aeroplane?
> Didn't your breath bring forth a city?

The town! How could we have known that Wanja's extension to
Abdulla's shop would start it all? Even when we saw that people
were driving from afar just for roasted goat meat, avidly drowning
it with Theng'eta spirit, we still thought it a temporary boom, part
of the magic brought by the aeroplane.

Within a month we witnessed even more amazing things. Surveyors pulling clanking chains along the ground came and planted
red pegs. Just like the ones who came many years back. But this time
these were soon followed by caterpillars and a cheering team of
workers of all nationalities and we crowded around them and
listened to their nonsense work songs:

> Brave one of my father, Njamba ya Awa,
> Work is done by a full stomach, Wira ni Nda,
> A man cannot be eaten by work, wanoraga uu?
> Except he be carrying an empty stomach.
> I throw the pickaxe into the earth
> And I plunge the spade into the earth!
> Long ago forest-paths were our only road –
> Do you hear birds of the air saying it?
> Road
> Ga – i – kia Ngu

Wa – thii – ku
Road
Ga – i – kia Ngu
Wa – thii – ku
Road
Ga – i – kia Ngu
Wa – thii – ku

Abdulla's place, well, Wanja's place, became the centre for talk: the road-workers drank and ate roasted meat and ugali and told gossip. Ilmorog market, which before had been an on-and-off thing depending on need, now became a daily affair with women selling onions, potatoes, maize and eggs, listening to stories and drinking in the suggestive eyes of the strange men. We asked: what lies far far beyond Donyo hills? Would the caterpillars, the D4S and the D8S, eat the earth with the same relentless power beyond the horizon of our eyes? Was it true what the MoW people said: that the road would reach Zaire and Nigeria, and onto the land of white people across the red sea? And the road workers would raise their voices above the roar of the earth-eating machines:

> The Akamba brothers sing it like this:
> Up to the rooftops raise the dust
> Ooh Mutumia wa Kibeti – iii
> Let's work with all our strength
> Mutumia wa Kibeti – iii
> The old ones wait at home
> Mutumia wa Kibeti – iii
> And the children wait to see us of the road
> Mutumia wa Kibeti – iii
> So let's try harder
> Mutumia wa Kibeti – iii
> We are opening a highway
> Is it for good?
> Is it for evil?
> It is for both,
> Mwana wa Gacimbiri-i

And the machines wallowed and whined and roared in the mud, clearing bush and grass and occasionally huts that stood in the way of trade and progress.

So we stood and watched as the machines roared toward Mwathi's place. We said: it cannot be. But they still moved toward it. We said: they will be destroyed by Mwathi's fire. Just you wait, just you wait.

But the machine uprooted the hedge and then it hit the first hut and it fell and we were all hush-hush, waiting for it to be blown up. Even when the Americans landed on the moon and we thought the earth would tremble or something would happen, we were not as scared as when Mwathi's place was razed to the ground. The two huts were pulled down. But where was Mwathi? There was no Mwathi. He must have vanished, we said, and we waited for his vengeance. Maybe he was never there, we said, and the elder who might have helped, Muturi, had become suddenly deaf and dumb at the sacrilege. But what the machine revealed made the strangers pause, and they called people from Nairobi who came with books and cameras and measuring instruments of different kinds. Mwathi was a guardian spirit: he had been sitting on a knowledge of many seasons gone: rings, metal work, spears, smelting works – all these. A wire fence was put round it and later a big sign: ILMOROG: an archeological site. Mwathi's power had worked after all. The road skirted the site. But who was Mwathi? We kept on asking the question. Muturi did not long survive this and died with the secret of Ilmorog's guardian spirit, whose place was now only a site for the curious about the past, long long before East Africa traded with China and the Indies.

Long after the road had gone beyond the plains and hills, and the workers had moved their camp, Abdulla's place continued to grow, becoming a 'stop' spot for big lorries and cars that were now using the tarred road. The drivers and the turn boys would often spend the night there, drinking Theng'eta which produced the lightness of hashish and Mairungi!

Abdulla and Wanja added more extensions. There was now a shop, a butchery, a bar, a beer-hall which was also a dance place, and five rooms where those in need could spend the night: for a fee.

Shop. Butchery. Bar. Lodgings. Everything was happening as if working to some invisible pre-ordained plan.

Even then we thought of it as a temporary measure, an alien thing which would soon disappear and leave us where we were before the aeroplane crashed into our lives.

But the road: it was our road.

We prepared for the opening of the Ilmorog section with proud though vague anticipations. Why! A minister of the Government would visit Ilmorog. We had never before seen a minister in our lives. We all helped in tidying up Abdulla's place. The school with its new teachers prepared a choir.

As it turned out, no minister came: it was not an opening ceremony but rather an inspection tour by high government officials accompanied by Nderi wa Riera, and his two lieutenants: *Fat Sto-*

mach and *Insect* who once came to our village long ago. Nderi spoke to us and apologised for the inconvenience and the false expectations. But what he said more than compensated for our failure to see a live minister. He talked about KCO and what it would do for the area if people listened to him.

He started by arguing that an MP could only be judged by how far he had brought and could bring development to an area. He, Nderi, had already done that by having a road pass through Ilmorog. Now people would not, as had been known to happen in the past, have to walk for miles through dry and dangerous plains on donkey-carts: there were now matatus and buses and lorries. The road had brought trade to the area: small shopping centres were springing up on either side of the road. In order to prevent a mushrooming of mere slums and shanties, he had proposed – and indeed the plans were under way – for Chiri County Council to set up a properly planned, sewaged shopping centre at Ilmorog. A few acres of land would of course be taken from the people for the purpose, but the County Council would pay adequate compensation. Then as a result of his representations and remonstrations with the central government, it had been decided to develop the whole area into ranches and wheat fields. A tourist centre would be set up and a game park further on would be enclosed and made out of bounds for the herdsmen. People, whether herdsmen or ordinary farmers, would be given loans to develop their land and their ranches. But first people had to register their lands in order to acquire title-deeds which in turn would act as security with the banks. He had promised that he would bring development to Ilmorog. The road was only a beginning.

How times were changing! We could not believe our ears, nobody could take in fully what they had heard. But he was our MP and we had indeed seen the surveying aeroplanes come and go: we had seen men on foot with measuring chains and theodolites: and now, the new road. Why should we not believe him?

Elections were coming, he warned us, and it was a wise man and woman who knew how and where to cast his vote. They should give him the chance to complete what he had started.

Progress with Nderi! Fat Stomach shouted, and we sang back the words:

> Go with Nderi!
> Grow rich with Nderi!
> Develop and fly high with Nderi!
> Drive on new roads with Nderi!

267

It had been a year of changes and progress!

Why had we once doubted him?

We were all happy except the old woman who felt uneasy about something and said she could not tell what it was because it was not clear. Maybe it's the words of the road-singers that stay long in my ears, she said, but I feel a trembling in the stomach, just a tiny trembling in my belly!

❀

Progress! Yes, development did come to Ilmorog. Plots were carved out of the various farms to make a shopping centre. Shops were planned and people were asked to send in applications for building plots to the County Council. A mobile van – African Economic Bank – came to Ilmorog and explained to the peasant farmers and the herdsmen how they could get loans. They crowded around the man fascinated as much by the up-and-down motion of his adam's apple as by the rounded voice coming out of the loudspeaker. Demarcation. Title deeds. Loans. Fencing the land. Barbed wire. One or two grade cows. Kill or sell or cross-breed the others. A Farmers' Marketing Co-operative. Ever for instance heard of the successful Dairy Farmers' Co-operatives in other Districts? African Economic Bank would do similar things here. Milk. KCC. Wealth. From this one would pay back the loans at a small interest. Not in one lump sum. Oh no. Paying back would also be spread over a number of years. No steady farmer need ever feel the pinch. Only one condition: payment had to be regular. Easy. It was a year of hope. Mzigo came to the area. The school, being now more accessible, would expand. New buildings. New classes. New staff houses. More trained staff. Really, it was another year of hope in Ilmorog, except for Njuguna, who was almost ruined. His fours sons had suddenly returned and they all demanded their share of the ten-acre farm. What could he do with the two acres that remained to him? The younger son used the title-deeds as security for a loan to start a kiosk in Nairobi. Later he returned to Ilmorog once again and set up the old man in a kiosk business and later in a shop. But in the year of demarcation, with the sons almost coming to blows with one another, Njuguna was a sad man. The road. Trade. Progress. We saw the new owners of plots bring stones and concrete. We watched the trenches being dug and we were glad that at least two of us from Ilmorog, Wanja and Abdulla, had secured a plot and so would show these outsiders that even Ilmorog had people who could put up stone buildings. Flowers for our land. Long live Nderi wa Riera. We gave him our votes: we waited for flowers to bloom.

2 ❀ They talked against light and shadows from a hurricane lamp – his electricity had been cut off – Munira trying to make him traverse the five years of separation. Much had happened. So much had happened. Ilmorog and everybody was changed, utterly changed.

Who would have thought that he would return? Only the old woman who had retained faith and said that he would return. Kumagwo ni Gucokagwo, she had maintained. And it was she who now was not there to see him: or maybe she was seeing him from the limbo world of the living-dead.

He sat back on the chair and rested his hands on the table between them.

Five years, Munira was thinking, five years since he went away and left a curse behind him, as if he knew that with his going the old Ilmorog would also go. His face was gaunt, his fingers kept on moving on the table as if in a nervous energy of impatience. There was light and fire in the eyes. And yet his face was still, still but hard, skin held tight against the bones. He had travelled more, seen more, grown more but what it was that had brought him back, Munira could not tell. He had a way of asking questions without any frills at their edges and he had a way of listening as if every detail was important and he had to compare it against other details.

The way Munira told it was as if things had happened in a neat sequence of time and place. Yet Munira had experienced the events and the changes as chaos inside and outside himself, and he a comic spectator with the comic passions of an old man, unable to act. It was only in Theng'eta that he had found personal reality and he was then able to view the burnt-out cigarette-ends of his life, his illusions, his desires. So in telling it to him who sat so still, despite his fingers that seemed to wander in search of things to do, he knew that he was falsifying history. But how could he recount his own descent into a five-year hell at Wanja's feet?

She had somehow gripped him, possessed him, turned his head and made his heart beat with a thousand pains and sighs. She was exacting her vengeance: she was his ruin. She watched it, supervised it, coldly, detachedly, and yet, somehow, she always seemed vulnerable, dancing just within reach, just outside of reach. His heart would miss a beat, oh the menacing emptiness, he would drink more Theng'eta and dream of heaven.

She had turned her energy and time, after Karega had disappeared, into work. She was seized by the devil spirit of brewing and selling and counting and hatching out more plans for the progress of her trade/business partnership with Abdulla. In time, she employed three barmaids – Kamba, Kikuyu, Kalenjin – who seemed to speak the same language with their eyes and fingers and movement. She also – what a stroke of genius – hired a live band composed entirely of women from many Kenyan nationalities, and this brought more customers flocking to see for themselves. Wanja presided over all this: she had money and she was powerful and men and women feared her. They talked about her, they sang about her, and the many people who drove in to eat roasted goat meat and enjoy music issuing from the delicate fingers of the women, and touch the breasts of the barmaids who would cry out in studied pain of loving protest, also came to see the famed proprietor. But she remained aloof, distant, condescending, willing and commanding things to happen, but herself remaining inaccessible to a thousand hungry eyes, fingers eager to touch, and arteries throbbing with hot blood of desire.

The gang of road-workers had given her and Abdulla a head start. She and Abdulla were really the only local people who had successfully bid for a building plot in the New Ilmorog and started work on it. The rest who either had plots carved out of their consolidated holdings or had successfully bid for one, later sold them to outsiders who could afford the cost of building. The builders, carpenters, masons, owners, contractors, all fed her thriving business in Theng'eta. One or two people in emulation tried to set up Chang'aa and Kiruru shops but the drinks never caught on. Nothing could beat Theng'eta.

Munira had thought that with the departure of Karega the understanding which had earlier existed between him and Wanja would be rekindled. He tried a reconnection, a reconciliation, but he only met with eyes that bade him no welcome. Defeat spurred him to redoubled efforts and more failure. How close to Abdulla she seemed! Munira felt like a schoolboy bully who, ousted from a group, was now hovering around itching to rejoin it and be accepted. Unwanted, excluded from their communal rite of making money, he felt a tremendous loneliness descend upon him and he was haunted by the past that had always shadowed him. An outsider. A spectator.

He drank more Theng'eta: he felt temporarily lifted out of himself, sailing on surging clouds of vain expectation. Looking at her from cloudy heights, she appeared even more desirable. He waited for a sign, a hand, a tender beaming smile, beckoning. None came. She was pure, indifferent. Her business boomed. Buildings in New Ilmorog went up, up, up.

Theng'eta. Deadly lotus. An only friend. Constant companion. The trouble with drinking was that he felt he needed a little bit more to get back to yesterday's normality and, in time, to prevent his hands from trembling so that they would remain firm enough to hold another horn. Theng'eta. The spirit. Dreams of love returned.

Something was the matter with him. If only Mwathi's place had not been razed to the ground! He certainly would have gone there for a love potion or else for medicine to cure the ache of loving.

He started reading star-charts and horoscopes, even in old, torn magazines and newspapers. He followed the doings and predictions of Francis Ng'ombe, Yahya Hussein and Omolo. He even thought of writing to them to ask them to set up an office at Ilmorog. He did not know the day or the month of his birth but every reading seemed to apply to him. He read:

CAPRICORN, Dec. 22 – Jan. 20: You can be turned on quickly by others who are unique in some outstanding way.

He thought he must have been born or conceived under Capricorn.

SAGITTARIUS, Nov. 23 – Dec. 21: Since you tend to fall in love with love, it is not surprising that at times you are more or less blinded to the reality of many situations and people: being something of a dreamer when it comes to matters of love, you have a tendency to fantasise most of your love and sexual experience.

He was sure that he had been born under Sagittarius.

GEMINI, May 22 – June 21: Once you develop an emotional interest in someone, you are inclined to persist in your pursuit until you are either totally accepted or totally rejected.

Gemini was really his star.

So that, depending on his moods, he variously imagined himself born or conceived under every star: practically every prediction and every advice seemed to apply to him. Sometimes he would try to act on different starry guides, hoping that one at least might prove true and prophetic. But nothing seemed to happen. Wanja was still chilly and distant, oscillating between her business establishment in old Ilmorog to her stone building going up in the New Ilmorog.

He decided to stick to one star. He chose Leo. He read:

This week is marked by the movement of Saturn into your solar ninth house of intellectuality and emotionality. Under both influences, you'll be inclined to lay a course which will both be challenging and promising of heaven. Keep on smiling. Romance may come your way.

He kept on smiling. He waited. Romance and love came his way.

Leo, Lillian, my star!

He saw her coming toward him and his heart gave thunderous beats. Could this be true? He listened to her unlikely story. Somebody had given her a lift from Eldoret, she claimed, and he had abandoned her in Ilmorog. Munira smiled at her. He knew her: he had seen her. He hummed the tune she once played at Ruwa-ini. She smiled back. They talked. He reminded her of the day, years back, he had found her playing a religious hymn sung by Ofafa Jericho Choir at Furaha Bar in Ruwa-ini. Wanja gave her a job. She was very fond of singing or humming religious tunes, especially after a drink or two. She would sing in a husky voice, her eyes dilated, her eyes and neck raised in heavenly expectation:

> Nearer my God to Thee,
> Nearer to meeeeeeeee,
> Even though I be a sinner
> I want you still nearer to me.

She had a way of making up words and phrases so that they fitted in without much seeming strain on her part. And yet with her obvious gift in words and voice, she would not hear of joining the band or singing what she called irreligious songs. She would only change from one hymn to another of her own making but they were beautifully seductive:

> Come, come unto me, Jesus,
> I am waiting for you.
> Come quickly unto me, Saviour,
> And fill me with thy holy spirit.

For a time Munira was intrigued by her and almost forgot the pain of being possessed with Wanja. Lillian: she was a strange case of a girl who maintained that she was still a virgin even after he had entered her and she had screamed and scratched his back, bitten his hand and cried in ecstasy and delight: Come, come, Lord, into me.

Munira had hoped that his involvement with Lillian would provoke Wanja's jealousy. But she did not seem to be moved. He gave up starry charts. Lillian, the 'virgin', was not a substitute for Wanja.

He resumed his lone walks across Ilmorog ridge, now cleaved into two by the Trans-Africa Road. He watched cars go beyond the hills: he would even count them to while away the time. Often, after school, he would walk to the building sites, and for a time become lost amidst trenches with pools of dirty water, piles of quarry rock, the cry of hammers on stone, nail and wood, the ribald chatter among the masons. What was happening to sleepy Ilmorog? What happened to the land of trios of children singing, paving the way to sleep with lullabyes? He stopped and rubbed his eyes clean: Wambui, Muriuki's mother, was staggering behind the handles of a wheelbarrow piled high with stones. The demarcation and the fencing off of land had deprived a lot of tillers and herdsmen of their hitherto unquestioned rights of use and cultivation. Now they were hiring themselves out to any who needed their labour for a wage. Wambui, a labourer! Now she had joined others who had been drawn into Ilmorog's market for sweat and labour. He quickly passed on and only stopped when he came to Wanja-Abdulla's building. This would soon be the New Theng'eta centre. He was racking his brains for ways and means of endearing himself to her when the idea struck him. Soon the place would be opened. There might even be other licensed bar facilities. He would help her increase her sales of Theng'eta. He would pull in more customers for her!

Munira had always liked advertisements. But now he started reading them even more avidly. He now had a mission. He studied them, the words, the phrasing, and the difference between the intended and the possible effect on the readers and hearers. He collected a few:

Put a tiger in your tank. Healthy hair means beautiful hair. Everytime is tea time. Be a platinum blonde: be a redhead: be a whole new you in 100% imported hand-made human hair. Join the new Africans: join Ambi people. Beautiful ones not yet born? You are joking. They are, everyday, with beautiful silky wigs: Man can get lost in it.

He tried his head at making up a few. Maybe he could sell them to whoever was going to set up businesses in the New Ilmorog. Munira: seller of beautiful ads and slogans. Want to go into Parliament? Buy a slogan! Be successful! Buy a slogan. For Wanja he would try to create a special one. For free. One that would so popularise Theng'eta that she would be known as Queen Theng'eta. She would then *have* to notice him. Author of her new fame.

Do you have what it takes? Drink Theng'eta. Increase your potency: Drink Theng'eta. Beautiful people, beautiful thoughts, beautiful love: Drink Theng'eta. Join the Space Age: Drink Theng'eta. On your way to the moon with Armstrong: Drink Theng'eta. Three T's: Theng'a Theng'a with Theng'eta.

He was now ready. He tried the last one on a few customers, suddenly standing up in their midst, during a lull in the music from the band, and shouted: Drink the drink of three letters and increase your potency: Theng'a Theng'a with Theng'eta. He shouted it again and raised a glass to his lips. They all looked up at him and thought him drunk. They laughed and continued their drinking. Wanja looked at him and shrugged her shoulders. But the slogan remained in use – as a joke!

That night he took Lillian home, and when she pretended that she was a virgin being taken against her will he beat her. They fell out. Lillian left Ilmorog. He was alone. Theng'eta.

He would always remember that year as the beginning of three years of shameless enslavement to naked passion. It was as if the completion and the opening of the New Ilmorog shopping centre also saw the complete unmaking of Munira, the hitherto respected teacher of their children. He could see it; he watched the decline, a spectator, an outsider, and he could not help himself. Or was he punishing himself for another kind of failure?

It was this that he could not quite tell him, he, who, in part, was the cause of it.

But Karega's eyes were insistent, his whole being seemed waiting for an answer to a big question he had not yet asked. It was all very much like their first encounter. Then Munira had sworn that tarred roads would only be built when hyenas grew horns. He would like to have swallowed back the words. For the changed circumstance under which they now met was in part a product of the tarred road. Trans-Africa Road. Even the school had changed: it was now built of stones; it had full classes and full teachers, with a new modern headmaster, and Mzigo came regularly, in part to inspect the school but largely to look after his shop in the New Ilmorog. Mzigo, Nderi wa Riero, Rev. Jerrod, they all had shop buildings in Ilmorog.

'What happened to Joseph?' Karega asked.

'He passed all right. 3 A's. He went to Siriana!'

'Siriana?'

'Yes. Siriana.'

A silent moment followed Munira's disclosures, both he and Karega maybe remembering what Siriana had meant to them in earlier times. Munira, still weighed down by anxiety, eyed Karega who looked at the same spot, a concentration of light in his eyes, his hands still moving, but his face refusing to smile. Munira could not tell if Karega was pleased or not with Joseph's success. But it seemed there were some problems pressing him and it was five years since he left Ilmorog.

'And what happened to the old woman?' Karega asked, as if he was completing a thought dialogue with himself.

Munira was visibly relieved that the big question did not come. But even this was hard to answer, because everything had happened so fast, a chaos in a drunken dream. Nyakinyua. The old woman. Even Munira did not wish to remember, to think of her fate. What could he now say about Nyakinyua and himself and not weep again?

He recalled, without telling him, that he had somehow continued looking for a slogan, for a catchy ad which would bring him Wanja's favours – even for a night. He would go through the newspaper and read, not the news, but the advertisements. He read of course about the lawyer and his thunderous speeches in Parliament and how he was calling for a ceiling on land ownership and other reforms. But that was only because there were memories attached to the name. His main interest was in ads – he had to get the slogans ... to beat all the slogans, the slogans that would finally buy him Wanja.

He would always remember the evening he read about Nyakinyua – with pain ... He was drunk but the Theng'eta in his head seemed to evaporate when suddenly he saw it. His hands and the newspaper trembled. He sobered up and looked at the announcement. It was not possible. It could not be possible:

KANUA KANENE & CO
Valuers & Surveyors, Auctioneers
Land, Estate & Management AGENTS
Acting on instructions given to us
by Wilson, Shah, Muragi & Omolo Advocates
on behalf of their client, African Economic Bank, charged with
powers of sale as conferred upon them. We shall
sell by public auction ... all that piece of land
situated in New Ilmorog ... property of Mrs Nyakinyua ...

She was not alone: a whole lot of peasants and herdsmen of Old Ilmorog who had been lured into loans and into fencing off their land and buying imported fertilisers and were unable to pay back were similarly affected. Without much labour, without machinery, without breaking with old habits and outlook, and without much advice they had not been able to make the land yield enough to meet their food needs and pay back the loans. Some had used the money to pay school fees. Now the inexorable law of the metal power was driving them from the land.

Munira folded the newspaper and went to Wanja's place to break the news. He felt for her and Nyakinyua. He did not expect favours. He just wanted to take her the news. And to find out more about it. She was not at her Theng'eta premises. Abdulla told him that she had gone to Nyakinyua's hut. Munira walked there and found other people. News of the threatened sale must have reached them too. They had come to commiserate with her and others similarly affected, to weep with one another. They looked baffled: how could a bank sell their land? A bank was not a government: from whence then, its powers? Or maybe it was the government, an invisible government, some others suggested. They turned to Munira. But he could not answer their questions. He only talked about a piece of paper they had all signed and the red blotched title-deeds, another piece of paper, they had surrendered to the bank. But he could not answer, put to sleep, the bitter scepticism in their voices and looks. What kind of monster was this bank that was a power unto itself, that could uproot lives of a thousand years?

He went back and tried to drink Theng'eta, but it did not have the taste. He remembered that recently he had seen Wambui carting stones to earn bread for the day and he wondered what would happen to the old woman. She was too old to sell her labour and sweat in a market.

'The old woman? Nyakinyua?' Munira echoed Karega's question, slowly. 'She died! She is dead!' he added quickly, almost aggressively, waking up from his memories.

Karega's face seemed to move.

Nyakinyua, the old woman, tried to fight back. She tramped from hut to hut calling upon the peasants of Ilmorog to get together and fight it out. They looked at her and they shook their heads: whom would they fight now? The Government? The Banks? KCO? The Party? Nderi? Yes who would they really fight? But she tried to convince them that all these were one and that she would fight them. Her land would never be settled by strangers. There was something grand, and defiant in the woman's action – she with her failing health and flesh trying to organise the dispossessed of Ilmorog into a protest. But there was pathos in the exercise. Those whose land had not yet been taken looked nervously aloof and distant. One or two even made disparaging remarks about an old woman not quite right in the head. Others genuinely not seeing the point of a march to Ruwa-ini or to the Big City restrained her. She could not walk all the way, they told her. But she said: 'I'll go alone ... my man fought the white man. He paid for it with his blood ... I'll struggle against these black oppressors ... alone ... alone ...'

What would happen to her, Munira wondered.

He need not have worried about her.

Nyakinyua died peacefully in her sleep a few days after the news of the bank threat. Rumour went that she had told Wanja about the impending journey: she had said that she could not even think of being buried in somebody else's land: for what would her man say to her when she met him on the other side? People waited for the bank to come and sell her land. But on the day of the sale Wanja redeemed the land and became the heroine of the new and the old Ilmorog.

Later Munira was to know.

But at that time only Abdulla really knew the cost: Wanja had offered to sell him her rights to their jointly owned New Building. He did not have the money and it was he who suggested that they sell the whole building to a third person and divide the income between them.

So Wanja was back to her beginnings.

And Mzigo was the new proud owner of the business premises in Ilmorog.

3 ✿ Wanja was not quite the same after her recent loss. For a time, she continued the proud proprietor of the old Theng'eta place. Her place still remained the meat-roasting centre. Dance steps in the hall could still raise dust to the roof, especially when people were moving to their favourite tunes:

> How beautiful you are, my love!
> How soft your round eyes are, my honey!
> What a pleasant thing you are,
> Lying here
> Shaded by this cedar bush!
> But oh, darling,
> What poison you carry between your legs!

But Wanja's heart was not in it. She started building a huge wooden bungalow at the lower end of her shamba, some distance from the shanty town that was growing up around Abdulla's shop, the lodgings and the meat-roasting centre, almost as a natural growth complement to the more elegant New Ilmorog. People said that she was wise to invest in a building the money remaining after redeeming her grandmother's shamba: but what was it for? She already had a hut further up the shamba, hidden from the noise and inquisitive eyes of the New Ilmorog by a thick natural hedge. She went about her work without taking anybody into her confidence. But it was obvious that it was built in the style of a living house with several spacious rooms. Later she moved in: she planted flower gardens all around and had electric lights fixed there. It was beautiful: it was a brave effort so soon after her double loss, people said.

One night the band struck up a song they had composed on their first arrival. As they played, the tune and the words seemed to grow fresher and fresher and the audience clapped and whistled and shouted encouragement. The band added innovations and their voices seemed possessed of a wicked carefree devil.

> This shamba girl
> Was my darling,
> Told me she loved my sight.
> I broke bank vaults for her,

I went to jail for her,
But when I came back
I found her a lady,
Kept by a wealthy roundbelly daddy,
And she told me,
This shamba-lady girl told me,
No! Gosh!
Sikujui
Serikali imebadilishwa
Coup d'état!

They stopped to thunderous handclaps and feet pounding on the floor. Wanja suddenly stood up and asked them to play it again. She started dancing to it, alone, in the arena. People were surprised. They watched the gyrations of her body, speaking pleasure and pain, memories and hopes, loss and gain, unfulfilled longing and desire. The band, responding to the many beating hearts, played with sad maddening intensity as if it were reaching out to her loneliness and solitary struggle. She danced slowly and deliberately toward Munira and he was remembering that time he had seen her dancing to a juke-box at Safari Bar in Kamiritho. As suddenly as she had started, she stopped. She walked to the stage at the bandstand. The 'house' was hushed. The customers knew that something big was in the air.

'I am sorry, dear customers, to have to announce the end of the old Ilmorog Bar and meat-roasting centres, and the end of Ilmorog Bar's own Sunshine Band. Chiri County Council says we have to close.'

She could not say more. And now they watched her as she walked across the dusty floor toward where Munira was sitting. She stopped, whirled back, and screamed at the band. 'Play! Play! Play on. Everybody dance – Daaance!' And she sat down beside Munira.

'Munira, wouldn't you like to come and see my new place tomorrow night?'

Munira could hardly contain himself. So at long last. So the years of waiting were over. It was just like the old days before Karega and the roads and the changes had come to disturb the steamy peaceful rhythm in Ilmorog, when he was the teacher.

❀

The next day he could not teach. He could not talk. He could hardly sit or stand still in one place. And when the time came, he walked to her place with tremulous hands and beating heart. He had not been inside the new house and he felt it an honour that she had chosen him out of all those faces.

He knocked at the door. She was in. She stood in the middle of the room lit by a blue light. For a second he thought himself in the wrong place with the wrong person.

She had on a miniskirt which revealed just about everything, and he felt his manhood rise of itself. On her lips was smudgy red lipstick: her eyebrows were pencilled and painted a luminous blue. On her head was a flaming red wig. What was the game, he wondered? He thought of one of the many advertisements he had earlier collected: Be a platinum blonde: be a whole new you in 100% imported hand-made human hair. Wanja was a really new her.

'You look surprised, Mwalimu. I thought you always wanted me,' she said, with a false seductive blur in her voice. Then in a slightly changed voice, more natural, which he could recognise, she added: 'That's why you sent him away, not so? That's why you had him dismissed, not so? Look now. They have even taken away my right, well, our right to brew. The County Council says our licence was sold away with the New Building. They also say our present premises are in any case unhygienic! There's going to be a tourist centre and such places might drive visitors away. Do you know the new owner of our Theng'eta breweries? Do you know the owner of the New Ilmorog Utamaduni Centre? Never mind!' She had, once again, changed her voice: 'But come: what are you waiting for?' She walked backwards; he followed her and they went into another room – with a double bed and a reddish light. He was hypnotised. He was angry with himself for being tongue-tied and yet he was propelled toward her by the engine-power of his risen body and the drums in the heart. Yet below it all, deep inside, he felt a sensation of shame and disgust at his helplessness.

She removed everything, systematically, piece by piece, and then jumped into bed.

'Come, come, my darling!' she cooed from inside the sheets.

He was about to jump into bed beside her and clasp her to himself, when she suddenly turned cold and chilly, and her voice was menacing.

'No, Mwalimu. No free things in Kenya. A hundred shillings on the table if you want high-class treatment.'

He thought she was joking, but as he was about to touch her she added more coldly.

'This is New Kenya. You want it, you pay for it, for the bed and the light and my time and the drink that I shall later give you and the breakfast tomorrow. And all for a hundred shillings. For you. Because of old times. For others it will be more expensive.'

He was taken aback, felt the wound of this unexpected

humiliation. But now he could not retreat. Her thighs called out to him.

He took out a hundred shillings and handed it to her. He watched her count it and put the money under the mattress. Now panic seized him. His thing had shrivelled. He stood there and tried to fix his mind on the old Wanja, on the one who had danced pain and ecstasy, on the one who had once cried under watchful moonbeams stealing into a hut. She watched him, coldly, with menace, and then suddenly she broke out in her put-on, blurred, seductive voice.

'Come, darling. I'll keep you warm. You are tonight a guest at *Sunshine Lodge*.'

There was something pathetic, sad, painful in the tone. But Munira's thing obeyed her voice. Slowly he removed his clothes and joined her in bed. Even as the fire and thirst and hunger in his body were being quenched, the pathetic strain in her voice lingered in the air, in him, in the room everywhere.

It was New Kenya. It was New Ilmorog. Nothing was free. But for a long time, for years to come, he was not to forget the shock and the humiliation of the hour. It was almost like that first time, long ago, when he was only a boy.

4 ❀ Indeed, changes did come to Ilmorog, changes that drove the old one away and ushered a new era in our lives. And nobody could tell, really tell, how it had happened, except that it had happened. Within a year or so of the New Ilmorog shopping centre being completed, wheatfields and ranches had sprung up all around the plains: the herdsmen had died or had been driven further afield into the drier parts, but a few had become workers on the wheatfields and ranches on the earth upon which they once roamed freely. The new owners, master-servants of bank power, money and cunning, came over at weekends and drove in Landrovers or Range Rovers, depending on the current car fashion, around the farms whose running they had otherwise entrusted to paid managers. The peasants of Ilmorog had also changed. Some had somehow survived the onslaught. They could employ one or two hands on their small farms. Most of the others had joined the army of workers who had added to the growing population of the New Ilmorog. But which New Ilmorog?

There were several Ilmorogs. One was the residential area of the farm managers, County Council officials, public service officers, the managers of Barclays, Standard and African Economic Banks, and other servants of state and money power. This was called Cape Town. The other – called New Jerusalem – was a shanty town of migrant and floating workers, the unemployed, the prostitutes and small traders in tin and scrap metal. Between the New Jerusalem and Cape Town, not far from where Mwathi had once lived guarding the secrets of iron works and native medicine, was All Saints Church, now led by Rev. Jerrod Brown. Also somewhere between the two areas was Wanja's *Sunshine Lodge*, almost as famous as the church.

The shopping and business centre was dominated by two features. Just outside it was a tourist cultural (Utamaduni) village owned by Nderi wa Riera and a West German concern, appropriately called Ilmorog African Diamond Cultural and Educational Tours. Many tourists came for a cultural fiesta. A few hippies also came to look for the Theng'eta plant, whose leaves when dried and smoked had, so it was claimed, the same effect as hashish. The other was Theng'eta Breweries which, starting on the premises owned by Mzigo, had now grown into a huge factory employing six hundred workers with a number of research scientists and chemical engineers. The factory also owned an estate in the plains where they experimented with different types of Theng'eta plants and wheat. They brewed a variety of Theng'eta drinks: from the pure gin for export to cheap but potent drinks for workers and the unemployed. They put some in small plastic bags in different measures of one, two and five shillings' worth so that these bagfuls of poison could easily be carried in people's pockets. Most of the containers, whether plastic or glass bottles, carried the famous ad, now popularised in most parts of the country through their sales-vans, newspapers and handbills: POTENCY – Theng'a Theng'a with Theng'eta. $P=3T$.

The breweries were owned by an Anglo-American international combine but of course with African directors and even shareholders. Three of the four leading local personalities were Mzigo, Chui and Kimeria.

Long live New Ilmorog! Long live Partnership in Trade and Progress!

5 ✸ 'What ... what happened to Abdulla ... and Wanja?' Karega asked, interrupting Munira's catalogue of the changes.

At last ... at last the question he had dreaded. Is this why he had returned from a five-year exile and silence? Could it be that he still retained a spark of the memory of times past? Of her?

'She is the most powerful woman in all Ilmorog. She owns houses between here and Nairobi. She owns a fleet of matatus. She owns a fleet of big transport lorries. She is that bird periodically born out of the ashes and dust.'

Suddenly Munira remembered his shock and the humiliation of being a guinea-pig. Bitterness returned. Why should he spare him?

'Would you ... would you like to see her?'

'Now?'

'Yes. Now.'

'Isn't it late?'

'Well ... it is not ... for her ... though we could ring her if you like.'

They went through the neon-lit streets. For Karega everything was familiar in a strange kind of way: he had seen similar towns all over Kenya. In any case, Nairobi, Thika, Kisumu, Nakuru, Mombasa were larger and older versions of the New Ilmorog. But both were conscious of an earlier journey to Wanja's hut: how long ago it all seemed now! Munira often interrupted the silence by telling him who owned what: and it seemed as if every prominent person in the country now owned a bit of Ilmorog: from the big factory to the shanty dwellings. 'Yes ...' Munira was saying. 'Even these falling-apart workers' houses ... you'll be surprised to see the landlords who come to collect the rent ... No shame ... they drive in their Mercedes Benzes ... and they have been known to lock the poor souls out. Occasionally, the Town Council has a clean-up, burn-down campaign ... but surprisingly ... it is the shanties put up by the unemployed and the rural migrant poor which get razed to the ground. And do you see those kiosks by the road? A year ago there was a big scandal about them. Some County Councillors and officials were allocated them ... free ... and then sold them for more than fifty thousand shillings to others who rent them out to women petty traders ... and now let me take you through our New Jerusalem,' Munira continued with his chatter.

He was like a tourist guide and he seemed to enjoy the role. Karega walked beside him in silence, turning over the comments in his mind. The story he listened to, so cruelly illustrated by what he saw with his eyes, contained a familiar theme, a common theme shared by the other places he had been to all over the Republic. But it was no less depressing. Munira abruptly stopped by a mud-walled barrack of a house with several doors partitioning it into several separate rooms.

'Here ... Here is Abdulla's place,' he announced. 'As you can see, it's right at the centre of the New Jerusalem. Do you want to greet him before we proceed to Wanja's place?'

'Yes,' Karega said.

Munira knocked at the door calling out a loud hodi, and Abdulla, from the inside, responded in a drunken voice. They heard the bolts creak. Abdulla threw open the door, but instead of welcoming them with greetings of recognition he went on with complaints against 'people who keep on waking up and disturbing peaceful citizens'. Then he saw it was Munira.

'Ooh, it's you ... my friend ... come in, come in. I have a few five-shilling packets of Theng'eta. Theng'a Theng'a with Theng'eta. Ha! ha! ha! Come in.'

He sat on the bed and invited Munira to take the folding chair, the only chair in the place.

'And don't knock down the hurricane lamp,' Abdulla went on. Then he noticed that Munira was not alone.

'Oh! Oh! And you have brought a visitor. Let him take the chair. You, Munira, my friend, come and sit on the bed. And be careful. Rubber straps make up the springs. And you know some time ago I sat too heavily on it and the straps broke. I was really sprung up and then brought down, onto the floor. And who is your visitor? Does he also take Theng'eta? Mwalimu's formula. $P = _3T$. Drink the drink of three letters.'

'Do you not recognise him?' Munira asked when they all had sat down.

'Who? This silence?'

'Karega ...'

'Karega.'

'Yes.'

'Karega! Karega, Nding'uri's brother ... But how ... You have really grown. A Mzee like myself ... you only need a few tufts of grey ... But which corner of the world did you spring from?'

Karega explained briefly. But he saw that Abdulla was not really following him. He had changed: hollow tired eyes in hollow caves. They tried this and that subject but nothing seemed to flow freely.

'All the same, welcome to this bachelor's corner,' Abdulla repeated. 'A bit different from my old place! But that was old Ilmorog. They made us demolish the house. And now look at the place they have brought us to.'

'And whose house is this, then?' Karega asked.

'This ... and a few others belong to a very important person in authority.'

'You mean, Him? This?' Karega asked.

'Yes. He charges a hundred shillings for this one room. So from the block he makes a thousand shillings a month. And he owns about ten blocks. That's ten thousand shillings. Just for putting up a few poles and mudding them. He comes in a Range Rover and he parks by the road. He sends his driver/bodyguard to collect the rent.'

'But he comes ... he earns more than sixty thousand shillings a day from transporting sugar and hardware for the McMillan sugar works. And this on top of his official government salary!'

'Well. That makes it sixty thousand plus ten thousand and that comes to seventy thousand shillings,' Abdulla said.

'It's the way of the world,' Munira added. 'He probably owns other slums in other cities. In our Kenya you can make a living out of anything. Even fear. Look at the British company that owns and runs security guards in this country. Every house, every factory has a Securicor guard. They should set up a Ministry of Fear.'

'A Ministry for Slum Administration and Proper Maintenance of Slum Standards, would be better,' Abdulla added. He turned to Karega. 'You left me a shopkeeper. I am still one – an open-air shopkeeper. I sell oranges by the roadside.'

'Munira told me that Joseph went to Siriana,' Karega suddenly said, as if to brighten up the conversation. 'It is very good news. He was a bright boy. I hope he will not go the way Munira and I went.'

'All the ways go the same way for us poor,' Abdulla explained. 'Oh, I forgot to give you something to drink. Theng'eta. I have one or two packets.'

He leaned over the bed and picked a packet of Theng'eta. 'Did you ever taste it, Karega?'

'Yes. In Mombasa once. I was surprised to see it on sale ... but it did not taste the same. I used to wonder how it came into commercial use.'

'Then drink it again. It almost made me ... well, almost made us. But it ruined us.'

'I think these drinks are made to keep people drunk to drug their minds, so they don't ask questions or do something about their misery,' mused Karega aloud, recalling in his mind all the places that he had been, and all the potent drinks that were brewed there: Changaa, Kang'ari, Kill-me-Quick and Chibuku, the last now run by an African director of a London Rhodesia company.

'It's as I said,' Abdulla continued with his train of thought, 'all ways for the poor go one way. One-way traffic: to more poverty and misery. Poverty is sin. But imagine. It's the poor who are held responsible for the sin that is poverty and so they are punished for it by being sent to hell. Hell to hell. Ha! ha! My only bright spot in this hell has been Joseph. That's why I think there is hope. And to know that he is not really my brother,' Abdulla suddenly let out and this jolted them all from their seats.

'Not your brother?' Karega echoed.

'What, what do you mean?' asked Munira at the same time.

'Yes. Not my brother. He is more of a son to me. And yet he is not my son. But what does it matter?' Abdulla asked. A change came over his voice, over his face, he was more introspective and now there was no foolery or bitterness in his tone, and they listened as yet another Abdulla emerged before their very eyes.

'Before you left Ilmorog I told you about my return from detention ... well, I did not tell you everything. My father used to own a shop at the old Rongai market at Limuru. It was a famous place because he owned a radio, and in the early days of the Emergency people crowded the shop to hear the news read by Mwangi Matemo. My father belonged to the KCA and he always liked to tell how it was they had sent Kenyatta to England, defying the colonial Government, how they used to raise money to maintain him in comfort in England in order to agitate properly for our land. Well, after I had been forced to flee to the forest before my time was due, I somehow kept contact with him. You know our place in Kinyogri area. It was just across from the settled area where tea bushes often formed our hide-outs. But after they were moved to the new concentration village at Kihingo I lost all contact. So you see that during my days in detention I really missed my family and I longed for the day that I would return. Our day for a Family Reunion. Well, friend, the day never came. Or rather, it did come. And I trembled at the sight of Limuru land, at the sight of Kihingo hill, Manguo valley, all the green land. I went to the new village. I urgently inquired about my father and about my mother and about my brothers. And people turned their eyes away. My heart beat with the pain of wanting to know, and they would not tell me except at last for one woman who said it bluntly: "You are a man, you have suffered ... But you can bear it!" "Bear what?" I asked, somehow knowing the truth. "During the digging of the trenches ... one night ... all wiped out ... British soldiers and their Home Guard running-dogs ..." I did not know how to bear it, and for days and weeks I hobbled about with the same song in my head: so they had killed all my family and I alone was left. I thought ... aaaa! But what's the use ... what's the use ... then I recalled that Kimathi had lost his brothers and that his mother had gone crazy and that he himself was later killed and all this for the sake of our struggle ... But still ... the wound ... it was hard, and only the knowledge that all that which we had fought for would soon be done ... land of honey and wine ... kept me a little alive. Well, you know what followed the raising of our flag ... It's good so, I mean our flag, but ... Anyway I bought my donkey ... I carted women's goods to the market and there at the place where the big shoe company throws the factory waste it is also where the shopowners who had taken over from the Indian traders threw their rubbish – anyway there, one day, I found him. He was a child ... scrounging for something to eat in the rubbish heap. He got a piece of bread and the others fell on him, claiming that he had caught the piece from their own corner in the heap ... He was pleading with them, they chased him, and he ran away toward Limuru sawmills. My donkey almost ran him over ... anyway I caught him and the others ran away. "What's your name?" I asked after he had told me the cause of the war. "I have no name, I mean, I don't know ..." "What about your father and mother?" They had gone away. "What about your brothers?" They too had gone away. None had returned, but he always hoped they would return! I thought, no, I did not even think about it, but the lie seemed natural and the words came out sure and smooth. Even the name. "Joseph Njiraini," I called out, shaking him by the shoulder. "By little brother ... I am the brother, the one who went away, and I am back ..." I took him home and he did not protest or anything and I have never really known if he believed me or not. After a few weeks, I had my doubts ... but I hoped that what with my one leg he would be useful ... errands here and there ... It was like that until Wanja saved me from looking at him that way ... and I must say now I never regret ... not these last days anyway ...'

❀

They moved on toward Wanja's place. They did not discuss Abdulla's extraordinary story.

Wanja's wood mansion was really impressive, a contrast to Abdulla's hovel. A hedge of well trimmed pines and creeping plants and bougainvillaea and other flowers surrounded it. A nice aromatic smell hung about the courtyard of beautifully neatly mowed grass with a pattern of words, LOVE IS POISON. A girl opened the door and showed them into a spacious sitting-room. She brought them drinks on a trolley: Tusker, Pilsner, Theng'eta Gin, whisky, Kenya Cane. Karega took whisky: Munira helped himself to Theng'eta Gin. It always pained him that his slogan had been taken from him: but at the same time he felt a secret writer's thrill whenever he read the slogan in newspapers and on the labels. The girl sat down and told them that 'Mama' would soon see them: meanwhile did they want music? Jim Reeves ... Jim Brown ... Kung Fu Fighting/Bumping ... Sukusus ... Ali Shuffle ... Theng'eta Twist ... anything ... Without waiting for an answer she put on *Huni cia Gita*, composed by Elijah Mburu:

Huni cia Ngita	*Young loafers with guitars.*
Ndigacienda ringi	*I'll never like them again.*
Ndacietiire Party	*I invited them to a party.*
Ikienda kundakaria	*They angered me.*
Igikua muhiki	*They took away my girl.*
Wakwa Ndethuriire	*Mine that I had chosen.*
Huni cia Ngita	*Young loafers with guitars.*
Ndigacienda ringi.	*I'll never befriend them again.*

On the wall hung old paintings of an English countryside ... the inscription: 'Christ is the head of the family' ... Martha anointing Christ with oil. On the table were wooden Akamba carvings of giraffes and rhinos. Almost as soon as the record was over, the girl had somehow vanished and Wanja in an almost see-through dress stood before them. Her lipstick was now less crude and merged with her face, and her Afro-wig matched her big body. She had grown. She had put on weight and this gave her physical presence and power.

For a few seconds she and Karega looked at one another. She stood still, very still, otherwise she did not show any surprise. Karega on his part did not expect this stranger ... this lady. Munira had not prepared him for this. As for Munira, he seemed to enjoy the whole scene ... the discomfiture which he knew both were trying to hide. She sat down on a sofa, facing them all, and her first words were addressed to Munira.

'Mwalimu ... you could ... at least have warned me.'

'He came about six.'

'It's my fault,' Karega explained ... 'I ... I thought ... it was not so very late.'

'Of course it isn't ... How are you? I must say this is a pleasant surprise. A ghost from the past.'

'I thought him a ghost too ... the way he looked ... so grown ... changed.'

'Where have you been? But you must be hungry: did Mwalimu give you anything?'

Without waiting for an answer, she leaned back and rang a bell, and another girl suddenly appeared.

'Lucy ...'

'Yes, Mama.'

'Make some food ... and be quick about it.'

It was a dream-fairy world and Karega did not know what to make of it ... she repeated her question.

'Places ... All over the republic ... I worked with the lawyer ... for some time ...' His voice was rough, rugged.

'He is a famous politician now . . .' said Wanja.

'In fact, that's how I came to work with him. I had wandered in the city for some time doing odd jobs here and there. Then I joined his election campaign. People in the slum areas remembered him for all the help he rendered to the poor. I think his rescue of the ill-fated journey to the city long ago had made him quite famous even among those who had not met him in person. He won despite the whole KCO machinery working against him.'

'Champion of the poor . . .' added Munira. 'He should be careful . . . all that talk about land ceilings . . . all those contributions to Harambee projects . . . don't always make everybody happy.'

'Charity . . . charity . . .' Karega suddenly thrust in his voice rather aggressively. 'I kept on reminding him about these same words because it was he who first used them that time we found him in the city. We disagreed a great deal. When he talked I could see that he saw all the wrong. He could capture it all in an image. He had the gift of the tongue. You should read his speeches in Parliament. He could see the wrongs so well, so clearly, that it pained him that others could not see. But after a time . . . I thought . . . he was putting too much faith in trying to make people see the wrong and repent . . . he was very sincere, you understand . . . but he had too much faith in the very shrines created by what he called the monster. He argued that his contributions . . . well . . . they were only a gesture . . . I said to myself: "There must be another way . . . there must be another force that can be a match for the monster and its angels. Ng'enda thi ndiagaga mutegi: that which is created by men can also be changed by men . . . but which men?" In the end I left him. He could not understand me and I could not understand him. But he had opened my eyes and I was grateful . . . I moved to Mombasa . . . Dockworkers . . .'

'Mombasa? Do those ships still come? And the sailors? Coconuts . . . sandy beaches . . . Fort Jesus . . . I would like . . . It's such a long time . . .' Wanja enthused.

'We loaded and unloaded the ships . . . handled all that wealth . . . with our naked bodies sweating in the steamy sun.'

'But they pay well . . . the dockworkers are the best paid workers . . . They have had a tradition of good responsible union leaders . . .'

'Responsible union leaders? I don't know. The trouble with our trade unions is that too often they are led by businessmen . . . Employers. How can an employer lead that which is fighting against employers? You cannot serve the interests of capital and of labour at the same time. You cannot serve two opposed masters . . . one master loses . . . in this case labour . . . the work . . . the heat . . . crumbs from the table ... I left ... I walked from Mombasa ... on foot ... looked for jobs amongst agricultural plantation workers ... But I could never stay more than two months ... slaves ... slavery ... they are paid one hundred shillings a month ... and for that they sell their whole family labour ... man, wife, and children ... living in one hut ... condemned to picking sisal and tea-leaves and coffee ... Many times I would sit and think: we people ... we built Kenya. Before 1895 it was Arab slavers disrupting our agriculture. After 1895 it was the European colonist: first stealing our land; then our labour and then our own wealth in the way of cows and goats and later our capital by way of taxation ... so we built Kenya, and what were we getting out of the Kenya we had built on our sweat?

'The lawyer was right about the monster demanding more and more sweat and giving only very little of that which it had demanded. I would talk my thoughts with the other workers on the plantation. They would say: suppose we are kicked out ... and I said ... unity in labour ... unity of sweat ... sweat power ... word would get to the African owners of the plantations ... I would be dismissed and I would move on my way ... And so I kept on moving, working here and there, on this or that farm, tracing, as it were, my father's footsteps until I found myself in West Kenya. I was lucky. I got a job with a sugar milling company. I worked as a store-keeper – something between a messenger and a store issue clerk.

'My work was simple, supplying the fitters, the turners, the welders and other mechanics with spare parts for the farm machinery. Pumps and motors kept on breaking. They needed constant repair and maintenance. The store also supplied Europeans and top Africans with household needs, toilet paper, gas, things like that. But there were times when the machines would go for a long time without breaking. Anyway I had time to look, to see, to think. This particular sugar mill was owned by a British company McMillan sugar works with extensive interests in South Africa ... Sudan ... Nigeria ... Guyana. The company's sugar plantation was started soon after Independence ... to develop the area ... to raise the standard of living. A number of peasants were driven off their land to make room for the company's nuclear estates. The peasants who were not driven off the land were encouraged to grow sugar on their plots instead of food. But the company buys the sugar at whatever price they deem fit! The peasant growers are not organised to protest and to bargain. So they lead miserable lives. Some cannot even send their children to school ...

'Oh, yes ... the company has an African manager ... Mr Owuora Wuod Omuony ... in fact, a few locals own shares in the company.

The transportation of the company's goods – sugar, rollers – was for instance in the hands of a very important person in authority – I think half Masai and half Kalenjin ... he had a long name ... Mr Innocent Lengoshoke Ole Loongamulak ... so you see African participation was extensive. The middle level managerial positions were in the hands of Africans. Otherwise all the top jobs on the technical side were held by European expatriate experts – mere schoolboys, I would say, lording it over African graduates training to be sugar technologists.

'The workers were in two categories. There were those who worked inside the factory. And there were the others who worked in the nuclear estates. Among them were immigrant labour from Uganda. They all had very stinking pay, considering the work they did. But those in the fields had the worst. Often they were beaten by their European and even their African overseers. They could not organise because the management had managed to divide them into tribal cliques and religious cliques and even according to the place of work. Those who worked in the factory felt they were more privileged than those in the fields. But those in the factory seemed better organised. They did not seem to care if the management was African, or if the directors came from their own region or tribe, they protested all the same and stood up for their rights.

'Anyway I watched everything – I saw how the European expatriate experts carried themselves. I said to myself, no European or any boss in free Kenya will be rude to me and I keep silent. So this European expert technician comes when I am attending an African trainee technologist. He demands to be served immediately. He wants a roll of toilet paper. I told him to wait his turn. He said SHENZI. I took a bearing and threw it at him and it hit him full in the face. I was called before the African manager and a few of the white foreign bosses. The technologist was a truthful witness. But instead of the Kaburu being reprimanded I was dismissed from my job ... no appeal ... so I said to myself; let me go back to Ilmorog and see what's happening there!'

'That's a real life of a wanderer ...' They were all speaking politely, avoiding the present, avoiding the past they shared, putting off questions and answers. Munira and Wanja could see that Karega had changed, but they could not tell in what way. All they could see was that he was different from them. Lucy brought meat on another tray and they ate quietly.

'What are you going to do in Ilmorog? Or are you only passing through?' Wanja asked. What he had described about the sugar mills in western Kenya had the familiar ring of a recent happening.

'A worker has no particular home ... He belongs everywhere and nowhere. I get a job here, I do it ... I carry my only property – my labour power, my hands – everywhere with me. Willing buyer ... a seller who must sell ... It is the life under this system.'

'Yes ... it's life,' echoed Munira, without realising the full import of the words.

They ate in silence. Karega and Wanja avoided each other's eyes. She urged them to have yet another drink. She poured them out what they chose: Theng'eta and whisky. After drinking, Karega suggested it was time they went away. Munira agreed. Wanja did not say anything. She kept on turning over the story Karega had told and it seemed that some of the features were part and parcel of what had happened in Ilmorog. They rose to go. She stood up to see them off. Then her eyes met Karega's: and there was a flicker ... a naked moment of recognition.

'Sit down,' she asked them. 'Please ...' They resumed their seats. She poured them yet another drink. She poured herself a gin and tonic.

'I don't drink ...' she started, slowly, a little hesitant. 'But I'll keep you company. Well, I also need company ... Truly I am glad to see you ... I have thought about you a great deal. At one point I thought you must be dead, or something. My grandmother ... she was always sure you would return. I suppose she never knew you would find me, well, all of us under these circumstances. You have told us a little about yourself ... your journeys. No doubt you are wondering what has become of us. I'll tell you, partly, I must confess for your sake. I can see that ... well ... that concern for others has never really died in you. There is a fire in your eyes ... A spark ... illusions. You may blame me ... I ask neither pity nor forgiveness nor any understanding excuse. This world ... this Kenya ... this Africa knows only one law. You eat somebody or you are eaten. You sit on somebody or somebody sits on you. Like you, I have wandered, I don't know in search of what: but I looked for two things in vain: I have desperately looked for a child ... a child of my own ... Do you know how it feels for a woman not to have a child? When Mwathi was here, I went to him. His voice behind the partition said ... woman, you have sinned: confess! I could not tell him. I could not quite tell him that I was once pregnant, that I did have a child ... that the world had suddenly loomed so large and menacing and that, for a girl who had just left school and had run away from home ... that ... that ... that I did throw it, my newly born, into a latrine ... There! I have said it ... I have never said that to another person.'

Both Munira and Karega started a little. It was shocking precisely because the disclosure was totally unexpected. There was an awkward silence. They both avoided her eyes. But she went on in the same voice.

'I was young then. I am not saying that I was right. It was only that this seemed the only thing to do: for how, I asked myself, was I going to look after it? Where would I get food and clothes for the child? Later I felt this guilt sit on me. Every night . . . sometimes even today I hear the delicate cry of that child . . . I have tried to atone for it . . . I've prayed to God for one more chance . . . one more chance . . . it has never been possible . . . I have even tried to get out of this life . . . God knows I have tried . . . Every time something has happened to thwart me in my desire to escape.

'I have searched for love, too . . . it has escaped me . . . except . . . except . . . I will say it . . . but don't think I am begging or asking for anything . . . except with you. That time I felt my womanhood come back . . . I felt accepted as I was . . . For the first time I could make love without the burden of guilt or the burden of a search . . . Then you went away . . . I kept myself to myself . . . God knows I am speaking the truth . . . I wanted to live honestly, an honest trade, an honest profit if that's possible. Theng'eta . . . there was memory to it too . . .

'And then something happened . . . My grandmother died . . . I had to redeem this land . . . I felt it the right thing to do . . . I sold the house . . . I continued making Theng'eta . . . and then one day I went to the site where they have built this utamaduni village. Have you been there? You should go. Women go there to sing native songs and dance for white tourists . . . they are paid . . . well . . . that's another story . . . anyway, I went there and found Nderi wa Riera . . . and the German I once met in Nairobi. I relived the fear and the trembling of that night . . . I almost screamed . . . until I realised that he did not recognise me. He is one of the owners of this tourist village, with huts built as they imagine our huts used to be before the Europeans came. Our utamaduni . . . a museum . . . for them to look at. I went away, thinking about this strange encounter. Later I went to see Mzigo. A by-law had been decreed that all brewers must get a licence. I thought Mzigo would help me since we had sold our building to him. After all Ilmorog could cater for two brewers. He was very uncomfortable . . . very evasive. Then he gave me a piece of paper to read . . . my English is not very good . . . but I could get the general drift of the writing on the wall.

AN AGREEMENT MADE THIS FIRST DAY OF – BETWEEN
Chiri County Council (hereinafter called "The

Licensor") of the one part and International
Liquor Manufacturers (Kenya Ltd) (hereinafter
called the Licensee) of the other part WHEREBY
IT IS AGREED AS FOLLOWS ...
IN Consideration of the Royalties hereinafter
stipulated the Licensor grants the Licencee sole
licence to manufacture THENG'ETA in accordance
with patent of invention NO. ROB 10000.

'And the directors of the Kenya branch were Mzigo, Chui, and Kimeria. I could hardly accept this twist of fate ... I don't even know
how I came back here ... But I started thinking ... Kimeria, who
made his fortune as a Home Guard transporting bodies of Mau Mau
killed by the British, was still prospering ... Kimeria, who had
ruined my life and later humiliated me by making me sleep with him
during our journey to the city ... this same Kimeria was one of
those who would benefit from the new economic progress of Ilmorog. Why? Why? I asked myself? Why? Why? Had he not
sinned as much as me? That's how one night I fully realised this law.
Eat or you are eaten. If you have a cunt – excuse my language, but it
seems the curse of Adam's Eve on those who are born with it – if you
are born with this hole, instead of it being a source of pride, you
are doomed to either marrying someone or else being a whore. You
eat or you are eaten. How true I have found it. I decided to act, and
I quickly built this house ... Nothing would I ever let for free ... I
have many rooms, many entrances and four yards ... I have hired
young girls ... it was not hard ... I promised them security ... and
for that ... they let me trade their bodies ... what's the difference
whether you are sweating it out on a plantation, in a factory or lying
on your back, anyway? I have various types for various types of
men. Some prefer short ones, tall ones, motherly ones, religious ones,
sympathetic ones, rude ones, tough ones, a different nationality ... I
have them all here ... And me? Me too! I have not spared myself ...
It has been the only way I can get my own back on Chui, Mzigo, and
Kimeria ... I go with all of them now ... I play them against one
another ... It is easy because I only receive them by appointment ...
If there is a clash, the girls ... they know how to handle the situation ... and, strange ... they pay for it ... they pay for their
rivalry to possess me ... each wants to make me his sole woman ...
'As for me, it's a game ... of money ... You eat or you are eaten
... And now I can go anywhere ... even to their most expensive
clubs ... they are proud to be seen with me ... even for one night
... and they pay for it ... I have had to be hard ... It is the only way

... the only way ... Look at Abdulla ... reduced to a fruit seller ... oranges ... sheepskins ... No, I will never return to the herd of victims ... Never ... Never ...'

She ended on a kind of savage screaming tone, as if she was answering doubts inside her. Karega sensed the doubt and now looked at her more intently. There was a hardness on her face that he could not now penetrate. He felt the needle-sharp ruthless truth of her statement: you eat or you are eaten. Had he not seen this since he was forced out of school? Had he not himself lived this truth in Mombasa, Nairobi, on the tea and coffee plantations? On the wheat and sugar estates and in the sugar mills? This was the society they were building: this was the society they had been building since Independence, a society in which a black few, allied to other interests from Europe, would continue the colonial game of robbing others of their sweat, denying them the right to grow to full flowers in air and sunlight.

And suddenly it was not her that he was looking at, seeing, but countless other faces in many other places all over the republic. You eat or you are eaten. You fatten on another, or you are fattened upon. Why? Why? Something in him revolted against this: deep inside, he could not accept the ruthless logic of her position and statement. Either. Or. Either. Or. In a world of beasts of prey and those preyed upon, you either preyed or you remained a victim. But there were some, the many in fact, who could not, who would never acquire the fangs and the claws with which to prey. Yet what was the alternative to the truth she had uttered?

'No, no,' he found himself saying. 'There is another way: there must be other ways.' And suddenly in that moment, remembering in a flash all the places he had been to, he was clear about the force for which he had been searching, the force that would change things and create the basis of a new order.

'In this world?' she asked, half contemptuously.

'Must we have this world? Is there only one world? Then we must create another world, a new earth,' he burst out, addressing himself to all the countless faces he had seen and worked with from Kilindini through Central to Western Region.

'H'm! Another world!' she murmured.

'Yes. Another world. A new world,' he reiterated.

'We must go!' Munira suddenly shouted, standing up, He reached for the door and rushed outside, as if driven by a demon.

Karega stood up, walked to the door, and then hesitated and looked back at Wanja.

She had not risen or raised her head. She remained sitting in one place, truly queen of them all under the electric light; her head was bowed slightly and it was as if, under the bluish light of her creation, the wealth she had so accumulated weighed on her heavily, as if the jewelled, rubied cord around her neck was now pulling her and her very shadow to the ground, so that she would not rise to say good-bye, or to shut the door.

Karega went out. He could not find Munira outside but he walked determinedly toward the town centre, the heart of New Ilmorog, where light and smoke and the roar of a distant machine announced that a night shift of workers continued the relay to keep the factory roaring its pride and power over Ilmorog.

In his own place, Munira fell down on the bed and repeated: Another world, a new world. Could it really be true? Was it possible?

Chapter Twelve

1 🏵 'And what does this rather ... eeh ... poetic business mean, Mr Munira?'

Munira leaned over the table to see what the officer was pointing at, what it was that he had picked out of all the things Munira had scribbled. Munira was relieved that after almost nine days of isolation they were now face to face.

'Oh, a new earth, another world?' Munira queried in his turn, sitting back on the hard bench, eyeing the office with immense pity at the earthly film of ignorance that covered his face, making it seem hard and totally removed from what Munira saw as the overriding need for the acceptance of sins and salvation through grace.

'Yes,' the officer said, the aloof, tolerant boredom in his eyes. 'What did it mean to you that night?'

Munira thought a while. He momentarily relived that scene two years back in Wanja's blue-lit sitting-room on the night of Karega's sudden return: he felt as if the jewelled, miniskirted body seeming so far away, so lonesome, and yet to him now carrying the power of satanic evil, would raise the head and pierce into his weakness, his fragile defence. It's me, it's me, oh Lord, he heard an inner voice calling, and he felt more secure and able to face the police officer. It was now his tenth day in the remand prison. He had been expecting this second visit with some dread, true, but at times feverishly looking forward to it, to his release from bondage, and yet when the time came for a second encounter he was surprised, wanted to put off the final confrontation to another day. After the usual breakfast of porridge in enamelled tin cups, he saw that instead of locking him back inside the cell or else letting him loose in the exercise yard as had been the established pattern, the policeman was taking him straight to the bare desk and walls that they called the office. Munira protested that he had not completed the document but this protest was faintly voiced because he was rather tired of the whole business. Inspector Godfrey had ignored his demurs, and had gone ahead with questions, perfunctorily turning over the pages of his prison notes.

'This ... eeh ... this new world ... what was it? You keep on referring to it ...'

Munira tried. It had always seemed clear to himself except when he tried to communicate the vision to somebody else. And now, with mounting despair, he realised how difficult the task before him was: how was it possible to impress on a man administering the corrupt laws of a corrupt world, the overwhelming need and necessity for higher laws, pure, eternal, absolute, unchanging? How was it that even the wisest in the kingdom of this world could not see what was open even to a child? The tune that had altered his life and outlook vibrated at the nerve centre of his spiritual being:

> Tukiacha dhambi, Mfalme mwema
> Hata tukifa, Tutawala tena
> Halleluya, Halleluya
> Hata tukifa, Tutawala tena.

He wanted to sing it loud, but instead he found himself talking calmly about his new-found land.

'It was not a sudden thing, you understand. It was that the words coming out of his mouth, amidst that perfumed squalor, and this after five years of exile and wandering, were strangely disquietening. Out of the mouth of babes, saith the Lord. And uttered after that story, after the tortured self-revelation of a sinful woman. I believe now that the word of God is revealed to us not in a context of our choosing. I had heard those selfsame words from Ironmonger, froɪ my mother, from my wife, but they had never really rung a bell. A new earth. Another world. I kept on turning them over in my heart and mind. I couldn't thereafter drink Theng'eta in peace. My body thirsted for it out of a five-year habit, but my heart was not there. At the bottom of Wanja's story and experience was an injustice that did not make sense. I knew her story now and yet ... yet ... Teaching became even more tedious how could I continue teaching them how to fit into a world I was beginning to reject, a world that was fundamentally illogical and evil? How could I explain this: that Iron-monger was replaced by Cambridge Fraudsham, that Fraudsham was replaced by Chui, that Chui owned a factory in Ilmorog, that he was one of Wanja's lovers, that he sold beer, with a slogan that I had first invented? How ... how ... how could it be that Wanja had run away from Kimeria only to fall more fatally into his arms? He too was now her lover. And Mzigo ... and Karega ... and the breaking up of the Ilmorog that I knew? Nothing made sense. Abdulla had fought for independence ... he was now selling oranges and sheep-skins to tourists and drinking Theng'eta to forget the forced demo-lition of his shop. Yes. Nothing made sense. Education. Work. My life. Accidents. I was an accident. I was a mistake, doomed to a spectator's role outside a window from a high building. I started going to church. The New Ilmorog Anglican Church was built with donations from Christians in Kenya, and from churches abroad, and it was an impressive affair, only a few yards away from the ashes of the once proud homestead of Mwathi wa Mugo, now, as you can see, an archaeological museum. Rev. Jerrod Brown was the head and the spiritual shepherd of this New Anglican parish community in Ilmorog. There were many cars outside: all the makes from all over the world. I would listen to him preach from prepared texts, admon-ishing people about drinking, too many divorces, too fast driving, the need to give to the church, and other sins of omission and com-mission. Nothing had changed from the content of the prayers except that for the 'King' they now put 'President'. Once I wanted to go and announce to him: I am so and so, son of so and so, whom you once turned away from your house hungry. Now I am not hungry for earthly food, I am burning in a hell of molten fire – help me. But remembering my experience in his house in Blue Hills, I thought he might be equally mean with his spiritual diet. I con-tinued going to church. I was weighed down by a sense of guilt, as if I had contributed to Wanja's degradation and the evil of the world, and I felt a tremendous need for forgiveness. Once I even wrote to my wife. I said that I was beginning to see that her way was indeed the right way. Walk your way all the way, I had ended it, and then suddenly tore it up. I would occasionally join Abdulla where he was selling oranges and sheepskins and mushrooms to passers-by on the Trans-Africa Road and tourists. Maimed. Wanja had once said that we were all like Abdulla but instead of our limbs it was our souls that were maimed.

'It was at this time we heard the terrible news: the lawyer had been murdered. He had been taken from a big hotel and taken a mile or so from the Blue Hills and he was shot and left for the hyenas to eat.

For the first time in a long while Karega, Wanja, Abdulla and Njuguna met. We had not planned it: it just happened that we all
strolled to Njuguna's iron-roofed house. His wife gave us milk and
nobody touched it. We talked about everything else but the murder
of the lawyer. Except Njuguna. The words seemed to just escape his
lips: "And it was on the same pass where we once trod on our way to
the city."

'Nobody answered him. How, I kept asking myself, how could they
murder a man who was only a help to the poor? He had contributed
to every Harambee effort in the land: he had wealth, but he did try
to share it out without regard to class, religion and tribe. How?
Why? We all dispersed to our different hovels and I asked myself:
How could I let this mistake continue, standing outside the gate of
things, and I a teacher? I was on the verge of a decision. And that
Sunday I did not go to church. I suddenly hated the very sound of
Jerrod's voice, his sermons and his prayers. I walked from my house
toward Ilmorog ridge, ready to end the accident by another accident.
The game could not continue. And then suddenly I saw the group.
They were dressed in white kanzus and they were drumming. They
were surrounded by curious children, a few women and men. I
stopped to listen. She was now preaching and her voice cut into me:
We have all sinned and come short of the glory of the Lord. I could
not believe my eyes: it was Lillian, transformed Lillian leading a
group of men and women in prayers and sermons and speaking in
tongues. She talked of a new earth, another world, that knew not
classes and clans, that levelled the poor and the wealthy, once they
accepted the eternal law of God. Not churches; not learning; not
positions; not good works: just acceptance, in faith, and behold: a
new earth and a new heaven. I trembled. It was too simple. Yet, yet
what else could be true, could make sense? We have all sinned and
come short of the glory of God. She spoke with all the power of many
voices gone, of many voices to come, of a world to be. Only accept:
only accept: my heart beat with her voice and the authority of joy
behind it. Not learning, not wealth, not good works, only accept.
The law. The eternal law. Will you now accept this new life with
Christ? It was as if the question was directed at me: It was as if she
could read my heart. How strange that Lillian should have crossed my
path at that very day, that particular hour. I looked at her, at her
eyes, her transformation and I asked myself: whence from this power
in her who only the other day was using the same religion as part of
the amorous game? In that second, everything was revealed to me.
And I truly beheld a new earth, now that Christ was my personal
saviour. He would level mountains and valleys and would wrestle

Satan to the ground and conquer the evil that is this world. New life with Christ in Christ. I accepted the law. My knees trembled. I humbled myself to the ground and cried: "I accept, I accept." I felt tears of gratitude and joy. My years of agony and doubt and pursuit of earthly pleasures were over ...'

There was a quiet but firm conviction in Munira's voice that somehow carried Inspector Godfrey. It had made him listen without the usual boredom that had characterised his investigative relationship with Munira. Behind the boredom was of course a questioning, calculating mind sifting words, storing phrases and looks and gestures, also looking for a line, a key, a thread, a connection, an image that would help tie everything together. He now sighed back into his chair and the boredom returned:

'Interesting – very interesting. And yet, Mr Munira, I believe you were always to be seen either with Karega or Wanja or Abdulla ... I thought that you – please excuse my curiosity – but you being no longer of this evil world would ... eeh ... well ... abandon it and keep the company of the holy ... Lillian, for instance.'

'You don't understand. It is enjoined upon us to bring others to see the light. I wanted each one of them to discover this new world ...'

'Mr Munira ... isn't it true ... and again excuse me if I am a little mixed up ... isn't it true that Karega also used to talk to the workers about a new world?'

'That was it,' Munira said excitedly. 'You are following, you are beginning to see. I wanted to save him ... I wanted to save him first from it—!'

Inspector Godfrey suddenly clutched at the sides of the table and interrupted almost hoarsely:

'It ... what ... what do you mean?'

'His dreams ... his devil's dreams and illusions ... save him from committing the unforgivable sin ...'

'What sin? Please, Mr Munira, don't talk in parables! What scheme? What sin? Please tell me ... and be quick about it.'

The officer's lower lip was trembling. He was like a hound on a hot scent. Munira looked at him, at his bloodshot eyes, and said:

'Why, of pride. Of thinking that he and his workers could change the evil ... could change this world ...'

The officer let out his breath and suddenly looked exhausted. He had lost the scent and he felt like kicking the holy fanatic of a teacher outside the office.

'Did he say how he intended to change the world, apart from inciting strikes, go-slow, work to rule and all that communist nonsense?'

'It is his pride I am talking about. His pride in even contemplating that one man unaided by God through Christ could change himself, could change the world, could improve on it.'

'I now understand your "IT". But this I believe was only at first . . . what other evil were you going to save him from?'

'Her!'

'Whom?'

'Wanja.'

'What do you mean?'

'He had started seeing her secretly. I am sure of it.'

'How?'

'I saw him.'

'When?'

'About a week before the fire. They were meeting at her old hut. But Abdulla—'

The officer was on his feet again. His lips were trembling. He stared at Munira.

'Are you sure, very sure?'

'Yes. I saw them. I saw them,' he said quietly, as a doubt darted through his mind. Suppose, he thought, and he was about to add something when the officer suddenly stood up and rushed to the door. He had picked up the scent and this time he was determined not to lose it. Munira shouted at him.

'Stop . . . wait . . . I've not finished.'

The officer looked back over his shoulder and waited, on legs ready to spring on in the chase. Munira approached.

'What have you done to him? What have you done with Karega?'

'Stupid fool,' hissed the officer and shouted an order. ' . . . Take him back . . . I'll be seeing him later.' And he hurried on toward the other cells.

2   To Karega the morning of his arrest, ten days earlier, was still doubly bitter because he had just listened to the six o'clock news bulletin only to hear that because of the tense situation in Ilmorog after the killing of Kimeria, Chui and Mzigo, the planned strike was banned. They always take the side of the employers, he reflected in anger. I knew they would seize on the excuse of the arson to ban the strike and aim yet another blow at the fledgling workers' movement.

He was in a cell all by himself for a whole day and night. He wondered what fake charges they would bring against him. He had only been arrested once: that time that he and Munira and Abdulla had led a 'donkey' delegation to the city. Then they were saved from prison by the lawyer. Such a long time ago, he thought. And the lawyer had been killed. He had not quite been able to understand the lawyer: he genuinely loved people: he could see and even analyse what had happened in a way that few others could do: yet ... he seemed at the same time fascinated by property and the social power and authority that this gave him. 'You see,' he had once explained to Karega, 'they can't fault me on education or on professional qualifications. They can't fault me on involvement in the struggle. I had as a boy taken the batuni oath and used to be a go-between for the fighting units. I would dress as a Boy Scout so I could go to places unmolested. They can't fault me on property. They can't say I am a Kaggia.' He had laughed at the pun. 'So I can speak fearlessly for the poor and for land and property reforms – put a ceiling on what a person can accumulate ... one man, one kiosk, that kind of thing. One shamba, one man, that kind of thing. One job, one man, and so on.' His brutal death had shocked Karega as it had shaken the whole land. Such a fine stock ... with all his faults, he represented the finest and most courageous in a line of courageous and selfless individuals from among the propertied men and women of Kenya; from some of the feudal mbari lords at the turn of the century who, despite bribes of beads and calico and the lure of white-protected power, would not side with the hordes of colonial invaders but died fighting with the people, to others in the thirties and fifties who, despite education and property, refused to betray the people for a few favours from the British. Oh, a long time ago, he thought again as he recalled how the lawyer had effected their release from the Central Police Station and from the law court. Those scenes now appeared as faint outlines of distant landscapes in another country. Even in himself he could not recognise the dreamer who once could talk endlessly about Africa's past glories, Africa's great feudal cultures, as if it was enough to have this knowledge to cure one day's pang of hunger, to quench an hour's thirst or to clothe a naked child. After all, the British merchant magnates and their missionary soothsayers once colonised and humiliated China by making the Chinese buy and drink opium and clubbed them when they refused to import the poison, even while the British scholars sang of China's great feudal cultures and stole the evidence in gold and art and parchments and took them to London. Egypt too. India too. Syria, Iraq ... God was born in Palestine even ... and all this knowledge never once deterred the European merchant warlords. And China was saved, not by singers and poets telling of great past cultures, but by the creative struggle of the workers for a better day today. No, it was not a people's past glories only, but also the glory of their present strife and struggles to right the wrongs that bring tears to the many and laughter only to a few. The Ilmorog whose past achievements had moved him so after listening to Nyakinyua was not there any more. Within only ten years – how time galloped, he thought – Ilmorog peasants had been displaced from the land: some had joined the army of workers, others were semi-workers with one foot in a plot of land and one foot in a factory, while others became petty traders in hovels and shanties they did not even own, along the Trans-Africa Road, or criminals and prostitutes who with their stolen guns and over-used cunts eked a precarious living from each and everybody – workers, peasants, factory owners, blacks, whites – indiscriminately. There were a few who tried their hands at making sufurias, karais, water tins, chicken-feeding troughs; shoemakers, carpenters; but how long would they last, seeing that they were being driven out of their trades by more organised big-scale production of the same stuff? The herdsmen had suffered a similar fate: some had died; others had been driven even further out into drier parts away from the newly enclosed game-parks for tourists, and yet others had become hired labourers on wheatfields or on farms belonging to wealthier peasants. And behind it all, as a monument to the changes, was the Trans-Africa Road and the two-storied building of the African Economic Bank Ltd.

He had noticed and picked out these changes within the first days of his return, because he had known the Ilmorog of Nyakinyua, of the mythical Mwathi and of Njuguna and Ruoro. But on looking back on all the places he had been to he could discern the same pattern: rapid in some places, slow in others, but emerging all the time in all of them. There was no other place to which he could turn. Further education? He had lost his chance: besides, what else was there to learn besides what he had experienced with his eyes and hands? Land? There was no land – he was born into a landless home. But even those with land: for how long could it continue to be subdivided into plots and sub-plots so that each son could own a piece? Why, anyway, should soil, any soil, which after all was what was Kenya, be owned by an individual? Kenya, the soil, was the people's common shamba, and there was no way it could be right for a few, or a section, or a single nationality, to inherit for their sole use what was communal, any more than it would be right for a few sons and daughters to own and monopolise their father or mother. It was better for him to get reconciled to his situation: since the only thing that he had now was his two hands, he would somehow sell its creative power to whoever would buy it and then join with all the other hands in ensuring that at least they had a fair share of what their thousand sets of fingers produced.

At least he would not, he could not accept the static vision of Wanja's logic. It was too ruthless, and it could only lead to despair and self-or mutual annihilation. For what was the point of a world in which one could only be clean by wiping his dirt and shit and urine on others? A world in which one could only be healthy by making others carry one's leprosy? A world in which one could only be saintly and moral and upright by prostituting others? Why, anyway, should the victims of a few people's cleanliness and health and saintliness and wealth be expected to always accept their lot? The true lesson of history was this: that the so-called victims, the poor, the downtrodden, the masses, had always struggled with spears and arrows, with their hands and songs of courage and hope, to end their oppression and exploitation: that they would continue struggling until a human kingdom came: a world in which goodness and beauty and strength and courage would be seen not in how cunning one can be, not in how much power to oppress one possessed, but only in one's contribution in creating a more humane world in which the inherited inventive genius of man in culture and science from all ages and climes would be not the monopoly of a few, but for the use of all, so that all flowers in all their different colours would ripen and bear fruits and seeds. And the seeds would be put into the ground and they would once again sprout and flower in rain and sunshine. If Abdulla could choose a brother, why couldn't they all do the same? Choose brothers and sisters in sweat, in toil, in struggle, and stand by one another and strive for that kingdom?

These thoughts matured as for six months he worked in the Theng'eta Breweries as a counting clerk. He kept a check on the bottles that came off the production line. He also helped in counting the number of cases put on a customer's lorry. They called him the silent one because he worked in silence, observing, annotating, now and then arguing with one or two workers, but no more. He also stopped drinking because alcohol sapped his energy and reduced his power of concentration. But he frequented the bars, where he would insert a shilling or two in a juke-box and listen to his favourites as well as keeping up with the latest singers and poets. The juke-box had driven out all the live bands. In one or two places he met some of his old students, now young men. They would call him Mwalimu, but he discouraged them from calling him so. The only bars he avoided were those likely to be visited by Chui or Kimeria or Mzigo, who liked staying on after inspecting the workings of the factory. Once or twice he went to the Tourist Village. He liked the songs and dances of the older generation. But when he saw how Nderi wa Riera and his managing consortium of German and Greek proprietors had so mummified them and drained them of all emotion and meaning; when he saw how the fat tourists carrying cameras, chewing gum and adjusting their safari hats clapped and cheered at this acrobatic nothingness, he was disgusted and swore he would never return. He observed how the workers were disunited: in their talk he could see that they were proud of their linguistic enclaves and clans and regions and tended to see any emergent leadership in terms of how it would help or hinder the allocation of jobs to people of their own clan and language groups. Men too seemed to think they were better off than women workers because they got a little bit more pay and preference in certain jobs. They seemed to think that women deserved low pay and heavy work: women's real job, they argued amidst noise and laughter, was to lie on their backs and open their legs to man's passage to the kingdoms of pleasure.

He now knew his line of attack and approach. These divisions had to end if they were going to successfully demand recognition and a fair share of their own sweat. From nowhere, so it seemed, pamphlets started appearing: and they all carried the same theme: workers were all children of the machine and the New Road. Those who owned the machine did not care where a worker came from in the game of exploitation. But the machine and the New Road were the children of the workers, for it was their sweat that built the road, the factory, and it was they who sustained the whole complex by their energy and consumption. The machine was no less their father than they were its father, and the struggle in future would be fought on who should own and control the machine and the products: those whose sweat made it move or those whose power was the bank, and who came to reap and harvest where they had not ploughed or planted. Every dispute was put in the context of the exploitation of labour by capital, itself stolen from other workers. Why should so few wield power of life and death over so many?

Suddenly, after six months, people realised that something was happening in this factory. Workers would argue and discuss in groups of two and threes. Every pamphlet was the subject of heated discussion and it would secretly pass from hand to hand in the factory. Except for the few in the inner circle nobody knew the source. But what the pamphlets said was true and so to the workers its origins and source did not worry them. As a first step the workers decided to form a union. The directors and the management were taken by surprise: whence this whizzing noise from those who only the other day were docile and obedient and spent their salaries on Theng'eta and fighting amongst themselves?

The first contest came over the recognition and registration of the

Theng'eta Breweries Workers' Union. The workers stood together. They went on strike. The Board of Directors gave way: after all, other unions in the country had been effectively neutralised by employers. But they had to look for a scapegoat. Karega was dismissed, even though on paper he was only a committee member. The management had somehow dug up his past. But the dismissal gained him popularity and he was immediately elected full-time paid Secretary-General of the Union.

The victory of the Breweries Workers' Union had a very traumatic effect on the hitherto docile workers of Ilmorog. Suddenly even barmaids wanted their own union. The women dancers formed themselves into a Tourist Dancers' Union and demanded more money for their art. The agricultural workers followed suit. Something big was happening in Ilmorog and the employers were shaken and worried.

And then Karega's real problems started. The employers went out of their way to sow discord. They encouraged national and regional chauvinism. When this did not work, they promoted some workers, especially the more outspoken, and labelled them management. By law these were not allowed to go on strike. Other workers were encouraged to buy one or two shares so that they would feel that the company was theirs. Despite this, or because of the increase in discussions, study groups and pamphlets, the workers' union remained strong.

But the biggest threat came from a new charismatic religious movement which sprang up and spoke in very egalitarian terms. It opposed the hypocrisy of the organised church. For them, there was no difference between the poor and the rich, the employer and the employed ... the only thing was acceptance of Christ. Jesus saves. Love was the only law that they needed to obey. They were to avoid the strife and struggles of this world. This world was a distorted image of the other world. Distorted by Satan. Therefore the only meaningful struggle was a spiritual battle with Satan. They held rallies in which girls claimed they could speak in tongues, communicate with Jesus and heal by faith. Lillian led them.

For a time this wave carried off many workers. Some even resigned from the union, believing that the Kingdom of God was near at hand.

Karega knew that this too was to be fought. He would often quote the verse 'Give unto Caesar' to show the separation between the secular and the religious struggles, that one need not exclude the other. But inwardly he knew that religion, any religion, was a weapon against the workers!

Munira especially annoyed him. He would not leave Karega alone but would seize every opportunity to ask him to give up the path of earthly struggle and first change people's hearts. If all employers were converted and turned to Christ, then selfishness would end. Karega was very impatient, and with him he would use strong words. Once or twice he bluntly asked him to leave him alone, but Munira would not hear. He persisted all the more until Karega began to wonder if Munira was employed to trail him. Later Karega learnt that the whole movement was financed by some churches in America which made a lot of money by insisting on the followers giving a tenth of their salaries as tithe. A bit of this would later be given back as the American parent movement's contribution to Harambee church-building efforts. The kinds of books the followers were encouraged to read were interesting: *Tortured by Christ* by Wurmbrand; *World Aflame* by Billy Graham, and other tracts published in America and speaking of communism as the Devil: they also warned of the immediate second coming of Christ to root out all the enemies of freedom.

One night Wanja sent for him. The note simply asked him to meet her in the old hut: he was not to fail. He wondered why she should call him. For two years they had not spoken much . . . and now she had called for him . . .

That was almost a week before the fatal accident . . .

As Karega waited in the cell he wondered what had happened to her, whether for instance she had recovered from the fire.

Three days after the arrest, the officer started questioning him. He seemed well informed. What Karega did not know was that Inspector Godfrey was using Munira's notes. And it was immediately obvious to Karega that the Inspector wanted to connect him with the arson. For a start he seemed particularly interested in certain incidents in Karega's past. How, for instance, did he lose his elder brother? He explained that he did not know the circumstances, that it was Abdulla who had told him what had really happened.

'Did it make you perhaps a little bitter?'

'It happened so long ago. Besides, in a struggle one has to be on a particular side. Nobody can stand on the fence. A struggle is a form of war. One side wins or loses. But even the side that wins has to lose individuals.'

'You seem to be fairly knowledgeable about struggles.'

'It's common sense.'

'Tell me: why did you leave Siriana?'

'I was . . . I was asked to leave.'

'Why?'

'I was involved in some sort of strike.'

306

'I see. Who was the headmaster?'

'Chui.'

'The same one as the late Director of Theng'eta Breweries?'

'The same.'

'I see. And did it make you a little bitter perhaps?'

'Listen. Why are you asking me all these questions?'

'Sit down, Mr Karega. I'll not hide it from you. Look at it this way. Three Managing Directors are burnt to death in the house of a woman who was known to have been rather partial to you. You are the General of ... I mean ... General Secretary of a union that had called for higher wages. The directors meet to decide on your demands. They come to the conclusion that your demands are too high; that should you declare a strike all your people would be expelled and new workers engaged. On the same night, the directors are all burnt. I am a police officer. Unlike a judge, I start with the assumption that anybody could be guilty, even myself.'

'But I've told you that I was at an all-night executive meeting to decide on tactics for the strike we had called.'

'I know. I know. I am not saying, I am not alleging anything. I work – like a doctor – on the principle of elimination. Let me ask you another: you once were a teacher in this school?'

'True!'

'Why did you suddenly give up teaching?'

'I was asked to leave.'

'By whom?'

'Mzigo!'

'The same as the late ...'

'You know. Why ask me?'

'I must be sure that we are talking about the same thing. Tell me about your relationship with Wanja!'

'I knew her. In the past.'

'Did you resume your cordial relationship after your rather unexpected return?'

'No. We lived in two different worlds.'

'You never met?'

Karega hesitated.

'No. For two years we never really met.'

'I see. Let me now play you something.'

He walked to the wall and pressed a button. A tape or a record started playing. Karega heard his own voice during the last meeting of the Executive Meeting of the Union saying: We can lay the basis of a New World.

'How ... how dare ...' He was really staggered by this and

wondered who the traitor could be. The officer waved him to silence. He switched it off.

'You see, Mr Karega, we have our own way of working.' Suddenly Godfrey banged the table and stared at Karega as if he would hypnotise him. 'Tell me: who killed Kimeria, Mzigo and Chui? Who gave the orders?'

'I thought you had your own ways of working,' Karega said acidly, sensing the man's uncertainty.

For the next eight days they played that game. Sometimes he was kept away for two days. Then suddenly Inspector Godfrey would spring questions at him. He would needle him with sharp-pointed comments: sometimes he would sneer at Karega's involvement in trade unionism; and at times he would issue direct threats. On the tenth day the officer came to his cell wearing a cruel, triumphant smile.

'Mr Karega . . .'

'Listen. I am tired. I've been kept here for I don't know how long, answering the same stupid questions. I have told you, I know nothing about the arson. I'll not pretend that I am angry, sad or anything, except that the incident gives all of you and the employers a chance to kill the union. But I had nothing to do with it. I don't believe in the elimination of individuals. There are many Kimerias and Chuis in the country. They are the products of a system, just as workers are products of a system. It's the system that needs to be changed . . . and only the workers of Kenya and the peasants can do that.'

'Oh, that's a good one, Mr Karega. But we shall see by the time I finish with you. I'll now ask you only two or three questions. Answer me truthfully and I'll leave you alone. I promise you that. You have been telling me that for two years you never really met with Wanja.'

'True, except on the night of my return.'

'Did you know – between us we don't have to hide these things – did you know that she used to have an affair with all the three gentlemen?'

'It was common knowledge.'

'You say you never met her again?'

'Yes.'

'Not even secretly?'

'No.'

'At Njuguna's once . . . after the lawyer's death?'

'Yes. But it was not really a meeting.'

'Did you know the lawyer?'

'Yes.'

'Worked with him?'

'Yes.'

'Were you a little bit – but it does not matter. Now, Mr Karega, I want you to refresh your mind. Did you meet Wanja a week before this fire?'

Karega hesitated. Then he said,

'Yes.'

'I see. Why did you hide this?'

'It's not important.'

'Why?'

'It's personal.'

'Mr Karega: what did you discuss that night?'

'That I can't tell you. It's personal.'

'Did you hold any other secret meetings?'

'No.'

'How should I believe you now?'

'You choose what to believe and what not to believe.'

'I see. Mr Karega, was Abdulla by any chance part of these secret personal meetings?'

'I've told you it was only once. And Abdulla was not there.'

'Mr Karega, you are a liar.' With sudden rage, he struck Karega twice on the face. Blood came out between his teeth. Godfrey shouted at the policeman.

'Take him below – to the red chamber. Give him a little medicine, a taste of what he will get from me. Have you ever heard of the famous whip of seven straps? Leader of the workers! I will myself work on you, drop by drop of salted medicine from a cowhide whip, until you talk, until you wish you had never travelled on any Trans-Africa Road to any factory in Ilmorog. Out with him.'

3 ❀ Abdulla sat huddled in a corner. He still felt surprisingly light and calm inside, despite nine days of questioning, being made to record one statement after another and occasionally being roughly handled. He felt in his present position the guiding hand of God, who had suddenly lifted – or so it seemed to him – a load of many years: somebody had clearly acted out Abdulla's own wishes and fantasies and intentions and so in a sense had saved him in more ways than one. His only disturbing thoughts were of Wanja: had she recovered fully from the shock? Had she, anyway, come out of her coma, or out of the hospital? Otherwise he felt sober and able to look at his life without the bitter feelings which had earlier always clouded his vision and his appraisal of the past and the present.

What had he really expected from the struggle? His expectation had always taken the form of a beautiful dream, a hazy softness of promises, a kind of call to something higher, nobler, holier, something for which he could have given his life over and over again. It had fizzled out now and toward the end, in Ilmorog, the bright flames of his dreams had died and only ashes had remained. With his donkey as his other leg, in the old Ilmorog, he had only wanted a restoration – a little restoration – a shop, even, like the one his father had had in old Limuru-Rongai Market, before the punitive closure of the shops after Ragae – a notorious collaborator with the enemy – was shot dead in Kiambu Hospital. There was a time in Old Ilmorog – a brief period, true – when Karega, with his talk of the past deeds of African heroes in their four hundred years of resistance to European domination, had stirred the ashes, and he felt as if the embers had not really died, that a little flame flickered. Even this died with Karega's sudden departure from Ilmorog. Abdulla had resumed his search for a restoration, solely missing his donkey as if it truly had been his own child. The one thing which had continued to give him increasing pleasure was Joseph's progress in school. When the results of the school's first attempt at CPE came out Joseph was top – and he had found a place in Siriana! Kenya, he could not help thinking, after this turn of events – this strange coincidence and repetition of history – Kenya was a small world!

Wanja had been his other source of joy in the wilderness of his bitterness, of his consciousness of broken promises, of the wider betrayal of the collective blood of the Kenyan fighters for land and freedom. Since her arrival in Old Ilmorog she had always accepted him without qualification, without the concessions of pity which with many were evidence of subtle rejection. She had made it easier to live, to look forward to the dawn of the next day. Working together with her on the Theng'eta project, he had felt: maybe things are all right ... maybe with a little money ... here and there ... maybe ... the memory would not hurt. Money could act as a soft feather-filled cushion for any fall. Maybe ... maybe ... this was what they had all really fought for ... chance ... opportunities ... what else could a human being want? Only a break ... the rest would be determined by his capacity for hard work and by his native wit. So he had rationalised it to himself and he had worked hard, completely trusting in Wanja's practical sense and puritan control. Under her firm guidance, Ilmorog suddenly seemed to expand: new roads, influx of workers, banks, experts, dancers and numerous small trades and crafts. He saw the changes as something being brought about by Wanja's magic. What a woman! One in a thousand! For she seemed, to him anyway, the true centre of all the numerous activities that were working in obedience to an invisible law. Then disaster had once again come into his life just when success and victory seemed so near, within his grasp. He applauded her selfless act of honour in redeeming her family land. But he feared the effect of this on her. For suddenly it was as if she had lost that firm grasp, that harmony with the invisible law. He had hoped that after the sale of the building they would still be able to make more money on their old premises and buy or build yet another place. Why! They could even move further up the Trans-Africa Road. He always felt something personal about the road, not only because it had for him eased his problems of moving, but also because he felt as if his donkey had been a sacrificial offering to its new coming. Wherever he could set up new business premises near the road, he would always feel it was home. But fate decided otherwise. The opening up of the New Ilmorog was the ruin of the Old Ilmorog and now, once again, Kimeria's shadow had crossed his path.

For a week after the order to close their dirty premises, Abdulla had stayed in his shop, Dharamshah's shop, and thought hard without anything definite and coherent forming in his mind. Maybe it was Nding'uri cursing him from the nether world for not keeping his word to avenge his death and betrayal. If during that and the following week Kimeria had come to Ilmorog, Abdulla would have killed him. He was sure of that. But Kimeria was already such a tycoon that his many negotiations for business takeovers and property deals were handled by the banks, insurance companies and estate agents. After one week, Abdulla had gone over to Wanja's place, her whorehouse. He knew the changes that had come over her. He felt somehow personally humiliated by what seemed her irrevocable and final entry into whoredom. It hurt him, but he understood. He stood at the door, then sat down and went straight into business. He stammered, slightly confused, but he went on. 'Listen. Please. Stop this business. I have a little money. I still have my share of what we got from the recent sale. Marry me. I may not be much to look at: but it was fate.' He finished, almost swallowing the last sentence in his embarrassment. She stood up, turned away and walked into an inner room. Then she came back. She was calm. 'My heart is tearless about what I have committed myself to. You know I have tried. Where was I to throw these girls that were part of the old Theng'eta premises? To others who too would profit from their bodies? No, I am not doing this for their sakes. From now onwards it will always be: Wanja First. I have valued your friendship. And I hope we can remain friends. But this is my cup. I must drink it.' He had expected this but it did not make it any easier.

He tried various businesses on his own. He went into illegal brewing of Chang'aa and Theng'eta. But a new police station had been built in the area and he was arrested several times, buying his way out of conviction with wads of notes. He next tried to rent a building in the New Ilmorog. He put in almost all the capital that he had accumulated during his prosperous partnership with Wanja. But many workers took things on credit and they were not always prompt in paying so that his stock was decreasing rather than expanding. A supermarket was opened nearby: he could not match the rigorous competition. He closed the shop and he was back in the streets, almost a beggar. He watched the new Theng'eta complex go up, and he felt it was fate mocking at him and his kind. He had only enough to buy oranges and sell them to passing motorists. Oranges and occasionally sheepskins: how Karega would laugh at me, he kept on thinking, contemplating this new twist of fate.

He started drinking – to get drunk. He did not want to know anything or remember anything or to think or feel much about whatever was happening around him. He sold oranges and with whatever little profit that he made he would buy himself a drink. He would, on weekends, go to the New Ilmorog Bar and Restaurant because that was where Kimeria and his group went for a drink and roasted goat's meat on their occasional visits to Ilmorog. The bar was owned by a former administrative officer and he employed juicy barmaids which was always an attraction. Abdulla did not now want to kill Kimeria or to curse him. He only wanted to feed his eyes on a man so beloved of fate. What was the point of any other attitude or posture? Kimeria had been right. He had chosen wisely. Abdulla once again became a well-known character – but this time, as a drunk and seller of oranges and sheepskins. He was so well known that even Kimeria would once or twice nod an acknowledgment in his direction – without of course knowing who he really was. The only thing Abdulla never did was to let anybody treat him to a drink. Reaching his hovel late at night, he would lie on the bed, and in the solitude and the darkness he would start mocking, sneering and making contemptuous faces at Nding'uri: So you thought that I would avenge you. Ha! ha! ha! You were even more foolish than I was. What right had you to die? Die! Die! Die again and again, die alone and don't you even expect a burial from me or from anybody. I, Abdulla, will live and live it up with Theng'eta. Theng'a Theng'a with Theng'eta. See now. We rejected Munira's advertisement and now it is a national slogan. Munira – a fool but not a bad chap. No, not bad at all. We now drink together and tell jokes and he does not mind my reminding him of that mountain of shit in the schoolyard. You laugh? Laugh. But now I know it's better to shit all over people's heads and live. I will enjoy the fruits of freedom: Theng'eta, Chang'aa. My torn, dirty clothes? What does it matter, provided I can drink and pay for my allotted share? Let Kimeria and Mzigo and Chui enjoy my shop. They didn't steal it. It's only that they were wise – at least Kimeria was wise. I will not blame him for his wisdom. No, not I, not Abdulla. Let him too eat his share, fruits of his freedom, including Wanja. Wanjaaaaa! Can you in your grave, could you have ever imagined that she would take him on again? After all she claims he had done to her? She too is wise. Because of money ... Because of money ... Nding'uri ... Give me money and I shall avenge you a thousand times. Without coins in my pocket, no action. Then he would beat his breast ... No, don't take it too badly. I too was foolish enough to lose a leg for a national cause. I say: what right had mothers to send their children to the battlefield when it would have been wiser to make them run putrid errands for the European butchers? Fools all. Let them take a leaf from Wanja.

He rarely saw her, but now and then he would run into her – a lady. But she never acted the lady in front of him – in fact she always greeted him warmly. Once she tried to offer him money to buy clothes. It was in a street. He tried to stand firm on his leg, took the first note and tore it to pieces and hobbled away. He would have been a dog to dress with money probably given her by Kimeria. But later he felt ashamed of the action. He knew very well that it was her who was now paying school fees for Joseph. In any case, he did not blame her: she was turning the way the world was tilting.

Once he saw her at one of her rare public appearances and he had to admit that in the game she had chosen few women could beat her. It was at a party thrown at the premises of a new golf club to celebrate the completion of the course and also to welcome Sir Swallow Bloodall, the General Manager of the parent Anglo-American Gin Company that had invested money in the Theng'eta project. It had turned out to be one of their most successful ventures in partnership with the locals. There were many dignitaries: European, Asian, African, including the MP, Nderi wa Riera and his KCO henchmen; of Fat Stomach and Insect. The Ilmorog public was allowed to peep in through a loose fence of double ropes. Wanja was there in a long cocktail dress, a big Afro-wig on her head, her fingers studded with rings and cheap stones. She had a way of keeping everybody on tenterhooks, now whispering to this one, brushing lightly, carelessly against another, smiling at that one while resting her moon-eyes on yet another. Everybody clapped when Sir Swallow Bloodall talked about golf and cricket as creating a climate of stability and mutual goodwill so necessary for investment. They all clapped and stood up to drink to the health and the future of more joint ventures between foreign capital and technical know-how and local businessmen with their acute knowledge of the market and the political situation.

Abdulla walked away.

In those days his best companion was Munira. Together they would drink and occasionally Abdulla would burst into a song in praise of Wanja, detailing how New Ilmorog came to be.

And then Karega returned and Munira became a fanatic. Abdulla was now alone. Munira would follow him and talk about new worlds with Christ. Once, arguing with Karega about the Mau Mau war – whether it was only for the return of the white highlands to black owners and the end of the colour bar in big buildings and in business or whether it was something more – Karega himself had talked of new worlds. Fools both. There were no other worlds. There was only this one, and he, Abdulla, would continue drinking cheap Theng'eta and singing in this one and only world.

All this he told truthfully, trying to show the officer that he had lost all thoughts of vengeance. Except on the fatal day when all those feelings rushed back and became an irresistible force. But he somehow could not tell him that this was because he too had, only a week before, discovered his own world, a new world.

A Friday it was when he received a letter and put it in his pocket and only read it in the evening just as he was about to go to bed. It was from Joseph. The results of mock EAACE were out and he was leading with six points. Abdulla did not know what 'mock' was or what six points meant. But he knew that Joseph was tops in Siriana and he felt a sudden warmth and joy at this turn of events in the gloom that was his life. He wanted to share this with somebody and Wanja came to his mind. He remembered the day he had torn her money and here was a chance to show that he appreciated her timely rescue. He went toward her wooden whorehouse but on the way he met Karega who greeted him and told him that Wanja was in the hut. He found her crying. But when he told her the news, she suddenly stopped, laughed, amidst her tears. They talked late into the night like in the old days. But this time he took her and she did not resist, and it was his turn to feel the old world roll away.

❀

That was why on the fatal Saturday he had woken up feeling great, vibrations of joy in the air. He had been like that for a whole week.

He had not even drunk anything. Wanja had given him back his life and he did not see why he should now waste it in Theng'eta. And to crown it, she wanted him back tonight. It would not be in the hut, but he did not mind her other house. In time, he might even persuade her to give up the whore business, seeing that she was now wealthy – she could even burn the house – and put up a stone building. He whistled and sang: how could he ever have mocked Munira's talk of another world? Only that for him now, a woman was truly the other world: with its own contours, valleys, rivers, streams, hills, ridges, mountains, sharp turns, steep and slow climbs and descents, and above all, movement of secret springs of life. Which explorer, despite the boasts of men, could claim to have touched every corner of that world and drunk of every stream in her? Let others stay with their own worlds: flat, grey, without contours, unexpected turns, or surprises – so predictable. A woman was a world, the world. He shaved and tried on various clothes to see which were less dirty, torn and ragged. He did not know what he would do with himself before night-time, before commencing on a second journey of exploration. At noon, he went for a stroll in the streets. He climbed up to New Ilmorog Bar and Restaurant to play a few records. And then, looking down, he saw Kimeria's Mercedes with a waiting chauffeur. Then he saw the other cars that belonged to Mzigo and Chui. Today was the day the Board of Directors was meeting to decide on the demands put forward by Theng'eta Workers' Union. A thought flashed across his mind like a sudden wave of heat: if it had assumed the form of words it would have been something like: and Kimeria might go to Wanja's place tonight.

He felt dizzy. His head went round and round and a world of chaos and injustice whirled about him. He thought he would fall, and he clung to the balcony. For a few seconds images followed on images as if he was not in control, as if he was nothing, a shell of a man. No. He was a dog panting, wet nose, and saliva flowing from a tongue thrust out. He was now yapping at the call of the master. No. He was not a dog. He was Mobutu being embraced by Nixon, and looking so happy on his mission of seeking aid, while Nixon made faces at American businessmen and paratroopers to hurry up and clear oil and gold and copper and uranium from Zaire. He was Amin being received by the Queen after overthrowing Obote. No, he was his own donkey hee-hoo-hee-hooing and dutifully carrying any quantity of load for the master. He was so many things, so many different people, but himself. At the same time he felt weak, as if he was losing the last shred of his manhood. He fought hard, clinging to himself, clinging to the balcony, trying to master those images, bring them under his control and into some perspective, instead of their looming so large and threatening. A barmaid passed by and asked him: What is it, Abdulla? He did not answer, he could not answer. Gradually, strength returned to his one leg, the sun-heatwave melting the brain went away. He hobbled down the stairs, past the waiting cars, and onto his place. He sat down on a box. He took out the letter he had received from Joseph the other Friday and read it again. Then he put it back. A tear, a single tear, ran down his face. He rubbed it off, rather impatiently. He poured water, cold water from a cup, into one hand, and washed his face. He was suddenly very lucid, calm inside. A sixteen-year mist had cleared. He was not jealous or anything. It was only that deep inside he knew that tonight, this Saturday, Kimeria would die. Only then would he regain the right to call himself a man.

He did not know what it was. He just knew that tonight he, Abdulla, would kill Kimeria, that he could never face Wanja or Karega or Munira or Joseph or himself unless Kimeria was dead. Not tomorrow ... not the day after ... but tonight. He was so certain, and it was so clear and simple and logical. He did not tremble with rage or anything. He did not even feel that moral outrage he used to experience as a substitute for action. Call it justice or fairness or jealousy or vengeance. But he had made a decision: the time, the day and the place was not of his making, but to act was his freedom. He had not yet thought what he would use or how, but he knew that he could throw a knife to the heart, even from several yards away. He had killed many enemies and even animals with his famous knife-throw. Or he could burn up the house, cleanse the whole mess. Yes, he could that. It did not matter how: he would do it.

He went back to the streets, now that he had regained his strength and a sense of purpose. Ilmorog as it used to be passed through his mind in a series of motion pictures. He saw himself arrive in a donkey-cart twelve years ago. Then Munira, Karega and his youthful inquisitive innocence. Every picture – of Wanja, Nyakinyua, the drought, the aeroplane, the new road, New Ilmorog – was very sharp in outline. He joined a crowd of workers who waited for news of any decision arrived at by the Board of Directors. If their pay was not raised, they all would come out on strike – in eight days time. Reporters were waiting around with their cameras – for a snap of the directors. He now had time to marvel at Karega. So calm. So involved. It's in the blood, he muttered to himself, remembering Nding'uri in his youth. Yet standing there he felt odd, and recalled his arguments and disagreement with Karega. Now he thought: these same workers led by Karega could as likely have been gathering there against him and Wanja. It surprised him that only a few years back he too had been an employer of labour, though on a small scale. Would Karega have fought them too with the same ferocity? He was tired of waiting, after all an increase in their pay would not make much difference to the sales of his oranges. Well, they might spend more on oranges, but he was also sure that they would spend even more on Theng'eta. The Directors were fools not to increase the pay, he thought, feeling generous to both the workers and employers. After all, the workers would return the money to the factory. He started walking toward Ilmorog Bar and Restaurant. He knew that after the meeting, they would surely call at the bar. He walked along the main street and passed by the junkyard near the market-place where dirt and paper and bits of oranges and other remains of rotten food were thrown. He stood and watched hordes of half-naked children with bloated stomachs as they fought it out, asserting their different claims to territories of rot and discarded rubbish. He shook his head. This eternal interminable cycle of destitution and deprivation amidst plenty! He resumed his walk toward his chosen destiny.

And indeed at about seven, they all came to the place. They looked a bit too self-consciously triumphant. It was Chui, looking at his watch, who was the first to excuse himself, Then, after a good interval, Mzigo did the same. An irresistible devil now seized Abdulla. He felt he wanted to speak to Kimeria. He felt this power and authority in himself because he had already sentenced him to death. Kimeria was surrounded by other local dignitaries. Abdulla moved a step along the counter and then loudly called out.

'Kimeria wa Kamia Nja!'

There was immediate silence in the whole bar. Kimeria was taken aback because he did not like his father's name. He had used various names in various places: at Blue Hills for instance, he was only Mr Hawkins. Who in Ilmorog could know his past?

'Kimeria: it's me. How are you?'

'Oh, it's you ... Abdulla ... I'm fine,' he answered uncertainly.

'Do you remember me?' People laughed, thinking it was one of Abdulla's drunken antics of a ruined man.

'Of course ... Abdulla ... Get a drink. Waiter! Give Abdulla, my friend, a drink.'

'I am not your friend: I don't want your drink. Do you remember ... the people you once arrested in your place at Blue Hills? People from Ilmorog?'

Aah! Kimeria sighed with relief: so that's where he had seen the man ... maybe that's how he had come to know his father's name! Nevertheless he did not want any awkward embarrassing exposure.

'That? It was only a joke – between men! Ha! ha! ha!'

'Ha! ha!' Abdulla joined in the laughter so that both were laughing. People in the bar also started laughing – although they did not know what the joke between men was – because they were all relieved that nothing unpleasant had occurred. But then Abdulla continued:

'You are rather fond of jokes, Bwana Kimeria. Jokes between men. Do you remember another joke you once played on Nding'uri ... your sister's lover ... sold him bullets ... jokes between men can be costly.'

Kimeria was trembling inside. He wanted to bolt right out but somehow he forced himself to stick glued to the chair. He ostentatiously searched for a handkerchief, took one out together with a pistol – a small pistol – cleared his nose and returned both to the pocket. He ordered another drink. It was so coolly done. But nobody missed the point. They waited for Abdulla's next move. But Abdulla only laughed and started moving away, a voice inside him saying: Look at me carefully, so that even after your death you can remember me.

He hobbled out slowly. Noise returned to the bar. But he knew that people were watching him. He deliberately walked toward his place. He still retained that clarity of certainty of a victory to come. How was it, how could it be that he was not afraid of the consequences? Kimeria would be at Wanja's place. Again he was sure of that. Kimeria was the kind of person who would rather be caught swallowing all, than leave out a few nuts for another to pick. He took out a knife and a box of matches. Then he hobbled slowly toward Wanja's place, for an encounter with his chosen destiny. He stood and listened to the news by a neighbour's hovel. It was nine o'clock. The workers' pay would not be altered because of inflation. This was followed by an item on a meeting of the Oil and Petroleum Exporting Countries to increase prices of crude oil. Yet another small item on the increased profits made by oil companies. This world! He moved on. He could now see Wanja's place. A Mercedes car moved away. It was probably Kimeria's car. But once again, he was not worried. It was normal in Wanja's place. Big shots were driven in by their chauffeurs. The chauffeur would be sent away and given a time at which to return for the boss. Whatever the case he did not worry. An invisible hand of destiny guided him. He would walk into Wanja's place knife in hand, or maybe it would be better ... better ...

He could not at first believe the evidence of his eyes. Was it happening in his mind? Was he under another stroke of heat in the brain so that what he was seeing was only an illusion? Red flames of fire issued from Wanja's place. He remained rooted to the ground. But only for a second. For suddenly he heard a chilling scream issue from the house. He started moving, cursing his inability to run. He hobble-hobbled, as fast as he could. In no time, however, people had come out of their places and rushed past Abdulla. But he found them only standing and arguing about the best course of action. He was Abdulla, in the forests of Longonot and Mount Kenya, making decisions in death-and-life tight corners. With his walking-stick he broke the glass window to the sitting-room. He put his hand through, pulled the latch and then lifted himself up and fell into the room. He searched with hands and feet, groping, until he touched a body near the door. He again groped in the choking, smoking heat, found the door-knob, and opened it, at the same time dragging the body along through fire and smoke. He did not stop to wonder whose body it was: it could even be Kimeria or one of the other girls. He did not care. He dragged it through, crawling on his hands, just managing to escape the tongues of fire as he collapsed outside. But the crowd, which was throwing water in a futile gesture of putting out the fire, saw this heap of two human bodies and pulled them to safety.

❀

On the tenth day after his arrest, Abdulla saw the officer burst into his cell, and knew that the man was in a hostile mood. But Abdulla still had this clarity in the heart and he felt calmly ready for any eventuality. He had answered all the previous questions without hiding any but the most intimate events. The officer did not stand on ceremony but went straight to the business:

'Mr Abdulla. You have so far been most truthful in your answers. You have even volunteered information. You have not hidden your hatred of Kimeria and your intention to kill him. You have shown me the knife and the box of matches. I will be candid with you. I have a feeling that you might be shielding somebody else, for reasons best known to yourself. Now I want to ask you a few more questions.'

'I have nothing to hide and I am not shielding anybody. I have told you everything.'

'I want you to cast your mind back a little. Did you ever hold secret meetings with Karega in Wanja's hut?'

'No. Not there, not anywhere. Karega and I did not always agree, especially after he came back from his five-year exile.'

'Why? What were the differences?'

'I thought he was going too far in overstretching the importance of workers' solidarity aided by small farmers. What about the unemployed? The small traders? I believed, and I told him so, that land should be available to everybody; that loans should be readily available to the small man; that nobody should have too many businesses under him – in a word, fair distribution of opportunities. But he always argued that loans would only hasten the ruin of the small businessman and the alienation of the small farmer ... that workers as a force were on the increase and were the people of the future and that—'

'Interesting ... but I think we can have that lecture when we have more time on our hands. Just now I want you to cast your mind back to a week before the arson. Did you or did you not visit Wanja?'

'I did.'

'In her whorehouse?'

'No.'

'Where?'

'In her hut.'

'Was Karega there?'

'No ... I don't know ... somehow I never asked.'

'What do you mean?'

'Well – I wanted to see Wanja for reasons that – anyway I wanted to see her. But on my way to her place, I met Karega. We greeted one another. He asked me where I was going at night. I told him. He told me she was in the hut, but somehow it never occurred to me to ask how he knew it.'

'I see. What did you discuss?'

'Well, it is ... It is personal.'

'Interesting. Very interesting. Why didn't you tell me this before?'

'I didn't think it was important. Besides, it was rather personal.'

'Personal! Personal! Personal!' he almost shouted, walking round the tiny cell. Then he abruptly stopped and faced Abdulla.

'Why are you shielding Karega?'

'I am not ... There is nothing to shield.'

'Nothing to shield? We shall see. Warders! Warders! Give him medicine ...' He walked out toward the red chamber.

4 ❀ It was only on the tenth day that Wanja recovered sufficiently to talk without that animal terror in her eyes which would suddenly plunge her into visions of fire and smoke and make her scream: See, see, put it out, put it ooooout ...! The shock, the

burns on the hands, the lack of sleep had weakened her. On the twelfth day, the police officer was allowed to see her. He was convinced that somewhere between the three of them was the answer, and he was determined to get it. He had found out a number of things: that Wanja, for instance, had specifically invited Mzigo, Kimeria and Chui for that night: that she had given her watchman and the girls a free day and a free night; and now Abdulla had claimed that she had asked him to come! But why should she want to burn herself and her house? For he could see, anybody could tell, that her trembling was real, the terror that even now lingered in her eyes could not have been faked. He spoke to her gently.

'You will soon get over it. Don't worry too much about the matter. We shall get to the bottom of the whole thing. We shall definitely apprehend the culprits. We are not doing too badly. One or two links are missing. Perhaps you might help us.'

'I would rather not talk about that night. But if I must, please, you must give me time to recover – inside.'

'I am really sorry to have to open old wounds – but – you understand that this is a very serious matter. It is arson. It is murder. You should see the papers. There is a lot of tension in the country. And we suspect some political motivation. You understand then that much as I would like to, I can't spare you the memory. I must be able to record a statement from you about two nights in particular.'

'Go on.'

'First – do you suspect anybody at all?'

'No . . . nobody . . . It has always been so.'

'What do you mean?'

'I suppose it does not matter. But fire is a nightmare in our family. My aunt died of arson. I left Bolibo Bar because a room I rented there was burnt. So you see I have been running away from one fire into greater flames.'

'I see. A week before this fire: did Karega come to see you?'

'Yes. I had wanted to see him.'

'In your place—'

'In my hut.'

'And Abdulla: he too was there.'

'Yes, and no.'

'Meaning—?'

'—that Karega came first. Then later Abdulla. It was a – a strange coincidence.'

'Perhaps you might care to explain. Both Karega and Abdulla have flatly refused to answer questions about that Friday. They say it is personal. But you must understand that there's nothing so personal that it should stand in the way of the truth about arson and murder.'

'Have they? I suppose – it was personal, but really there's nothing to hide.'

And yet as she tried to tell him about that Friday she found that there was quite a lot to conceal. She tried to tell him the main facts, leaving out only intimate details. In her youth she had moved with a few policemen and she knew some of their fixations and suspicions even about the most minute details, especially where they had already constructed a theory however erroneous. She also knew that Abdulla and Karega could be obstinate and lead themselves into trouble over nothing. So she edited the story as she went on. After all, a coherent narrative depended on knowing what details to tell and what to leave out.

But even to herself she could not tell why she had decided to call Karega that night rather than another, or why she had chosen the hut, in particular. Maybe it was the warm memory of their past intimacy. Or respect for his feelings about her whorehouse. She had removed her lipstick and her wig, and she had only her beads and a few bangles round her hands. As she waited for him, she found her heart beating in a kind of vague expectation. She was surprised that she could still feel this way: she had been so used to a heart-beat because of the money sliding into her hands, at her cleverness in manipulating situations, at her abilities to read a man's face like an open book, knowing precisely what illusions he wanted flattered, what frustrations he wanted to work out, and the excitement of being proved right: so used to this kind of thrill, that she had imagined her body and heart now dead to other possibilities.

When he came and stood at the door, it had all the illusions of old times. Only now he was big and hardened in body and famous in the area and, she imagined, in the whole country. It pained her, this purity of pleasure she felt at his arrival – something struggling to be born and reach out to the light against the debris, rust, and squalor of a junkyard.

Karega, too, felt this illusion of a return to the past. He noticed that it was the same bed; the same sheets; the same lamp and furniture. She had preserved it exactly as he had known it: a moment trapped in frozen space. Ilmorog had changed: everybody had changed; new forces had been born and the lines of battle were more clearly marked. Nevertheless, looking at her, he could not help marvelling at how Wanja could be different people in different times and places and situations. That, he supposed was the secret of her continuing success: that she could appeal to so many different people at different times, as if each could find reflected in her the condition of his being. He could not help sighing at such a wasted talent.

'It reminds me so much of Nyakinyua and the night of our first Theng'eta drinking,' he said as he sat on what had once been his favourite folding chair.

'Yes,' she said. 'Shall I make you tea?'

'A cup. That would be fine.'

He watched her, haunched, on knees, putting pressure in the stove, her bangles and beads making a noise to the rhythm of her movement. She was completely absorbed in the act – and really, she was beautiful. How could such a woman have thrown a child, a life, into a latrine? How could such a woman be trading on the bodies of other girls? It was not for him to judge her, nevertheless the intrusion of these unpleasant thoughts broke his admiration.

'Why have you retained the hut?' he asked, just to say something.

'I don't want to forget the Old Ilmorog. I never shall forget how we lived before the Trans-Africa Road cleaved Ilmorog into two halves.'

'What's the point?'

'It is remarkable how you have changed. You used to argue that the past was important for today, things like that.'

'True ... but only as a living lesson to the present. I mean we must not preserve our past as a museum: rather, we must study it critically, without illusions, and see what lessons we can draw from it in today's battlefield of the future and the present. But to worship it – no. Maybe I used to do it: but I don't want to continue worshipping in the temples of a past without tarmac roads, without electric cookers, a world dominated by slavery to nature.'

'You are too – you sound like a preacher to me, so earnest! And yet you used to sit at the feet of my grandmother and other older folks and you would keep on asking: and what happened, what happened? And you would be so rapt in thought ... lost in the power of her voice and narrative ...'

'She was a great woman. I was really very sorry to hear how they drove her to her death. There is your system of eat or you are eaten.'

She poured tea into cups – the same old cups – and sat down.

'She always said that you would return ... even on her deathbed ... strange ... She called me and for two days we really talked: or rather she talked, making me relive my childhood afresh, and so many things. At one time, she put her hand on my head, and said, without looking at me, there's so much sorrow and sadness on your eyes and in your heart ... I know why you grieve ... but he will return, he will return, only I fear that you may not be *there* to receive him ... I told her: I'll never leave Ilmorog. She did not answer. I waited for her to continue – but she did not say any more about it ... Otherwise she did not discuss the future or the present. Instead she kept on talking about my grandfather. And now I asked her the question I had once asked her: "Tell me how my grandfather met his death!"

' "He was a man – he belonged to a race of men such as will never be. I know it: didn't he take me under the millet growth and I felt his power making a woman out of me, a girl? Didn't we make Theng'eta together? Not this concoction you and Abdulla are cheating people with. But he was always troubled by memories of the past and fears for the future. It is, he told me, because of what as a boy – a young man on the verge of manhood – he had seen and witnessed with his own eyes. He had heard of what once had happened in Ilmorog market. He had also heard of other deeds but only about lands afar. This was a time when pitched battles against the strangers were fought – you know the whole of that side of Dagoretti was then dominated by Itungati led by Waiyaki: walk on through Wangigi, leaving the ridges of Koinange to your right, and you come to Githiga, the clan of Muniu, where your mother came from. All this he had heard but thought it would never happen in Ilmorog. And then it did. The women and children were hidden in caves and in the forests. The young men of Ilmorog were determined that they would never again be taken asleep; that they would always defend their goats and land in obedience to the curse of Ndemi. Your grandfather ... he hid in a barn ... he refused to run away with the women and the other boys. He wept because he was not yet circumcised to join in the defence of this soil. He told me how he saw a thousand spearblades of our warriors catch the afternoon sun and turn red like flames from a burning house ... marching against the enemy. A thousand brave men walking to their death, mowed down by fire and noise from those sticks ... but they fell on the enemy, screaming defiance, until the enemy was forced to flee ... but on the ground lay the flower of Ilmorog manhood ... He had wept ... at his own inability to help ... and he swore ... next time ... next time ... But next time he was already an elder ... and it was only to be a porter ... It was there that he heard it whispered how in a land called Russia, peasants had taken spears and seized guns and drove out the enemy. Were they black like him? Was it Europeans that they drove out? In one camp ... he stole something ... He swore next time ... but next time – it was his sons who were taken. But he kept the secret hidden, even from me ... He was growing old ... and dreams troubled him ... the animal of the earth ... he thought your father would be interested, seeing that he had been to the Big War ... and other young men were talking of another war like in India, like in China. But your father ran away ... and it hurt him ... and for him it seemed there would be no next time and his dreams kept him awake so that he would groan ... He had given up ... he told me the secret ... Forget your foolishness, I told him. I thought he had forgotten. And then the fat Waitina mzungu – you know – the one who would ask people to dig their own graves – came here ... wanted to know who was helping the group led by Ole Masai ... we were all in the Baraza. Then he said he would set an example and selected two young men: they would be killed. He said two old men would dig graves for the youth. He asked for volunteers ... and it was – we all thought him mad – your grandfather volunteered. And I was so ashamed: I was so ashamed I wept: so my man was a woman after all? To go and get a jembe to dig a grave for the young? So all those dreams were because of urine and shit in his bones? We all watched him go to the hut ... into the barn ... and came out, a jembe on his shoulders ... And women were going to scream at him ... I knew they would and I wanted to stop him from doing the traitorous thing ... then ... I'll never forget the hour ... he dropped the jembe and pulled the secret from under his blanket and pointed it at Waitina ... and Waitina trembled, we saw a white man tremble, and we all waited for the bang ... You should have been there ... I was so proud, so proud, I would now lift my head among other women ... Well ... It did not fire ... It was too old ... He pulled and pulled ... well they caught him and hanged him ... but he never uttered a word of 'sorry' or cry for forgiveness ... He was a man, my man ... he was a man!" '

'She died the same night ... and I shall never forget her words of pride and joy ... "I am coming to join you, my warrior ..." and she closed her eyes.'

Karega felt as if he had been present amongst those who watched Wanja's grandfather walk to a heroic death, keeping honour to a promise made in his youth way back in the last century.

'It was then I understood why my father never came back and why he and mother always quarrelled and passed the burden of their tension on us children ... Tell me, Karega, tell me, how could I have let this land go to the African Economic Bank, after that? Even if I had to sell myself over and over again,' she ended bitterly.

He felt the old fire flicker ... he reached out to touch her ... she waited suspended ... but in mid-air, he felt the futility of the action and scratched his head as if searching for fitting words.

'That is the kind of lesson we can learn from our past ... as a guide to action . . . but also learn from your grandfather's tendency to act alone—'

The magic string between them was finally broken.

He wished he could swallow back the words. He had hurt her less by the didactic triteness than by a combination of tone and gesture.

Wanja suddenly let him go: she too felt and knew that this was the end: she was not there when he returned and she would not cry over it. Let him go and preach to his workers and the crowds. She had treasured a dream: it was gone. She became businesslike:

'You are once again wondering why I called you. I wanted to ask you to be very careful. They have sworn to kill you – to eliminate you . . . the way they did the lawyer. All those who are against KCO must be eliminated. Just like the lawyer.'

'Who?'

'Kimeria . . . Chui . . . Mzigo . . . all . . . I know it. Don't ask me how. It's part of a big plan. They want to encourage the formation of various tribal organisations. Each tribal union would have its oaths binding its members, on point of death, to an absolute loyalty to the group. Then the leaders from all the unions would form a National Front with KCO as the main power. It would be the duty of each union to eliminate disloyal elements under the pretext that such elements were betraying the tribe and its culture and its wealth to other tribes.'

'And how does one qualify for leadership?'

'Property . . . but I don't think they have worked out all the details. But KCO is a good model. It's led by those with property.'

Karega was quiet for some time. Then he said, more to himself:

'They are bound to fail. Can't you see: we, the workers, the poor peasants, ordinary people, the masses are now too awake to be deceived about tribal loyalties, regional assemblies, glorious pasts, utamaduni wa zamani, all that – when we are starving and we are jobless, or else living on miserable pay. Do you think we shall let foreign companies, banks, insurances – all that – and the local rich with their Theng'eta companies, the new black landlords with their massive land-holdings and numerous houses – do you think people will let a combination of these two classes and their spokesmen in parliament, at universities, in schools, in churches and with all their armies and police to guard their interests – do you think that we shall let these owners of stolen property continue lording it over us for ever? No . . . it is too late, Wanja . . . we shall no longer let others reap where they never planted, harvest where they never cultivated, take to their banks from where they never sweated . . . Tell them this: There are a million Karegas for every ten Kimerias. They can kill the lawyer or ten such lawyers. But the poor, the dispossessed, the working millions and the poor peasants are their own lawyers. With guns and swords and organisation, they can and will change the conditions of their oppression. They'll seize the wealth which rightly belongs to them. Why – it's happening all around us – Mozambique, Angola, Zimbabwe. Just now you thought I was not touched by your grandfather's story. I would choose your grandfather ten times ... not your father ... Never! The workers and the peasant farmers of Kenya are awake.'

He stood up to go. 'But thank you for warning me. I really mean it. It touches me ... and I am only sorry, really sorry, that you are on their side. KCO and Imperialism stand for the rich against the poor. They take from the poor and that's why they hate to see the poor organise and you are helping them.'

She stood up and faced him, hatred in her eyes, anger in her voice, proud in her bearing.

'No ... It is not true, it's not true, I've tried to fight them, the only way I can. What about you? What I am, you made me. You went away, you went away. I pleaded with you, shed tears, but you went away and now you dare blame me.'

Then as suddenly her voice changed and she spoke softly.

'I have been so lonely ... so lonely. This wealth feels so heavy on my head. Please stay tonight ... just tonight, like in the old times ...'

Yet again she changed and this time she cried out to beyond Karega, beyond, a savage cry of protest:

'Oh, it's not true. It's not true. I have loved life! life! life! Karega, give me life ... I am dying ... dying ... and no child ... No child!'

He did not look at her. He felt callous but it was also, for him, the only way. He was firm and sure!

'Whatever you are, you have chosen sides. I don't hate you, I don't judge you ... but I know that we cannot fight Kimerias by being them ... by joining them ... we can't beat them at that game ... No, we want a world, we must struggle for a world in which there are no Kimerias and Chuis, a world in which the wealth of our land shall belong to us all, in which there will not be parasites dictating our lives, in which we shall all be workers for one another's happiness and well-being.'

He left her standing by the door where later Abdulla found her.

❧

For the next few days Wanja thought about what had happened. It seemed that it had all been inevitable: her final break with Karega and her union with Abdulla. Abdulla's news about Joseph's success in Siriana coming so soon after Karega's censure had given her a measure of pride and a little hope. It seemed to her that it was the only good thing she had ever done, at least the only thing she had initiated without adverse repercussions on her own life. And what a life! She had carried dreams in a broken vessel. Looking back now she could not even see a trail of the vanished dreams and expectations. It was Kimeria who had bored a hole into the vessel. That was true. But she had let him. She had chosen. This she could not now hide from herself. Karega was right. She had chosen, and she could not blame it on her parents and on Kimeria. At least she could have chosen to fight differently. Her grandfather had chosen. Her father had chosen. Karega had chosen. Everybody chose to accept or not to accept. The choice put one on this or that side of the line-up in the battlefield. She had been, it seemed to her, the warrior in the story who came home to tell and catalogue his defeats, not in shame but in pride, as if defeat was itself an achievement. She, Wanja, had chosen to murder her own child. In doing so she had murdered her own life and now she took her final burial in property and degradation as a glorious achievement. She tried to look at this coolly, without this time shifting the blame onto others.

She could not now return to a previous state of innocence. But she could do something about her present circumstances. She did not know what she would do: she only felt the need to do something. For a start she could end her relationship with Kimeria. Yes. She must end it. But this second time it would be on her own terms. She would choose the hour, place and atmosphere. She would have her vengeance. The more she thought about it the more she liked the idea, which soon became an obsession. It was as if the manner of ending it was more important than the act. She did not see any contradiction in her choice of Abdulla as her instrument of vengeance. It seemed only natural now that she had accepted him into her life. The idea was simple. She would invite Mzigo, Chui and Kimeria: she would then introduce Abdulla, in his rags, as her rightful man. She would then expose Kimeria. She worked out the plan. She would send all the girls away, and the watchman, for she really was determined to end her present life-style and means of earning a living. She would later work out ways of employing the girls in her other ventures. But for the night of her vengeance, they had to be away. Her plan was to keep Mzigo, Kimeria and Chui in different rooms until Abdulla's arrival. She trusted her long experience and her tongue to manage separate but simultaneous entertainment. It would be a kind of grand finale to a career of always being trodden upon, a career of endless shame and degradation.

Everything worked according to plan until the last day. Chui was the first to arrive. She put him in a room, talked to him a little, and then excused herself to make supper, and carefully locked the door after her. She went into the kitchen and started cutting meat into small bits. She cut enough for four, put it into a sufuria. Mzigo was the second to arrive and she put him in yet another room, talked to him a little and then excused herself to go to the kitchen. Cooking and the kitchen became the most important link in the drama and she was beginning to enjoy it. To the question why she could not let the girls cook, she would tell each the same story: this was a special evening for him and her. Otherwise it would not be difficult to entertain them: Chui liked to be listened to as he talked of South Africa, England and America. He also liked casually dropping names of other big men. 'The other day, talking to so and so . . .' or 'the other day, having goat meat at so and so's . . . I tell you, if a bomb had been dropped all the Kenya elite would have gone.' He liked it most when one showed constant amazement at the places he had been to, and if one showed a little jealousy at all the English girls he had slept with. Mzigo liked talking about cars in a deprecating manner as if the car, and especially a Mercedes, was the greatest evil in the world. He liked it best when one praised cars in proportion to his running them down. Kimeria liked to be made a little jealous and then he would try to woo her back by promising gifts. He also occasionally talked about parties with other big men: and at all his parties, people bought only rounds of whole bottles of champagne or whisky. 'You know, the big ones that cost nearly a hundred shillings each', as if it was the size of bottles bought and the cost that made the parties worthwhile. She now waited impatiently for Kimeria. And she found her heart beating suddenly, fearing that something would go wrong. She again thought about her life, wondering if it would have been different without her early encounter with Kimeria. Her thoughts shifted to her father: suppose her father had been like her grandfather, would things have been different? This and that, this and that, and it was the picture of her grandfather that now stood vivid in her mind as Kimeria knocked at the door. She opened for him: he breezed in, ready to be loved. She still held the panga she had been using in cutting the thick vegetables . . . He smiled at her . . . and she showed him to his room. It was when she was going to see if Abdulla had come that she suddenly saw flames and smoke and she screamed, screamed for help before fainting on the ground.

That in the main was what she told Inspector Godfrey. And it was true. What she did not tell him, what she would never tell anyone now that she was still alive and the evidence had been burnt, was that it was she who had killed Kimeria ... struck him dead with the panga she had been holding.

5 ❀ 'Tell me, Mr Munira ... you knew Chui well,' said Inspector Godfrey. He was very relaxed. The boredom and cynicism on his face had gone. The eyes were playful, lit by genuine curiosity.

'I have already told you that he and I were in the same school. We were expelled around – I think it was in 1946 – because it was the year of the age-group called Cugini/Mburaki.'

'That means black market?'

'Yes. Because it was after the war and things were in severe shortage. It was during these years that Karugo, the driver, became famous. He used to transport goods and maize from the settled area to the African Reserves and no police car could catch him.'

'That's why they say: Tura na Cia Karugo?'

'Yes.'

'Very interesting.'

'Today the same thing would be called Magendo ... But this time in ivory and rubies, maize and charcoal. Only that no policeman would chase some of the culprits.'

'Ha! ha! ha! Mr Munira, you seem to know a little bit about your culture. But I believe that your parents were Christians?'

'Yes.'

'And your brothers are all well off. One is now a big man in an oil company, not so?'

'Yes.'

'And your father is still – he is a big landlord?'

'Yes.'

'What was the relationship between you and your parents? Cordial?'

'Strained, I should say.'

'How would you describe yourself? A failure? The odd man, the black sheep of an otherwise white family?'

'There is no failure for those born anew in Christ. This world is not my home.'

'Quite right. But tell me ... did you meet Chui again after your little adventure in Siriana?'

'No ... not really.'

Munira stopped and thought for a few minutes. Then he laughed as if amused by sudden inward reflection.

'No. Actually ... you see, I saw him several times in Ilmorog. I thought of introducing myself. But I didn't, or rather I kept on putting off the decision. Then one day I did so. It was funny. It was during the opening of Ilmorog Golf Club. We teachers were also invited. This time I went straight to him. At first he could not remember me. I told him about Chui, the football player. I called him Joe Louis – Shakespeare. He burst into laughter. He felt his huge stomach with one hand, glass of champagne in the other. "How are you, my friend? Ha! Ha! I suppose today they would have called me Muhammad Ali or Bruce Lee, or Pele. So you became a teacher? Like myself? That Fraudsham ... did you attend his funeral?" We talked a little bit about the Ironmongers, Fraudsham, and Siriana in our time. "Schoolboys ... these days ... not at all like we used to be," he said. He asked me what I was drinking. Why didn't I Theng'a Theng'a with Theng'eta? Did I not know the modern algebra – P was equal to 3 Ts? "New maths," he said and laughed, slapping me on the shoulder with his free hand. That day I did not want to drink and I said ginger ale. "Come, come, wine is a good familiar creature if it be used well," he said encouragingly and slapped me hard on the shoulder. I still stuck to my ginger ale and quoted back. "O thou invisible spirit of wine, If thou hast no name to be known by, let us call thee devil." "So you remember Mr Billy Shakespeare," he said, and laughed again. An argument developed. Was ginger ale really an ale (Alcohol Livens Everybody) or was it a Fanta (Foolish Teachers Never Take Alcohol)? He said that it could have an alcoholic effect, depending on who was taking it. He told a story how once at a party in his place at Blue Hills, a lady did get drunk on ginger ales. She went to the door and screamed and fainted and later claimed that she had seen a ghost ...'

'I see. Very interesting. And Kimeria? Did you know him?'

'No ... not very well ... Except that he had ruined Wanja's life and betrayed Karega's brother.'

'And Karega ... did he ever talk in a way that might suggest – eeh?'

'What?'

'Bitterness. Or how he was going to bring about his new world? Could he have thought of hastening its coming?'

'I've told you how it was that I didn't believe in man's—'

He stopped. The officer was looking at him in a strange manner. Inspector Godfrey suddenly changed his tone ... he was not any longer the bemused onlooker.

'Mr Munira ... what were you doing on Ilmorog Hill on the Sunday morning after the arson?'

Munira looked at the officer. He read everything in his eyes.

'So you know?' he asked quietly.

'Yes, Mr Munira ... The rulers of every world have their laws, their policemen, and their judges and ... and the law's executioners ... not so? I am afraid, Mr Munira, that I am only a policeman of this world. And I'll now formally charge you with burning Wanja's house and causing the deaths of three men. I may warn you that anything you say may be used against you in a court of law. Tell me: why did you do it?'

'I – I wanted to save Karega,' Munira said.

❀

Munira had been so convinced that this world was wrong, was a mistake, that he wanted all his friends to see this and escape in time. That was why he had pestered Karega so much. In the end this had become an obsession. He followed Wanja; he followed Abdulla; he followed Karega. But it was Karega in whom he was most interested. It was as if he had a doubt in his mind which could only be erased by Karega's conversion. But it was sheer coincidence that on the crucial Friday he saw the shadow of Karega. He had followed him. He saw him enter Wanja's hut. 'So they have been meeting in secret,' it suddenly dawned on him. 'So they have been seeing one another in the hut!' He waited in the dark, thinking hard. He recalled his first arrival in Ilmorog: he remembered how Wanja had shaken his world, the world he had created around himself. He recalled and relived his involvement with her and his later sliding into sloth and drinking, and she looking so desirable like the fruit in the old garden. From nowhere, a voice spoke to him: She is Jezebel, Karega will never escape from her embrace of evil. In the dark, the message was clear: Karega had to be saved from her. He would otherwise descend the very same steps that Munira had himself descended and from which he had been saved by the return of Karega and Lillian. Save him ... save him, the voice insisted. Munira knew that he would obey the voice. Christ, after all, had beaten the traders who had been spoiling God's temple. What was important was not just passive obedience to the law but active obedience to the universal law of God. It was a tremendous revelation. He saw Karega move out. He wondered if he should act tonight and how he should act. He was going to follow Karega when again he saw Abdulla come and also go into the hut. 'Even he ...' Munira thought and moved away.

For a whole week he prayed that God would show him the way. He bought petrol on the Saturday evening ... He walked to Wanja's place. It was not he, Munira. He was doing this only in active obedience to the law. It was enjoined on him to burn down the whorehouse – which mocked God's work on earth. He poured petrol on all the doors and lit it up. He walked away toward Ilmorog Hill. He stood on the hill and watched the whorehouse burn, the tongues of flame from the four corners forming petals of blood, making a twilight of the dark sky. He, Munira, had willed and acted, and he felt, as he knelt down to pray, that he was no longer an outsider, for he had finally affirmed his oneness with the Law.

Chapter Thirteen

1 ❀ Inspector Godfrey sat by the window of a first-class coach and watched the fields roll away: neat man-controlled beauty of coffee and tea plantations on hillsides and valleys and ridges. His mind was not wholly on the undulating landscape between Ruwa-ini and Nairobi, but was still in New Ilmorog. He should now have been experiencing that inner satisfaction he always had felt whenever he put a crime jigsaw puzzle together: but instead he felt an inner discomfort, a slight irritability. He was a little surprised at himself because this kind of unease was hopelessly out of character with the equanimity with which he was wont to view the flow of social and political events. Not that he was interested in the likes of Karega. For such destroyers of order he had no feelings. Inspector Godfrey, a self-made man, for his formal education had not taken him beyond Form 2 and yet see where he was, the heights he had reached through study, application and through an instinctive fear of stirring the bottom of a pool, he had been brought up to believe in the sanctity of private property. The system of private ownership, of means of production, exchange and distribution, was for him synonymous with the natural order of things like the sun, the moon and the stars which seemed fixed and permanent in the firmament. Anybody who interfered with that ordained fixity and permanence of things was himself unnatural and deserved no mercy: was he not inviting chaos such as would occur if some foolish astronaut/cosmonaut should go and push the sun or the moon from its place? People like Karega with their radical trade unionism and communism threatened the very structure of capitalism: as such they were worse than murderers. Inspector Godfrey always felt a certain protective relationship to this society. It did not matter that for him, all these years, he had acquired very little. Still he felt a lordly proprietorial air to the structure: was the police not the force that guaranteed that stability

which alone made possible the unhindered accumulation of wealth? Everybody, even those millionaires that had ganged together under Kamwene Cultural Organisation, really owed their position to the force. The police force was truly the maker of modern Kenya, he had always felt. The Karegas and their like should really be deported to Tanzania and China!

But it was people like Munira who really disturbed him. How could Munira have repudiated his father's immense property? Could property, wealth, status, religion, plus education not hold a family together? What else could a man want? Inspector Godfrey decided that it was religious fanaticism! Yet from his own experience in the police force, such fanaticism was normally found among the poor. Human beings: they could never be satisfied!

And yet there was a way in which Munira was right. This system of capitalism and capitalistic democracy needed moral purity if it was going to survive. The skeletons that he himself had come across in the New Ilmorog could not very well come under the label of moral purity. Of course he had seen similar or near similar things in Nairobi, Mombasa, Malindi, Watamu and other places but he had never before given it much thought because, at least so he supposed now, he had never before come across a Munira who was prepared to murder in the name of moral purity. And it was not Wanja's *Sunshine Lodge* that Inspector Godfrey was thinking about. It was, for instance, the Utamaduni Cultural Tourist Centre at Ilmorog. Ostensibly it was there to entertain Watalii from USA, Japan, West Germany, and other parts of Western Europe. But this only camouflaged other more sinister activities: smuggling of gemstones and ivory plus animal and even human skins. It was a centre for the plunder of the country's natural and human assets. Women, young girls, were being recruited to satisfy any watalii's physical whims. The more promising ones, those who seemed to acquire an air of sophistication with a smattering of English and German were lured to Europe as slave whores from Africa! Inspector Godfrey was in no doubt that this lucrative trade in Black Ivory was done with the knowledge of Nderi wa Riera, the MP for the area, for did he not own the centre? He was in partnership with the proprietor, the man from West Germany. Black Ivory for Export: First rate Foreign Exchange Earner: but couldn't we do without it, Inspector Godfrey thought, recalling the storm that had burst out when years before a similar trafficking in young flesh had been discovered at Watamu Bay? Maybe he would talk to his superiors about this: maybe he would give them the separate report that he had made. But then remembering how many VIP's might be connected with such an

Utalii Utamaduni Centre, he desisted. He would keep the report and the knowledge to himself. It might come in useful should he ever be called upon to put together another criminal jigsaw puzzle. He was a crime detective not the leader of a moral vice squad! Tourism was after all one the biggest industries in the country and there was nothing good that did not carry with it a few negative things. His duty as a policeman was to help maintain stability, law and order, upon which depended the successful growth of all the industries and foreign investments. He chuckled to himself. He felt better. How silly of him to have let himself be drawn into moral questions of how and why! Was he growing weak with old age? He settled back in the carriage and his mind dwelt at the more comfortable formal questions of his investigation of the murder by arson of Kimeria, Chui and Mzigo. Wanja, Munira, Abdulla and even Karega passed through his mind ... as the train took him nearer and nearer the city of which New Ilmorog was only a tiny, tiny imitation ...

2 ❀ She thought about her father: what was it that made some take the side of the people in a struggle and others sell out to foreign interests while still others stood precariously on the fence? What was it? And recalling Abdulla, Karega, Munira, her grandfather and all the other individuals who had been in and out of her life, she decided that maybe everything was simply a matter of love and hate. Love and hate – Siamese twins – back to back in a human heart. Because you loved you also hated: and because you hated you also loved. What you loved decided what you would have to hate in relation to what you loved. What you hated decided the possibilities of what you could love in relation to that which you hated. And how did one know what one loved and hated? Again, thinking of the events in her life, she came back to the question of choice. You knew what you loved and what you hated by what you did, what actions, what side you had chosen. You could not, for instance, work with the colonists in suppressing the people and still say you loved the people. You could not stand on the fence in a struggle and still say you were on the side of those fighting the evil. Her father had wanted to make money and to accumulate property: he had chosen neutrality, and he hated any suggestion of being involved on the side of the people in case this ruined his chances of making money. The tragedy of her father, who by his neutrality had therefore chosen the side of the colonists, was that despite his selling out, despite his denial of self and of his father, he had ended up ruined anyway, the world disintegrating around him. His petty trade as a plumber was no match for the giant enterprises around him. She could see this

clearly because of her own involvement in the petty transport trade and she knew what pressures were brought upon the petty trader, the matatu driver, the owner of one bus, the shopkeeper – all these and more. So what was the difference between her own position and that of her father? Had she not, like her father before her, also chosen her side in the struggle because she had latterly opted for her thing to love: money and money-making? She had chosen, then, the side of the Kimerias of post-Independence Kenya: how could she then blame her father? She now wished she had really known him: she wished she had talked with him at some length! But what could they have spoken about? Had she not, after all, added to his humiliation? It could not now be helped. But was there a time when she maybe could have helped it? She thought of her many attempts to return home and all the failures. There was the time she packed all her things and told the other girls that she was definitely quitting the life. The following day she found all her clothes stolen. She became scared of going home empty-handed. There was the time her father called her a prostitute and, in word if not in deed, had chased her out of the house! There was the time the lawyer had asked her to return home. She would have done it. She had taken the bus, determined to go back home. But on reaching her place she had suddenly changed her mind. She had been stabbed with guilt, not only because of her being empty-handed but because of the memory of her very last encounter with her father. The memory wounded ... it still hurt. She had, before her first visit to Ilmorog, decided to make it up with her parents and seek their blessing: who knows the effect of the power of the parental curse? She had reasoned. She had gone home at midday and found him lying on the grass under the barn. She saw from his emaciated face that he was very ill; she suddenly felt kindly toward him. He was all alone. He spoke to her with difficulty. He asked her for water. She went into the house and poured some water into a cup and took it to him. His hands trembled. He looked up at her. Then he slowly shook his head. 'You look exactly like your mother when she was young,' he said, and his voice was soft. Maybe, she had thought, maybe he was remembering a time when it was possible to love. And indeed in that second she too remembered the time when she used to sit on her father's knees and he would sing to her. It was a brilliant sunny spot in her childhood before he became obsessed with the idea of making money. Her heart mellowed toward him. She wanted to confess all her failings and ask for forgiveness. He looked at her again. He said: 'Have you any money? Five shillings? Twenty shillings?' She picked up her handbag. She saw him suddenly beam bright on his face, his emaciated hands were trembling with eagerness. He started praising her in a most exaggerated tone, saying that he knew all the time she would later be his blessing in his old age. He complained to her how her mother treated him, cheating him out of his money. And not just his mother: it seemed as if all the neighbourhod had ganged up to deny him his share of the money in Kenya. Only Wanja was left. And suddenly her hands became frozen in the very act of pulling out a note. So only money, no matter how it was got, could redeem her in his eyes? And she had thought . . . She could not buy his love or his blessings or buy her way back to the home with money. She said: 'I have nothing!' and she shut the handbag. Then he started condemning everybody: he had known that all his children were useless . . . She walked away, went to the nearest bar and wept and drank all the money she had. Later she heard the news of his death and she did not cry. He had died of cancer.

She rested on her bed in the old hut, turning over these things in her head . . . these silhouettes from the past . . . these images that refused to be burnt right out of her life and memory. She wanted a new life . . . clean . . . she felt this was the meaning of her recent escape! Already she felt the stirrings of a new person . . . she had after all been baptised by fire. And to think that it was Munira and Abdulla who were instrumental in her double narrow escapes, in her getting yet another chance to try out new paths, new possibilities? Yet would there now be any better chance for her? Whatever would happen to her she would always shiver at the horror of that moment . . . she still wondered how or from where she could have got the strength to do what she had done . . .

Somebody knocked at the door. Who could it be? There was another knock, then the door opened and—

'Mother!' Wanja gasped.

'My child . . . fire again!' her now aged mother cried out. They wept together, maybe both weeping out their different memories.

'A whole month, and I did not know. I heard about it only the other day and that from a mere stranger!'

And she explained how an acquaintance had asked after Wanja's health, whether she had recovered from the fire. And Wanja's mother had felt very weak at the knees and she was only able to stand and walk because of her faith in the mercy and the infinite justice of Christ.

For the next few weeks they just talked, softly, treading toward the past, but never quite bringing it into the open. The only thing they discussed at length was their refusal to go to Tea. Wanja was thinking: maybe nobody could really escape his fate. Maybe life was

a series of false starts, which, once discovered, called for more renewed efforts at yet another beginning. Suddenly she could no
longer keep her fears and hopes from the elder woman:

'I think ... I am ... I think I am with child. No, I am sure of it,
mother.'

Her mother was silent for a few seconds.

'Whose ... whose child?'

Wanja got a piece of charcoal and a piece of cardboard. For one
hour or so she remained completely absorbed in her sketching. And
suddenly she felt lifted out of her own self, she felt waves of emotion
she had never before experienced. The figure began to take shape on
the board. It was a combination of the sculpture she once saw at the
lawyer's place in Nairobi and images of Kimathi in his moments of
triumph and laughter and sorrow and terror – but without one limb.
When it was over, she felt a tremendous calm, a kind of inner assurance of the possibilities of a new kind of power. She handed the
picture to her mother.

'Who ... who is this ... with ... with so much pain and suffering
on his face? And why is he laughing at the same time?'

3 ❦ Abdulla and Joseph sat outside their hovel in the New Jerusalem, talking. Joseph was now a tall youth in a neat uniform of
khaki shirt and shorts. He held Sembene Ousmane's novel, God's
Bits of Wood, in his hands but he was not reading much. The sun
was brilliantly warm over Ilmorog but it also made the smell of urine
and rotting garbage waft through the air to where they sat. But they
were used to the smells. Joseph was saying that he was confident of
passing his exams. He would have liked to go to another school for
his Higher School Certificate but this was not possible because he
had not applied to move. Abdulla's mind was elsewhere. He was glad
he had saved Wanja. But he still did not know what to make of the
experience. So Munira was capable of such an act? He did not know
whether to admire or to be angry with him: to loath his sneaking
cowardice or to praise his courage. After all, he had carried out what
he, Abdulla, had contemplated doing without ever bringing himself
to do it. Joseph was still chattering:

'It's very strange,' he said. 'It's very strange that Chui was killed
at the time he was killed.'

'Why?' asked Abdulla perfunctorily. But he was jolted by Joseph's
reply.

'Because the students were planning another strike.'

'Another strike? Why?'

'Chui ran the school from golf clubs and the board-rooms of the various companies of which he was a director, or else from his numerous wheatfields in the Rift Valley. The junior staff – the workers on the school compound – were going to join us. And one or two teachers were sympathetic. They too had grievances, about pay and conditions of work and Chui's neglect . . . This time we were going to demand that the school should be run by a committee of students, staff and workers . . . But even now we are determined to put to an end the whole prefect system . . . And that all our studies should be related to the liberation of our people . . .'

Abdulla lost interest in Joseph's catalogue of ills at Siriana. He was reviewing his own life. He recalled his own childhood at Kinyogori, remembered the many elders, men and women who used to come and talk long into the night. Ngang'a wa Riunge. Johanna Kiraka. Naftali Michuki. Ziporah Ndiri. True patriots of Kenya. They would talk and whisper long into the night, reviewing the history of Limuru, denouncing those who had sold out to the white foreign interests like Luka, but praising those who had stood up and fought against settler encroachment. They talked about how in years to come all the land in the area would be returned to all the mbari ya Limuru, the children of the soil. KCA. KAU. They talked about all this and they would end up singing songs of hope and songs of struggle. How Abdulla had loved those songs. How they had moved him to heights of glory to come! He saw Nding'uri, he reviewed his own narrow escape, his flight to the forest, his arrest and detention, his return home to loss and to a kind of gain. And suddenly Abdulla felt he should tell Joseph the truth about is past. He felt guilty when he remembered how he used to curse at Joseph, taking out his frustrations on the little one, and the little one bearing it, thinking that maybe it came from his returned brother. It was strange how Joseph had never asked him about 'their' parents and, except for his delirium during the journey to the city, never referred to his childhood. Maybe he knew the truth. Maybe . . .

'Joseph,' Abdulla suddenly said, as if he had not heard about the strike in Siriana. 'If I have treated you wrong in the past, forgive me.'

'Why? There's nothing to forgive,' Joseph replied, struck by Abdulla's sudden change of subject and tone. 'I am very grateful for what you have done for me. And also Munira and Wanja and Karega. When I grow up and finish school and university I want to be like you: I would like to feel proud that I had done something for our people. You fought for the political independence of this country: I would like to contribute to the liberation of the people of this country. I have been reading a lot about Mau Mau: I hope that one day we shall make Karuna-ini, where Kimathi was born, and

Othaya, where J.M. was born, national shrines. And build a theatre in memory of Kimathi, because as a teacher he organised the Gichamu Theatre Movement in Tetu ... I have been reading a lot about what the workers and peasants of other lands have done in history. I have read about the people's revolutions in China, Cuba, Vietnam, Cambodia, Laos, Angola, Guinea, Mozambique ... Oh yes, and the works of Lenin and Mao ...'

He was talking like Karega, Abdulla thought, but he did not say anything. Maybe ... maybe, he thought, history was a dance in a huge arena of God. You played your part, whatever your chosen part, and then you left the arena, swept aside by the waves of a new step, a new movement in the dance. Other dancers, younger, brighter, more inventive came and played with even greater skill, with more complicated footwork, before they too were swept aside by yet a greater tide in the movement they had helped to create, and other dancers were thrown up to carry the dance to even newer heights and possibilities undreamt of by an earlier generation. Let it be ... Let it be ... His time was over. He was fated by the present circumstances to remain a petty fruit-seller on the verge of ruin. But he was glad that he had saved a life when he was on a mission of taking one, and he would be happy to know that Wanja was happy and that sometimes she remembered him.

4 ❀ Just before the trial, Munira's father and mother and his wife, accompanied by Rev. Jerrod, came to see him. They all found it difficult to hit on an appropriate subject of conversation. Munira looked at his tall father who, despite having traversed Kenya's colonial history – he was more than 75 years old – was still very strong and healthy. What did he really think of this world? He who had seen the pre-colonial, feudal clan-heads and houses decline and fall; who had witnessed the coming of missionaries; of the railway; the first and second war; the Mau-Mau upheavals; the post-Independence trials – the murders of Pinto, Mboya, Kungu Karumba, J.M., the detention of Shikuku, Seroney, oathings to protect properties – all this: what did he think of it? Munira inquired about his brothers and his sisters and it was as if they were not blood relations at all, so remote and removed they seemed to be from the present circumstances:

'And where are the children?' he asked. They looked embarrassed. Munira frowned in anger. He snorted: 'You don't want them to see their father, a failure, eeh?' And suddenly his mother broke down.

'Why did you do it? How could you do such a thing?' she asked.

She had broken the taboo of silence on the subject. Rev. Jerrod chimed in:

'And to know you were here all the time and I didn't ... I might have helped.'

Munira more than ever before was struck by the hypocritical stances around him. He recalled the forthrightness of Inspector Godfrey, who at least was clear as to what laws he was serving, and he felt kindly toward the detective and his eccentric ways of investigating crimes.

'Return to the path ... turn to the Light ...' Munira intoned, standing above them, suddenly filled with pity and anger at the same time. The others looked at one another, except Waweru, who stood apart and seemed far away in his own past.

'You, my father—' Munira called with authority.

'Yes?'

'One question, only one question I want to ask you. Do you remember that in 1952 you refused to take the Mau Mau oath for African Land and Freedom?'

'What has that got to do with your—' and Waweru pulled himself short, wondering about the new Temptations of Satan.

'And yet in 196—, after Independence, you took an oath to divide the Kenya people and to protect the wealth in the hands of only a few. What was the difference? Was an oath not an oath? Kneel down, old man, and ask the forgiveness of Christ. In heaven, in the eyes of God, there are no poor, or rich, this or that tribe, all who have repented are equal in His eyes. You too, Reverend—'

'What has got into his head?' his mother cried out again, frightened.

'You remember that once in Blue Hills you received some people from Ilmorog—'

'I can't quite, eeh, remember—' he said, wondering what was to follow.

'A cripple among them? Drought?'

'Yes ... aah ... yes.'

'I was one of them: and you sent us away thirsty and hungry.'

'I didn't know ... If I had known ... but ...'

Munira coughed once: he cleared his throat and then dramatically pointed a finger at them:

'The Law ... Did you obey the Law of the one God? ... Depart from me, you accursed, into the eternal fire prepared for the devil and his angels; for I was hungry and you gave me no food, I was thirsty and you gave me no drink, I was a stranger and you did not welcome me, naked and you did not clothe me, sick and in prison, and you did not visit me. Then they also will answer, Lord, when did we see thee hungry or thirsty or naked or sick or in prison, and did not minister to thee? Then will he answer them: Truly I say to you, as you did it not to one of the least of these, you did it not to me. And they will go away into eternal punishment, but the righteous into eternal life.'

They went away weeping for him. At the Ilmorog Anglican Church they knelt down and all of them said prayers for Munira.

'It is these revivalist cults that claim to speak in tongues and to work miracles. Going too far ... They must be banned ...' said Rev. Jerrod, sadly.

'Yes ...' agreed Munira's father. But he was thinking about Karega and Mariamu and how it was the woman who had, through her sons, hit twice at him. Maybe ... it was his sin of attempted adultery ... weaknesses of the flesh ... But how could this be, seeing that he had not quite ... and in any case he had repented? Then he recalled a recent coincidence. Kajohi, who had sold him all of the Kagunda Mbari land in the 1920s and disappeared into the Rift Valley, had now come back, an old man half blind, to ask for assistance. Mr Ezekiel Waweru had, through his contacts and friends, found him a place at an almshouse run by the church in the city ... God works in mysterious ways his wonders to perform, Ezekiel muttered. He would know now how to write his will ... how could he then question God's wisdom?

5 ✿ Karega received the news and his face did not move. But despite attempts to control and contain himself, a teardrop flowed down his left cheek. He watched the drop fall to the cement floor. He was weak in body because of the early beatings, the electric shocks and the mental harassment. These, he could bear. But to hear that his mother was dead – dead! That he would never see her again ... that he had never really done anything for her ... that she had remained a landless squatter all her life: on European farms, on Munira's father's fields, and latterly a landless rural worker for anybody who would give her something with which to hold the skin together! 'Why? Why?' he moaned inside. 'I have failed,' and he felt another teardrop fall to the cement floor. Then suddenly he hit the cell wall in a futile gesture of protest. What of all the Mariamus of Kenya, of neo-colonial Africa? What of all the women and men and children still weighed down by imperialism? And for two days he would not eat anything.

On the third day the warder who had broken the bad news came again.

'Mr Karega ... there's a visitor to see you ... you had better come out ... Mr Karega, I ... we want you to know that despite what has happened ... some of us are glad to know of your struggle for us workers ... we feel with you ... only that we endure because, we must eat ...'

For us workers – Karega repeated in his heart. His mother had worked all her life breaking the skin of the earth for a propertied few: what difference did it make if they were black or brown? Their capacity to drink the blood and sweat of the many was not diminished by any thoughts of kinship of skin or language or region! Although she insisted on her immediate rights, she never complained much believing that maybe God would later put everything right. But she had now died without God putting anything right. She had got no more than what she had struggled for and fought for. Could Wanja have been right: eat or you are eaten?

He saw the girl from a distance and wondered who she was. As he approached the barbed wire, her face seemed vaguely familiar. Then he remembered that he had seen her at the factory: she looked after the seed millet for making Theng'eta – she spread it out to the sun to dry, and things like that. She looked shy and she spoke in Swahili.

'I have been sent to you. I have been begging to be allowed to see you. This warder helped me.'

'What is your name?'

'Akinyi. They sent me—'

'Who?'

'The other workers. . . with a message. They are with you ... and they are ... we are planning another strike and a march through Ilmorog.'

'But who—?'

'The movement of Ilmorog workers ... not just the union of workers at the breweries. All workers in Ilmorog and the unemployed will join us. And the small farmers ... and even some small traders ...'

He stood still ... so still. The movement of workers ... it must be something new ... something which must have started since he was held.

She told him more about the workers' protest and rebellion on the Sunday he was arrested and also about the condition of the workers wounded then. She told him about the death of a very important person in authority ...

'Really?' he asked.

'Yes. In Nairobi. He was gunned down as he waited in his car in

Eastleigh, outside Mathere Valley. He was waiting for his chauffeur-bodyguard to bring him the rent ...'

'He profiteered on the misery of the poor. It was probably robbers who did it, but all the same—'

'Not robbers. According to Ruma Monga it's more than that. They left a note. They called themselves Wakombozi – or the society of one world liberation ... and they say it's Stanley Mathenge returned from Ethiopia to complete the war he and Kimathi started ... There are rumours about a return to the forests and the mountains ...'

Mathenge back? He turned this over in his mind. It could not be possible. But what did it matter? New Mathenges ... new Koitalels ... new Kimathis ... new Piny Owachos ... these were born every day among the people ...

'What are they going to do to you?' she said, interrupting his thought-flow.

'Detain me ... I am suspected of being a communist at heart.'

'You'll come back,' she suddenly said, looking up at him boldly.

Her voice only agitated further images set in motion by her revelations. Imperialism: capitalism: landlords: earthworms. A system that bred hordes of round-bellied jiggers and bedbugs with parasitism and cannibalism as the highest goal in society. This system and its profiteering gods and its ministering angels had hounded his mother to her grave. These parasites would always demand the sacrifice of blood from the working masses. These few who had prostituted the whole land turning it over to foreigners for thorough exploitation, would drink people's blood and say hypocritical prayers of devotion to skin oneness and to nationalism even as skeletons of bones walked to lonely graves. The system and its gods and its angels had to be fought consciously, consistently and resolutely by all the working people! From Koitalel through Kang'ethe to Kimathi it had been the peasants, aided by the workers, small traders and small landowners, who had mapped out the path. Tomorrow it would be the workers and the peasants leading the struggle and seizing power to overturn the system and all its prying bloodthirsty gods and gnomic angels, bringing to an end the reign of the few over the many and the era of drinking blood and feasting on human flesh. Then, only then, would the kingdom of man and woman really begin, they joying and loving in creative labour ... For a minute he was so carried on the waves of this vision and of the possibilities it opened up for all the Kenyan working and peasant masses that he forgot the woman beside him.

'You'll come back,' she said again in a quiet affirmation of faith in eventual triumph.

He looked hard at her, then past her to Mukami of Manguo Marshes and again back to Nyakinyua, his mother, and even beyond Akinyi to the future! And he smiled through his sorrow.

'Tomorrow ... tomorrow ...' he murmured to himself.

'Tomorrow ...' and he knew he was no longer alone.

Evanston – Limuru – Yalta
October 1970–October 1975

FOR THE BEST IN PAPERBACKS, LOOK FOR THE

In every corner of the world, on every subject under the sun, Penguin represents quality and variety—the very best in publishing today.

For complete information about books available from Penguin—including Pelicans, Puffins, Peregrines, and Penguin Classics—and how to order them, write to us at the appropriate address below. Please note that for copyright reasons the selection of books varies from country to country.

In the United Kingdom: For a complete list of books available from Penguin in the U.K., please write to *Dept E.P., Penguin Books Ltd, Harmondsworth, Middlesex, UB7 0DA.*

In the United States: For a complete list of books available from Penguin in the U.S., please write to *Dept BA, Penguin,* Box 120, Bergenfield, New Jersey 07621-0120.

In Canada: For a complete list of books available from Penguin in Canada, please write to *Penguin Books Canada Ltd, 10 Alcorn Avenue, Suite 300, Toronto, Ontario, Canada M4V 3B2.*

In Australia: For a complete list of books available from Penguin in Australia, please write to the *Marketing Department, Penguin Books Ltd, P.O. Box 257, Ringwood, Victoria 3134.*

In New Zealand: For a complete list of books available from Penguin in New Zealand, please write to the *Marketing Department, Penguin Books (NZ) Ltd, Private Bag, Takapuna, Auckland 9.*

In India: For a complete list of books available from Penguin, please write to *Penguin Overseas Ltd, 706 Eros Apartments, 56 Nehru Place, New Delhi, 110019.*

In Holland: For a complete list of books available from Penguin in Holland, please write to *Penguin Books Nederland B.V., Postbus 195, NL-1380AD Weesp, Netherlands.*

In Germany: For a complete list of books available from Penguin, please write to *Penguin Books Ltd, Friedrichstrasse 10-12, D-6000 Frankfurt Main 1, Federal Republic of Germany.*

In Spain: For a complete list of books available from Penguin in Spain, please write to *Longman, Penguin España, Calle San Nicolas 15, E-28013 Madrid, Spain.*

In Japan: For a complete list of books available from Penguin in Japan, please write to *Longman Penguin Japan Co Ltd, Yamaguchi Building, 2-12-9 Kanda Jimbocho, Chiyoda-Ku, Tokyo 101, Japan.*

FOR THE BEST LITERATURE, LOOK FOR THE ⏀

☐ **THE BOOK AND THE BROTHERHOOD**
Iris Murdoch

Many years ago Gerard Hernshaw and his friends banded together to finance a political and philosophical book by a monomaniacal Marxist genius. Now opinions have changed, and support for the book comes at the price of moral indignation; the resulting disagreements lead to passion, hatred, a duel, murder, and a suicide pact. *602 pages   ISBN: 0-14-010470-4*

☐ **GRAVITY'S RAINBOW**
Thomas Pynchon

Thomas Pynchon's classic antihero is Tyrone Slothrop, an American lieutenant in London whose body anticipates German rocket launchings. Surely one of the most important works of fiction produced in the twentieth century, *Gravity's Rainbow* is a complex and awesome novel in the great tradition of James Joyce's *Ulysses*. *768 pages   ISBN: 0-14-010661-8*

☐ **FIFTH BUSINESS**
Robertson Davies

The first novel in the celebrated "Deptford Trilogy," which also includes *The Manticore* and *World of Wonders*, *Fifth Business* stands alone as the story of a rational man who discovers that the marvelous is only another aspect of the real. *266 pages   ISBN: 0-14-004387-X*

☐ **WHITE NOISE**
Don DeLillo

Jack Gladney, a professor of Hitler Studies in Middle America, and his fourth wife, Babette, navigate the usual rocky passages of family life in the television age. Then, their lives are threatened by an "airborne toxic event"—a more urgent and menacing version of the "white noise" of transmissions that typically engulfs them. *326 pages   ISBN: 0-14-007702-2*

FOR THE BEST LITERATURE, LOOK FOR THE 🐧

☐ **A SPORT OF NATURE**
Nadine Gordimer

Hillela, Nadine Gordimer's "sport of nature," is seductive and intuitively gifted at life. Casting herself adrift from her family at seventeen, she lives among political exiles on an East African beach, marries a black revolutionary, and ultimately plays a heroic role in the overthrow of apartheid.
354 pages   ISBN: 0-14-008470-3

☐ **THE COUNTERLIFE**
Philip Roth

By far Philip Roth's most radical work of fiction, *The Counterlife* is a book of conflicting perspectives and points of view about people living out dreams of renewal and escape. Illuminating these lives is the skeptical, enveloping intelligence of the novelist Nathan Zuckerman, who calculates the price and examines the results of his characters' struggles for a change of personal fortune.
372 pages   ISBN: 0-14-009769-4

☐ **THE MONKEY'S WRENCH**
Primo Levi

Through the mesmerizing tales told by two characters—one, a construction worker/philosopher who has built towers and bridges in India and Alaska; the other, a writer/chemist, rigger of words and molecules—Primo Levi celebrates the joys of work and the art of storytelling.
174 pages   ISBN: 0-14-010357-0

☐ **IRONWEED**
William Kennedy

"Riding up the winding road of Saint Agnes Cemetery in the back of the rattling old truck, Francis Phelan became aware that the dead, even more than the living, settled down in neighborhoods." So begins William Kennedy's Pulitzer-Prize winning novel about an ex-ballplayer, part-time gravedigger, and full-time drunk, whose return to the haunts of his youth arouses the ghosts of his past and present.
228 pages   ISBN: 0-14-007020-6

☐ **THE COMEDIANS**
Graham Greene

Set in Haiti under Duvalier's dictatorship, *The Comedians* is a story about the committed and the uncommitted. Actors with no control over their destiny, they play their parts in the foreground; experience love affairs rather than love; have enthusiasms but not faith; and if they die, they die like Mr. Jones, by accident.
288 pages   ISBN: 0-14-002766-1

FOR THE BEST LITERATURE, LOOK FOR THE Ⓟ

FOR THE BEST LITERATURE, LOOK FOR THE 🐧

☐ **THE LAST SONG OF MANUEL SENDERO**
Ariel Dorfman

In an unnamed country, in a time that might be now, the son of Manuel Sendero refuses to be born, beginning a revolution where generations of the future wait for a world without victims or oppressors.

464 pages   ISBN: 0-14-008896-2

☐ **THE BOOK OF LAUGHTER AND FORGETTING**
Milan Kundera

In this collection of stories and sketches, Kundera addresses themes including sex and love, poetry and music, sadness and the power of laughter. "*The Book of Laughter and Forgetting* calls itself a novel," writes John Leonard of *The New York Times*, "although it is part fairly tale, part literary criticism, part political tract, part musicology, part autobiography. It can call itself whatever it wants to, because the whole is genius."

240 pages   ISBN: 0-14-009693-0

☐ **TIRRA LIRRA BY THE RIVER**
Jessica Anderson

Winner of the Miles Franklin Award, Australia's most prestigious literary prize, *Tirra Lirra by the River* is the story of a woman's seventy-year search for the place where she truly belongs. Nora Porteous's series of escapes takes her from a small Australia town to the suburbs of Sydney to London, where she seems finally to become the woman she always wanted to be.

142 pages   ISBN: 0-14-006945-3

☐ **LOVE UNKNOWN**
A. N. Wilson

In their sweetly wild youth, Monica, Belinda, and Richeldis shared a bachelor-girl flat and became friends for life. Now, twenty years later, A. N. Wilson charts the intersecting lives of the three women through the perilous waters of love, marriage, and adultery in this wry and moving modern comedy of manners.

202 pages   ISBN: 0-14-010190-X

☐ **THE WELL**
Elizabeth Jolley

Against the stark beauty of the Australian farmlands, Elizabeth Jolley portrays an eccentric, affectionate relationship between the two women—Hester, a lonely spinster, and Katherine, a young orphan. Their pleasant, satisfyingly simple life is nearly perfect until a dark stranger invades their world in a most horrifying way.

176 pages   ISBN: 0-14-008901-2

FOR THE BEST LITERATURE, LOOK FOR THE 🐧

☐ **VOSS**
Patrick White

Set in nineteenth-century Australia, *Voss* is the story of the secret passion between an explorer and a young orphan. From the careful delineation of Victorian society to the stark narrative of adventure in the Australian desert, Patrick White's novel is one of extraordinary power and virtuosity. White won the Nobel Prize for Literature in 1973.

448 pages   ISBN: 0-14-001438-1

☐ **STONES FOR IBARRA**
Harriet Doerr

An American couple, the only foreigners in the Mexican village of Ibarra, have come to reopen a long-dormant copper mine. Their plan is to live out their lives here, connected to the place and to each other. Along the way, they learn much about life, death, and the tide of fate from the Mexican people around them.

214 pages   ISBN: 0-14-007562-3